KAM

Book Two

Glen "Rocky" Meyers

This novel is Dedicated to my mother,
Barbara Jean Hayes.
Thank you, mom!

By Glen "Rocky" Meyers

Feral Eyes: Book One

Feral Eyes: Book Two

Sara

Kara: Book One

Kara: Book Two

Covid 57: Book One

<u>The 'NIA' Series.</u>

<u>'KAM' Book Two is the fifth of 13 books in the NIA series.</u>

<u>I printed some Incomplete Manuscripts a couple of years ago to test the market, called ACR's…</u> which stands for Advanced Reader Copies, and I had some Beta readers preview some of the storylines in the NIA Series. In a word, they were '<u>Awful</u>' and needed editing and punctuation, and many of the plots were discombobulated. I have been working on cleansing these books for publishing since 2019; yes, it's been a journey! Today the fruits of my labor are here to be read and hopefully enjoyed. I will publish Six books at the same time in May of 2023.

<u>The First Amendment.</u>

Freedom of expression is a fundamental human right and a central tenet of an author's work, livelihood, and American Society. The First Amendment protects freedom of speech, the press, and citizens' assembly to protest or march in groups. Freedom of expression is the freedom for us all to express ourselves. It is the right to speak, to be heard, and to participate in artistic, political, and social life. I am a firm and staunch believer in our First Amendment! Using someone's name, image, or life story as part of a novel, book, movie, or other 'expressive' work is protected by the First Amendment.

<u>The NIA Series… Book Five …'Kane: Book Two.'</u>

<u>'A Preface.'</u>

<u>An introduction of how's and whys… with explanations.</u>

<u>'I'm a Felon… and enjoy using Disfluencies in my manuscripts.'</u>

Within most of my manuscripts, I incorporate the use of disfluencies. There are many reasons why I do so. Many purists will find this form of writing unprofessional and of a lower standard… which is fine by me. Some authors have distinctive writing styles, '<u>prose.</u>' In writing, prose refers to any written work that follows a basic grammatical structure. Prose simply means language that follows the Natural Patterns found in everyday speech. It isn't well known that disfluencies pop up in everyday speech or conversations in most languages on our planet. In conversations, it has been approximated that about every 4.6 seconds, a disfluency is used. I try and combine disfluencies to emphasize points or for the reader to slow down and reflect on what was just read. I have fun using disfluencies, and I use them to directly communicate concepts, ideas, and stories to my readers. If you were to really concentrate on a person's speech or a friend's conversation… uhm, or listen to an interview, you might find yourself amazed at how many of these 'placeholder words, filler words you hear. Even some highly esteemed professionals use an abundance of disfluencies.

<u>Please reference this great piece of work regarding disfluencies ("Well, um, you know, you're saying more than you think.) You can find this article in the November/ December 2022 'Psychology Today,' magazine.</u>

i

To paraphrase, some of the substance in this awesome article is that most of us use disfluencies; for example, have you ever been conversing with someone and lost track of where you were going? You pause momentarily and think of your next words… using Ah, Uh, Umh, then pick up where you left off. Disfluencies can be used to emphasize your topic of choice, aligned with appropriate expressions, and you see this at comedy clubs and in everyday conversations. We roll our eyes and pause and use 'Um'   . Disfluencies are common in humorous or even serious discussions. Stop for a minute and truly listen to someone's interview, either on TV or the Internet, Social media sites; you will hear an abundance of Disfluencies. We as a society have become immune to the dozens of common disfluencies many speakers use them for repeating a phrase or revising the sentence structure in midstream. I use disfluencies in my writing for emphasis, and because they're fun for me, I hope they aren't annoying to readers, umh, especially the purists. If so, I apologize, ugh, right up-front. Um, I don't want any of you not to enjoy my books. I do believe that over usage of disfluencies can become a nuisance, Uh.

Okay, umh, so here's the rest of the info that I'll share with you regarding disfluencies. Now I'm not defending my overuse of these words, or maybe I am? In many of my 13-plus written manuscripts, you'll read and see or hear words such as… 'um, uh, ugh, ah, umh, huh, so, uhm, ughhhh, ahhhh, and other variations like… oh, yep, yup, yay, yum, ahoh, lol, lmao, huh, and the list goes on…

The argument can be made; according to some Professors of Psychological Science, disfluencies help listeners and readers concentrate better on the narrative, and the use of a disfluency sometimes tells the audience there is likely new information about to be disseminated. Disfluencies seem to occur at discourse points or are used to indicate a Major plot change of direction. These educated professionals have said that disfluencies 'focus listener's attention' and sometimes allow the listener to analyze what has been said, sort of like a pause for reflection. In testing theories regarding using Disfluencies... when appropriately placed in a narrative, they actually increase a person's attention and memory of what they have heard or read.

Disfluencies have been used to help emphasize the topic being discussed. They are proven to help the listener or reader to remember storylines or points of contention better than most other deliveries of verbiage.

To sum up, highly esteemed intellectuals use disfluencies, from our Presidents right down to street urchins. They have been proven to increase listeners' attention. Please try and catch disfluencies either by yourself or others. You might be surprised at how many of them are used in a single day. Like... Well, heck, that said a lot, lol... Umh, okay. Yup!

How I became an author after my arrest for growing and dispensing Marijuana.

I'm sure you've heard the term 'to make a long story short,' which indicates that the story will likely not be short and concise. Lol. I've penciled over a thousand pages in a book named Sacramento County Jail, a harrowing non-fiction venture. Below is a short passage into what caused my life changes and thus led to my creative writing hobby.

In the year 2012, suddenly, health issues befell... my body and mind. I was beyond listless, with no energy or motivation to do anything felt like a Slug. I was a regular at the gym and in the past was active... this all stopped. I sought out professional help. First things first, I had to donate blood for a wide variety of tests. A sex hormone panel, 'SHBG' amongst other tests, was ordered since I was approaching the age of male menopause. The endocrinologist called me in and informed me that I had several anomalies. One was that I had extremely low… deficient testosterone levels, but what bothered her more was that I'd had the highest Estrogen levels she'd ever seen in a man. In fact, her words were with a smirk, 'Mr. Meyers, welcome to female menopause. Your levels are off the charts.' Thirty-five years of being an endocrinologist, she had never seen these numbers before. After checking with her colleagues, it was decided that I needed another hormone test because there must have been a mistake! My test numbers were impossible to comprehend. Well,… what would you know? Two weeks later, I was called back into her office. This time I didn't witness a smirk from her countenance, nope. She beckoned me to have a seat across from her magnificent mahogany desk. She folded her arms up elbows on the desk, clasped her fingers in a temple, and bent her head down. With her not saying a word, I'd automatically jumped to the conclusion, 'I WAS DEAD,' something terminal. I must be on my way out 😵.

>>>>Please visit '<u>Gembooksrock.com</u>' and finish reading… Yep.

<u>**Former Federal Inmate.**</u>

I am a former prisoner and felon sequestered by the IRS… Federal Government on Marijuana charges… was imprisoned and locked up in Terminal Island Prison for about Seven years. A short synopsis of the events that led to my writing career can be found on my website 'Gembooksrock.com,' please check out my homepage. You will find some interesting tidbits… along with links to my arrest 🌙.

<u>Kamryn at the Quickdraw competition.</u>

Kamryn was frolicking about in her mind, not in attendance, oblivious to the throng of people surrounding her. It was the largest audience she'd been around since last New Year's celebration with her honey Brock Dame. She looked out on the dirt road that was made up to be something from the 1800s. She'd supposed… wished she'd had earmuffs listening to the whistles and clapping. Kamryn wasn't in the mood to be cheerful only wanted off the NIA grounds, secya. The crowd seemed to be chomping at the bit for action. She wasn't paying attention to the loud announcer, lost in her thoughts having read the banners… Quickdraw challenge. Wendi didn't say much about what they were doing. She acted kind of unfriendly.

Rocky had taken over at the administration office. She'd finished the Physical and the hordes of paperwork and, thankfully, didn't have to drink that awful Green gel. She didn't have to go through body scans nor an extensive Physical, just her blood pressure was taken with her heartbeat and temperature, and all three were high… Sofie was friendly and accommodating and did precisely what Rocky asked of her. *The oddest thing happened while she was in the lady's restroom, pooping in a stall. What she overheard didn't make sense, but two women were washing their hands at the sinks. What they'd said was etched in her memory; for some reason, all the justifications expired.* <u>*Her rationale process couldn't equate to the phrase or question of what was whispered between the Lab Techs. Their words lingered stuck to her like Ter 'wasn't her younger sister just in here?' "Schhh, I was told that was a subject off-limits. All we're to do is qualify her, badge her up, and send her out to Wendi."*</u>

Kam wasn't keen on signing away two years of her life in a Bootcamp, but she had her outs. She planned to escape NIA. Knowing she'd disappointed her Uncle when she vehemently refused to meet with FBI Agent Rico Captor for the Sara interview. What Liz and Uncle were unaware of… unh, that when she was approached to help with the Doctor Garza predicament, uhm situation. Terrance had told Liz to give her the passwords to their exclusive network giving her freedom to roam through the NIA network. She'd accessed her own files, well, not hers only… nope, devious sister Sara's files finding useful information that she could use as leverage to get the hell out of this cesspool. Kam had copied numerous files to the disk she now had systemically hidden. When snooping, she'd clicked on the cameras. Lo and behold, in her designated cell was the evil bitch herself, Sara. One plus one is two Uncle Terrance and Liz have somehow convinced their sister to re-enter the prison and take part in the interview with Rico. For the life of her, she couldn't figure out any reason Sara would be back behind the razor wire. Again this proved Uncle never intended to let her go.

Kam had succeeded in copying the files only moments before Liz had slipped into her studio apartment, and Jax had beckoned her down to the basement Sally port… to join him in the Hummer. Jax drove her to this side of the NIA properties, and then she met and was taken under wing by Wendi. Rocky had helped her immensely… bypassing all the exams at the Admin building. Kam was slightly worried about riding the horse with Wendi to the Quickdraw contest being with child. But had to admit it was fun dressing in Western gear and being treated with so much respect by the staff. She couldn't get over the size of the outside arenas and was stunned at how massive NIA-U's complexes were.

She yawned, thinking over her options considering the circumstances first; would she be allowed to drive out or exit this place? My second thought was that Jax typically left the keys in his Hummer in the ignition… why not drive that out the gates? Although, with a quirky smirk, would that be misconstrued as Grand Theft Hummer? The third option was to get to a phone and call someone to help her. She'd memorized a few numbers. Brock Dame, her fiancé, was in the NIA hospital outside the prison complex, and she still retained his parent's phone numbers in her skull along with her BF, who was supposed to be her bridesmaid at the canceled wedding of Brock and her… ugh great all she needed was a cell phone.

Kamryn decided to get a drink from a snack bar in the foreground, "hey Wendi, I'm going to get something to drink and use the bathroom. You want anything?" "No, I'm cool, thanks." Kamryn stepped from the bleachers, struck with a sharp pang for vindication that slammed her silly. The betrayal by her Uncle and family was debilitating. She wanted to scream if she had an automatic machine gun. She'd shoot everyone; she didn't want to sit there and watch all the happy people gazing at this ridiculous Quick Draw competition. She felt like a pressure cooker boiling over… Yes, indeed, she wanted revenge and resented every person that she could see. She hated NIA for all the maniacal ways she'd been abused by the NIA staff. Drugged into zombie land on psychotropic pharmaceuticals, restrained and chained down. Given unwanted injections, beatings, sexual assault by the man-bitch giant guard, boots to the ribs, and slamming her to the concrete. The fight in the cafeteria against the fiend woman, straitjacket in irons, yeah, the beatings and scars that still remained on her epidermis that will linger for much more time… mentally, maybe forever, she had to escape.

Kam steadfastly decided, 'I'm going to call my soon-to-be husband's… past employer, the FBI, primarily Rico Captor… and tell them all, uh, despite Rocky's warnings. I will disclose all that I know, become an informant, and put my twin behind bars for the rest of her unnatural demented life. Uncle Terrance and the rest of the staff probably wouldn't get into trouble, but I'd try. I hope Rico will listen. They think they have their asses covered. Certainly, the company's stock and future would be affected. I don't give a Rats ass what they think. Sure, I signed all their paperwork and pretended to be truthful… ughhhh, vows of honesty, lol let me out of this piss-hole!"

Kam's exhilaration was like a natural high her adrenal glands pumped, and her mind was overwhelmed with a feeling of exoneration and control of self. Her vindication would be Sweet. Not a soul even looked at her twice. Everyone was entranced, um enthralled, at the gunslinger competition. This could be easier than expected. Spots a Golf cart, then in the distance Jax's Hummer. She'd take the cart to where his vehicle was, and if she had to ram through the gates with the Hummer, so be it. Now momentum picked up her pace, and increasingly optimism reigned. She hopped into the four-wheeled cart.

Suddenly the Golf cart tilted towards the passenger side almost at the very time the small ignition key was turned to the right. 'I nearly peed all over myself for the most enormous, meanest snarling Canine I'd ever seen was nose to his long hairy muzzle in my face. I literally could taste his breath and feel the wetness of his massive, flexing nostrils. It wasn't a Dog! Nope, it was a Timber Wolf. I dared not flinch or move… a vibration came from the Feral animal, a growl aligned with an unblinking stare. The Wolf in my peripheral vision… Oh no, with a swift movement to the left of where I sat in the driver's seat, there was a pack of wolves. Suddenly I shook like a leaf in a tornado. My smallish Golf cart was weighed down. A freakin hungry lookin Wolf grinned, teeth baring in the passenger seat.

'Nice doggy, ugh, nice puppy doggy.' Slowly I backed off, his nose turning like molasses in freezing weather… his fricken twin stood outside the small windshield, likely wifey Wolf or Mommy Wolf, whatever. Delusional was I on a reality show for the National Geographic? Uh, on my left side stood another hairy four legs fk a Wolf pack, maybe a brother or Uncle Wolf. I was trapped and initially thought to scream and holler at my vocal cord's maximum yield. But as I moved my legs slithering methodically out of the cart, the Wolf on my left, standing peering at me, seemed to back up like to allow me to get out, then a hard, sharp prod on my right thigh a paw pushing me like a freakin club. Then both front paws kicked out at me, the weight leaned me outward, a loud bark in my trembling right ear like, get the fk out of the Golf cart, so I did. Wthell would you do?"

Strangely no one came to my aid. My three unwanted Feral companions began a circuitous wag… one of the Wolfs led me with an invisible leash, another on my left and right on my heels was the third one… directly to the woman's restroom. Like a gentleman, they waited patiently outside the door. Well, two of them did. The other roamed by the windows as I washed my hands. I had never dealt with something so bizarre, and now fricken NIA had guard Wolves!

I stepped back out, closing the bathroom door while two chatty females walked by to use the facilities and didn't even give me a double take nor acknowledge the freakin Wolves or me. Damn, were they invisible etched in my imagination, dreaming nightmarishly? Aah, apparently not! Remember my stature? I'm like 5'1" tall and a buck 15 pounds. These were ponies for me, Naw, not the My Lil Pony variety. Herded in a bee-line or Wolf line, I was not rejoiced to be right back to where I'd planned my escape bleachers, hoots and yells, hollers, and the deep baritone of the M.C. 'well folks, whatcha think have you seen sharpshooters like this before?' whistles and stomping on the bleachers oh everyone was having a blast aah so much damn fun… not I.

Seven steps later, up in the V.I.P section club seats, Wendi cocks her head with an indiscriminate smirk, "you find your way all right?" "Yeah, with the help of your Wolf Pack," paused, then said, "Thanks a lot!…" "Oh, no worries, don't mention it!" Yes, I wished I didn't have to, but I felt compelled to return her re-greeting with a wryly… smirl, my combination smirk and smile. "Wendi, that was rude. Why…?" "Kam, your missing unreal action. Let me catch you up to speed!" I took my purse off my shoulder and spun to sit. <u>"Kammy, isn't this way fun?" wait, who said that?… my spine reverberated with sharp spikes down towards my sacrum before a set of frightful, ugh… undeniable eyes shrank me back into my seat.</u>

Looking down the aisle, all I saw was hulking masculinity, the Captains, leaders of the NIA teams, umh, was I sweating? Yep, I could suddenly smell my underarms stink of sour perspiration blended in with Wolf shavings. A thick blush upon my cheeks, teeth chattered together. I'm losing my mind. I'm not okay, 'Kammy' it has been forever and a day since anyone called me that pet name. Seldom meaning on rare occasions, Sara would call me Kammy, but that Red tinted-haired beauty with Hollywood round glasses leaning down on her nose wasn't Sara. Who was that person? I was freaked out again. I maneuvered up and sideways. Where were those eyeballs that I'd glimpsed? Last I saw Sara. It was on the closed-circuit cameras. She was going to the legal room for the interview to meet up with Uncle Terrance. I prayed Agent Rico Captor grilled the Snake Sara… to a crisp!

"Check it out, Kam. We're down to the last two combatants. One of them will be eliminated next week. The last four standing will shoot it out for the Gold, Silver, and Bronze medals!" I wasn't the least bit interested… in tunnel vision mode… as I elbowed Wendi lightly on her right side. "Hey, who's the woman that's sitting next to Jax…?" "Sshhh Kam, geez, I'll introduce you after the tournament. If you don't want to watch… go and take a stroll with my Wolves! Ssshh!" "Yes, Ma'am!" Needless to say, I remained seated on the bleachers.

<u>Kamryn decided to roll with the punches because she hadn't any other alternative, uhm, yet!</u>

'All right... if you can't beat 'em, join them,' so I refocused on the duel. A Cowgirl in a fancy Pink cowboy hat was facing off with a leather-skinned tall, lithe lookin man in a Grey cowboy hat. They tipped their bells... if that's what they're called, and sure as shit, everything froze.

A kind of 'still,' a solid squeamish hush closed over us, uhhh, the crowd, all of us. I must be on an LSD high or drugged because, slow-mo galloping on a Black Stallion sitting up high, entirely dressed from head to Cowboy boots in Coal Blackness, was a man... With a flashy Silver buckle, matching a Silver accented hat and vest. Streaming down each leg of his pants were Silver sequins. It was like Cowboy G.Q. had arrived. Yeah, right down to a chewed nub of a cigar, still smoking, itty bitty sunglasses Silver in color with a Silver and Black scarf right under his unshaven Black whiskers. Clint Eastwood could no doubt have pulled this entrance off, but he most likely was kicking it off the Coast of Carmel on one of his yachts, enjoying the Pacific Ocean with family.

Did I not mention that the Black Stallion was in the company of a spotted Brown and White Appaloosa, and in that saddle was a petite female dressed to the hilt... a hooting cowboy dream. Her exquisite feminine attire was sparkling with glistening Rhinestones, and she wore a matching Brown and Beige ensemble. Hot to trot, and that was what she was doing trotting up next to Cowboy G.Q. They were a pair from a distance, and seemed to relish in the limelight, her tight-looking ass in those jeans right down to her cowgirl boots and Beige Cowgirl hat had the crowd... crowing hooting and howling. The couple uncoiled off their prodigious horses, took the reins, and wrapped them over one of the 2-pronged round rails, and after his grand entrance, the hush over the crowd remained. He bowed his head, took his hat in his left hand, and motioned his right hand, showing a thumb forefinger. A metaphorical gun mimed as he bent down, waving his hand, pretending to spray the audience with a machine gun. Finally, a stirring chortle, cackles, people hooting and laughing, the M.C. dethawed saying. "Well, I'm honored to introduce to you all… our leader and Patriarch, Mr. Terrance Hallinan. Welcome, sir!" The crowd went bonkers Rockstarish Terrance was strutting onward in a calm cocky stroll like… Yep, I'm all that and with a chocolate Cherry on top!

As his boss closed in, the announcer continued, "I'm afraid I haven't had the pleasure to meet the lovely Cowgirl that's with you yet?..." Terrance snatches the microphone, beaming smile "howdy you all," most grinned back a howdy doody. "Sorry for the untimely interruption" then, he spun to the female with a swirling motion, bowed with one arm, and tugged her close. The girl took off her beige cowgirl hat… oh fk-no 🐎 "This is my lovely niece Sara Amaya… please give her a warm welcome." Well, warm, it wasn't. Ugh, lukewarm on the icicle side. Obviously, sis Sara's reputation had already arrived and preceded this occasion. She was booed in an uproarious chorus by some in the crowd even before she'd dismounted. The audience was garishly hostile, full-on negative, and didn't like my killer sister. She didn't care and mockingly gave the crowd a herky-jerky curtsy. Terrance took her paw, and they headed straight to where I sat with Wendi… Omg, I melted. 🐎

Uncle Terrance showed a tinge of respite respect, pouncing his butt next to me with the freak on his left. A quick ghoulish vulturistic scowl left her face like a dart on its way to strike me. I ducked! My posture arched like a gymnast gritting my White ivories back at the skank, wishing to display a wicked, tempestuously genuine bolt of utmost hatred… oh, for all my effort. Her retort was a left-eye wink and a puss-lipped air kiss.

How I even sat still was a miracle that behooved me still till this day. I didn't remember a single bullet fired who eventually won the Gunslinger match. Never that afternoon did I even think back to the Kammy statement that the Redhead had made in my direction, no nada remembrance. Nope, all of me became stifled, musing about why my Uncle would do this to me. Did he not so secretly despise me said he loved me more than any of his nieces, but fk, that's a straight-up lie bringing Sara here like she was his damn guest of honor, Please! Unforgivable. I'd be better off with the Wolves!

<u>Enjoying dinner hours after the Chopper trip over NIA…</u>
<u>Rico and Shanon.</u>

After the second bottle of wine, they analyzed the whys… how's…whens, and what's primarily the possible narratives for the motives for NIA, why would the organization try to keep this Sara escape or gate-pass from her cell on the sly, objectives goals which had to be diverse trying to isolate reasonable incentives other than the stock price. Shan asserted herself, saying, "come on, the world is about money. Can you imagine what would happen to NIA if we could substantiate that Sara had a gate pass?" Rico took another path, the fact that NIA recruited criminals from around the globe, the world's worst killers, psychotic insanity-laden humans actually lobbying other regimes with enticements to allow NIA to house their criminally insane within their walls… There is something corrupt going on inside the Razor wire."

"Shanon, it's like they catalog no wrong word. I mean, maybe they have a rating system. While we sit here, there are more mass murderers killers down the road from whence we flew over than in any seven prisons, maybe ten anywhere together!" "Rico," as she sips the luscious Shiraz. "In a course at one of the learning institutions, I attended a lesson that has resonated with me ever since… I will never forget it's inscribed in my mind the idiosyncrasy of the deemed criminally insane who, as a whole, are highly intelligent. Actually, psychopaths tested and compiled into a group study had I.Q.s off the charts, way above average and beyond genius levels. Rico, many times a tragic occurrence during childhood or during the stage of puberty caused trauma! Bam, the fine line broken in their psyche, they snapped like a switch. Resembling chameleon lizards, they live amongst us with Reptilian coldblooded grins, watching us… blending into our society, some with the added nuance of keeping to themselves. The professor used a manufactured descriptive word calling them the worse of the worse 'PsychoSociopaths.' They could be your neighbor, and you'd have no clue!"

He shakes his head, gulping, "I know… your speaking with the choir. If the public truly were aware of the fact that most serial killers die of old age-ugh. The average Joe has never even, by comparison, pulled up the graphs and charts of how many convicted serial child molesters and rapists live in their neighborhoods unaware of the site 'Megalaw.com." "Yes, I know. I recently put in my zip code and found there were 177 sexual predators in the near vicinity of where I lay my head," said Shanon. Frowned, "the distressing reality is that most the predators haven't been arrested, most never are." He adds "yes but on the positive side when they are arrested it's a lot harder now to win the insanity defense in court at least now when the predator is judged cured he or she is then taken back to court to be held responsible for their crimes in most cases, that is!"

He pours their glasses full with the rest of the bottle "uh, and it's like NIA, uhm, they're stockpiling these freaks that have obscene skills of survival. Yep, brilliant, warped minds shit, they should do tours exhibits of the famous inmates of the Who's Who, maybe like a Circus Museum." They laughed for a millisecond, then she stated, "yeah, but what's in that circus tent on the NIA training centers vast piece of land?" She sighs

"Well, what we do know is NIA is also behind a treasure trove chest of miraculous breakthroughs look at Agent Lucie Link. After her injuries falling from the third-floor balcony, unh, she was a vegetable certifiably guaranteed paralyzed and given up on by Neurological Hospitals across North America. Every doctor her parents took her dormant mind and body to for an evaluation concurred that Lucie was hopeless. Now she ambles along with the help of a walker, even feeds herself, and is saying some words because of the Scientists that NIA had hired... the finest in the world. Stem Cell Therapies a blessing!" Rico clinked his glass on hers. They sip he was affirmatively shaking his head with a smile "your right about that. It's like if you're a Free Agent Scientist or Neurologist, ahh Specialist yah want the most money, then NIA is hiring!"

"Heck, while you're on that narrative, how about your best friend, FBI Agent Brock Danne, again justifiably brain dead, nearly comatose, only drooling, displaying Grand-mal seizures, strapped down in a straitjacket wheelchair bound and shackled to a gurney for five months. The man couldn't blink a yes or a no or move his pinky finger. He's now exercising and walking. NIA has turned down... many awards and accolades from the Science and Medical communities. NIA has had many writeups, uhm, positive affirming articles from sources like the Mayo Clinic, The Science Digest, and The New England Journal of Medicine. And even new-wave magazines and websites are spreading their amazing successes, which further proliferates their esteem and admiration of medical professionals. Listen, Rico, haven't you witnessed Brock doing pullups and pushups, right? Lately, Stem Cell research has made leaps and bounds, with NIA at the forefront with the addition of bone marrow treatments. What they're doing for paralyzed victims is utterly astounding! And now there opening an entire floor for Fire, um, burned victims."

"Wham bam, thank you, ma'am, that's the rambling on of an advocate. Okay, you have valid points. Brock is now able to play a game of Chess with me... by every one of my visits, he's improving. He's working out saying sentences yep, amazing...." "Yes, both Lucie and Brock were Zombies. If they were any other place else in this biosphere, they'd be wearing diapers 'Depends' and being spoon-fed!" He nods expressively "yes, and I will not forget what they've achieved for Wendi after her wounds from her brother Mark, she was in a coma with a gunshot wound to her head, yea I 'gotta take my hat off...!" I'm impressed at what their Neurological center has accomplished." "Yeah, Rico, and the latest rumor is they are on the brink of an explosive innovation in treating spinal injuries!"

The Blueberry cheesecake was nearly gone. They ordered a slice of Carmel Carrot Cake, washing it down with some Blackberry Port wine-tapping... goblets. Glad they decided to take an Uber to their hotel about 13 miles away, they lounged comfortably in each other's company. "I shouldn't divulge this. It's highly classified," then stops speaking with a grimace. She leans in conspiratorial like, "tell me you can't start that crap... then stop. That's bullshit," frowning, "oh all right, check this out! Shan, no, I better not say another word. It's Highly Classified"

"Shanon, just forget it. I can't believe I just...." "Too late, Rico; as she wobbles over a couple of ounces of the delicious Blackberry Port, cheers, don't be a party pooper. You know you can trust me. You can't start like, 'Let me tell you a secret,' then stop, nope, no way we have no secrets between us, shit. That's what we'd promised one another years ago. Damn, I'm more open with you than with my own husband. Aah, every so often, Jaxon will say or ask, 'hey babe, should I be concerned about you and Rico? You seem to spend an inordinate amount of time together, way more than with our children or with me!...' so spit it out, guy."

Rico flashes a Red face; she can't decide if it's all the Red wine or a start of a blush. He breaks her train of thought.

"Sham, fine, this is from the Pentagon. Top-level classifications are necessary to have, um, even to get a whiff of this highly sensitive information. Only the uppermost individuals in the know. I'm only privy cuz I was the protagonist in this secretive mission that's been going on for the last 19 months we...." He stops, takes a look around the fancy restaurant then leans into her. "I have lost two operatives who had infiltrated NIA's training facility." She loudly gasped "wait, lost, how do you lose someone? where's the..." "Sshhh, Sham shit," he peers around nervously, "keep it down, will ya? I know where you're going, Sham. Where's the investigation? Why hasn't the Government intervened? Well, let me give you the axinine reasons. First, NIA is insulated, wrapped, and sealed as tight as a drum, like a CIA operation. Their connections are mind-blowing. It's like the fraternal organization of Freemasons or a clandestine agency. My investigators constantly run up against dead ends. Mind you, the expansion of the now conglomerate is all-encompassing worldwide. Um, it's the old adage 'not what you know but whom!" He slowly lifts his fork for another bite of cheesecake.

"You're scaring me. What are you insinuating, huh? Come on now, how can NIA be connected with our Government, and you lose two Agents gone under the carpet, both NIA spies? Rico, it's not adding up...." "They had accidents off-site one died in Hawaii on a dive... she was with her husband about 11 miles off of a beach in Maui, treasure hunting old shipwrecks. Somehow she got an embolism in her skull after returning from the depths in an ocean dive. She was a diving professional with over 700 dives, and the autopsy was done on the island..." Shanon was flabbergasted and yelped "why wasn't I called in..." "I'll get you the results. It was deemed accidental!" "Yes, please do so... but why wasn't I the lead M.E. on this?" "Because, my friend, you were already spread too thin. At the time of the so-called accident in Hawaii, you were busy working with Brock and Lucie on the serial killer Sara's case down in San Diego. Your skilled hands were analyzing Brock's dead wife, Patti Dame, on the slab, um homicides knee-deep in autopsies couldn't just snatch you up! Heck, you had three bodies on the slab at that time, ugh, on ice." She swirled the rest of the Port and slugged it down her esophagus.

He likewise drains the last of the Blackberry dessert wine. "So that leaves the second accidental death involving our Agents. Let me remind you that they were on the inside of NIA, working the system and training alongside the other recruits. He had just filed a report and was in the second phase of the training course. He was with his wife and two children in Costa Rico. It was a family vacation. He and his wife were out while the children were being escorted to a fun park arcade and a waterworks park. They were up in the mountains out of San Jose, Costa Rico... Zip lining a gorge and magnificent waterfalls. You ought to see the videos anyways. The cable broke, and he tumbled down onto the rocks 5,000 feet below." "My Gawd, how devastating for his family, but...." "They shut down the zipline company. It's still out of business today. The owner had cameras all in the trees and inset into the Rocky base ledges, big monies in selling the digital pictures and video to the tourists who joined the excursion."

"Okay, what did the pictures and video show?..." "Shanon, here's the pertinent detail every hour, an employee would run the whole course of cables that were just under 13 miles of ziplines. They'd triple-check the lines to ensure there wasn't any splintering or tears in the cables, any issues whatsoever, the lines were secure, this sudden splintering of a tension cable wire was extremely suspicious." She felt tipsy ahh, buzzed a touch past her comfort zone, yet couldn't resist taking another sip from her near-empty goblet. Being entranced and looking over at his handsome appearance, thinking, 'this man is single; R U Kidding me? Squirms in her comfy chair, embarrassed, dropped the thought off the cliff, quickly disturbed, having had the intrusive urge sneak up on her, she converted back to her disciplined life... mindset.'

Dropping back, intrigued with his storyline spanking her lack of discipline, she added, "cameras, video's hourly checks of the ziplines with your description, it seemed a well-run business...." "It was Shea it was, but coincidently all camera's video went on the blink covering 'Tom's' zipline experience. Tom Gomez was my Agents name, and the zipline company had no coverage of him, nada. The last shots were of him making it about halfway across a ravine. When Tom noticed the cable was shredded, he was filming his trip over the waterfall and was up over a mile above the water. The cable tore and ripped. Tom dropped from the sky... he tumbled, somersaulting down to the jagged rocks. Hey, and Btw... I knew Tom well. We worked out together and competed in handball contests. The guy was an athlete. He corrected himself in midair and hit the shallow water and rocks with a perfect dive!"

Shaking her pretty head at him morosely... he continued, "amazing truths. Tom's Nikon underwater video camera survived the plunge, never hitting the rocks below, landing in the mouth of the river at the base of a waterfall, and was found days later lodged in a fisherman's net a few miles from the ocean. We had five eyewitnesses who detailed what they had seen. Tom survived nine days in a coma. We flew him out to the Mayo Clinic hospital. He regained consciousness briefly, his children and Lora by his bedside... Sad!"

Shea saw emotions starting to brew, unwound on his face, and wanted to cease this hurtful line of conversation. The pain was full and present, but he stopped, eyelids dampening his head to the left. Staring straight through her, he said, "I talked Tom into going undercover. It should not have been him... being a family man. I was wrong and should have chosen a single agent... not a married person. He was my number 1 choice, now his widow and children...." Shea reaches across and touches his hand. "I'm sorry, OmLord, so tragic," silence as he raises his arm from hers, pantomiming to the server bill… check.

While in flux, he only stares, staring out waiting for the server to deliver the bill, "Tom came out of his coma briefly and was nearly certain that he'd seen NIA's Shon Peterson, who blended in with the Native Costa Ricans in the area. Shon is a special forces Op, the guy unit leader of one of the training teams at NIA. He's a Black man, an ex-Army Ranger. In the end, we couldn't trace Shon to Costa Rica nor… leaving Sonoma County. He had alibis all 'set up.' After a short investigation, we discovered that the cameras and video were destroyed by a sophisticated heat laser which also cut through the cable on the zipline, so there were no pictures or video available we figured out this weapon was shot from a helicopter. From estimates, perhaps 150 feet above the Zipline, uh, it was a high-tech assassination. Why? well, crap, we all knew why he was murdered." "I'm sad for you…" "don't be. Let's get out of here," he hands the server his credit card. Five minutes later, they hug, sitting out under a porte-cochere squinting into the early evening light, a mixture of exquisite colors, rainbows after another rainstorm. They sat close together on a bench, Bougainvillea flowers in bloom, vines roaming in crazy angles. Resting still in thought, a few moments passed.

"I'm terrified and curious at the same time. I can't wait to view all the digital pictures we took today from the chopper. Right now, we have three spies on the inside of NIA, one near her date of graduation and the others in their first semester. What we have determined without proof or solid enough data to substantiate a formal accusation… is, unh, were close Shan, although not conjecture or hypothetical assumptions, call it subjective truths. Rico slurs his words, his mouth, and tongue not in unison. He had serious Cottonmouth. She passes him her bottle of water, both inebriated, buzzed, and feeling no pain, and she adds, "Rico, what you just muttered made no sense to me," they giggle. "Uhm, what did I say?" they grin. He held the bottle taking the water down his throat with huge gulps.

They stare at the water fountain statues of Zeus and children enjoying the sprays and suds. "Where was I? Shan, I lost my…." "Aah, evidence or substantiation, umh, something like…." "Oh yeah, our Moles have discovered a network of militia camps bases across the USA. We believe they are backed by NIA. My Agents are tracking large encampments in Oregon, Washington, Montana, Nevada, and Florida… hell, and we've intercepted memos. That were initiated by NIA, which displayed a map, uhm, and saw 27 states on charts. There are hints coming from other trainees that there hoping to be chosen for certain states to become Staff Sergeants. The graduates are filtered off to these Militia bases. There's a civilian network already in place, with military precision, I'm telling you, Shanoa." "Please, Rico, relax. You're getting all worked up again…." "No Shan NIA is organizing and proliferating a civilian militia on American soil… the quirky misnomer is what NIA is doing is 101% legal. Were between a Rock and a hard place, I guess the real question that should be asked is why are they doing this? We need boots in their encampments on the ground, a spy to move up their hierarchy and gain a leadership role. Call him or her a Mole. Tom was gaining the respect he'd even felt that Jax was taking a liking to him, even met Terrance when he won a hotly contested semi-final match of Fencing."

The Uber driver pulls up; Rico gives her the hotel name. Sitting in the back seat, Shan fell asleep on his shoulder. They'd not sleep all night soundly… Nope!

<u>Back at the Quickdraw Competition.</u>

The Quickdraw gunslinger exhibition was winding down to the last winning combatant. She yanked her cowboy hat off, waving it at the bystanders. The audience cheered wildly, and most couldn't wait till the following week when the championship rounds would conclude. In an orderly fashion, everyone moved back to the main artery that was in between the three airplane-like hangar buildings. Many were animated, chatting it up about the heated competition. Some were speaking in hushed words about the advent of Sara Amaya, showing up with CEO Terrance Hallinan. The overall consensus was 'the nerve of him bringing a suspected serial killer out of the mental hospital to enjoy the festivities!'

Wendi turns in my direction. "Kam, how are you feeling? You have been extraordinarily quiet, barely made a squeak. Did you not enjoy the sharpshooters, unh, quickdraw?" "I don't know, feeling a smidgeon disoriented, um sick and confused ahh miffed at my Uncle in the mix, bet that all of you in the know have formulated conceptions of who Sara was and is. Wendi, you couldn't miss the jeers and negative response when Uncle introduced her, could you?" "Kam, no, I understand why you have an emotional reaction to her riding a Horse in with…" "not just that, I don't give a crap about that. Please look where I'm at. I've been trapped in prison in her freakin place for almost seven months, all because of her. Doesn't anybody get it?"

Wendi reaches out and puts her arm around Kamryn's shoulders "that's the reason why your twin is here this afternoon. Terrance is not filled with grandiosity. No, he, like us in the 'know,' understands that any healing will take a long time, or perhaps you're never going to recover; I'm sure it has been explained to you a dozen times. We cannot just switch you two out. We..." "Wendi, ur way off base. I will never ever forgive her. I'm scarred internally forever. I'm..." "Hold up, don't interrupt me. We're all empathetic and feel rotten. Yes, your intense passion for vindication is warranted. Your Uncle is going to meet with you alone in less than 19 minutes. Shall we go now?" I looked around. All the V.I.P. boxes were empty, but for us... most of them were going to the next competition at the Track and Field Arena. It was only Wendi and I and, unh, the three Wolves contently staring and waiting for us patiently like good ole Wolves.

I followed her down to ground level and asked, "so Wendi, I respect your opinion. What or how would you deal with this Sara thing with my Uncle?" She leaned down and matched eyes with the Wolf leader petting them all. Twisted about nastily with an ire of angst, she blaringly exclaimed, "Kam, what were you going to do in the Golf cart? Where the Hell did you think you were going?" I froze, and my stomach curdled. The damn snitch Wolves, I thought crap. I leaned back, freaked out could swear the Lead Wolf winked at me.

Wendi is standing, hands on hips "either tell me, or I will have to report this to your Uncle. I should anyways we sign pacts here honoring a code of integrity, Kam." Shit, I was fricken lucky the Rat-ass Wolf couldn't read my mind like Wendi could all animals, or I'd truly be busted because I was going to steal... lol Grand Theft Hummer. Jax's driver, "well, we don't have all day, Kam!" "Simply, I panicked, Wendi. I was going to take a ride and hopefully find an exit that wasn't locked or guarded. I know, so ridiculous wanting to drive to freedom, that's it!"

Wendi, Shar-Pei... unh, wrinkled her forehead, "that's why I had my Wolf pack watch you, Kam. Let's go, girl, and discuss all of this with your uncle!" "Crap, you don't have to tell him all about this...." "Again, I have sworn oaths of integrity. I will not betray this organization nor myself by being less than forthright remember, a _Lie of Omission is just that, a LIE!"_ "Thanks for nothing, Uncle will be major league pissed off at me. I don't understand the importance of informing and snitching me out. Really I told you the truth. Should I be punished for doing so?" "Listen, Kam, your Uncle has a lot bigger fish to fry. Although I can commiserate with you for what you have been through with ur messed up twin sister, this may not be difficult to differentiate or understand blatantly... You want to hear the bare facts, huh?" Wendi didn't wait for acknowledgment just kept rolling on. "Here it is with full transparency. Sara is much more valuable to our cause than you. My dear, her skills are superior to what you have to offer your Uncle and NIA. I'm sorry everything will work out for you, I'm sure!"

This was when it dawned on me whew slammed down hard, epiphany intruded "Wendi Feral was admitted into NIA's outpatient mental hospital after she came out of a coma caused by her older brother Mark Feral who had shot her in her head while she was in her car. I'd read that serious head trauma resulted while driving to her business Feral Feedback that a bullet was lodged in her skull, and this calamity hit all the headlines. Since Wendi had already gone Viral several times on social media sites, call it like it was, Wendi Feral was famous, she was a celebrity along with Jax Foul, and there had been books written about the way they'd dismantled the Cuban Mafia's child pornography ring, who had made sex slaves of poor children.

The hatred towards her from her brother Mark couldn't be quantified from my perspective. I'd read that Wendi had been in a coma for months and was so traumatized that she reverted to her childhood and invisible friend. Her alter ego, "Sunshine,' yes, that was her name, Sunshine. Wendi was then diagnosed with a severe case of Dissociative Identity Disorder. Her parents and deceased husband, David, had signed the admittance forms at NIA, and the poor woman had been here ever since. It was apparent I was just now talking with Sunshine, not the kind and compassionate loving Wendi Feral!"

She then pushed me along "let's move, Kam; it's no time to linger and waddle and dawdle. I was supposed to have you at your Uncles office at the Admin. building a while ago. Get in the Golf cart!" While being obedient, I mused with pursed, pouty lips thinking that many people and organizations shunned or frowned on what NIA stood for. Stigmatized from its inception in the early 1900s, it was called the Napa Insane Asylum. Now an unpopular title, not politically correct, so they Whitewashed it with the acronym NIA.

I sat alongside a freaking Nut, tossing caution into a tornado, being cocky without a penis, pretending no fear. I made the statement to my civilian guard. "Can I ask you something, Wendi?" "Sure doesn't mean I'll be able to give you the answer that you want!" "Uh… am I speaking with Wendi, or are you Sunshine? I'm <u>Betting the holder, your Sunshine Feral</u>, right?" She didn't say a word back. She had just parked the Golf cart at the Administration Building,… a feeling of hostility was in the air from the Wolf leader in the back seat. The first words she said back to me as she opened the double doors "good luck, you would have won the bet, Kam!"

I was led to a Bronze plated inscription that read CEO Terrance Hallman. The doors swung open; I was intimidated by the giant cathedral-arched ceiling. The furniture was right out of a medieval castle at one end of a ridiculously long table made out of exceptional exquisite hardwood, possibly Cherry, not my forte. Ugh, wood, geez, my mind is muddled.

Besides the Ivory blocked walls, what else stood out to me was the stark vulturistic sense that I was on the platter being munched, a sacrificial appetizer to the NIA Gods or Devils. Sunshine yanked a highbacked matching chair out for me. We sat in unison. I took account of who was in attendance trying to calm my frayed nerves and thought I'd controlled this childhood curse, but no... I suffer from a hyperactive brain combined with a hyperattentive mind, not a duo I'd wish upon anyone. Ugh, well, except Sara... gosh, I felt nauseated. Whatever ailment or acronym the psych doc's wanted to label it as... I'd own it. I needed to keep my composure and blood pressure down for my baby.

Uncle T, at the number 1 position alongside him, was Jax, Shon, and Jaybird. On my side were Wendi, Rocky, and Liz. Another woman dressed in a Pilot's uniform sat in a seat kitty-corner from me. I bent forward, squinting my eyes. Over her left breast pocket was the name Agent Klite. The rest of the chairs were occupied with people I'd not been introduced to, leaving about five chairs empty. Directly across from my seat was the Reptilian smacking hatred entrenched Snake herself, Red eyes glaring in my direction. I imagined a stench coming from her rotting flesh, dear sister Sara. Who tried in vain to lock into my eyes, leech-like a Frowl (growl & frown) exposed imagined her fork tongue. Instantly I knew I was in the wrong place at the wrong time.

Jax said if anyone needs to use the restroom or wished to have a drink, this was the time to do so, pointing to gender-based doors and a wet bar in the corner with a glass-doored refrigerator that seemed full of miscellaneous stuff... a mini kitchen. Sara took up her glass, drained the rest of the Reddish fluid, and declared, "think I will refill my Cranberry," then sarcastically said, "Sister, can I grab you anything?" Suddenly all eyes were upon me minus two.

Like the bitch she was, placing me awkwardly in a complex situation only wobbled my noggin. No... I felt like an intruder and didn't belong here at this table. I shyly got up to use the restroom and took a bottle of unopened water, remembering the last drink Sara had served me, ugh, given to me laced with poison. While I visited her at NIA prison in her makeshift salon... sister dear had given me Iced Tea to drink. Little did

I know the tea had disabling psychedelic sleeping agents, unh, chemicals that totally knocked me out. That's how I got here; my twin stripped me, putting on my clothes, uh... stop this memory. I gawked an evil stare at the Vulture's back. Thinking Nah, fool me once fine not my fault yours but fool me twice my problem and my weakness uhm, my fault!

<u>Valerie Amann is a Voyeur.</u>

Alone on the other side of the 8-inch walls was Valerie. She was watching the different screens captured by the five cameras. She watched the group of NIA Brass. Her Uncle Terrance had asked her to analyze and compute all the information dispersed. Of course, all was recorded for prosperity's sake and further discussions. The two-way mirror was placed next to super-large screens in the adjoining conference room where she relaxed. She was glad as hell she wasn't invited into the War room, grinning mischievously at her two older sisters, Sara, and Kam, who showed utter disgust towards one another. Val laughed out loud. Wow 'my sisters are together for the first time. It had been over 27 years since she'd seen them, both in the same room!

<u>Terrance Halliman brings the impromptu board meeting to fruition.</u>

Terrance stood; "thanks for joining us this afternoon. I believe we're all familiar with each other; if not... We soon will be. Please be cognizant of what is disseminated here.... Please stand, and will you address this forum, Cassie Klite?" Terrance grinned "this is our FBI Pilot Cassie Klite... Ms. Klite is a graduate of our fine facility and a 2013 alumni member. She's here to report some alarming news that could harm and affect all of us. Without our intervention, we're facing serious consequences. Our due diligence and circumvention are essential…" A loud chime is heard; Terrance flashes annoyance and pushes a button staring into the distant camera that hovered over the entrance of his office "nice for you to make it for our 5:15 meeting, Floyd!" He's buzzed in and takes off his ball cap. Strides in raises his arms to speak Uncle stifles that, "please take a seat!" turning to the others. "Floyd is also in the class of 2013. His expertise is in surveillance and counter-surveillance. He graduated at the top of his class, not often tardy. It will be forgiven this time."

Terrance seemed to have a change of venue and said, "Ms. Klite, can you take your seat for now? Floyd, will you do us the honors and start today's proceedings!" His compact build of sturdiness was the first thing I noticed. He had a round face, big blue eyes, and long eyelashes that some women would die to have. That was the only feminine thing about this rugged brown-haired Marine cut-styled man. He wore a dark brown suit without a tie and an off-White dress shirt rolled up on some popeyed forearms like a prototypical clone at NIA.

"Boss, first let me apologize for my late arrival. I had to meet with our Uber driver for the recording chip of Rico and Doctor Roble. My team followed them to the Residence Inn Marriott here in Napa after they had a 3-hour late lunch at one of your Wineries." Terrance nodded affirmative others fidgeted in their chairs. Floyd continued, "for years, we've tracked Agent Rico Captor placed bugs innovative devices in many of his hotel rooms. Even knowing he will use a scanner to check for such devices. For years we've camped next door to his hotel rooms, monitoring him, um, or trying to do so. The man is a suspicious and paranoid person, always checking his rooms for cameras and listening devices. He never fails to run a scanner to detect our gadgets. After re-entering his rooms, most people run one scan, not Rico."

Floyd chugged some water down, "we couldn't succeed in gaining anything of importance until today. This morning I engaged our Phalanx probe directional satellite tool. We point the unit on whom we want to eavesdrop on ahh... Those of you that are unfamiliar with this tech..." "go on, Floyd, not necessary," said Terrance. "Not only were we successful at recording them at your winery, sir! But we also followed Rico and Doctor Shanon Roble out of your establishment and pointed the Phalanx probe at the backseat of the car that they were sitting in. Our listening probe and our Uber driver's recording device... combined, here is what we heard... mind you, Rico had already cleared the Uber car of listening devices, then I'd ordered the driver to switch the recorder back on. Rico had asked for some music to be played... even fricken drunk, he was a weary soul!"

Floyd tapped down... on his phone, which was synced with the speaker system in the conference room. *"Shan, I'm now even more convinced that Sara is allowed to leave the prison. I caught her and Terrance in several contradictions. Sara even had tan lines yet was locked down supposedly for the last five weeks!" "Rico, that could be explained by spray on tan's___" "No way; if you're going to use spray for your legs, wouldn't you spray your entire leg? Huh, not going to leave sock lines? Hey, it was the same on her arms, sleeves, tan lines___" "You got me on that? Tell you what, I will take the hair follicle samples and check for any chemicals used in tanning sprays___" There was a pause in the recording, then; he slurred, "I went all-in with the Judge, who worked with me on the warrants for her DNA. You will see the video... pay special attention to Sara's expressions before she flipped the fk out. She's guilty as Sin___"*

Kamryn felt like shit; ugh,... 'I drifted as I do at times, having trouble focusing on subject matter I didn't give a crap about. I wasn't feeling like myself, and heck hadn't since I'd been drugged to oblivion since being wrongfully incarcerated... uh felt kinda jittery. Floyd summarized the conversations between Rico and Shanon. Then I blinked awake when I heard... *Rico yelps loudly, "Terrance is guilty of collusion. We're going to have the proof after we print out all the pictures and videos we took together on that helicopter flight over their off-site training facility. Our informants have reported that this was a good day to catalog video and take pictures of the audience at the NIA games, with many V.I.P.'s in attendance. It's the semifinals this week. I'll tell you, Shon. I was so fricken glad to be out of that closed room earlier this morning with the freak show of Sara, Ama, Al, and Donny. She's definitely insane, and Terrance is the Puppet Master!" There was a pause, we waited, then "Sadly, you couldn't make it to the interview, I sure could have used you in that attorney room with Terrance and the psycho, but I'm happy you're here now, Shanon!" "Yep, I had to finish up with my family, sorry!"*

Not a soul at the table wasn't affected. Disturbed expressions ran all gambits in the negative connotations sphere, mouths covered, shaking of heads, fists slamming the table, all were catatonically magnetized eyeballing Terrance.

Floyd raised his hand's palms out "ah, let me start from the beginning. We overheard an earlier conversation. Rico was speaking to Doctor Roble inside the hotel's elevator, planning to meet her at the Napa executive airport for a flyover of NIA-U. I had to go into warp speed!" he sipped his water. Floyd went on, "my next linear movement was to contact one of our FBI Agent pilots, Ms. Klite." He pulled out a chair, saying, "Ms. Klite, you have the floor," and sat down. She arose slowly and began to speak in a forceful, no-nonsense tone, "I also recorded their conversations, giving Rico and Shanon headphones to use for communication in my helicopter. Rico knew that his scanner would go off like crazy if he checked for electronics, so he didn't check for recording devices. Heck, the chopper is only used for Law Enforcement, anyways Rico ordered me to fly over to the NIA training facility where we're meeting now. We hovered above for a total time period just this side of 37 minutes." Terrance's scowl became entrenched.

"They were clicking their telephoto lenses away like hyper Paparazzi photographers down on the training facility concentrating on the Quickdraw contest; Rico asked me to engage the outside camera's video on the helicopter. Ahh, let me say this if it weren't for Floyd's warning, Rico would have had a different pilot. I was at the gym working out and rushed back to the airport and finagled my way into being his helicopter pilot." "Cassie, please, I can respect that move on. Get to the pertinent facts, or we're going to be here all night," mentioned Terrance. "Umh, all right, without further ado, here's the full recording of the 77-minute flight. Oh, before I push play, I believe it's imperative to understand Rico and the Doctor were far more reserved with me being nearby, but some helpful information can be gleaned from their discussions."

I was lost again, like most individuals who are aroused with inner conflicts, consumed with self-inner chatter, um, realizing that never would I ever forgive the ugly face that was my image across from me. How couldn't I... not have nervous tension? Despite the room being around 67 degrees, my underarms were sticking. Omigod, let me escape this predicament. I don't get it. Sara was here so she could resume her 'Life sentence.' I should be free to go; why am I here anyway? This has nothing to do with me. Wendi already said that Sara had so much more to offer NIA, so Wtf? I spun out of my stupor. An angry, hungry shout, "Play that back and turn up the Volume," bellowed my Red-faced Uncle. My attention focused on current affairs, not like my issues weren't present or relevant, well, at least to me...

The helicopter recording is played back. Everyone seemed hypervigilant. *"Shan, zoom in on those Horse riders. Hey, pilot, drop down as low as is legal, no screw it, lower legal or not get us as close as you can over those Horses...." "Oh man, it can't be...." "Will you believe this if that ain't that lying prick Terrance and the slimy killer Sara herself riding Horses dressed in fancy western clothing? Ft solitary confinement, my Ass!..." "Hold up, Rico, you forget her twin. It could be Kazarpa. We'd have to have conclusive evidence to bring to the Judge!" he sighs. "Your right, I'm jumping to conclusions. Take as back over the Cowboy show," he demands* of Pilot Elite. "Let's take some more shots." There was a breather. Nothing was said, then Shaun blurps, "oh damn, no way. Look at the female 2nd from the end in the V.I.P. section. That sure appears to be the other half of the set of identical twins. This is bizarre Rico-like phantasmagoric, we umh. I can't make out her face, but her hair is entirely blonde, and she has a similar body type. Maybe we can get a close-up of the one on the Horse if she takes off that Beige cowboy hat; whoa, just got a great shot of the one on the bleachers."

I sat a little taller in the high back seat, thinking if the Feds knew I was here and Sara was on the loose, that could be my way out. 'Get out of prison card... yes, go open the gates now!' I returned my attention to the group... watching the NIA group's reactions. Most were agitatedly alert, waiting for the recording to continue. "I will have to go to one of our Labs and have the technicians enlarge and sharpen the pictures and do their magic with our videos. But Shanon, there isn't, umh... ain't no way in hell that's not one of the twin Amaya's. Did you see when she tipped her hat? It was none other than Sara... in my book. She's out there with that lying prick, Terrance, man I knew something was wrong with that dude. I never liked that asshole. Remember, I just saw her this morning..." "If so, then we might have proof, and we will raid NIA with my Swat Team." Then we hear an earsplitting shout, "Oh No Way... sitting up next to, oh no, is that whom I think it is? That's not Wendi Feral; OMGod, she's supposed to be in the hospital with Brock and Lucie."

Rico couldn't grasp what he saw and turned his glasses back into the bleachers. He was gasping for oxygen, wheezing, nearly fainting, shouting, "no, that's not my girl Wendi. Uh oh No, what, please tell me? I'm seeing things God No!" Rico's shock mortified his cardiovascular system as he fell backward. On the radio, we hear a panic from Shanon yelling, "Rico ahh Rico, what's wrong Rico OnLord, he's grabbing his chest take us down now pilot to Napa General Hospital at once."

I leaned over to my side and focused on Wendi's reaction, nada... who sat beside me on my left. Ahh, I mean Sunshine's. She seemed unmoved but subtly put on a display of concern for the rest of the consortium with a parody of placing her palm over her mouth and bowing her head. I thought, what a Fake bitch!

FBI... NIA Agent Cassie Klite stands again, leveling her eyes on my next-door neighbor Wendi uuhhh, Sunshine Feral, who sat composed, seemingly without a care. The limelight upon her for all, dare I say she spun a don't give a flying fk look. A garbled inaudible mumble came over the speakers. No one could make it out, Klite said, "Rico fell down across Shanon's lap. I quickly spun the chopper back around and headed to the hospital, but after a short while, Rico recovered and was A-Okay. A few minutes later, he regained his composure and nixed the hospital flight, with Shanon arguing with him to go get checked out. He became intense, snarling, and like chomping at the bit. I could tell the man was angry by his aggressive tone. He ordered me then to fly the perimeter of the NIA Institution. Uhm, I have nothing else to report. I dropped them off at the Executive Airport. That's it for me. I've turned in all the data to Floyd" she sits abruptly.

<u>Terrance stood and addressed Wendi/Sunshine and Pilot Klite.</u>

Terrance stated... thank you, Cassie, for your professionalism ... I'm proud to call you an NIA team member, and you undoubtedly excelled in trying to control the caustic situation with Rico and the doctor. He then rolled his head towards Sunshine inquisitively, "Wendi, you are aware that Rico tried in vain to visit you earlier at the NIA outpatient hospital, where he spent some time with Agents Brock Dune and Lucie Link. We had him informed that you were in a therapy session. Since you were escorting Kamryn, you weren't available. Could you discern what Rico was trying to say before he lost consciousness?" Wendi bent her head upwards. "I caught some of it." Cold as a razor-shard dagger, Sunshine replied, "sure, Terrance, he said that's Wendi. I'm sure of it. We're in love, no, unh, maybe it's Sunshine. Uh, help me…" Terrance let loose an uncustomary howl "well, well, I'll be. We got ourselves a card to play here. He's still smitten with you under a trance or romantic spell. This can only improve our chances… like an Ace in the hole. There's still a chance of bringing him to heel." "Yes, Terrance, I feel that soon Rico will propose we get hitched. I mean married; it's how he looks at me…" Terrance grinned widely "we need to play him like a fiddle. Get him off our backs."… I couldn't believe how cruel Sunshine could be with sweet Wendi right there under the surface, listening to her alter ego say these words with Iceberg cold matter-of-factness.

I periscoped around. Most in the room smiled along with my dear ole uncle, going along with the protagonist, the Admiral, and the Leader smiling with elation because Terrance was The Man! Only a specific few in numbers were aware Wendi wasn't under control, vexed ah subservient to her more dominant alter ego, Sunshine. Who was devious in my book, although she was way far behind in second place in our collected space inside this room today, for The Anti-Christ… lingered within… Sara is the Devil.

Floyd retook the floor. Gawking at Uncle… "I'm afraid we're out of sequence, no excuses, but remember this all happened today just hours ago. I played the Uber trip phalanx recording from after the flyover and their early dinner. Sorry didn't have time to align…." "Damnit, what's wrong with you? You're confusing all of us. Where the fk is the chronological reports? Uuhhh, you're discombobulated, Floyd?…" "I'm sorry, Sir, I ugh okay, the storyline gets even worse from this point, the degree to which each of us can determine and analyze in our own ways." He moaned with a distraught grimace staring at Terrance. "Sir." Terrance, visibly stressed, stood, "Floyd cut the dramatic caricature of disaster. We aren't in drama class. Leave the semantics at the door, now just facts, no more embellishments get with it. This was only hours ago. The present tense is happening now. We have to be proactive. I'll remind you we're going nowhere until we formulate a plan of attack."

Floyd kowtowed uh, "Yes, sir, well, earlier, we followed them to your restaurant winery. Obviously, Rico and Shamen were unaware the ink hadn't dried yet with your buyout of the establishment, nor I believe they would have chosen it, so boss...." Uncle slams his fist knuckle down. "Floyd, no conjecture, just fricken facts!..." he flashed a Red countenance. "Umh, in the Uber on the way back to their hotel, they didn't speak much, or the better description is we couldn't pick up anything discernable. We were pointing the listening device at the Uber, but we were in traffic and moving in and out of lanes. So what I've already disseminated to you is all we got in the vehicle. They had the music on in the vehicle; as I said, we tracked them to your winery. They took a VIP booth in the back. I snatched up Jordan, a first-year cadet here at NIA, to take the section that they decided to dine in, umh, for him to be their Waiter. He brought a pitcher of water lemons and a bug that he stuck to the underside of their table. This was when Rico and Shamen got obliterated on your wine Mr. Halliman three bottles of Red and then a bottle of Blackberry port."

I almost released a chortle for Floyd.... didn't get it. My Uncle didn't give a fk what they drank, nor anything else. He wanted Floyd to get to the meat and potatoes, the evidence, duh. This guy apparently liked to talk, and it was funny to me.... I waited impatiently for Uncle to explode again, one of his hands in a fist touching his chin, the other knuckles down, tapping the wooden table.

Floyd continued addressing the group, "they spent three hours and about 13 minutes dining and chatting. Our

Laboratory has broken much of it down. We could not discern a lot… with the glasses clanging, dishes banging, and the surround sound playing smooth Jazz. Here are the excerpts that were considered crucial let me start the recordings."

All the characters around me had one thing in common! I decided they had a lifetime bond of commitment or were loyal to one another; alliances melded. I'm in the other camp. The contrarian way of thinking enthused me and motivated a powerful dislike for all of them. The wool came off of my Uncle a "WereWolf" was all that remained. I tried not to stare at Rocky, who was my only Ally at the table and inside NIA. I, of course, was paranoid; even when it came to him, the stories he told me at the Gazebo before he helped qualify me to get my NIA badge still resounted in my skull. Primarily the segment he described regarding NIA Teams working for our Government, like Black Ops, having accomplished not one but many missions overseas. The last covert or clandestine… objective was in Iran. He was part of an assassin group, and the US Government would disavow any knowledge of them if caught. Rocky had intimated that NIA wasn't what I believed it to be and that, sure, there were bad Apples working on the grounds of NIA. But NIA was endorsed and sanctioned as a clandestine army that covertly assisted our government in endeavors that were never to see the light of day! Rocky had joined NIA to fight for an old way of thinking… for what our Founding Fathers had constituted the actual 'Constitution of America,' which, in his words, had been trounced on.

I wondered if others suffered from a lack of attention and did what I do and blasted off in my mind, like losing incremental periods of time, twirling lost, again not making excuses. Still, if I'm not interested in the topic that was being discussed, I drifted. I even did so lately while reading books like floating off in a spaced-out abyss enthralled in separate unassociated thoughts. Sort of wandering about in your subconscious while comprehension wanes in the present tense. Where was I?

Felt as if I was watching a movie losing the plot and not focusing on the conversations. Ahh, the motormouth runs at the mouth about a need-to-be interesting subject or topic. There's a pause he-she they all stare at you, probably asking you a question, but you don't give a hoot. You were not paying any heed… nothing of value interested you…Suddenly I bounced out of my carousing mind… A Scream accompanied by glass shattering on the table. "Kamryn, where the Hell are you? What do you have to say? This pertains to you. We need your damn input, Niece!" dazed and confused played in my inner ear. This can sort of be embarrassing, that is, if you care, and because I was a captive, I best give a shit, right? But how do I recover from this precarious ledge… help me?

Thinking quickly or maybe not, should I cop that a brain fart occurred while suffering from debilitating severe spinal pain or my leg fell asleep, and it was twitching? I decided, "I'm sorry, Uncle Terrance, I need to use the restroom. I'm dealing with horrible cramps and am concentrating on not pooping my pants. Excuse me, please!"

Rather proud of my resourcefulness, I swerved my chair to the right, bumping into Wendi, missing my twin's glare as no one had a retort like my Period stopped the flow from all their mouths. With a frowning nose curling grimace, Terrance exclaimed, "Kam hurry up if you can," not showing ill will. "Yes, Uncle, I'm sorry…." "Sara, all right, I'll pose that same question. What would you suggest" slowly, I waddled to the door. This was my chance to save face, stalling ever so slowly. I tried to learn what I'd missed that was so darn important.

I hear Sara's similar voice rap, "we all heard Rico he's going to be asking for a warrant to take a sample of Kamryn's DNA to compare against mine. There's a breakthrough in Mitochondrial DNA where Science can now differentiate cells of identical twins. He's going to start reconnaissance on my Beauty Salon and

Kamryn's house and try to interview her. On top of that, he will scrutinize my Uncles homes…. Law office, pulling camera video from all available sources, including civilian security systems and stores shops by my Hair Salon. Also, he's going to have Cal Trans video for the roads to and coming from NIA…." Impatient, Terrance wails, "Sara, please, why are you repeating what we heard from Rico? Unh, what do you suggest to remedy at least a portion of…." "Uncle. I was running that back by Ame, sorry" … Sunshine nodded with a grin.

The only perplexing expressions came from Floyd and Pilot Kkite, the first-time attendees of the upper-scale NIA conference gathering. They weren't versed in the multiple personalities that Sara embodied! Ame spoke, "well, sir, it's apparent that if the Feds are going to be tracking and running reconnaissance on Kamryn…. encompassing her vehicles, homes, and her hair salon business seeking DNA samples. Uh, we have only one option as I see it, Kam disappears. We cannot afford for Kamryn to be caught outside of NIA…. unh. With the advent of this innovative next-level testing of this newly discovered form of mitochondrial DNA, it's too dangerous. This is a perilous situation we find ourselves in. We must certainly be diligent, sir!" "Thank you, Ame…" "oh sir, as far as Rico's infatuation with you, it will be short-lived, in my opinion!"

Standing at the cracked door… great, did I hear what I thought? Um, please, can't it be true? Instantly I was pumped and felt like leaping in the air and doing a pirouette. Did I eavesdrop that I got this bitch Sara? She can't leave this institution, for the Feds have the warrant to test, oohhh yes, she's history now. Science can differentiate our DNA. Ahh, yep, they need me to play along on the outside, unh hey, wait, what was that about Kam me uh, the disappear stuff? I washed my face with cold water staring into my gaze. The mirror showed back my emaciated former self. Gosh, I'd gone through the wringer here at NIA. I looked like shit warmed over. Sara was the better version of me now. I rubbed my baby bump, 'I'll get us out of here, babydoll.' How did I know I was carrying a girl? Ah, mothers can tell sometimes *

When I stepped out of the bathroom and back into the humanity-filled office, two things had been altered the subject matter had a hostile tone, 'testosterony' a word I made up describing macho men in a rage. Shon was debating on the words he'd heard Rico on the recording say while he spoke with Shanon at the restaurant. It regarded him and was about the accidental Zipline accident where there were witnesses who thought they'd seen him there!

Jax waved his concern away. "Shon, just like the accidental drowning in Hawaii, the FBI still hasn't changed the death certificates to homicides...." "True, Jax, but you heard him. They have found other pictures of the assailant... I'm the assailant that is me, and they are trying to raise the pixels and use a newer version of facial recognition. Even with my fake mustache and change of hair and body type, there's something to worry about!" Terrance jumped in "that's the least of our concerns" he lurched forward and stood up, growling. We just heard that there were Spies here on NIA grounds under our watch. They're on-site right the fk now working for the Feds. Furthermore, they've somehow cracked or hacked into our security system."

He pounded the table... "This is a Code Red Alert. We need to know who they were like yesterday and where they got the information about our militias... locations. This is unfathomable and unacceptable. Only the people in this room have that information. We need to check our network terminals to see where the breach is immediately..." Jax waved his head with approval "we have a list of suspects we've had under wraps. They're free to roam about, but we have them under watch. It's good to know the exact number of infiltrators, Terrance. We need to eliminate them at once, uhm, carefully," then Jax stopped in his tracks.

Jax stands as Terrance takes his seat "actually, we face a precarious dilemma with knowing they suspect that we eradicated the last two spies believing we murdered them. This is a surprise because the death certificates had been documented as accidental we must tread lightly like on Eggshells and really think this out. The first step is setting the informants up with some false information and tracking the results after they disseminate the info to the Feds or Rico. Decloaking them will be a pleasure, so three spies are living amongst us, with at least one of them having access to our internal network with keys and some of our encrypted codes. Whomever it is... has the passcodes to subvert our firewalls. This sabotage has to be traceable hell, whoever it is ripped a fricken hole in our Firewalls."

Jax raises a bottle of water and drinks it down... "Listen, this is invaluable information, and I, for one, want to thank Floyd and Cassie for their input and expertise!" 'I hear that, yes, for sure, no doubt Youmans work, awesome job, stunning were some of the remarks tossed on the table for the pilot and surveillance expert.' Wendi/Sunshine holds her hand up, and Jax sits as she stands to address the group. "Rico, unbeknownst to him, had left us a marked trail. He stated that we were developing militia encampments in 27 states, leading us directly to whoever had pilfered that data. We just need to find which computer was used to violate our network. There will be a record of when the information was accessed, and we will have a video for our cameras are everywhere! Hell, to start with, the level of classifications they had to have bypassed is scary. After gaining this knowledge this morning, I called for a conference with NIA's top tech wizards. Alec's team is on board and working on this anomaly as we speak here. I would also request Kamryn to join us after this meeting in the technological laboratory. She has considerable talents in computer espionage, as we all saw with her breakdown of the Doctor Garza and New York Times debacle."

Terrance stood "from euphoria to the gutter. We will convene tomorrow at the same time. This is a scary time for us. We will overcome this intrusive invasion in our way of life. Whoever did cyber-sleuthing in our network will suffer for weeks. We have three infiltrators on site. Therefore, we have Death wishes. Let's move out and do this!"... Yep.

Everyone left the room with determination, feeling empowered, except for Terrance, who waved Valeria to come in the room from the 2-way mirror. He stood over Kamryn, who had her head resting on her arms on the table. He shook her. Kam didn't respond. Suddenly Valeria was at her side, lifting her head with Terrance steadying her. That's when they saw the Whites of her eyes. "Oh, Fk, she's dead...." screamed Valeria. Terrance hits the silent alarm on his phone. Red alert emergency. The GPS would lead the paramedics to where they stood!

-40-

<u>In a Medical Emergency... Kamryn is down and out, hospital-bound</u>

<u>I, ugh, Kamryn...</u> *'Lost but not found in a bad loop. I keep repeating this, fear is what I eat, breathe, and swallow. Am I finally succumbing to the family curse of derelict genetics? Yeah, I'm alive and mutating.... my hyperactive mind is broken, busted, Damn... cracked? Terminally filled with anxiety and madness. I feel highly frightened, umh petrified and insecure, and vulnerable. Is this just a bout of acute anxiety like I had when I was like ten years old when baby Valeria was kidnapped at the daycare center at five years old? I was already in therapy, umh, counseling sessions after my baby brother drowned. I'm unlike Sara, who was delusional with caustic episodes, rants, paranoia, and panic attacks. This*

mania manifests itself mentally and physically and absolutely cannibalizes your mind, uhm, my mind. Am I going nuts?"

Sweat dripped, couldn't rationalize, and hearing became warped as underwater muffled words fell in together, merging syllables like railcars in a 3-mile pileup. Realizing my head was on the table on top of my folded arms, in my Uncles conference room... who am I? aah, Kamryn. I didn't have a split personality, not diagnosed with one of the genetic curses of my ancestors. Schizophrenia was predominant in my bloodline. Ah, no, I was normal... or, for that matter, didn't suffer from any of the other hosts of mental disorders. Peering up past a crack between my arms, I saw the room was vacant.

In typical instances, textbook Dissociative Identity Disorder occurs way before my age of 37 years old. At least a person that suffered from this predisposition, ugh, mental disease, would have had some symptoms before now, not I. Because my family tree was a sprawling mass of psychotic psychopaths, I was a diligent... prudent individual. I did follow-ups and checkups with medical practitioners uuh Psychologists until I was in my early twenties. It was decided I was home free.

I was not complaining to myself. Nope, it wasn't until I was locked up and drugged here at NIA, this fricken insane asylum, did I start not to function properly, not feeling like me. I wonder what any of you would become if you'd worn my shoes? Doctor Liz Honcho, the Forensic Psychologist in charge of NIA's psych wards, once called it... 'de-realization' ahh, I'd had a mild case... Symptoms of de-realization, which meant feelings of altered states of being, which could have been brought on by stress combined with psychotropic drugs. That triggered the dormant compartmentalized schizophrenia that hid within my skull. The anomaly of not accepting my surroundings even though I was in my present state, even being so, I pretended that I wasn't locked in a prison cell. No, it wasn't real. But of course, it was because I was having a bout of mental disturbance… proof enough. Confirmation was with my next peek from under my folded arms on the conference room table. No one had left this meeting, yet moments before, I was alone!

"Kamryn do you want me to call the medical department" then *I hear Uncle Terrance say into his phone, "Liz, can you send a Nurse over to the facility? We have an emergency; we need help at my main office. Kam is unconscious. Hurry, thanks!"*

Like a TV show, emergency room drama played out, then, all my surroundings seemed to blend together like a kaleidoscope of hallucinations and distortions. I couldn't focus; a reeling noise reverberated in my ears. I was embroiled in a seizure wailing my arms and gesticulating like a jumping bean. Uh, I had blurred visions of all attendees of this high-level conference standing petrified against the walls as I was strapped down on the gurney. Liz was there with Renae and two paramedics. I was trembling, shaking, my tongue glued to the roof of my mouth, dehydration Death Valley-like. The only occurrence that I remember from that time period was how dark and cold it was outside… and Renae kept telling me Kam, baby, it's going to be all right. On the other side, Liz said something to one of the paramedics. 'Need an immediate blood panel'… 'I.V. inserted a Saline drip.' Oxygen mask on with a blood pressure cuff then out went the lights. Ugh.

Fun times… most pleasurable memories…that could have been 😢.

Kamryn flashed to fun times months prior… 'Brock was dripping wet skin shining Roman Brown. Kamryn watched him gliding across the water, jumping… and skipping across the wake. 'Oh, how Kam enjoyed this man.' He whips up the ski rope and drops it… his pointed slalom ski dropped below the water's surface, and she heard him hoot with excitement.

She quickly holds up an Orange flag flipping a circle and protecting him from other boaters. Brock starts to paddle over towards her. She puts the boat into idle and walks out on the open deck to snag the ski. "Hey, Kam baby, did you see me get that air? I cleared both wakes. That was so much fun. Your turn, babe!"

The dream was the highlight twilight of their sizzling love affair. It was less than 23 days and nights to their final glorious union on Shasta Lake. The Wedding party was staying at the park campground named 'Shangri Lala,' owned by Brock's other best man Rocky Blake. Then from the corner of her eye, she sees two Sea-Doo's skipping across the rolling wake of the lake. As they got closer, she recognized Rico Captor, who was going to stand up at their wedding, his best man, and Rocky Blake standing up waving excitedly; they were grinning from ear to smiling ear. Hey, you two, lunch is waiting over at my campground. Come on; it's a fricken feast, yelps, Rocky!

A needle in my arm blasted me back… I saw my evil arch-nemesis sister Sara; her laughing eyes looked down upon my head, which I couldn't lift from the tabletop. She blew me a wicked kiss and then waved her left-hand Karate style across her neck like I was dead meat! She evidently wasn't finished even after stabbing me in the back, drugging me and switching lives, nearly killing Brock, and destroying who I am….'

Awareness out of a fugue state, ahh dream state beeping medical devices, medical ward no not again Deja-Vu trying to regain traction memory recall button… eyes were closed mind locked. Someone was talking 'she was in a meeting with all of them. She'd had a seizure and medical emergency,' faintly recalls vagueness, ears perked up. <u>'Kamryn had an episode. Her genetic flaws had finally clawed her, tearing into her mind a De-Realization.</u> She was losing her mind. There was no other explanation' who was speaking, huh, understanding it wasn't just today with the Wolves of Wendi's? Something internally was skinning her with a potato peeler. She was sick with schizophrenia. Kam wondered, her back flat on the gurney. Do I choose the other voices Umh, my alter egos, how does it work? Or does the entity speak to me within and say, 'hey Kam, I'm Bob. How ya doing? Don't mind me sharing your body and head. There are a few things we need to get straightened out, Kam, the do's and don'ts... I will not tolerate....' Uuhhh...

I believe I've met all of Sara's personalities Anne, Don, and Al. Where do they hide when she is in charge? This is scary shit. Do they cling to the underside of her tongue, waiting to be heard or to speak? Then how do you shut them up? Do you have control of these other egos? Are they like spirits? What happens to my inner voice, my inner-spirit Ego, to whom I can generally speak to? Will there be interference? To whom can I talk to? Is my conscious state of being going to be available? Will I remain integrity based flat-out recognize all the people I am taking the masks off of, umh, reconcile all, or will my multiple entities merge... Scared into Silliness!

Example: I am Kamryn. I walk into a crowded convention center. I'm handed the microphone. The M.C. looks out at the large crowd saying, 'and now let me introduce you to an extraordinary lady who will present the winner of the Horseshoe Championship, Ms. Kamryn Amaya' cautiously, I take the mic. "hello to all of you. I'm Kamryn, Bob, Debbie, and Victor. How are you'll all doing tonight... we're just fine!'

With effort, I try to control my motor skills molasses-like slow. I open my left eyelid, afraid like a Chicken with a reflection of a cleaver, umh, hatchet at my beak. Yep, I'm in a white clinical room. Am I chained, shackled once again? Wiggle toes, fingers all there Wtf I go for it, kick my feet up, arms out, instantly grabbed by strength 'stop it... you will pull your I.V. out of your arm. Ms. Amaya, stop,' the Nurse pushes the call button. She hands me a paper cup with a straw from a small table by my gurney 'here, slowly... take a sip. Don't gulp it down. You are a lucky little lady,' said the kind elderly Nurse.

"Where am I?" "silly Goose, you're in NIA!" ah, oh no, silly Goose, not good. Did she say Daffy Duck? Did I fly over the Coo-coo nest, my mind whirling; I say, "how appropriate is the silly Goose statement, Nurse?" She stares at me perplexed, pestered, maybe with pity. "I'm freaking out, but why?" she finally breaks the silence "missy, your B.P. is going up with your heart rate. Please relax. Help is on the way...." "Like hell, helps on its way, nope like a flan straitjacket, are they rolling in a Guillotine? Ugh, get me up out of here. This ain't no Fairy tale!"

A frown is bestowed and directed at me, admonished. I thought I saw dentures chip at me. I have to get out of this place and kick the sheets off as Liz and Renae shove the swinging door open. Ah, oh, now I'm screwed. Something was amiss. I reached down by my side and pushed the gurney remote, sitting up, and inhaled a double breath blowing out my cheeks like I did when I was a child. *Was it the drugs in the I.V.? Geez literally felt in total like a million dollars couldn't remember the last time I could envision a positive outlook of any sort. It was always highs with super lows couldn't maintain an even keel. Um felt nervous all the time. Before now, I hovered in anxiousness.... but at this exact moment in time, I felt glorious. Lately, it was as if... daily, a mechanical shovel dug more dirt up then the Earth covered me up inch by inch, slowly and mercifully buried me alive like quicksand. Um, my depression was at every waking moment.*

Liz was on the right side, Renae on the left at the foot of my bed. Their expressions mirrored one another, an unknown amusement like a surprise birthday party. I was the centerpiece. Collectively they apparently had news that appeared to be elation related, not the vibes that you just won the lottery or that I was cancer free, or that Sara had an aneurysm that exploded. She's dead nothing this mind-blowingly wonderful... Nope!

Liz asks, "Kam, how long has it been that you've felt like a Black cloud of despair clung to your insides, confused, nervousness hyped up, apprehension unh? Call it morose like, uh, anxiety-laden being nervous with severe headaches and tell me, aren't you always thirsty…." Renae interrupted rudely while I mulled over… that of which Liz had inquired. "Kam, at this moment, how are you feeling?" I felt my cheeks grinning. They smiled like the shots of anti-depressants had kicked in, and I should be invigoratingly high as a kite. I felt if I waved my arms out flapping that, I might take flight

I placed both palms on my bare thighs, realizing some person had taken the liberty to confiscate my clothing. All I wore was a thin, lightweight hospital gown tied at the nape of my neck, my pregnant-filled boobs hanging without any support. Of course, that was no prob, for I had a petite rack that sat up high and proud yep, heck felt like I could dance.

"Kamryn, I asked you how you were feeling. Are you all right, girl?…" "Actually, this is the best I've felt in maybe a couple of months, at least before I was incarcerated in this…." "Kamryn, you nearly lapsed into a diabetic coma. Your blood sugar was off the charts; you're a type one diabetic. We administered a full vial of insulin. You must have felt like death warmed under, you poor girl." "Kam," Renae adds, "you're lucky it's 2018…" Liz was chomping at the bit, grinning nearly giddy "not long-ago diabetes patients had to poke themselves in their fingers for blood-sugar tests constantly. Not anymore. Thankfully, technology has caught up with diabetes. We're going to fit you with the newest innovative medical device, a small, implanted insulin pump. You will then be able to check your blood sugar at a whim with a digital readout L.C.D. on your wrist."

Liz pats my thigh "you're going to have to change your diet, sweetie. We will get you up to speed. I cannot believe that we didn't catch this. There are no excuses. You have been treated in the infirmary many times since you've been here.

This will be a life changer for you, Kam. I've read that your disposition and energy levels will be a wonderful change for you, we...." I bolted up, grabbing my toes with my fingers, similar to Christmas morning as a child seeing the presents under the tree for the first time. I am overwhelmed. I wasn't going insane! Omigod instantly... out of whack, emerging emotions released pent-up laughter, giggling uproariously.... followed by tears covering my mouth as I openly semi-howled and cried out of control. They came over to me, holding me and comforting me "you're going to be just fine now, Kamryn!"

I couldn't shut up and told them, "I thought I was going insane afraid the family curse had pierced my brain, schizophrenia at times couldn't rationalize what was real, or make-believe and I was residing within La La Land...." 'I didn't tell them that I let my mind contribute with negative momentum to the very worst scenario. Ugh, psychosomatic renderings or a form of hypochondria. I started reconsidering all that I am or was, and worse... fear of the unknown had set in.' Liz cocks her head to the left "that's the good news now, the bad news, if it could be construed as so.... your sister Sara and your Uncle are waiting to meet with you if you're up to it? Oh, ugh, if it's any form of consolation, Terrance was ecstatic to hear your diagnosis and to know you're okay. He was beginning to worry about you. Ahh, Sara wasn't fazed; she just wanted to get on with her life. I could put them off till tomorrow if you want to rest. Relax, Kam, it's up to you!"

"Thank you both for the awesome news by default. I'm not entering the dimension of delusions. Sure, I'd rather not have diabetes, however. My Grandma and Aunt did have diabetes... now that I think of it. It's all about genetics, isn't it? Surely wasn't gifted in that department!" I take another long pull on the straw, the cold water down my throat, pausing to consider my next move "no, I want to rest now and figure out where my best opportunities are... tell Uncle please that tomorrow any time after 9 am." "I sure will, Kam. Oh, your new diet tray for dinner is on the way," exclaims Liz.

They left me alone. The kind Nurse was also gone after telling me to push the call button if I needed anything. Amazing was how I felt, not confused, clear as a bell was my thinking. With clarity, whoa, Diabetes is a serious ailment. I never gave it much thought, for usually, Type 1 diabetes appears in adolescence. I had blood tests into my 20s and was in great shape wondered how long I'd suffered from this imbalance. I was able to do math equations again in my head, multiplying 3-digit numbers and formulating and analyzing the present situation, unlike yesterday or even a few hours ago. I needed to re-assess all, constantly forgetting where I'd left off, like having a thought or memory, then they'd collide, ugh, vanish, couldn't maintain any concentration, totally discombobulated. I pushed my recline button and closed my eyes with a smirk. Ahh, life isn't all that bad. The Worm is turning in my favor finally.

<u>"The Cat jumps out of the bag, Uh!"</u>

My hospital room door bursts open, and she says into a radio attached to her side, 'I will be indisposed. I'm going offline. I will check in later.' Liz stood over me with a ghoulish glare "well, missy, when were you going to come clean about your current situation? You're about six months pregnant and not showing much yet, but that will change, Kamryn. You're in dire need of prenatal vitamins. I've called in our in-house Obstetrician-gynecologist; you have an appointment tomorrow morning." I was, of course, not shocked. I lay naked under a thin gown, and my baby bump was the highest part of my prone body.... no use in denial, and yet I was mum. Liz paced back in forth in front of my gurney, "So I have a few questions for you, Kam. First, who's the father? Second, who knows that you're with a child? I won't bother asking the obvious of why you have kept your pregnancy a private matter!"

She stopped grabbing my feet in her hands, waiting for my reply. I glared back catatonically and said, Nada. My only thought was one word that reverberated Gynecologist. I had to get that baggie out of my cooler that had the egregious evidence against NIA.... umh, the memory disk I'd used to download all the information from the NIA proprietary network.... umh, had to hide it somewhere safe.

Liz shook her head slowly, not in the least bit happy, then nodded at me like she'd made some sort of conclusion and turned abruptly towards the door. I was compelled to try and mitigate what I knew was going to happen... "Liz, uhm, wait a moment. I'm not being fair to you. I am afraid of being forced into getting an abortion if I divulge the daddy. Do you think you could keep my pregnancy a secret a little longer, or at least until I'm about to..." Liz rolled her shoulders and reapproached me, "Kam, it will not be long till the baby drops, and it will be evident that you are pregnant. I will keep your secret as long as it is feasible. We will see how your visit goes with the Gynecologist in the morning. Okay, who's the pappy?" I groaned and sighed. "I appreciate your integrity here, Liz. The daddy is no other than my husband-to-be and Fiancé Brock Dame, whom I've heard is recovering next door at the Stem-Cell hospital. We conceived, I believe, in the ladder part of June." Liz couldn't hide her surprise, sticking her tongue out and wiping her upper lip, "well, I must say I'm glad it wasn't one of our Correction Officers, we've had a spree of that happening, as of late. Wow, I must say congratulations, little lady, and yes.... it's our secret for now!" She squeezed my shoulders while giving me a much-needed hug...

<u>**Sisters Valerie and Sara reunited after 27 years of living apart on separate continents.**</u>

Valerie was amused and intrigued at how her life had abruptly been flipped upside down like a three-hundred-and-sixty-degree reversal. Everything had changed in just a couple of months. She vamoosed umh and bolted out of London; she'd been living like a recluse being hunted like a rabid dog by Interpol and Scotland Yard... well, wait, hunt, not the proper word. No, they zeroed in on me; ugh, Law Enforcement from all over Europe knew precisely where she was located. They had suspicions and assumptions without DNA proof. I'd just eliminated the only living eyewitness just before they'd concluded that I was the serial murderer responsible for killings all over Europe. They watched her openly and tracked her not a moment of alone time out of her flat... um, apartment. When in public, the only place to hide from the vultures was inside a closed bathroom. I'd lock the door. The police were glued to her. They made it obvious and didn't care, even walking beside her at the mall and sitting at the counter right next to her at her favorite bar and grill. One bold fellow joined her at her table at her favorite restaurant. Lol, and hey, I couldn't get restraining orders.... against the cops. It was a 24/7 haunting experience.

By no means did the majority of Inspectors/Detectives have proof that she was the notorious Vampiress killer, although obviously, this aligned with some of their theories. Valerie, for self-preservation, decided it was time to vacate England before the simmering frying pan of scrutiny had full-on started sizzling, and she ended up with a charred ass. Ughhhh, before she was locked up in one of those dreadful archaic dungeons famously hideous throughout Europe.... she was threatened that her bones would rot in the Wakefield penitentiary in West Yorkshire, England. The pressure of the continued investigators tracking her blatantly finally took its toll. She had sent for her birth certificate proving she wasn't deceased and entered the U.S. Embassy. She'd befriended one of the Diplomats wanting a fast track back to the USA. She claimed to have a breakthrough with regard to her memory, a flashback. She pretended that all the pent-up trauma-based events of her life came to the forefront. Her amnesia dethawed. She remembered everything, along with fake buckets of tears and running emotions displayed for the Diplomat told him how she was kidnapped at the young age of five years old and never heard of again. It was her Uncle Terrance that was able to cut through the Red tape and pull the strings. Who knows where she'd be without him, perhaps doing Life inside one of the worst prisons in Europe. In Valerie's distorted mind, she didn't put past the 'Ministry of Defense Police and Civil Nuclear Constabulary' of planting evidence with her DNA attached. In fact, she was threatened by a Chief Superintendent in the United Kingdom who told her he would be precisely doing that; uhm, he was going to set her up! Yep, the prick was scandalous.

Valerie faked friendships with paper-thin annoyance and despised people... having loyalty for any human was never in fashion, um, en vogue. She never gave a damn about any person, lovers, boyfriends, or girlfriends. Val could just as easily slice their carotid arteries... or, ah, hug them. When she was done using them, they became expendable history seeya wouldn't want to be yah. Back here in the USA in Napa, all of that superficiality was halted, belonging to a cause to a man, a dream. Uncle Terrance and NIA were the real deals. The militias, every single gear and moving part of this organization enthused her... Val was all in. It was time to give back, with due respect, that she never understood. Val was a new human being in every way. They even looked different in the mirror.

That is where she'd fight her inner demons daily, with nighttime the worst time to stare at her inner selves. They'd remain locked up, divided, um, compartmentalized unless needed.

Val had shoved the chair to the side hours ago in a rage; three spies who meant to destroy not only Uncle and NIA, no.... She was the offspring relative who would inherit and ensure that NIA would prosper and flourish for decades to come. She remembered being enraged, listening on the other side of the see-through wall... without being able to give her feedback to the contingent of NIA royalty. She grew tired of staring through the 2-way mirrored window hiding on the other side of a wall while the delegation discussed how they were going to move forward. Why wasn't she in her proper place in the room with the NIA hierarchy, duh? It was because of her sisters; gotta get over it. It's way past time to confront them with the realization that 'Baby Val' lived, and here I am. Her 5-year older twins would be initially shocked. Then they'd take her in. What big eyes you have... said Little Red Riding Hood!... Lol.

She got up, paced, stared at the group, took up her phone texted Terrance, 'my dearest Uncle. It is time to break my silence. Let's start with Sara. Can you keep her after the meeting, umh, of course, with your permission, Uncle?' Time had lapsed by.... my uncle was busy with the passionate group of intense individuals... then a vibration, a text 'yep, it's time, Val!' Then he called her to come into the conference room...just before Kamryn had gone unconscious... everyone around was checking on Kamryn... Who had her head on the table, feeling sick. A few moments later, Kam goes into a tizzy and nods out is strapped on a gurney and taken by ambulance WTHeck!

Watching this unfold from the open doorway, Valerie, unseen... quickly bounced back into the adjoining room from whence she came, staring once again through the two-way mirror. She felt oddly nervous and went to work in her calculating mind on some algorithms waiting on Uncle, who followed the paramedics out. Felt oddly some feelings as Kamryn disappeared. Thinking perhaps I was human, Nah, smiling whimsically, wondering who was the most coldblooded between us. This would be a shocker for coldhearted Sara, for, in minutes, the meeting with Sara and Terrance was all that remained in her evening plans. However, she wanted to hang out with Jax a little later, um… after her enlightening reunion with sister Sara. But unfortunately, Jax was on a mission and had something he had to take care of.

Then loudly over the speaker system like a UFC Primetime main event announcer, "It's Time!" Terrance walked over and unlocked the party door between the rooms, and I casually strolled out, spying on Sara. Sara was still talking about the ugly mess that they would clean up regarding Rico and the FBI investigations. She leaned back in her chair, watching uninterested as Uncle led in this effervescent Strawberry Blonde beauty. Sara at once sits up straight. Terrance, with a wry expression, "my Niece Sara Amaya, why don't you refamiliarize yourself with my long-lost niece and your younger sister Valerie Amaya!"

Terrance watched Sara's mouth open huge… hands to her face. "I will leave you two sisters for now and go and check on the last of my family, niece # 3. Call or text me so we can get a late dinner… toodaloo!" Valerie stands on her tippy toes, kissing both his cheeks. Out the door, he struts, smiling magnificently outwardly and internally. He felt a slight relief grin on his exterior, although a touch of apprehension prevailed 'will they get along or be like Water and Oil mixed? Or Fire and Ice…. ah, hopefully like Steak and Potatoes,' wishing for the ladder.

Strange as it was, Val, pulled out a chair across the table from Sara, who remained seated, staring without looking down or away. This is how matching eyes met slowly for the first time in over 27 years. Deliberately and gradually, their eyes rotated without head movement. It's when the analysis began in earnest hair, chin, nose, cheeks, ears, facial structure, irises, unblinking eyebrows furrowed with suspicious overtones. It had been a quarter of a century plus since Sara had seen her younger sister. She was dead in her mind, and everyone else's Wtf. There would be no reality show semantics… with the dramatics of leaping in the air, hugging, and screaming, ugh, histrionics. No, quiet solitude. Oddly at almost the exact same time, they cocked their heads to the left, pursing their lips.

Neither had the emotional bonds or pretenses, meh, impulses to jump into each other's arms. Hush church-like silence had been both their friends. They suffered from the derealization of some of the mental disorders that had cannibalized their hereditary lineage, uhm… the prominent and dominant genetic syndrome, ughhhh, inborn schizophrenia. Valerie had better control, uh, restrain of this malady. Her other entities visited in times of strife or survival issues called upon ditto, similar to <u>Wendi and Sunshine's</u> existence. Since childhood Val regularly attributed her surviving the sadistic molestations by the demented couple who abducted her… by escaping into her other personalities; she'd visited painful hell too many times to count. Primarily Rudy was their savior. Valerie, ugh… she'd disappear high above her body into the ceiling, leaving her other selves to keep her amongst the living. Constantly praising her alter personalities, although still she could at a moment's interval summon her inner selves to the forefront sort of like a trance, since breathing in American oxygen, she had become grounded, nearly at peace for whom she was and had been. Val would morph when violence and killing for retaliation or revenge were necessary. Her vengeance knew no bounds if it was for survival… or protection. These emotions… brought out her advocates, who would take her physical self to the next level and then ascension to the peaks of brutal insanity.

The clock ticked... nada words were spoken after 7 minutes... Val realized she'd have to incinerate the frost. Almost perturbed, where should she start the topic launcher, nah icebreaker? I nearly said... to Hell with it and got up and left the room. Besides the same DNA blood coursing through their veins, paternal and maternal ancestors.... their kin, and sisters, yet strangers and would remain so if it were up to Sara. No doubt, if they didn't communicate, how would they ever realize any commonalities? Stare-off continued with minimum blinking. Why did it matter? Well, shit, the reasons weren't Nuclear Science, ughhhh equations worthy, no pretty fkn basic if we were going to be main players inside NIA. I didn't want to lobby for my position or have my sister Sara as a competitor.... for what I wanted to accomplish here at NIA. I had to win her over to dominate or eliminate her. It was up to her... In the end, I'd be in charge of this entire...? Sara coughed and moved her chair. Val finally decided that she'd have to be the one to end this awkward non-reunion.

Val pushes herself upwards and walks straight out towards the door before opening it to leave and declares over her shoulder at Sara. "You should never have killed daddy, our father!" Sara sprung up angrily, tossing the chair to the tile. "Mommy wasn't even in the ground yet. Her funeral was three days off, and daddy and that tramp slut neighbor was...!" "hey huh hey, what do we have here, sisters? Wait, stop!" Terrance stands straddling the threshold blocking Val's exit holding two of his favorite bottles of Merlot and three wine glasses. "Whoa now, whoa, we must celebrate. I have some good news!"

Valerie rolls her head in disdain and backs away cautiously, keeping her sister in view. "Uncle, I'm not sure I'm in the mood for wine!..." "nonsense, it's always a good time for Vino. Go sit down, sweetie" Val does as he wishes. Sara snapped, "Uncle Terrance, it's not good to drink on an empty stomach. I haven't eaten anything since breakfast." "I've got that handled girls a load of Carne-Asada tacos... Guacamole, salsa, chips, yellow rice, and refried beans smothered in Habanero cheddar cheese coming right now from the café. Relax now, not another word!" As he pops the corks out of the bottles to let the wine breathe, the nieces, unlike before, refuse eye contact, sitting like insolent spoiled brats.

He swaggered over and stood in front of the pouting sisters. This is flat tragic for me to be part of this trio, ugh family, were like blood where's the excitement here Sara from out of the Blue your sister Baby Valerie is resurrected from the dead and you Val…." "Uncle, didn't you say we need to celebrate? Did you already catch one of the three spies? What's to celebrate we…." "No, Val, it's not that of which we need to celebrate, but be assured we will pin the tail on those Donkeys; the spies will be caught. Nope, our celebration is about your other sister Kamryn. She's going to be all right, actually better than okay. What has been ailing her is Type 1 diabetes. I was going to our hospital to visit her, but she's spending the nite, so I high-tailed it back here to see how you two loving sisters were doing?" He repeats since neither woman acted like they gave a shit about Kam "the good news is Kamryn will be just fine this explains the last several months her highs and lows, and in just the last few weeks the mood changes have been off the charts. I'm extremely upset with our medical department. This is a rather simple test, and it should be a part of her regular checkups that your sister has had… since you swapped her out for you, Sara!" Sara cackles at that with an evil sneer, licking her glossy lips.

He stares down his nose at the two sisters as he takes out a rectangle cartridge and a small package and walks over to Val "all right, which finger?" she looks up at him. "I'm fine," and yet unfurls her middle finger. Terrance cleans it with an alcohol pad "you girls do have diabetes in your family's genetics on your mother's side. True, it's abnormal for Kam to have this diagnosis at 37 years old. She jumped right past Type

2 diabetes to the worse." Val inquisitively looks at the tester, slight concern on her face… digital display blood-sugar 127.

"Uncle Terrance, well, how's that 127?" he takes out a little pamphlet "umh, not terrible, but not terrific either. Where you want to be is between 60 and 101. You might already be a borderline Type 2 candidate; I'll schedule more testing with Renae for you…." "Okay, geez, it can't hurt, but it depends on what I've eaten… right? and I've not had much today!" Val, this is all new to me. Let's get a blood panel on you!" "All right, Uncle Terrance."

Sara approaches them, now the closest in proximity to Valerie in 27-plus years, with no concerns… with her forefinger exposed, ready for the pinprick droplet of blood. The testers…. LCD screen shows: 79. She smiles genuinely, "so I'm cool," gloating at Val. "That's within the guidelines," says uncle. He takes out the testing strip, pokes his pinky finger, and sticks the strip into the tester 63, grins at the curious girls "now that's what we're talking about… Yep!" There were smiles all around… Knocking on the door, interrupting their pleasant exchanges. He pushes the intercom, "come in" 3 first-year students at NIA University enter, all of them with a Hispanic heritage "this is Chef Manny. His family owned a Mexican Restaurant franchise and were lucky to have him here at NIA." Terrance enjoyed Mexican cuisine eyeing the Tamales excreting saliva as his mouth savored the taste he'd soon relish. The table was set "thank you, Manny, for such prompt service," bending his head at the other two acknowledging them. "Your welcome, sir. If there's anything else you'd like, let me know," Val raises her hand, "a Margarita pitcher." Manny smirks "well, of course, Senorita" Terrance wondered about Val's 127 number and how alcohol would react with blood sugar remembering the fermenting process wasn't many alcohol products made with sugar, 'oh well, he let it go' much more important things he needed to address.

Terrance sat in his customary seat, the sisters right next to him on both sides, Margarita's tipped against his Red Merlot. He exclaims, "this is tastebuds bliss" they were chewing yum. In the interim, savoring each swallow, he chose the hottest Habanero blended salsa. There were three different heat variances in bowls, "listen, girls, the last thing we need is a family rift. I don't expect a love fest or immediate bonding, but besides your sister Kara, your all that's left of your genetic tree!"

Valerie chomps down on a loaded tortilla chip "well, that's a positive thing without negativity," she looks at Sara, who also shakes her head affirmatively "that's for sure, sister," said Sara. Terrance sensed the ice in the Margaritas melting along with the sister's dislike for one another. Watching them eat, even in their idiosyncrasies, there was an uncanny quirky reproduction of mannerisms... it was astounding to me looking on. Knowing Valerie and Sara had been separated for upwards of 27 years. No question they were, but imitations with the same body types, Val perhaps 3 inches taller. Beauty contest winners or runners-ups... both had cocky dispositions and confident struts as if to show the world with the fact that their Shit didn't stink. Downright cute killers... lol, taut tight, strong figures, and eyes that tore through you, leaving you weak with desire, Lionesses without fearfulness. These felines could play on both sides of the Razor wire, charming killers, mysterious and seductive, ensuring they'd cum out on top!

He sipped another glass of Merlot, not a fan of Margaritas. The triple sec and lime juice mixed with Tequila bothered his stomach, causing severe bouts of indigestion. Terrance remembered lessons he'd learned while reading about world history, 'Femme Fatale' or maneaters. Kings, Emperors, and Princes were taught at young ages to beware of the mesmerizing lure of the 'Femme Fatale' types. Nothing could drop a man's guard down quicker than a tantalizing sex-dripping luscious vixen unsatiated or satiated and then assassinated with a long-lasting smile scintillatingly so.

Terrance put his fork through a Chicken Enchilada, musing about his good fortune. Sara was supremely talented. Her Ventriloquist skills unheralded a once-in-a-generation aptitude inherited from her Grandpa. She could mimic the voice of anyone. Al was valuable in any mission. Arne was the mastermind, the thinker, then lastly, the perverted Donny who fell on the lascivious side with an added shrewdness, uh, a perspective leaking out... debauchery at its finest... or worst... he was a sexually devious entity. In total, Sara was a cold, calculated murderess.

Valerie took the art of killing to another level. She was an experienced serial executioner with many of the same attributes as sister Sara. Ugh, with the exception of Val's unmatched Archery expertise, they were close in comparison. Val was a silent killer with the Crossbow... blow dart guns, and spear guns. Val was a 3-time reigning Olympic Gold medalist Champion. With the attractive gorgeous persona to meld in chameleon stealth like swiftly an arrow piercing the heart. Sara, for her part just as fiendish, was also a Silent Femme Fatale... wicked and heinously malevolent... killing with poison elixirs sprays and so forth.

Smiling, Terrance adored them already... taking another pull of his Merlot, the two of them were essential to him. He grinned from within, for only he knew the true nature of the final impact of what NIA would become... Uh, his vindication of what the global-based soon-to-be conglomerate NIA would evolve and manifest into a morphing that would stun the world. These musings brought forth a perpetual throbbing hard-on... he was the ultimate power broker... smirking, and he almost choked on a bite of Sopapilla Cheesecake.

Even though it was a quiet dinner, the concession by his nieces to sit five feet... apart across from one another was clearly the plus now... if they would only speak. Terrance decided on another tactical approach instead of the Vanguard, yep, change of venue, he'd use a diverse proactive protagonist POV 'point of view' and come at them with a direct assault. Or wait, how about engaging the attack from their flank come at them from behind 'sexy' or the sides? He had a hard time, like many testosterone-secreting animals.... trying not to allow lust or the anticipation of devouring the sexiness of an enticing body that thoroughly turned your endorphins into a tizzy of Heat. The whirlwind of fantasies imagining you inhabiting,... nhm-yum dwelling inside the body that was overwhelmingly insatiable... driving your manhood... plunging into the luscious skin. Terrance's warped mind was constantly fantasizing about what the conquest would be like looking at them. That's why men were the predominant porn watchers. Heck, he grinned can't help it. We've been set up! 🦷...unh testosteroned based ejaculations personified!

But Lord/Devil knew incest wasn't best! It wasn't just a mindset with ill underpinnings. No, never in the cards...a fallacy of a sick mind, it was gone. Terrance shook his head without moving it. I have to see my favorite secretary tonight for some dipping action, and Lord knows I'm fricken Horney. Oh yeah, gotta still deal with her. I hadn't spoken personally to her since she'd left the card about her untimely pregnancy, unh, mine too.... ahhhh! 🗯

With that being expounded on internally... and vanquished, he continued his assessment that the siblings were of a strain of Hollywood skilled professionals, top 3 % in disguises makeup artists extraordinaire when in camouflage they could literally walk past you without you having a clue that you knew them. He thinks how disarming a woman of their physical attributes will be in the future for his business, now how to mend fences.

Cell buzzed, he answers, wiping his chin fully satiated, maybe a bit too full "excuse me, nieces," he listens attentively, walking away from the table. Saudi was on the phone. They had a quirky relationship. Sandi was Wendi Feral's original partner in the mega-successful business endeavor they'd developed together… she was speaking. He respected their entrepreneurial vision and concept called 'Feral Feedback,' which was founded when, started up in Vancouver, Washington, and the Portland area Northwest, USA. Sandi said, "I just got off the phone with Wendi's parents. They are coming down to visit this weekend and haven't been able to get her on the phone. Terrance, we need to talk about what else they divulged. Can we meet later this evening?…" Terrance purposely taps the speaker on and says to Sandi, "well, of course, when I finish with my nieces, let's say 8:15 pm at your suite…" "Unh sounds good, seeya then, good luck with those two firecrackers!" lol.

He pushes end, thinking Sandi was a decent change up to ordinary people… her looks and thought process were purely enlightening. A good friend for sure, an Albino, an anomaly of extremes nonetheless, another beautiful woman with far more allure within her cranium. Alas, beauties come and go. Personalities and brains stay till death do… they part! What's more exhilarating, a one or a dozen night stands… or a person that continues to turn your body and mind on years later? unh… multiple? Sandi had been useful in bringing the sinister dead husband David to the Wood-chipper!

Terrance pulls out his chair, wise-cracking, "hey, sorry to interrupt you" this did bring out a 'chewing cud cowish' response. Each of their eyebrows curled up at him. He frowned "what was wrong with what Sandi said calling you firecrackers?" before either replied, thought… 'Hey, screw 'em if they can't take a joke,' he muttered silently. He was switching gears and mulling over their competitive nature, contrasting lifestyles, and innate similarities. No matter… he'd set up the UFC cage if they wanted to entertain a few of his trainers, betcha Jax and Wendi would enjoy seeing Val and

Sara blew out their dislike for one another with a 3-round 15-minute fight.

"Listen, you are both going to get along and work together despite what you may think. You're so alike, unh, 2 Peas in a pod...." Val pounded the table with her fork and went off on a tirade, rambling on in a couple of German, Italian, and French sentences... ending in a slurry of assertive Russian. Terrance's temper riled up. He replied back at her in Russian. She wiggled her head, looking at Sara. Who throws her napkin, turning on both of them. "How fricken rude I'm sitting right here... speak fkn English. We're in America if you haven't fricken noticed." Val barks, "older sister, if you weren't but a mere pagan, unh, American Princess who was uneducated in the languages of this world...." "English is all that matters. I don't need...." Terrance slams his fist down on the table 'ouch,' he kept that to himself "shut-up stop it, damn it. Okay, what you two already have is enough for a strong bond three things in common one, you both are homicidal maniacs. Two, you have a sibling named Kamryn. Three, you have an Uncle who loves you immensely and needs us to be a family again!"

Shock value 9.1 on the Richter scale... graph. He had them backed up and decided to roll with slight momentum "what do you propose I ahh we do about Kamryn? We have options, but which one is clearly the proper course to take, unh salient, viable without repercussions? We've already got three males to deal with. Is your sister a liability?...." "What about her? What is she guilty of? Look, Uncle. I can only remember little of her up till I was abducted at five years old... Kammy, as I'd called her, was like miss prim and proper Goodie 2 shoes. still to this day, I will say she was mommy's favorite...." "Yeah, I agree," postured Sara, "but you were daddy's favorite. Val, where do you think that left me, huh?" "You know right where that left you, Grandpa's favorite. Papa adored you... you two were inseparable, and you murdered him, too!"... yelled Valerie.

Terrance stood hastily "enough, no more barbs; the past is the past...." "Yes, Uncle. True, we can't alter the past. If you don't learn from it, we risk the possibility of repeating it!" "Okay, Val, history will not be repeated now. Back to Kamryn..." Sara took up the gauntlet. "Kam was always the Lil tattle teller snitch. You could never trust her with a secret when she was young. She was a player, always playing mom against me. Sure, as Valerie said, I wasn't an Angel." Val sneers in her direction... Sara growls, "you know what, little sister, we can settle this, you bitch. I've had enough of your high and mighty attitude, and you're flim scowls, your arrogant filth, and you can stick that fake English accent... for I'm going to kill...." "Let's do it, you old hag. Come on Bitch!"

Terrance pounces back up, spilling his wine, and throws his palms up, done with this crap. "No worries, I can and will set up a duel for you both. We can also pick from straws or numbers what kind of duel we'll decide, but for certain, it will incorporate fair-mindedness. Your combat fight will be without any favoritism. We will have to decide how you'll fight it out, perhaps wrestling in the deep end of one of our Olympic pools...." "To the death," shouts Sara, "Suits me fine," says a bored-looking Val. "Okay, I'll discuss this tomorrow with the team leaders will even enjoy some wagering and have a select audience, but until then, focus. I will not sustain another outbreak, um, interruption, or temper tantrum, or the two of you will be locked into a cell tonight. Is that clear?" With A flinch of fear, and a flash of annoyance, they wince rather than argue; they replied, "Yes, Terrance"... "All right, Uncle."

Valerie nodded at Sara, then raised an open palm at her Uncle. "Okay, you asked what to do with Kamryn. Why? What did she do?..." "Wendi reported that she was trying to leave the grounds this afternoon. Kamryn openly admitted this, your sister, like yourselves, is a highly intelligent individual who's analytical, but trying to escape NIA would constitute idiocy, even madness. But we may have revealed why she'd be so

so

sketchy and irrational. She'd been suffering... for Lord knows how long and nearly fell into a diabetic coma. With that being said, I cannot allow anyone to spoil or ruin and despoil what we have accomplished here at NIA. We will change history. We will make a difference. We must figure out if Kam is back to herself and not a threat to what we're going to achieve here... we are family. Rico, as you just heard plans to interview her and request a sample of her DNA, the question is, will he have to search her out, or will Kam go to the Feds herself, not seeking gasoline on the fire but when you swapped places with her Sara something has snapped in Kam she's not the same and...."

The first expanse of ill-witted humor exposed Val chuckling, "now that was fkn brilliant sis OmGod you were perfect completely diabolical unuh when Uncle divulged what you did to Kamryn OMLord. I was busting up; I want to hear you tell that story. I mean, when Uncle told me you're magnificently orchestrated and gruesome tale... oh man, I was on the edge of my seat, masterminding mission impossible whew escaping NIA Prison leaving your twin holding the Life sentence." Val bowed her head and nodded. "Kudo's to you, Sara..." who was wildly grinning with her teeth full on showing and rocking back and forth in her chair, giggling ferociously till tears cascaded down her cheeks.... then instinctively, she raised her right fist for a bump the sisters hammered bang. Suddenly an atmospheric biotic metamorphosis resulted, and a rotation of feelings systemically adhered. Uhm, let's just say simply that the sisters let their guards down with a form of acceptance and admiration... Lol.

Then Sara was off and running at the mouth "so baby Val... it all started one day like a Lightning Strike, an epiphany Bam, like, I was walking with Kam after I was sentenced to ten years to Life here at NIA's mental institution and ...." "Yeah, I watched the trial broadcasted live in Germany." Valerie smirks... grinning hugely, and elbows Terrance "man, dude, you were a stud heck. What did those suits cost you? Women around me in a lounge or wherever I was… kept saying what a handsome attorney that serial killer had."

Sara let loose of a grin, wrinkling her pert nose with a gleam in her eyes. Terrance was sitting up straight… now engaged and enthralled 'he liked to hear how handsome he was, smiling large.' "Yeah, I imported them from Sicily, Italy. It was a worldwide event… right Valerie? It was sensationalized, huh? Didn't the trial, uh, it go viral on all social media levels." He then twisted his head towards Valerie. Sara continued enthused to tell her amazing feat to her younger sister. She couldn't brag to anyone else, she thought, without getting arrested or in trouble. But Terrance interrupted and said, smirking, "Kamryn had so much heat and negativity on her during the trial that she needed to change her looks. Being Sara's identical twin and all, she went brunette Black with a Raven hair color." Sara didn't miss a beat, animated now "so okay, Valerie, this guard, who was enamored with me, uhm, the one I just killed. Carl joked a while back, 'man, girl, if you could dye your sister's hair blonde,' you could just walk the hell out of here pretending you were her!" They laughed. The three of them were on a roll with the ice-melting a warming trend en-vogue, and the healing began forming aah's, oh's, wow's no ways, ughs, umhs, fx no's yah gotta be kidding me woe's their real-time tales were relived without embellishments.

Terrance broke away from the table while Sara became even more spirited, and with Valerie entrenched, they didn't even notice him slipping away. His ego had been boosted, massaged felt like the strategy he'd employed would pay dividends, although, on the other side of the coin, they could kill one another before the night was over …Yep!

He stepped from the building, concerned with Sandi's wavering voice. Her phone call had an ominous forewarning of upcoming trouble. It was in her voice. He groaned and rubbed his tummy, man. I ate too much heck; there was enough already on his plate. He pats his stomach again and puts the wrapped plate of Mexican food leftovers on his front seat for Sandi. He checked with Tabby to see if she was willing to jump into his Limo and have Jacob drive her here to join him in his suite. Tabby agreed quickly, saying they had to discuss this pregnancy. His ulterior motives were sexual… he didn't want to talk about a fricken baby… dammit but she'd satisfy as a backup. Terrance then drove to meet the Albino beauty. He texted her, letting her know he was running a bit late. She'd texted back… I'm going for a swim. You know my code, seeya… in a bit.

_—42—_

    Terrance let himself into Sandi's Suite using her keypad code. Remembering his nieces drank Margaritas, he still had an entire bottle of Merlo and what remained of a bottle minus two glasses of wine he'd inhaled. At NIA, all the Leading Trainers Uh, Shotcallers, had suites on the property. Sandi was a top-notched superior athlete and intellect. Terrance gazed around at her uncluttered domicile. Sandi lived like a plain Jane type of person; just the basics were all she wished for. Looking only at essentials, no paintings, montages of photos, in fact, as he scanned the room, not a picture frame, one was amazed at how simply she lived. Her suite hadn't changed at all from his visits prior. It appeared the same as when she'd first moved in after being graded out and honored with being selected as one of NIA's team leaders.

    Sandi was a tall woman, a fine physical specimen with street-smart cunning and intellect. Having to deal with her incongruity being an Albino throughout her childhood, she'd accepted her anomaly and became comfortable within her own skin instead of buckling under public scrutiny. Having dealt with being castigated, isolated, and tormented. The teasing by children was unmerciful if you listened to her when asked the most often asked question, "hey Sandi, what is it like growing up as an Albino?" She'd answer, nah. It's impossible to have you or anyone understand. It's not like being the only Black, Asian, or Hispanic person in a school or in a room, or in a crowd. Nope. Most people couldn't stop staring at her. She was always on Blast like an Alien. Either she had to come to grips and accept who she was or climb under a rock. In early life, she was ostracized and shunned as a weirdo freak who was never invited to birthday parties or other fun activities. Still, instead of allowing others to cause introversion or dictate who she'd be, she found inner strength with much soul-searching. She learned to like who she was, galvanizing a new her, rousing an inner strength with a never give up persona motivating her to not only be proud to be a one-of-a-kind human but the best that she could be in any and all things she inspired to effectuate with abundant invigoration and self-mobilized motivation. Well, thought Terrance, it didn't hurt that she was drop-dead gorgeous with a killer body... huh?

Sandi had an open mind with an uncanny genius to mold and transform herself into any situation to be creative with analyzed contingencies. Her prowess for leadership with calm and stoic resolve is unmatched. He could hear the music out on the wrap-around deck of the large expansive one-bedroom suite of 1,375 square feet that came stocked with a barbeque and hot tub. He went to the small wet bar and found two wine glasses with dust remnants. Remembering she wasn't much of a drinker these days; she'd partied back in the day and had many drinking war stories with Wendi and her going out on the towns and cities in the Northwest... United States. Vancouver and Portland were where they were raised. He smiled and believed she must have sewn her roots back then, for she wasn't much into cavorting around like many of the other Team Leaders. Sandi was more of an introvert, uhm, or maybe an Ambivert mulling over a book he'd read by Malcolm Gladwell.

He placed the glasses on a nook... shelf within easy reach, then undressed and went out to the playing music, looking forward to seeing Sandi, but she wasn't there, sadly went back and grabbed his phone, replaying their texts. Wasn't she going to relax in the hot tub? Yeah, well, I guess I'll get started... oh, well, she was out doing laps at one of the swimming pools on site. The inviting tub took impetus, and he turned it on... Time for a bit of relaxation... Oh yeah.

After a few minutes had elapsed... Sandi traipsed onto the deck, "why is it I knew I'd find you out here?" he didn't answer, pointing to her wine. She had a beach towel wrapped around her, covering a Red and Gold bikini, and held his hand out "hey, I love your soothing Jazz music... before you hop in. I gotcha some delicious Mexican food. It's on the counter, just made fresh tonight. She bowed her head and left with a lingering smile.

A little later, while soaking in the tub, he wondered if he should check in on his nieces, then switched topics of worry and thinking of how he would deal with the Rice thing and Kamryn... the sisters, would have to take a back seat. The three FBI informants, the upcoming board meeting on and on... ducked his head under the bubbling jets as Sandi entered the tub. Comes up to see a sour puss expression and a wine glass in her left paw and asks her, "so what brings me here tonight, darling?" "Terrance, let me have a few more sips of wine and unwind. I just finished a 3-mile swim after we texted, I decided to blow some steam off and go to the pool, but yes, before anything else, we shall discuss upcoming events...." "Come closer to me!" she ignored this request "upcoming problems, Terrance, yeah, we need to plan out next week, please dude, relax for now!" "Woman, I'd be asleep if I were any more relaxed." She snarled for a second.

Sandi was a no-nonsense woman, not much for humor unless it was warranted. She intensely disliked superficiality or small talk. Some people were affronted by her approach direct to the point mode, didn't waste time, and had no manipulations. Zero games for him. It was the way all people should be. All humans wear masks portraying what they think you want to see, a portrayal of beneficial selfishness hiding beneath their disguises, uhm, masks, not she. It was stimulating to know there would never be ulterior motives with Sandi. Everything was upfront and out in the open.

Terrance watched her through cracked eyelashes. Maybe tonight, she will let me spend the night and sample my first-ever Albino woman. What a delectable sight, uuh, Yum. He'd been smitten the millisecond that Wendi had introduced her Ohyeah Sandi could flush out the pipes really good. Well aware he was a couple of decades her senior, but what the hay, he grinned to himself as he imagined touching her skin. I'm a horny old man, lol.

Her Hawkish luminescent eyes caught him "whatcha grinning about over there? I certainly could use an induced smile. Indulge me, will yuh?" He pushed himself straight up, feeling the jets pumping from the seat which sucked him in, unsed, looking at her nodded 'what's good for the Hen is good for the Rooster' he decided to throw steam over the hot tub. He answered her with likewise honesty, why not?' "I was only self-indulging, um, amusing myself with a fantasy of mine. Would you genuinely like to hear about it?" "I wouldn't have asked you if not…." "First, would you consider us friends, Sandi?" she closes her eyes as if in contemplation. "I'll answer with a question, Terrance, do you think I make it a practice to get into hot tubs with naked, not friends of the male gender?"

He almost stutters and grabs the wine glass to power on, "well, I suppose or guess not. Why don't you get more comfortable and take your bikini off?" no reply. She decided to leave the last question alone, "I'm here because I want to be Terrance, so let's shelf your blatant intent won't you humor me?" Feeling like he was losing ground and sliding into lurking muck. "Sure, Sandi, what's up?" "We must discuss Wendi. I know you're aware that we've been wildly successful with 'Feral Feedback' as you know, we've been awarded many prestigious honors for our staple of seeing eye dogs guide dogs, DEA snigging Canines, ATF for explosives, Airport security officers, our Canines are world renown courtesy of the Lyons Club who advocate for the blind all over the States and Worldwide we...." "Whoa, woman, aren't we getting off base here? I'm not looking for a resume. Or a damn commercial about Wendi and your business successes. I'm well aware of all that you've attained with Wendi. What jumpstarted you on this subject? Weren't we talking about my fantasy and you losing your freakin bikini?"

The bubbles bounced from the surface, steam arose, and all that was heard was the meditational smooth Jazz and jets blowing the water around. He soldiered on, "Sandi, can't you relax for a moment? Always hypervigilant on edge, huh?" his plaintive stare felt her sigh. "I wish I could. I'm feeling a little better, thanks to the wine. It's been a month since I've indulged in any alcohol. Ahh, before I permit you to evolve this tête-à-tête into your seductive amorous self-professed yearnings, I can either put up barriers or tear them down. There are guidelines..."...he snorts. Geez, you sound like a damn AUSA or District Attorney during litigation or a deposition. Your wound so freakin tight let me loosen you up?" Inside he was satisfied with those last clever lines, right around the point of what he wanted to achieve. How would she mitigate his finesse and skillful subtlety?

She released a pent-up wide-ass grin wobbling her chin and bending her neck toward him. "Oh boy, Terrance is ever pressing forward... onward, aren't you with your euphemisms on the prowl 2nite? I see, and I feel the mini hunt. Am I the prey this evening, huh?" she paused! He closed his mouth showing puckered lips. She ducked her head under, coming up with her tongue stuck out. Cobra playing with the Muskrat, cackling, "yeah, before I can let my guard down, unlike you, my mind must be clear and devoid, uh stress-free, it's different for males, I know, but...." "Wait, but I'm here to try and give you some much-needed stress relief, woman. I betcha I can have you purring like a kitten... call me Captain Stress-release. Ahh, there should be a bottled prescription with my picture below the word Relief...." He giggled at his last proffered line, as did she, "I appreciate your way of thinking, and that may be achievable, but first, can we discuss why I've invited you over here? Unfortunately for both of us, as it may turn out... it's not for your sexual conquest of me?"... she winks!

"Okay, you win. Yeah, got me. Let's blow through your concerns Darlin" he pours some more wine after she gulps the rest of the Merlot, holding out her glass for a refill. "Let me start with Rico, who contacted Ed and Barbara Feral earlier this afternoon." Terrance's complexion altered as his butt clenched, sitting up erect at attention. "Why did Rico contact Wendi's parents? What does this have to do with..." "her parents will be here tomorrow night. I spent over 30 minutes on speakerphone with them. You know I'm like a second daughter to them, and well, it goes both ways. I love them as well. Anyways it's obvious Rico had insinuated to them that Wendi is being manipulated here at NIA and isn't herself. Rico had told her parents that she was not being treated for schizophrenia and told them the three last visits to the outpatient hospital here, Wendi wasn't around or available and was missing. The bastard also told them he didn't think that Wendi was still in sessions with psychotherapists and that he had proof of otherwise. Having pictures of her at a training center... nah facility on another piece of property owned by NIA."

Terrance now was flushed, not from wine nor steam or jets "how could he make such an accusation, uh, unsubstantiated statement? His opinion shouldn't matter what a piece of shit I'm going to…." "Hang on, don't get upset with the messenger, okay? Rico sent digital pictures of Wendi to her parents of her sitting on bleachers and walking with Wolves, and another few pics showed an outdoor animal training center. He intimates that Wendi was working here as a trainer, her split personality had morphed and taken control ala 'Sunshine Feral' in a sentence, he wants the parents this time to sign her out of NIA post-haste." Terrance lets loose a howl…

"Rico has arranged for the parents to fly out from Portland, and he promised to pick them up in a limousine… they will be here tomorrow night!" "What, Sandi, that doesn't give us much time, does it? Oh shit?" She replied, "Wendi is my age, born minutes apart, actually 37 years old. How can they still have control of her? After we erased her conspiring husband David, that will never be found, wasn't he the person who had power of attorney and had signed her into NIA?…." "Duh, woman, yes, for sure that was the case, but her mother thenceforward has been reassigned power of attorney since David disappeared months ago! Sandi, have you followed the freaking head trip that Britney Spears has been dealing with? Sandi, all you have to do is read up on the bizarre happenings of the Pop Star Britney Spears case. Some of my colleagues that have been hired to advocate for Britney have filled me into the insanity that ole Britney has to deal with…." Terrance slurps the rest of his drink. "Sandi… Britney Spear's life has changed dramatically since one of my fellow attorney's law practitioners took her case. Have you followed the doc… #FreeBritney…." "Sshh Terrance, let's stay on point please, geez…." Sandi dunked her head again and emerged from the bubbles squirting from her succulent lips, a stream of hot water across the tub.

"Terrance, I might live reclusively, but I'm not dead yet, and I don't live in a damn culvert. Sure, I've followed Britney's debacle! She's freakin 39 years old and fighting for changes in her court-appointed conservatorship, which has controlled her career and finances for like 15 years. Poor thing has been like a puppy on a leash. Her parents are despots and power-mongers. Let's stay focused on what is going to happen tomorrow."

Sandi leaned forward toward Terrance as the bubbles stopped blowing... "surely I remember Wendi signed over all Power of Attorney to her husband David, giving him all control of her finances, health, and well-being, umh wherewithal. She wasn't aware that now her mother, Barbara, was in control. Heck, Terrance, this is just another fkn move by Rico. The only privilege she's got is her freedom at the facility. In essence, they could sign her out of here tomorrow, and her parents could take her elsewhere. We need her. She's irreplaceable, a commodity unlike even me. I..." "Hold up, Sandi..." "No, Terrance, it gets exceedingly worse. Ugh, I haven't a clue as to why Rico even brought this next stuff up. It has nothing to do with my BFF Wendi. For a man like you that is incredibly calculating, it stuns me that we are having this conversation, and you haven't already handled the Rico situation...." "Stuns you, huh, Sandi? Now you're getting under my skin. That's not part of my master plan. Rico the bastard, I should've offed him long ago but forget it. Tell me all right. I can't guess what's 'exceedingly worse' what else did he say to Wendi's parents?" He abruptly stands, reaching for a beach towel. "I'm getting out. Let's continue this in the living room!"

While waiting for Sandi to change, he tried to make sense of how to avoid the inevitable confrontation with Wendi's parents, but what of the other damage that Sandi had intimated.... umh could it have to do with the Video and digital pictures from the unplanned helicopter ride over the training facility by one of NIA's planted Pilots Ms. Klite. Dammit, seeing Sandi sit across from him supposing… uhm, knowing the romancing was kaput. Truly he now didn't have an amorous bone pulsating.

Having uncorked one of her reserved bottles of Cabernet, he'd cut her aspersions off at the gate, saying, "here comes the sequence of this morning. For sure, it was risky. I'm a gambler risktaker. How did I know the prick was doing a scenic flyover with his side-chick… kick Doctor Shanon Roble? The Pilot had no forewarning and no time to alert us. It was wham-bam, thank you, ma'am. Rico showed up at the executive airport and said to the pilots of the FBI planes, let's go." Sandi frowned and declared, "Sara and Kamryn were photographed, Terrance. How the hell could you have allowed that to happen? Jeesh, what were you or anyone else thinking having both the Twins in the same vicinity at the 'Quickdraw Competition.' I've asked myself why Rico would share that with Wendi's parents other than for shock value… and it did work. Barbara and Ed were shocked seeing you riding horses with a serial killer."

Terrance bolted up, stalked towards the door, swiveled, then shot back entrenched in the 'Love-Hate frenzy of chaos that enveloped him.' "I don't owe you or anyone else any explanation, and yet I'm compelled to do so… The FBI, CIA, you name it could be unwelcome raiders with warrants to enter our NIA gates. This changes the game just like that… I've, unh, we've worked so hard for where we are today. In a single afternoon of horseback riding with my devious niece… could change everything and take us from the penthouse to the sewer! I don't think so, woman. The short and not sweet of it concisely uah dammit woman… I'm going to have to call for an emergency board meeting. This is Hazmat Dangerous… Toxic!" Sandi had never seen one of Terrance's temper tantrums. He was disconcerted and was jumping to negative inclinations, and she took it upon herself to bring him back down to a simmering tea kettle.

"Terrance, we are already trying to mitigate what Sara has done after swapping out her innocent sister Kamryn and going on the killing spree...." Sandi stops midstream, thinking, when, she's adding kindling to the fire and only mutters, "we will survive." He sneered at her, "this ain't no disco song...." Downs his wine and walks to the wet bar, takes a bottle of Maker's Mark Whiskey, and pours a crystal glass full 'bottoms up' wow, he exhales, stepping over towards her, slowly pacing with his hands gesticulating. "Sandi, here's a fast overview. Sara and I hit it out of the park in the interview room. IMO.... in my opinion, Anne is the better quarter of Sara's inherent characters, was astoundingly proactive, and had poor ole Rico cowering in the corner of the interview room. Next thing you know, Sara wants out of NIA and back to the streets. I'd promised her that if she performed with me on the invasive warranted visit by Rico, I'd let her go back to her salon and life of freedom. She promised up and down to stay out of the limelight and assured me she'd me no trouble. Sara knew Rico would try and interview Kamryn and sample her DNA. Believing her to be the owner of the San Rafael Beauty Salon, he was going to set up surveillance and confront her." "Wow, how do you sleep at all, Terrance? You have so many irons in the fire, dealing with complications on so many fronts. You're an amazing guy!"

Terrance took a needed breath while Sandi just folded her legs and placed her clasped hands on her lap... he felt compelled to finish his soliloquy. "As you know, Sara had duped everyone and traded places with Kam, who refused to be interviewed by Rico, so I relented and literally begged Sara to do the interview, um, leaving both twins here today. I couldn't consent to Sara leaving or Kam until we came to an understanding and a meeting of the minds, including both sisters. I piqued Sara's interest and asked how she would like to go on a Horseback ride to visit our facility, mind you. She signed a contract the night before for two years in our program. She became excited, so we geared up and went to the Horse stalls, took off, then had our dramatic entrance while the Quickdraw contest was in action heck, you were there, Sandi, and that's how it went." He poured some more Makers Mark into his glass and gave it to Sandi, "here take a sip, I'm sorry for losing it, I feel like a pressure cooker sometimes, and needed to blow." He grimaced, "it wasn't the way I wanted to explode this evening!" She took the crystal glass and knowingly grinned, "well I'm flattered...." He tossed up his palm.

"What I didn't know could surely destroy us. Ugh, umh, after Rico left NIA from the interview, he met with Doctor Shauon Roble, whom we'd had tabs on. She had flown into the Napa executive airport. Rico had picked her up, and they made a day of it... We picked up surveillance later that day... Uh, Floyd was the lead dog on the surveillance team. We were lucky his team intercepted Rico's request for an FBI Chopper in a split second. We substituted pilots. How were we to guess the location he ordered our Pilot to fly over was the fka Quickdraw damnit then this fiasco began to gain momentum. Ms. Klite had no choice but to fly him where he demanded. Seeing the huge crowd out for the semifinals NIA championships, he ordered her to drop and hover above. 'Darnit pilot Klite' had no options either she followed his orders or be fired for insubordination. In hindsight, I wish she would have... acted out an emergency, such as a mechanical failure or a serious problem, and flown back to the airport, but alas, she didn't. With the forethought of a simple malfunction faked, none of this would be relevant or come to fruition. Then she could have broken away and alerted Floyd about Rico's intentions." "We can't go by what might have been, Terrance, we need to move on and..." Terrance reached out and tugged on her leg, nodding.

"Floyd, for his part, sent eleven texts and tried to call to alert me that Rico was in the air and called our private line seven times. My cell phone was in the side bags behind the saddle of my horse… like a perfect storm. Somehow with the handling of my phone, the Mute button was hit. Yep, mute, I didn't hear a chirp as Sara and I leisurely rode around the lake towards the games…." "Why didn't Floyd call Jax, Liz, Wendi, or even me?" asks Sandi.

"We haven't grilled Floyd over proper protocol or how the chain of command is aligned. Sadly, we failed on that, although he did try a group text to the three you mentioned, who, in turn, texted me. You have to understand that no one knew Sara and I would come riding up to the tournament. It was purely impromptu. We originally were going to trot around the lake… but hearing the hoots and laughter. We were drawn to the contest and crowd. Beyond that, I hadn't a clue that Kara would be sitting in the audience with Wendi. Think about it at least five simultaneous competitions were going on at different venues. Who's to blame? This was an unprecedented situation with many in our hierarchy at the Quickdraw contest, with even Liz and Renae in the stands. Let's face it, the dazzling show of skills had everybody mesmerized. Some had turned their ringers off, not wanting to interrupt the proceedings."

"Terrance, sad to say you pinned it correctly earlier. It was the perfect storm that you rode your Horse into, but we were fortunate, were we not? For if not for my communication with the Feral's we wouldn't know that Rico and they were visiting in less than 24 hours, so we can brainwave like Wendi always used to say and figure a way to alleviate the pressure and obviate the ending results, here's what has to happen in my opinion the parents have been convinced that Sunshine has taken control of Wendi's being…." "Well, yes, she's the protagonist and…" "Hold up, Terrance, the reason Wendi is in therapy and taking the psychotropic designer drugs invented by NIA is to put Sunshine out to pasture. They want their daughter back as well as Rico also does. This is the problem if Wendi isn't here to meet and greet them when they get off the plane, then they're going to take her body from NIA, that's what I think, and by the way, you can't fake out, Mom she raised Wendi/Sunshine, so yes we have serious problems, Terrance!"

Terrance struggles up and takes another glass out of the cabinet so they'd have their own and hands her a glass of whiskey… with his shaking in his left hand. Sitting next to her and leaning back, they slowly sip in silence. After a few moments, "Let's face it, there are no excuses, woman, in a nutshell, were cornered. Now, where do we go from here? I need to find a direction!" Prolonged suppression of words "Terrance, I prefer being referred to as Sandi or darling or something in that vein, not 'Woman' which, by the way, you have referred to me as… more than a half dozen times, no not being overly sensitive nor politically correct but…." "Sorry, Sandi, I'm frustrated for once. I'm grasping for slippery straws!…" she places her palm on his thigh and squeezes. "Ok, I agree. Let's call in our troops to analyze what we can do to solve this issue. Also, I will contact Wendi and set up a meeting for you and me to discuss this problem with her right away!"

-43-

<u>Rico and Shanon discuss his upcoming meeting with Wendi Feral and her parents.</u>

On the flip side, the other side of the same coin was Rico striding pumping, sweating the top 50 songs vibrating in his AirPods, climbing the last mountain ranges, racing in the Tour de

Mont Rosa, crossing through both the Swiss and Italian Alps, pedaling like a maniac currently in 5th place on his stationary bike. He couldn't recall when his energy level was on max output, his legs burning, lungs gasping, his entire body convulsing, every cell in his body on fire, yet his spirit and heart wouldn't accept failure, no quitting. He dug deep, not wanting to break-weak!

Later a short shower, he exited to meet with Shanon to brainwave a later meeting... an afternoon gathering before Judge Delaney and a Federal team of experts flying in from Washington DC... A special task force was in the infancy of forming an objective. Finally, his agenda and investigation into NIA's improprieties would be addressed, with his input and evidence from Rico's three spies. This should go down without a flaw. When this hits social media, there will be a new word that surpasses 'Viral' Yep!

Way before Doctor Roble got out of her Lexus, Rico had spied her with a glimmering grin from his spacious 3-room suite at the top of the San Francisco Federal building. He couldn't wait to see her and show the overwhelming evidence they'd discovered because of the pictures and video they'd taken on the helicopter flight over NIA the other day. It was definitely electrifying.

He'd had his tech team project the relevant pictures with video onto the massive screen on his wall and had each appropriate image printed out 8x10s for them to scrutinize up close. He touched the intercom to his secretary 'yes, sir,' Rico chuckled 'why so formal, Bethany?' In her voice, he could imagine her smiling. 'Mr. Captor, it's just that this morning I've had a dozen or more calls from D.C. such Quantico and the Pentagon, got caught up in the officiality of it all. Oh, your brunch is on its way, and yes, I'll let Doctor Roble in when she gets here." "Thanks, 'B.' Hold all calls until I tell you to let the faucets flow again, okay?" "No prob, I sure will, Rico." Moments later, Shanon busts through the door "okay, I'm dying to hear this... fabulous news. I rushed over here,"...

tossing her purse and taking her jacket off, slinging it on a chair.

Rico was calm, wanting not to miss one of his pre-planned details. The topic's aligned in his mind, "I hope you're hungry. I have a platter of fruit and croissants with...." "I had something earlier this morning, not here to eat. Stop stalling, show me, dammit." The first picture was a blowup of a woman who appeared to be Sara, the serial killer sitting in a cordoned-off section at the top of a makeshift arena. Shanon was still standing and walked over to the 75-inch photo display "she's terribly beautiful, high, proud cheekbones, Greenish flecked eyes, and short blonde hair that seemed to have been just growing back. Shanon remembered that Sara used to have lustrous blonde locks. There she was, no question… her pouty lips, nose, and ears symmetrical a damn Doll." A quizzical look back at him, "this could easily be Kamryn, their identical twins, Rico; what's the crime if Terrance invited his niece to the NIA games?" He said 'nada' and moved on to the following pic. On the left side sat Wendi Feral. No doubts here. Rico bit his lower lip. Shan stared over at his dry, painful expression knowing full well he pined for Wendi, recalling some of the toxic past between Wendi and Rico. They had a brief dalliance, then a continued romance a while ago. The Mexican Cartel, with Rascal Savage and Doctor Anita Sparks with Sandi's former lover Rubio Animl, had conspired to kidnap Wendi. She and Rico were vacationing… they were assaulted right under Rico's watch at a deluxe cabin on Trinity Lake. Wendi Feral has never been the same person since. Leaving Rico heartbroken and grasping and clinging to a Wendi that was….

Shanon kept ruminating over Wendi's tragic history, remembering that after she was rescued in Mexico City, her life had nearly returned to some sort of normalcy. Working in her business Feral Feedback with her partner and best friend Sandi, she was attacked again. An attempted murder of Wendi on the I-5 Hwy at the hands of her brother Mark Feral who shot her in the head… lucky to survive her injuries. Wendi nearly died…. she landed in the NIA Hospital, and her lead Neurologist said that the latest trauma had caused her alter-ego to come to the surface, protecting her. Wendi had an intense childhood and was nearly killed falling into a Gorilla cage as an infant and thought to be drowned. Lack of oxygen affected her brain, resulting in schizophrenia, aka 'Sunshine Feral,' was born and became her Savior and another identity.

Finally, Shanon broke the stillness "sorry Rico, I suppose Wendi isn't in the rehabilitation center where she was reported to be. She was supposed to be at NIA's outpatient hospital for her mental disorder. I get it, and again I'm sorry I know how you feel about her. Rico, I felt scared to death up in that helicopter when we saw Wendi. I'm truly sorry! Ughhhh, It's quite possible that Sunshine's alter ego is whom we see here… right?" His chin rested on a fist, peering over from his desk "yes, I spoke with her mother and father last night. They are the ones that signed the admittance paperwork to have Wendi committed to the outpatient psychiatric ward at NIA after her husband, David, went missing. They have total and absolute power of attorney when it comes to Wendi. I want to attempt again to move her to another clinic that is owned and operated by a Forensic Psychologist, an alumnus of Stanford University."

Rico tapped a key on his laptop next picture popped up. It was of Jax Foul, an inmate found guilty years ago in Federal Court, where Wendi testified for the defense, standing with Attorney Terrance Halliman… and supporting Mr. Jax Foul. Jax was surmised to be temporarily insane and interpreted to be so by five different psychologists and sentenced to NIA Prison for between 10 and 15 years. This always ate at Rico's craw. He couldn't wrap his mind around the fact that Jax was dubbed insane, not culpable mentally in killing a dozen or more of the Cuban Mafia in South Florida. Jax found himself in a power struggle to stop the child porn ring he was associated with. Jax was reaping a windfall of cash from his dastardly actions. What was forgotten… Jax was the original kidnapper of the children!

He asked her, "what was wrong with this shot?" she twisted several strands of her hair "nothing that I can surmise, listen, Rico, I'm playing Devil's advocate here. Any attorney would say Jax is still behind the gates of the prison. He's now a trustee. They could call this a form of his therapy if I recall his Federal sentence's directives. Wasn't he supposed to be locked up until he was considered sane enough to be put back on trial? Is that correct?" he nodded affirmatively. Rico stopped on the next photo. It was a handsome Black man in fatigues. "I had sent these photos off for facial recognition applications, and I await their complete assessment. We were able to discern his name, waiting for his resume. I can venture to say many in the V.I.P. section in the stands are the 'Who's Who' of our military's finest. This man is, in fact, unh, meet Major Shou Peterson of the Elite Delta Force 1, a Commander and possibly the assassin of my friend Tom who was my undercover Agent in Costa Rico." He points to the Major's right side "there is Jaybird who was arrested with Jax but exonerated… another military specialist Ops… Sniper. Jaybird is the leader of one of the largest militias on US soil. We haven't been able to figure out how many belong to his factions ughhhh, the numbers are not definable, but the estimates of his active forces are in the tens of thousands. His organization has strongholds in Montana, Idaho, Utah, and Nevada and now stretches to the Pacific Ocean, Washington, and Oregon. The guy is like a magnanimous dictator or General… and is a Team Leader at this so-called NIA-U."

Shanon finally takes a seat while Rico keeps tapping out the photos, stopping at another blown-up shot "this woman in the Sombrero hat next to Jax, we took four pictures with her in it… only can get her chin and nose unh, lips nothing else…."

"So why is this lady of interest then?" He slid the next photo out, which showed the blonde twin Sara or Kam frowning with a glare... as their eyes seemed to frown at one another. The unknown woman was caught staring at one of the twins in several other pictures. Her gaze wasn't friendly. Both had scowls of dislike as the sombrero female covered her face. "They seem to have a history or dislike for one another. That's Beth's and my take. What do you say?" Shanon walks over to the blow-up. "I could agree with you but can't tell really anything definitive from a one-look picture."

He starts flipping through more of the 515 pictures they'd taken that were usable and not too distorted. Shanon hops up in the air and shouts, "oh, no way," he replies, "yes way, it is him!" "Wow, he was one of my favorites... rumor was he bought a huge spread up in Shasta County on Shasta Lake. Haven't seen Rocky in a coon's age... now that guy is...." "Yeah, Shanon, that's the exceptional Mr. Rocky Blake, Ex-FBI Ex superstar of the Police games and a special Ops Seal Team leader, and his accolades go on...." "I must ask, Wtf is he doing there?" "I'll find out, believe me, Shanon. I'll definitely find out. He is one of my best friends and was going to stand up with me at Brock and Kamryn's wedding, and I hadn't seen him since Brock was found unconscious on that beach up on Shasta Lake!"

He sped up, flashing pictures "ask, Doctor Liz Honcho next to Head Nurse Renae on and on pic's in the grandstands in the standing crowd of hundreds of snapshots. He stops again with a blurred photograph "oh, she's an Albino woman. That's a___" "Her name is Sandi, the partner of Wendi's business Feral Feedback. I didn't know she was in Napa wonder who's running their company? I met her years back. She is a wonderful person. Why was she at NIA?" he asks no one in particular, speaking to himself aloud.

Knocks at the office door. Beth enters, waving in three employees from the dining hall restaurant down on the 3rd-floor platters with a pitcher of iced tea "thank you so much. Can you put everything on the table over there, please?" Shanon smiled, adding 'thanks.' Before the door closed, Rico declared to a server he'd recognized, "put it on my tab and add a 20% tip" she grinned 'thanks, Mr. Captor.' After they were left alone, "seriously, you have called for a high-level meeting this afternoon. I have to tell you I'm rather concerned… from my perspective. I've seen nothing criminal or illegal. But yes, it's truly terrifying to have so many skilled men and women, Ex, military… and law enforcement officers engaging in the now notorious NIA Games. I don't know Rico… how are private competitions and contests different from other exhibitions and competitions that our military branches engage in? Hey, pal, you have been involved in the Police Games, competitions, and championships. Sniper shooting contests, and so on. I don't know what, if anything, you can glean or prove is wrong or unlawful here, I a…." "Excuse me, I know where you're going with this. I'll say this it's all above my pay grade… I'm the Director of the FBI for California, just passing the information on to the D.C. Pros."

"What about my DNA proof that Sara assassinated Carl and Bianca Sparks, and when will we have Kamryn's DNA to compare with the collected…." "Shanon, we have surveillance on her Salon and home. She has yet to emerge; we believe she is still on the grounds of NIA. We also have all entrances and exits under scrutiny… believe me, no one enters or leaves the NIA grounds without video." Shanon nods, "sorry to get us off topic. Still, I want closure on Sara's latest homicides, including her poisoning of the attorney." He acknowledged her with an affirmative shake and moved to the brunch carts. They quietly chose some nourishment and silently melded over what had been promulgated thus far.

Rico reenergized, sipping an espresso "without a doubt, the latest info garnered from my spies inside NIA's training facility justifies the reason the D.C. brass are flying out. We can presume that the training facility is churning out skilled infantrymen & women and officers to man militias across the continental USA. While we were flying over the Quickdraw competition, unfortunately, we didn't get any telephoto still shots, but the video cameras caught these images. Let me run them by you then I will back them up to separate clips. Dammit, if I'd seen these horses, I'd ordered the pilot to drop even lower for closeups!"

They'd watched it in silence three times and slowed down the moving video... neither said much, except Shanon... who exclaimed, 'that's Terrance Halliman for sure' as he took his Black hat off, waving to the incensed crowd. The female rider appeared to be the other twin, Kam or Sara. Both were indeed there together on the facility grounds; she wore a light Brownish Beige Cowgirl hat. Curiously, she never took it off, just did the cowboy thing like pulling the bill down like ma'am or a howya doing greeting.

"All right, you've convinced me we've finally caught Terrance in a compromising position, having validated on video recording his words that Sara was in solitary confinement locked inside her prison cell for 23 of 24 hours a day." Rice showed a gratifying full-faced smile "yeah not even the great attorney litigator that he is, can worm his way out of this one Horseback riding on the other side of NIA's razor wires, confines not inside the prison but on the training grounds with a notorious killer. Indeed Terrance was in trouble legitimately. The fact must be addressed: Sara indeed had escaped her cell and was off joyriding with his ass." Rice, enthused and wide-eyed, said, "oh, what I'd give to tighten some handcuffs on Terrance, that would be glorious!"

They stopped and moved over to the food trays to indulge in more snacks. She filled a bowl with some fresh fruit. He interjected, "on the record from two of our sources, when Terrance pulled up on his Horse, he introduced the female rider with him as Sara Amaya to a chorus of mixed cheers and boos, jeers and hisses of antipathy." Whew, he clenched his sphincter, grabbing his abdomen ugh, bending over "my stomach just cramped up. I'm going to the bathroom...." "What, oh my, do you have an ulcer? You're working non-stop, Rico. You need to take a vacation; you're working yourself jagged! When was the last time you had a full-on checkup and physical?" She was speaking to an empty room. He crab-walked into the restroom.

His pants were down, and his stomach was whirling, yet just fumes burst out alone with just the vent fan causing a racket. He fell into a natural soliloquy. He was the narrator bouncing feelings and musings across his Cerebral Cortex and Amygdala. He normally found this state of being while listening to music or driving. It was his sort of inner chatter of introspection. As a child, when he was caught in a trance-like state. His dad would joke that it's all right to talk to yourself. Just as long as you don't answer yourself out loud, then you're a lunatic and a crazy person.

Aww, some relief as he does a courtesy flush for his olfactory senses... thinking about a few things that were bothering him. Sick that he allowed his heart and mind to fall in love with a mental case, a woman with a personality disorder? Was it Karma for whatever? Knowing Wendi was of 2 opposite minds, Sunshine the leading role, proactive identity, ugh personality, why didn't I protect myself unh my inner-self let me down. Where were my boundaries, the alarms of my heart knowing to this day he'd visited her at least twice a week. He was there when Wendi's parents showed up at the psych ward and advocated for them to sign her admittance papers after David, her husband, had been adjudged MIA. David hadn't been seen for almost a year, and his credit cards were not used... his bank accounts only accrued interest.

Rico squeezed his sphincter and fidgeted angrily, recalling... It was his suggestion that they fly her down to the NIA Neurological Hospital, rated the best at that time in the

Western United States. From the start of their visits, they heard screaming rantings and shrieking in other rooms down the hall with patients restrained. He'd used his pull and got her off the main floor into her own suite, his inner conflict similar to Yin and Yang. The contrarian's voice repeated, "if you're looking for pigs, go to a pig farm looking for fish, a hatchery looking for alcoholics, go to a bar, looking to buy a car... go to a car lot. If insanity is what you want to observe, go to an insane asylum, duh, and that's where I was. NIA had thousands of lunatics, umh, maniacs all caged behind the walls right next door at the NIA Prison. Wendi was at the outpatient hospital and had been for... bang knocks. "Hey Rico, you all right in there? did you fall asleep or fall in... huh?" "Ahh, yes, I'll be out in a sec." Flush.

His afternoon and evening were already planned out... had a meeting with Wendi's parents at the outpatient hospital. The question was, where would Wendi be? Grimaced, thinking this was like a personal attack all arranged by him to manipulate her parents to sign her out of NIA, he looked at his wristwatch. It was hours away, but he better prepare for the 8:15 pm appointment. Perhaps he'd have to put that off till tomorrow. First on his crowded plate was the conference with the D.C. Brass. Depending on how... Enough had to prepare mentally for this highly classified conference with the Government officials rumor was that the A.G. Attorney General of the US was part of the entourage. Judge Delaney would be watching via video conference. Washing his hands and face, wow felt better until he stared into the mirror, 'muttered it's my head locked into the wooden block of the Guillotine! Ugh.'

He was about to walk back out of the restroom when he heard his unique notification sound associated with his Agents watching NIA. He quickly stepped out to see Shanea holding some pictures in her hands, bent down, and read the text. 'Terrance's Limousine has just left NIA grounds and is heading towards the highway!' Texted back, 'stay on him....'

<u>**'Sunshine'… had control of Wendi's body and mind.**</u>

Wendi paced like an animal caged in the Zoo and texted her mother, telling her it wasn't a good time to fly down from Portland, Oregon, to visit. They had called several times, and dad left a message 'Hey Pumpkin, I love you, can't wait to hug you. It's been almost three months, golly. Where does the time go… anyways? Your mother and I are excited we're staying for a week.' There was no stopping them. Terrance was frantic and stood to the side of the door with Sandi, only observing her. They'd already had a desperate conversation, neither with an idea of how to stop the inevitable confrontation with Rico and Wendi's parents… Sunshine was irate. "I don't need this pressure. What the hell are you staring at, White girl…" Sandi twirled around in a stand-off. "Woa now, Sunshine, don't be disrespectful. I'm here to help you; keep a level head. I know that's difficult…" "That's quite enough from the both of you, and verbal in-fighting isn't goin to solve anything. Please think!" Sandi exits the doorway a few feet… with the statement, "good luck with this Wendi imposter."

Sandi knew there would not be a farewell party. Wendi/Sunshine was going nowhere unless Sunshine could somehow fake out her parents and Rico… and make them believe they were communicating with sweet little Wendi. Ahh, good luck with that storyline. Nope, the last seven weeks, Sandi and Wendi/Sunshine had been training on the 'A' squad that had been handpicked by Jax, another Mission Impossible, and Wendi was an intricate key piece in overcoming their extreme odds. They were hired to extract a Ukrainian leader who was under duress from Putin and the Russian hierarchy. Without her, Jax could and would possibly fail, which would hurt NIA dearly.

Terrance watched Wendi, uh Sunshine… pace from one corner of the room to the other; then, she slowed down. She stopped cold, "what are you looking at?" she asked. "You… Wendi, can you please sit down so we can talk…" "Why must

I sit? I think much better on my feet... dammit, you and I know what's about to happen! When my parents arrive to meet me with Rico, they expect miss congeniality to be a loveable squeezable happy go lucky fku, sensitive, and sweet, naive Wendi, not me, her alter-ego Sunshine! This is an end game, our End." Terrance hit a wall with his fist, "I'm not going to allow anything...." Knocking then opening the classroom door was Liz staring uncontentedly at the three of them, standing with grim and gloom-ish expressions. "Well, hell, this isn't the end of the fricken world. We still have cards to play. Remember, nine/tens of the law... is in favor of possession, and Wendi is in our possession. We still have her onsite. Now sit down. You're making me nervous. You to Sandi and you also Terrance, let's get to this. I have some ideas!" Terrance tossed up his left arm. "I have an idea and want us all to take a ride in my limousine. We have one stop that could bring about a peaceful resolution. We need to alter the ambiance, unh... or at least realize what our future could look like!"

Wendi remained sitting, with her back to the group, looking out a window onto the courtyard at NIA-U, and spoke in a low monotone... "Terrance, I'm not in favor of going for a ride out the gates. If what we've learned is true and there are three infiltrators, uhm, spies, then this would be reported to the Feds and Rico. We haven't a clue as to whom are watching us..." Sandi rubbed her chin, glancing at Terrance "yea, I have to concur with Wendi's assertion. This isn't the time..." Terrance watched Liz's expression, her mouth gawking open and shaking her head in agreement... not a good idea to leave out the gates. Terrance quickly decided to nix the idea of taking the group to Liz's favorite Winery for brunch uhm. Sadly... they wouldn't leave the facility in his limo. "Okay, I'll admit that I was rather too spontaneous and irrational in thinking we could go anywhere anonymously, so I will change my plans in midstream...."

Terrance, Liz, and Sunshine… Scheming on how to handle Wendi's parent's visit.

Sunshine's eyebrows flipped up a dashing swirl across her cheeks: "Doctor Liz Honcho, my favorite psychologist who's pawned me off on a half dozen half-ass psychiatrists, ahh, group therapies. It's nice for you to make some time for me… First, oblige me, and let me ask you why it is always considered non-productive to be pacing back and forth. I've heard it said… Sit down so we can talk or discuss this or that, and secondly, Liz, I enjoy the law bit you espoused earlier. Regarding the 9/10s of the law, the bit about it equaling possession, I think that law is more about drugs or weapons. Therefore, let's rationalize this variable right now. I own and control this body; Wendi has one-tenth of me, and I own nine-tenths. How about those Apples?" Gloating smugly, impressed with her own wit.

"I'm not here to defend myself or to be counterproductive. You've made tremendous progress from being shot in the head and the subsequent car crash and coma, Wendi. I'm not pretending to understand your dilemma; I have a ton of experience treating complicated, multifaceted mental disorders here at NIA. It's a breeding ground. We undoubtedly have hundreds of patients with multiple personality syndromes with a profusion of depressed, morose inmates living in a myriad of imagined universes within their heads. Some of these inmates live each day like the fantastic movie 'Ground Hog Day' living in a loop day in and night out. We have, at last count, a laboratory onsite with 7 Scientists that work feverishly to understand what it is that causes your inflictions um ailments. Certainly, it's a chemical imbalance that affects your retention of sanity and causes episodes of severe anxiety, stress, and depression. I have a detailed chart with full psychiatric evaluations on this laptop right here! Many patients use alternate personalities as a sort of Fail-safe escape." "Stop, Liz, who makes you God or your precious Scientist's holier than thou… who's truly the judge or jury or individuals who can make determinations of someone's insanity levels, huh? Who's not to say the so-called normal people working and moving about in the Rat's maze of life aren't fricken natty as bed bugs…trained Weasels. Who died and made you Queen Bee or God?" Liz throws up her hands. "Go ahead, Wendi, or let's call you Sunshine, for your now in charge of Wendi's shell! Yeah, I'm the one that's disheveled along with Terrance and Sandi, and we have split personalities, sure I suppose an argument can be made. All humans are somewhat Schitzo, Sunshine…." "Liz, I'm severely tired of hearing your grandiose ideas and concepts; you're a fricken Quack!" She barked.

"Liz, I'm not a freakin shell; I am and always will be in control mentally and physically of who I am. I've decided to disregard your statement and abhor your reference to me sarcastically as Wendi. Furthermore, I don't give a flying fk about any of this. Don't you and Terrance understand, huh? Screw your Scientists, who still no nothing about how human brains function? It's guesswork at best. Hell, no one has even figured out what causes or cures Bipolar disorders. All these bullshit cognitive behavioral therapies, uh, scientists, who are using my ass, making Millions of dollars experimenting on us like Rats. Don't either of you think I'm fkn naive to the testing of so-called patients, unh, inmates here who have no support on the outside of these walls? Decades since they have even had one visit, these are people, not inmates, whom family, spouses friends have forgotten. Those are your test subjects locked in the Dungeon below the main prison, yeah, and your so-called Scientists constantly experiment on these poor souls. Yeah, I'm not naive at what goes on around here with your archaic torturing treatments. I bet you… your still doing Lobotomies here, shock treatment therapies, and drilling holes, uh, perforating the skulls of poor souls here under your control. Like I said, why don't you let the outside world in to investigate the Maximum Penitentiary down in the dungeons that date back from the 1800s, ft." Liz and Terrance let her vent no use agitating this wild woman any further.

"When are you going to comprehend that these mental disorders, such as manias and extended episodes of dissociative phobias, none are the same, Liz? There are no unified applications… there is nothing synonymous with one person's delusions or disassociations from the next person… were all different, like Sand on the Beach. No magic pills theory… here. Take this fricken pill. It fixes everything! Dumb-ass Psychiatrists prescribe pills unwittingly, not admitting that none of their patients have the same mental illness… Nope, not one of us humans is the same inside our brains. Human brains cannot be labeled no way of explaining the multitude of diverse mental syndromes… Apples to Oranges to Walnuts. Don't you get it, damnit? Your methodology is flawed. It's not like a simple Insulin shot for a diabetic. We all have different chemical imbalances percentage wise various chemical displacements. We may look from our dermis like one another, except for our skin colors and the various size differences of our features or appendages. Internally we are not the same, and humans can differ in extremes; for instance, I can eat a peanut butter cracker, and another person allergic to peanuts can die; their esophagus closes down from a damn peanut. The stagnation of chemicals in my body may be harmless and easily flushed from my system, but your body with the same chemical concentrations can be deadly. Ugh, our brains and biochemical secretions are all divergent. Even identical twins have different biological and genetic variances. Remember, chemicals create Bombs!"

Terrance and Liz can only watch and listen patiently with subtle nods between each other, trying to figure out what the hell she was rambling on about, concluding that what she's said somehow must make sense to her! They'd silently telepathically decided to be submissive and acquiesce. While Wendi/Sunshine goes off on her rant like a temper tantrum, letting her unwind and speak her 'minds' inside her world of frustrations. Their eyes meet several times as the angry words are continually expelled. She is barely seen breathing, not stopping her tirade. No, she wasn't sitting down. She was moving faster, sometimes pointing her fingers within inches of their faces, gesticulating wildly. Terrance wondered if she'd start foaming at the lips soon, like a rabid Canine.

"Scientists, screw you all. Schizophrenia isn't a biological, environmental, or behavioral condition. A split personality isn't a Neurologically contained visual condition. You people truly have no… Zilch about the human brain or, for that matter, even animal brains and how they analyze, um, formulate hypotheses, or think… or fooling yourselves. Check it out. If a negative trait is predicated predominantly or pervasively prevalent, ugh, inherited in humans, it's called a genetic disorder. Just pull up the family tree insanity propagated, put this in your fricken pipes, and smoke it. I'm not giving up, guys. I've taken the body, I own the shell, I am Sunshine, and fka Wendi is in for the ride of my life, so fk off. The only time I feel free, wild, lucid with euphoria is when I'm… uhm, I am grounded, surrounded within My epiphany. Clarity is crystal clear when I'm with Jax Foul on a mission to kill or torment other human beings for a true cause. Get the fk with it. I'm a soldier; I work and belong to the NIA Army, happy ecstatically with Blood and guts dripping from my fangs. Nothing engages my endorphins in a sublime reality…." "Stop that no." screeched Terrance. He'd heard it all before in sporadic segments. He swallowed, "enough, you listen to me!" Liz frowns at him holding her hands up like a mediator.

Liz bounces up, trying to quell the toxic situation… "all right, Sunshine, there hasn't been a cure for these disorders yet. I'll concede that our team of disparaged Scientists are close to breakthroughs on many fronts despite your irreverent statements... let me remind you that the last tests on inmates have shown positive effects with prescribed medications. They've called the treatment 'Chemical Equilibrium Reset!' Having manufactured a new miracle designer drug taking the chemicals that instigate the brain to coalesce in the subconscious state of being manifesting subliminally into a reconditioned awakening. We've proven in EEG scans that in the conscious state, chemicals from Risperdal, Lithium, Lexapro, Valium, Seroquel, and a half dozen more isolated drugs that our Scientists here at NIA have combined testing in selected increments... Uhm, I'm here to enlighten your...." Liz ceases to speak and stares across at Terrance, then at Sunshine, who is now leaning forward, slouched over... sound asleep. Whoa, snoring loudly!

Terrance stands, spins around, and slams his fist on a wall... attention regained "okay, Sunshine, it's your way you win! NIA and I ahh we need you your ability to communicate with all animals because of Wendi's tragic experience at 18 months old nearly drowning at the San Francisco Zoo where Rocco the Gorilla blew breath back into your body..." She scowls " ugh, I don't need a history restoration duh... remember I was there and who I am...." "Wrong Sunshine, you weren't present nor a living personality. You didn't manifest into being until Wendi was about five years old. That's when you hitched a ride on the little girl, and we need you to understand what we're trying to perpetuate here Sunshine. There will be dire consequences if you don't change your focus and attitude." She opens her mouth, hopping up. He adamantly points at her with a vicious grimace. "Ssshh you Ssshh, your parents will be here with Rico in under five hours at around 9:15 pm if you are as defiant, rebellious, and pigheaded and inflexible, your history Sunshine. Ugh damnit, the short and sour of it is if you show them your Sunshine and not Wendi, we all risk losing you!" She smirked, grinning broadly, and bowed like on a stage, looking down at her subservient admirers. "Well, it's incumbent on you folks cuz yah don't wanna lose the Star," she cackles loudly! ☀️… ☀️.

"Listen to reason, Sunshine. Fire up your brain, please, woman. Sandi, Wendi's best friend, had a lengthy conversation with Ed &Barbara, your parents, last night. They are moving you within 48 hours to another psychiatric hospital by Stanford University. This is certain, not fabricated nonsense or bullshit. Rico is behind it, so this act of yours is expiring. You and Jax will never be again… no longer be the Dynamic Duo. Sunshine, regarding what your beliefs are on what we do here, you referred to it as archaic testing on our inmates, huh lol wouldn't want to be in your sandals. Wait till you get to your new hospital cell. You will be prodded, poked, and injected, and probably end up in a fkn strait jacket in a rubber room drooling and pissing yourself, so either work with us or pack the fk up!"

The room instantly had lost wind… sails limp. Sunshine blushed for the first time in her existence, "unh uah, but I'm 37 years old. I am an adult in charge of my life. They can't…." "Sshh," he unfolds a magazine article from a side pocket and places it on the table. A pretty woman's image… the centerfold was of Britany Spears. "You know of her, right Sunshine? She's a super successful Pop singer, unh, artist with number-one hits, an actress, and a gorgeous, talented woman." Sunshine picks up the wrinkled centerfold… "Britany is embattled and under siege… for her very own sanity and who controls her money. And therefore, much of her life. Because of Britany's mental wherewithal and addictions, her parents and attorneys are all set up under a stealth-like guise."

Terrance lowered his voice conspiratorially, "Wendi shouldn't have signed likewise legal contracts over to her parents. Then a judge took your life's rights away… get with it, or don't… mom and dad control you, Sunshine your committed here at NIA and soon will be a lab Rat elsewhere if you don't stand up and take fricken control of the situation!"

Finally, with momentum, Liz jumps into the fray and interjects, "if you love this life, love Jax Foul, all of this can continue...." "Wait, I never said I loved Jax in a sexual way. I prefer females. I adore Jax and admire him and would take a bullet for him. Ah, maybe I'm a touch Bi-Sexual and haven't figured it out... but be sure I will. Yes, I love him but 'not in love' with him." Terrance, like a sniper, sees his shot. "Sunshine, if you cannot sell Rico and your, uh, the parents that what we've done here with you psychotherapy-wise, that our techniques aren't showing improvements or working, then you're gone, whm toast. I'm not warning you like Liz here; I'm telling you in no uncertain terms that in 48 hours or less, you'll be living in a rubber room cell elsewhere! This isn't a threat. No, it's a promise and out of my control."

She sighs, leans back, sways her head, shouts 'fk,' and pushes the chair out, a hand on her forehead. "WTHeck happened? We were on a long run with no problems for like three months, two successful missions. All's well then, Bang!" He once again takes the floor. "Rico has been to your room in the outpatient hospital three times in the last two weeks to visit you. Ugh "Wendi, that is... we had him informed that you were in therapy twice and the other time that you were in the gym working out. No big deal, for God's sake, you're not in jail here, but the other day, he was spying on us from a helicopter taking aerial pictures of the QuickDraw semifinals, and Walla, you were in many of the pictures look sliding the photo's over...." "So what? I'm not in prison here like you said I can..." she paws the pictures of the V.I.P. sections. There she was, sitting and smiling. "How'd you get these pictures...." "Never you mind Sunshine, just like Britney Spears. She's in the same boat loop, not in jail or prison, but it's all relative. You're in that song, um lyrics of 'Hotel California' The 'Eagles' great melody 'You can check out, but you can never leave.' The guards at the gates would apprehend you, same as Britany metaphorically "<u>Stab it with the steely knives, but you can't kill the Beast…</u>." "Enough of the song Terrance. Not amusing, I know the lyrics well. Who the hell doesn't? I'm surprised, though, at your memory being so clear from way back then. I heard you were an Ancient party animal, Terrance!"

He played into it "whew, that hurt, yeah sure, I've lost a ton of brain cells," miming sad puffy lips pushed out cheeks. She grinned, obviously finally conceding, "okay, I'm screwed. I'm all ears. What's the plan, as you know? Jax and I head up that quest up in Seattle in February, a month or so away!" Liz squints her eyes; Terrance nods "well, the fix isn't simple. Ain't no way to transform you back into 'goody two shoes' loveable Wendi with all her innocence personified surely without you… Sunshine. Neither of you would have survived your life's ordeals. With that being said, can you fool Rico, mom, and dad and make them think you are Wendi? This is the main reason they signed the order to commit you to NIA. We plainly told them we would cure, uhm, solve your… personality discrepancy, ahh, deficit. You must be Wendi and stifle Sunshine. Think about that, please!"

Terrance adds that it's Rico, whom we have to sell. Remember, he was and maybe still is 'head over heels' in love with Wendi. The prick reminds me of like a celibate feeble peckerless Frog pining over his Fairy Tale Princess fix. It's sickening, ugh, Pathetic!… Yep!" Then Liz disagreed, "no, it's not Rico. You have to fool it's Ms. Feral um Barbara, who raised your ass, she can smell you, Sunshine." Sunshine bowed her head with a contorted grimace "problem is when Wendi is in charge and control of our body and mind. I'm squelched off, uh, out there in the peripheral compartmentalized. It's hard to explain, like being in another department in a huge store, everything is disconnected, ahh disassociated dimension I'm looking through a mirage or façade like colored distorted mirrors at one of those circuses." Liz and Terrance were fully alert, now seeing Sunshine's transformation and beginning to understand the importance of the meeting with Rico and the parents.

She continues, "only when Wendi's blood pressure rises, temper or fear, and stress levels secrete the hormone Cortisol, which is produced in our adrenal glands. Her autonomic nervous system puts me in an alert mode which is also known as the Freeze Fight or Flight response. That's when I'm called to the forefront. Especially when it's a fearful reaction, endorphins powering up, and fear hits her, uh, consumes her. This insecurity that's built into her psyche causes indecision overwhelming Wendi. Then I'm finally released. It is definitely a chemical imbalance. It's sort of like a Vacuum like sucked to the vanguard, and suddenly we're on the same plain… subconscious dimension sharing our existence. But this is temporary, a spate of dialogue. This is when we communicate on the same level, her stress-tension pressure going Viral blasting off. She relents behind the curtain of her mind Walla here I am 'Sunshine.' Now I'm here forever… Yep!"

Terrance twists his head from Liz to her "are you up to play acting with us, Sunshine…?" "For sure, if you think it will help!" "Okay, get something to eat or drink in the cafeteria, use the restroom or whatever you have to, and just prepare yourself to spend some uninterrupted time with us. <u>Meet us in Theater # 3. Liz and I will be there in 15 minutes. This is important. When you walk in, the Act begins. Your, then… 'Wendi,' feel us and throw it all at us. You're on Broadway. We need an Academy Award performance. We're going to be Mom and Dad…." Sunshine frowns ah, "Shit, that's freakin scary, dudes."</u>

Five minutes later, Liz and Terrance exit the elevator to Theater # 3 "yuh, think Sunshine will pull it off, Liz?…" "Do they sell snow cones in Hell? Absolutely not, no way!…" "I concur 99% and agree with your earlier sentiment; that's why we have our alternative action prepared, correct…." She raises a Syringe from her purse, "yes, Terrance, but as you said earlier, if we inject her against her will when she regains Sunshine's disposition, she will not trust us anymore. Unah could betray NIA... loyalty would be gone, and we stand the chance of alienating her and losing her forever. She will Hate us, Terrance!" "I realize this. That's why you must convince her of the necessity to let you inject our pharmaceutical mix, the hybrid that our Scientists have...." "Yes, Terrance, remember on the test subject inmates, it has been simply amazing the chemical Potpourri should do the trick, bring Wendi back for the night, then like a Yo-Yo when the drugs dissipate breakdown in her system Sunshine the stronger entity and more viral strain of the two will remain standing. The question really is will she swallow the medicine, or will I need to jab the needle into her?" "Liz, that's not my only concern. You might just underestimate Wendi's resolve and the internal battle that will result after the medication has its effect. The power struggle will be intense."

On-time Sunshine/Wendi opens the Theater door strutting confidently, then clumsily cowers and looks up at them, shrieking out, prancing forward. "Mom... Dad, OmGod, I've missed you so much. I love you... Thanks for coming to visit me!"

She tries to embrace Terrance, who holds her at shoulder length, smiling, "pumpkin, how have you been doing? You look great...." "I'm doing so much better, dad. I've confined Sunshine," a minuscule frown, "hi honey, come here give me a hug...." "I love you, mom..." "let me look at your face" Liz stares at her intimidatingly. "I brought you a bowl of your favorite.... Clam Chowder. It should still be hot. We put it in the microwave down the hall, or you can keep it for later." "Oh, mom, thanks, but I've lost my appetite. Just seeing you both is overwhelming!" Terrance throws up a stop hand. The three of them smile accordingly "well, Whatdayah thinks not bad, huh?" exclaimed Sunshine. Liz says, "No, not bad at all. Now Terrance will be Rico...." "Oh fk, I don't like that guy...."

"You're right, you don't like Rico, in fact, you despise him, but Wendi loves him, declares Terrance. Now go back out the door and re-animate yourself in three minutes. I wanna see love flow from your features."

She slouches backward up the aisle. She waddled, muttering, 'I can do this shit. Let me psych myself out.' Liz hides behind a curtain with a Birdseye view waiting for Sunshine's performance. She steps through the door and brings the palm of her left hand down from her forehead like changing faces. See's Terrance "aah Rico. I'm so sorry to have missed your visits; she lunged toward him with a kiss on the cheek and a long embrace and whispered in Terrance's ear, damn, I've longed for your touch. I missed you, baby. Let's go for a stroll around the ponds, Rico!" Liz claps and steps out. Terrance steps to the side. "I told you I could fool them," still using Wendi's higher pitched voice, "I was flu great, wasn't I? like a Tony, ahh Emmy winning porn-star unh Academy Award winner ain't no problem no worries ugh one thing that bothers me are either of you going to be there for moral support?"

They ignored her "come on, let's go over to that open table. The three of us are going to grade you out on your skit" they yank chairs out and cover the seats with their glutes, "I think there's potential; Dontcha agree Terrance?" "Yeah, she was good for a quick impromptu..." "so I flu sucked, huh? I'm getting perturbed the vibes you two are putting off aren't positive" she leans her head towards the tabletop. Once again, Liz slaps her iPad down. I'll let you be the first judge of your greetings. We just filmed you, but before you watch, let's take you back to an earlier visit when Wendi was in the leading role. Please, with an open mind, check this out. Maybe we should have shown you this prior, but it was necessary from our perspective for you to AdLib."

The three of them watched the earlier visit strangely. The atmosphere was far more subdued, Wendi's movement less then half speed, no jumping or gyrating or any rambunctious joy portrayed long hugs which seemed en-vogue. She spoke in a low, ambling monotone after greeting her parents. She turned ever so slightly and had an eyeball-to-eyeball gleam with Rico. Who winked 'welcome back, babydoll' 'hi, handsome,' he leaned over her. She bent her chin up, and he gently smelled her, nibbled her upper lip, then they kissed for a minimum of five seconds "oh fk no gross shit ewe ugh," expelling a gag look. "What did you expect me to do, drool all over your fricken suit, bro dude? I ain't French kissing you. I mean no disrespect, Terrance, I'm not doing that sloppy ass shit, dammit to hell." Silence took hold as Liz played back Sunshine's rendition. Ugh!

Afterward, Sunshine was resigned to defeat. Terrance starts talking calmly, carefully using appropriate language, saying, "we're still three hours to showtime. We can go through a second or third take. Some actresses need a half dozen shoots to get it right." He stops for a sec. Twirling his hips and bending forward, "some problems that I saw and felt you need to address, you called me. Dad… Wendi refers to me as father, and Wendi also refers to Sunshine with a deep-seated frown. In fact, Wendi almost never mentions Sunshine, for she knows how her parents feel about you. Furthermore, Wendi's always smiling when describing you like you are her savior." Sunshine shook her head "that's not the way I see it or feel…" He disregarded her comment, "another error. Wendi always hugs her father to the side. Never face his front in a hugging formation. This has been traditional."

Terrance nods at Liz. She begins, "it was an admirable attempt. I don't believe I could have done any better, although you can't call me mom or mommy when playing Wendi. I'm Mother on these visits. Ahh, you're allergic to Clam Chowder, and always embrace your mother first. You're the one that holds her face staring into her eyes, not the way you approached me…." "Unh, I think I can fix all of that. The problem is the kissing of that arrogant prick. I hate the dude. He disgusts me. I'm liable to chomp on his intruding tongue or lop it Plum off. The thought is sickening. I might vomit. How do I overcome him? He will, without a doubt, know that I'm not Wendi. Ugh, they've been wildly intimate. Remember, kissing or kisses are like fingerprints. No one kisses the exact same way. Shit why don't I have the flu? Yeah, I'm sick. That will work!_ Yep."

Terrance slips out a picture and then another, slapping them on the table "here you were yesterday. These are the pictures that one of our assets inside the FBI was able to copy from their labs." Sunshine picks one up and quickly shuffles through them. 'She and Kamryn on the bleachers,' another shot of her and the Wolves walking with Kam. One more, 'Jax and Terrance with her smiling,' she shakes her fist. Terrance adds, "again, not to be redundant, but you're going to be locked up in an observation tank. You think we experiment here at NIA where they're taking you will..." she hits the table with a crack, knuckles down, and stands up. "Then why don't I escape? You have a hundred places for me to hide, heck. Isn't there a militia in Spokane?" "Yes, but that's not going to work. The FBI is already down my throat. Can't have Rico going all berserk and personal on us Vendetta like.... Nope!"

Sunshine snorts into a snigger "well, damn, what's the plan, huh, our next move? Let me fricken guess you want me to give up control and let the sniveling brat out. Unah, sorry, it ain't going to happen here. It's my way or the highway. I'm here for good always. From now on, I own this body, and it's my mind that is in control till the end of this life! I will fight till the death screw Rico and this whole situation this ain't going to end mellowly." Liz looks at her purse. At the same time, the selected jingle plays from both their phones. Terrance acknowledges the private line, takes his cell phone out and frowns "now what?" A text from Renae. 'Rico and her parents have asked permission to bring a professor with them to interview Wendi and to analyze her improvements from our treatment programs here at NIA and so on.' He angrily sends back a text, 'what professor who?' he then flips his screen around for Liz and Sunshine to read. The mood went drastically ice cold, terminally morbid Terrance mutters, "Rico is pulling out all the stops. I won't be surprised if he brings a court order to take Wendi from here..." Sunshine yelps out "no, fk no, how do we stop him?" "One thing for certain," he replies, "we will not refuse him, and the professor, we have to play it close to the vest and act supremely confident that Wendi is at the best place she can be right here at NIA." He texted Renae... 'we need to know all we can about this, Professor... Renae.'

Before their faces, Sunshine's never say die optimism shrank... drained pragmatism reared its ugly head. Liz had seen this on several occasions. Contrary to whom Sunshine personified, she was acting weak and disheveled as Wendi had in similar conflicting situations. Was she entering a chasm of emotional incontinence trauma induced by aligned panic? Next, she'd be creating delusions and hallucinations piled high with paranoia, definitely all factors present. The situation was tense before, but now the three of them are slipping down and off a precarious ledge.

Sunshine whipped out her fist lightning fast and punched her left cheek; Terrance and Liz reacted quickly, grabbing her. "Stop it, stop, get a hold of yourself" they struggle with her Sunshine is way stronger than she looks, finally being able to hold her down onto the carpet. A wailing howling dark deep, growling chortle rotates, peeping up teeth chomping Red streaked blood dripping from her lips. She spits in anguish. Terrance and Liz have her from both sides. "Wendi is fkn dead. She is never going to reappear now. What do you two want to do?" Her mouth opens, and screaming indecipherable verbiage, doors pop open at the top of the stairs. Liz had already pushed the emergency button on her hip, and guards with medical staff entered. Terrance holds his arm up in their direction, palm up and out, and shouts, "Stop!" He held her tight, her arms now dropping as she trembled 'thinks geez, this woman is crazy.'

Eye contact telepathic renderings… he nods and closes his eyes. It's time for extreme measures; the only recourse available. Liz promptly pulled the cap off the hypodermic needle. Sunshine's teeth were now locked like a Pit-Bull growling and snorting "relax, Sun," shouted Terrance. "Everything will be okay soon, I promise!" Liz pumped the syringe deep into Sunshine's shoulder while he held her tightly. Her mouth opened in shock, giving Liz the opportunity she'd hoped for, shoving the Horse tablet down her throat… and then clenching her jaw closed as the victim fought and scratched. Three guards grasped her thighs and upper body, locking her down, yet she gesticulated like a nest of Serpents. Suddenly she collapsed with five people slowly lifting her to the waiting gurney.

Liz studied the welt beginning to bruise near Sunshine's left eye and the blood that was streaked down her chin, frightfully catching Terrance's glare. He sniffed derisively "well, this about does it… just our luck she'll have a shiner Black and Purple eye by 8:15 pm. This worked out worse than I had imagined. Please stay with her, Liz. I'll check in with you in an hour. We still have like 125 minutes, and if I have to, I will stall the oncoming entourage at the NIA gates. I have to visit with Kamryn now!" He could hear Liz order the guards to load her on a gurney and take her to Room # 3 in the emergency room, just then some more of the medical staff enter the theater, Liz means "it's been hell around here lately!"

Terrance brings the Clairvoyant to NIA.

Terrance steps out of the chaos and selects his private line to his Chauffeur, Jacob, who picks up on the third ring. "Hey, boss, how's everything going?" Jacob, I'm not into small talk. I need your cooperation and focus... what are you doing?" "Uh, well, boss, I'm playing some poker at the clubhouse. I..." "I need you to drive to the City and pick up my Clairvoyant. She's waiting for you. I just finished texting her your contact information. I need her onsite ASAP... "Yes, sir, I'm on it!"... Jacob grits his teeth, muttering, 'Terrance can be an asshole!'

-45-

<u>Valerie was visiting with her sister Sara.</u>

The last three days he'd aged three years, he felt exhausted; he texted Valerie 'how's it going? Val.' Terrance didn't even knew how her meeting ended with her sister Sara. He had fires to put out at every turn, and he chuckled, thinking being Uncle to his three nieces might just kill him. Thankful for no more family members. They were all dead and buried or cremated. No more bones left hidden in the proverbial closets.... unh no, that didn't make sense and wasn't true. Ahh, decisions had to be made, resolutions either favorable or harmful to NIA's future. He was in charge, and it was up to him to make firm, decisive conclusions. The pressure was above the boiling point. Why couldn't he think clearly? Val texts back, 'I'm in the Archery pavilion, Uncle. Working on instructing Sara, unh, she's a natural for sure, would say a chip off the old block, but I'm the younger sister. Lol, what can I do for you?'

Able to deflate his lungs, blowing out carbon dioxide until he was involuntarily forced to intake oxygen, stress kills, rubs his temples, closes his eyes okay, and decides to let her and Sara be, happy that they hadn't hurt one another as of yet. Texted back, 'let's hook up later for an early dinner or late lunch...' Moments later, 'A-ok, with a thumbs-up, Uncle seeya then.' Valerie and Sara can deal with Kamryn on their own. Val initially tried to introduce herself days ago. However, Kam had gone into a diabetic trance, didn't remember seeing her, and was still unaware that her baby sister lived. Sara would rather Valerie never meet with her twin. It wasn't a jealousy thing, or was it? No, Sara worried that Kam would paint an ugly picture of her and turn her against her. Terrance was always preoccupied with working advantageous angles, wondering how he could parlay the shock value of baby Valerie alive and having survived her horrific abduction. Maybe Valerie could convince Kam to get in line and play ball, but that would wait for now. Kam was a problem he'd have to address. She was anti-NIA, at least before her Diabetes diagnosis. Maybe she was discombobulated because of internal medical issues, he hoped. One thing was certain he must straighten out the young lady's mindset. She either was part of his empire or, uh, he didn't want to muse over the 'OR' enough for now. He swiftly expunged it… and it exited his mind.

He punched in a text to Kam she hit him right back 'hey, you got some time for me?' reply 'course!' 'where are you?' he 'walking the track by Swan pond' 'k I'll meet you at the entrance in nine minutes ✳' smiley face, he ponders could something go right today unh anything? He was well aware of Kamryn lobbying to visit with her ex-fiancé next door at the Stem-cell facility. She made it clear that she wanted to get back on with her life. How could he let her out to the streets and get picked up by Rice, where he could serve her with the warrants for her DNA! He desperately wanted to interview Kamryn and pit her against her sister Sara.

Suddenly someone grabbed his left shoulder from behind. He reacted deftly, slipping his Derringer 2-shot pistol from his right sleeve… mere habit, not expecting trouble inside of NIA. He was on his property. No one would dare to assault him here. Jaybird was cracking a pie-eating grin, "all right, boss, I have some enlightening news. After shaking the bush up sufficiently could have one of the infiltrator's identities, we've set her up, waiting for her to take the bait. I like to call it... shake and bake 85% confirmed. Ahh, sorry to shake you up. Got a bit enthused..." Terrance grinned "thanks, Byrd, keep me updated."

Terrance checked the monitors on his iPad after Walter, his security man, had informed him of where Kamryn was located. Terrance watched her find an empty Golf cart and start driving to the entrance of Swan Pond. Then Kam stopped and stood beside a park bench. He yanked out a set of mini binoculars and spotted Kamryn feeding some Mallard Ducks. She must have gotten sidetracked; he smiled. Oh, how he did love the little lady. She was quite a different person than her evil sisters. He zoomed in... her complexion was back. She looked great. A great big Goose was sneaking up on her butt. He laughed. Yep, he Goosed her, and she squealed up into the air, spinning, whirling, then giggling all at the same moment, yelling loudly; he heard her echoed words, 'Bad Goose!'

'Oh My' as he closed in on the path towards her. She's so damn pretty... it reminds him back in time, like 30 years Kam and him down in Half Moon Bay in a paddle boat. She used to be so full of life and fun that he might have his rarest of nieces back brought him a tinge of happiness. She is a believer in the Ten Commandments. She was pure good, ooh, the poor thing was straight-up lost. This World was Evil!

Kam, again it seemed, was having fun, and skipped over to him for a hug and peck on his cheek, "wow, I feel fantastic, the best ever in so damn long I was suffering in despair without any idea why depression consumed me it was Diabetes that encapsulated the whole of me I'll never ever be able to explain to you... or now, even me, Uncle... It's like the old saying I feel like a huge weight has been lifted off of me. OmLord, ahhhh anyways, how are you? Lol hate to say it, but you look like I felt before my episode what's wrong, my favorite Uncle?" This he hadn't heard in years used to be a regular statement of affection. Hence, he played along like in the past their facetious comical game "favorite Uncle huh I'm the only Uncle yah got!" they giggle with another embrace like long ago oh so cool he slides his arm over her shoulders. They walk away from the gathering birds.

February was just around the corner… thus far, 2018 has started up drearily. If it continued this way grimly… Terrance mused he might have a fricken heart attack damnit could anything work right for him and NIA? The sun was shining far from hot in Napa, but a fine crisp day was ending. It was a pleasant 67 degrees. They meander down the path stopping by a Weeping Willow Tree… listening to visitors with inmates along with the medical staff chatting it up. The guards stayed out of sight, trying to blend in. Many children were playing, building sandcastles, climbing jungle gyms and, going down slides, swinging in the deluxe playground. There were many trustees. This was the 'Camp side' or low-classification side of the prison.

Terrance was oblivious to everyone except his favored niece… they just enjoyed each other's company, mindful that Kamryn didn't belong here. When push came to shove, nothing could improve her disposition at this very second other than opening the gates of Hell. Yet Kam thought she'd be on the streets in no time, be free to live her life again, and her dastardly twin would be locked up where she belonged.

Deep breath, then let it go whistling, took up Terrance's hand, and started swinging it around. "I was so afraid, scared to death, really thought the curse of Sara, my mother, and Papa, so many of my relatives, inherited destructive genetics felt doomed as if it was psychosomatic knew woah believed insanity lurked at each turn Uncle so confused like living in another dimension." Terrance twisted towards her staring down with a red-faced stare. "I can't pretend, honey, to know that kind of internal pain that you were going through. The mind is a powerful thing… what you believe can manifest into your reality. Come, let's sit down on that bench; let me give you an example of when I was a little boy and what I'd learned."

He put his hand on Kam's shoulder, sat back, and relaxed... "I was taught a lesson that enlightened me about the power of the brain in an animal. I had a miniature Dachshund. Her name was Tara. Gosh loved that puppy. She wanted to be pregnant so badly that, psychosomatically, she willed it. I was a boy of 7 years old I'll never forget my mother, and I took her to the Veterinarian...." "What? Why?" Kam was laughing at his odd expression "did the dog talk to you" snickering, he beamed, "no silly pill, I'm no Wendi Feral" she laughed harder... "Touché Uncle!" Kamryn felt her stomach in her loose shirt, covered up with an oversized jacket. She wondered if Liz had finally broken weak and filled her Uncle in on her condition, but almost didn't care. The OB/GYN had told her a week ago that she was about seven months pregnant. Which mathematically made sense; her last loving session with Brock was in late June. It was weird that my uncle would bring up pregnancy. She felt a touch irritated, thinking, did Liz or the doctor betray her confidence, but then smiled and rolled with it...

He stopped leaning into her on the bench face to face "my Dachshund grew a hard stomach like she was carrying puppies. Her nipples swelled hugely with nursing milk, but the darn dog had never seen a male doggy, lol." "That's it, Uncle, your too funny... woe impregnated from the air?" He laughed. "No, the Veterinarian shook her head and told mom and me that Tara mentally convinced herself she was pregnant. She had a self-induced disorder in her brain, which communicated to her body Walla the dog Tara believed she was pregnant. Therefore she was." They chuckle, and he adds, "the takeaway was the Vet said it's not that uncommon...." "So your dog was off her rocker, a dog bone short of a.... ugh crazy. Maybe you should start NIA for Canines and Felines, or wait, how does this snippet relate to me?" "Kam, isn't it clear if you believe something strong enough and psych yourself out? It's not too difficult to imagine it being true, leading your internal imagination into a self-fulfilling prophesized resolution sort of self-fruition."

"So, where's the life lesson here, Uncle?" "Kam, I'll leave you to figure that out. Suffice it to say NIA doesn't stand for the evil you associate it with; my organization is a needed cog in this world. Why would you think otherwise, huh? What because of our leniency with your sister Sara? Or for my NIA hierarchical powers to be... that flagrantly have refused to let you leave here and get accosted by Rico Captor and the Feds? We have a lot to negotiate...." "Ssshh, I've heard enough, Uncle... it's like you're running a political campaign and want to recruit me...."

They again start down the path past a dock. "Uncle remember when I was a little girl, and you would take me to parks? We'd have so much fun. Come on, let's do it...." "Do what? Go down a slide in my $3,000.00 Armani suit," he frowned with a smirk looking around "heck, there's got to be 35 people out here..." "Come on, let's Skip to my Lou" holding hands, we can still do it come on let loose...." "Are you fricken kidding me? Huh, that would be insane. What would my guards think? The CEO hmm. Their boss is skipping merrily away. No, they'd have me locked up in a rubber room...." He let loose with a cackle, morphing into a hilarious giggle. "Please, pretty please, with Sugar on top, Uncle, come on...." "Wait a second did you have a psychiatric evaluation?" she tugged at him. My $30.00 outfit and your $3,000.00 suit can do it in unison, unh, lift your feet, and you won't scuff those fine ass shoes...." "Kam, no!" Whoops, she yanked his arm, and they went. Skipping to my Lou, suddenly, he burst into laughter... hysterics 30 yards into the skipping. They were balling and frantically panting at 35 yards. They fall onto the grass riotously, tears uncontrollably falling.

They pulled themselves up and sat on the wet grass on their asses, catching breaths and only grinning "you know I love you baby, Kam, you're the only person that could…." "I love you too, Uncle," they warmly embrace for this time; real tears fell down emotions with relief, a continuum of a new perspective called Happy tears.

His phone beeps, breaking them out of their gaiety. He smiles at her again "looks like my afternoon is looking up," he lends a hand down, lifting Kam up. Grass stains, ugh, a mess. "I'll have to change now….." "Why not be like you are, Uncle" 'ahh' raising his eyebrows, "all right, why not." Back on the path, "Kam, this has been much more enjoyable than I'd expected. I sought you out for a serious discussion. I'm afraid we will not have the time now. I can't put off this important gathering…." "What meeting? Do you need my help? I can…" "Nah, it's a Wendi/Sunshine thing. They've put off this meeting until tonight. Her parents and Rico will be here at 8:15 tonight. Ahh, gotta check in with Liz. Hey, so I'm going to leave you around the next bend by the Rock fountain. Listen, suffice it to say I know you want the hell outta here. Your freedom is also of utmost importance to me, and Lord knows you deserve to be free. It's unfathomable what Sara did to you. Not going to dwell on that. I'd like to set up some parameters to give you freedom under a new paradigm shift, um, a new start. We'll go into the whys and who's all the logistics later. Nevertheless, my favorite Niece, I beg umh implore you to join your Uncle's dream and be a part of it and make it your own… will talk later!"

She squeezes his arm "so, Uncle, I don't want to disappoint you, but okay, I'll listen to your concerns and propositions. You knew I wanna return to my life; this has been….." "Kam, I want you to honor the contract and 2-year commitment for training here at NIA U… I want you to live at the facility and…" seeing her expression ruined, "but Uncle, I signed that when I was out of my mind, not myself sick, you said it yourself...." "Oops, gotta go; no worries, we'll deal with it. Love you..." then he sees them. Cautiously he allowed an optimistic smirk with a sideways, more prolonged, lasting grin to hit the surface of his face.

Kam was stunned, shaken, and nearly slipped awkwardly on an acorn... almost began dry-heaving. Nervous nausea instantly crawled up her esophagus for what the Uncle had requested no way she'd have to stand up and void that 2-year contract. He wasn't going to let her leave this prison. She followed his weird reactive expression and saw a person in the path who acknowledged him... with another female also nodding with a peculiar stare. The females were standing off the track directly in front of them.... who the heck were they?

She recognized the woman dressed in a Robinhood outfit, Green with an ancient, designed hat with a feather in it.... she had seen her days prior at the Quickdraw contest. Whoa, weird, she said to herself. Where's her bow & arrows? The woman was on a direct path toward her when she got within 15 yards. A noise exploded in the air. "Kammy, Kammy, it's me, Kammy jumping in her Green outfit. Kam stopped bending down, hands on her knee, remembering she'd heard her nickname from when she was a baby at the Quickdraw contest. The woman continued in motion, now about 7 yards away. Her heart fricken exploded, her mind at warp speed, trying to assimilate an impossibility. Blood pressure shot through her skull in a natural adrenalin rush, like 15 shots of expresso endorphins blasting. Valeria saw her reaction aligning with her own... tears stormed from stoically proud Valeria.

Kam went from Zero to infinity, frantically sprinting fast as she could. They met each other, arms out OmGod hugging bouncing, squealing twirling ear-piercing shrieks dancing in a circle giggling, hugging, holding sisterly reunion I love Luv you; Luv love you Kam was crying uncontrollably Baby Val no way OmLord no a long passionate embrace together again after over 27 years! Omg, OmLord, impossible, oh hell no...

Terrance stalled and watched the drama unfold like a reality show, walking the other way, a heavy sigh tightening his dark sunglasses. He murmured females, huh, uuuh, felt emotionally spent. I'm a man, ugh, a walking conundrum or oxymoron, right a contradiction as he slyly wiped his face with a kerchief pretending to be cleaning his glasses, fk I need my testosterone checked. My hormones have to be outta wack! His niece's reunion had vibrated his being. "Man, I'm getting soft in my formative years, snorted, then a blow of his nose that was the best set-up yet played to perfection. Uh, now onto a train wreck… highs and lows.

He Sucked a big breath in, knowing Liz awaited him with strife bubbling up. Ahh, how to deal with the 3:15 meeting 'sshh, calm down,' he mumbled, now knowing severe trauma was near 'where was the updated information that I'd ordered from Jax and Renae on this Professor Milo that's coming with Rico?' He'd always known that Professor Milo would become a problem, but no one listened. Now he'd have to deal with the wayward doctor once and forever. When he'd left the theater where Wendi went berserk, 'mad as a hatter,' his last vision was of her discolored face. Could Liz or her staff cover up the welt and bruise that had already started to swell on Sunshine's right cheek? That's all he needed, yeah, the parents and Rico to show up, and precious Wendi had a black eye, uh… or worse yet, the pill and shot had her in oblivion? How did that affect her? Wow, tons of unknowns, damn, he mumbled. If 'pressure makes Diamonds,' I'm a freakin 191-pound Rock, um, stone. No doubt he was down for Liz injecting Wendi. Sunshine was losing it, and Liz had shown him proof that the formula she injected into Sunshine had helped some test subjects significantly, all of whom suffered from Schizophrenia. It was our only alternative, but the fricken horse pill wasn't part of his plan. I wondered why Liz adlibbed and choked that down Wendi's throat. Oh well, you can't cry over spilled milk, right… wrong!

Back finally in the Golf cart, looking down, he had plenty of time to change clothes; worry strangled him… the human psyche, our minds an unopened book with no manuals, unlike an automotive engine or schematics, nope! With Wendi's personality disorder, who's to say she doesn't wake up? And drops back into a coma? I need her alive and fluent. Thinking wishing Wendi could believe she was an unstoppable Warrior like her alter ego. He chuckled. Wouldn't it be great if she could morph into, um, like she was Genghis Khan or Julius Caesar or Fricken Cleopatra? She had to find empowerment be strong and assertive… and help all of us to be able to keep her here at NIA.

He waits for the pneumatic door to open, seeing Liz standing over her gurney, numbers in digital Red flashing on machines hooked to Sunshine's body, and an I.V. taped to her left arm for fluids, heart rate fluctuating on the high side, which was worrisome B.P. 175/99.

Liz was obviously unhappy, displaying negative vibes and staring at her patient, whose eyes were dilated, unblinking. She was plumb out, coma-like. The experimental Horse tablet, in conjunction with the liquid form that she injected into her shoulder, had done some damage. Uh, she ruminated. Was that too much, dammit it like spontaneous combustion! When Sunshine showed her tonsils, I reached for the pill and crammed it down her throat… not a good thing. One of the leading Scientists who had invented the concoction stood on the other side of the gurney with an unpleasant countenance. Liz glared at the scientist… her arms folded over her breasts looked constipated, thought. Liz, then dared to glance at Terrance's gruesome scowl… jeesh he reflected a castrated 'Ken Doll' … Bad stuff

The squeaky voice of the Scientist, who had worked alongside the inventor Greg Walters who had developed the latest chemical compound that was injected into Wendi, said, "I texted Greg, who's on his way back here. He'd finished his shift a few hours ago. I have to say he was bewildered as to why you would give Wendi a triple dose. The syringe was of double strength, and then you forced the pill down her throat. Damn, we may have lost her!" Renae bolts into the room in time to hear the last words spoken, the importance not lost on her knowing an intense confrontation was soon to happen. Seeing Wendi's Red and swelling cheek and discolored eye lifts the ice bag immediately and replaces it with a new one from the nearby refrigerator unit. Terrance was breathing in easy inhalations, calming himself, and reading on his tablet the latest information sent to him about the extra visitor being brought with Rico.

A few minutes later, he sat in a vacant room adjacent to where Wendi lay. Professor Milo is the addition to Wendi's visiting list. He calls Liz in to discuss this latest information, "Googling Milo. I found that he and some colleagues have formed an L.L.C. partnership and have a clinic in San Mateo. The professor is in the book 'Who's Who' and he's the head of Forensic Psychiatry at Stanford University. He's an alumnus of Yale, a Cum Laude graduate who did a stint at the Mayo Clinic and two years touring European countries speaking at seminars and cajoling.... the cutting-edge Scientists. The dude has an impressive pedigree, Liz...." "Sure, I've heard about him from a couple of friends who worked with him at Stanford. The guy is known as an arrogant prick. The perception is he's a cutthroat megalomaniac."

"Wow, your right look at this article, <u>Doctor Milo is a Thief</u>,' they share the Laptop sitting close together. Liz mutters while reading, "the guy is a crook." "Well, to paraphrase, he was accused of poaching and stealing trade secrets, chemicals, and formulas from an institution out of Berlin, Germany. There were dozens of articles and writeups online, and they stopped at one named 'Rumor Mills.com.' *Terrance's phone vibrates. He hands her the laptop and steps away. 'Boss... Vadoma is getting antsy, and her daughter Bripa wants to*

Terrance turns to Liz, who stands and says… "Get this, Milo's family tree dates back to ancestors loyal to Sicilian tribes. The earliest records are from around 45 B.C. One of his ancestors was the Psychopath killer and betrayer General Marcus Brutus who was the protagonist and instigator in the outright assassination and slaying unh murder of Julius Caesar of Rome!" Despite the events of the afternoon and the pressure and stress, he tweaked a smirk "really look at you Liz your so animated here wow you are pumped maybe you missed your calling should have been a history professor tell me what's 2,063 years ago got to do with today I don't care about his bloodline but thanks for the anecdotal info."

Renae steps into the room, joining Terrance and Liz. They fill her in on the professor who was joining Ed and Barbara Feral with perpetual troublemaker Rico Captor. Renae was also familiar with Doctor Milo, but from another point of view, and started going off at what she'd heard "the good doctor was a narcissist who is known for experimental testing on patients. He has no qualms or reservations about injecting his test subjects with untried chemicals!" "Now that's useful information, Renae. Can we substantiate this? I mean, is it only from the rumor mill? It does us no good to elucidate on hearsay gossip darn, what do we really have to bite down on ladies?" He nearly cackled at Renae's words about Milo injecting untried chemicals. Isn't that like calling the kettle black… hah didn't they do that to Wendi?

Staring at Renae… "find me something we can use and verify." Renae continued, undeterred, saying, 'Milo is the equivalent of a mad scientist in today's world.' Terrance raised his voice "where's the proof in the pudding?' stop running at the mouth." Renae pouted after the admonishment and didn't quit pointing at her iPad "genetics is what makes us who we are, what we look like and appear to be… predisposed is a word that often describes these phenomena. This isn't Voodoo. It's scientific facts we are who we've been, for example…." Renae taps the screen to her photo albums while Liz rolls her eyes at her long-lost friend lost as in not being forthcoming with her plot with Sara. Umh, Liz could never forgive her for that impropriety, but let it be for now. The time would come soon enough for her confrontation with this would-be friend. Renae continued, "This is a picture taken in 1807, my Great Grandma to the 5th power…" "5th power what…" "5 generations back" she enlarged the pic, and low and behold, it was a woman of Renae's height, weight eyes right down to the cleft in her chin "whew." Liz exclaims, "you're not bullshitting me; you took this picture at one of the State Fairs in a picture booth. That's you with matching beauty marks on your left cheek. Come on, Renae? That's beyond crazy."

Renae zooms in on the ancient article and hands the iPad to Liz. The article was on… yellowing newspaper in large black fonts. She read aloud, 'Nurse Renae Hospice has opened a new clinic for terminally ill patients in our city of Boston, Massachusetts; please see the back page for lawyers who advocate for Last Will and Testament or power of attorney for bequests.' Liz had already felt faint, queasy from lack of sleep and worry "come on; you're fkn pulling my leg. Your descendant was the pioneer of the Hospice system?" "Yes, but that's not the takeaway here, Liz…" "R. U. kidding me, why haven't you ever brought that up before?" "I didn't know until my husband got all addicted to the ancestral internet crap. Ron would sit up all night tracking our family tree's sending out emails, checking registries and burial sites, sending out letters digging up birth certificates. I think it was 'Ancestry.com' anyways. We are what's in our bloodline… genes. Our DNA formed back from the Adam & Eve days. Check out the sisters Sara, Valerie, and Kam's lineage. The sister's psychopath killers go back as far as you can track them. You'll find a horde of mental cases disorders I'm willing to bet you..." Terrance yells "hey, stop, what's the point, okay Renae, you've got me in a quandary. Tell me why we are on this subject. Where's the relevance? I mean, it was a nice distraction, like who gives a shit if this Professor is related to the mutinous trader Marcus Brutus from Roman days." Silence personified... they just breathed stalled in time, bland expressions. It seemed like minutes passed, but it was... only seconds. Until Renae took up her defense of the topic, she'd become enamored within.

"Professor Milo is no doubt a snake-like Marcus Brutus, a Rat, and betrayer accused of pilfering innovative technical advances in Psychiatry, Psychology, and Science," she focused on Terrance. "The dude is the epitome of a perfect NIA employee. We should hire the Rat!" This was it... in harmony, they busted up hilariously, gagging, spitting, and howling like laughing Hyenas. Terrance regained his composure "uah, unh, okay, we needed that. Wow, that was good, Renae!" He wiped his face with the back of his palm "all right, great break, now let's get back to this real-time dilemma." They head back to Wendi's room. Renae couldn't help tossing this last statement out "my hubby Ron will soon be named the ex-hubby only wish Grandma to the 5th power was still around. She could have experimented on Ronny like they did when she started her Hospice program." She elbows Terrance, "and that's thanks to you. Yeah, Terrance, thanks a lot. Ron confessed to me, your one sicko dude betting that he'd jab that death needle into me...." "What are you talking about?" yelled Liz "not now!" said Terrance.

They strode in opposite directions. Renae was happy her shift was almost over, thinking of her daughter in Colorado, Candice, and the threats that were lodged against Candice by Terrance. Her daughter was innocent and not part of NIA. She was excelling in College. How evil can Terrance and NIA be? Her husband had gone along with it and plunged the killer needle into her to save his own skin. A game played out at her expense by Terrance and niece Sara and his prick bodyguard Angel. As she violently punches the down button in the elevator, one thing is for certain: they will rue the day they should never have fixed with _Mama-Bear! Fruit doesn't fall far from the tree if they only knew that my other Great Grandma was the infamous 'Bridget Bishop,' the first so-called 'Witch' convicted on June 2nd, 1692, in Salem Village and hanged eight days later on what would become known as Gallows Hill in Salem Town, Massachusetts. Lol_

-46-

Terrance had to break away and get some guidance from a Gypsy Queen.

Terrance turned his back on Liz, who was showing Renae something on her laptop. Renae's last words meandered and lingered in his head, although he could understand her resentment and anger towards him for pitting her husband, Ron, against her. I guess it was inappropriate for Angel, Sara, and him to bet that Ronald would stab her within the wagered time frame with the benign hypodermic needle. But hey, it was what it was, a spur-of-the-moment bit of fun. He would have to keep tabs on Renae. She could be trouble for him and NIA. Luckily, she'd already inhaled the mono-filament GPS tracker in her bottled water so he would know where she was.... at a click of his phone. He had to thank his niece again for bringing that invention to his attention. Hey, I believe that rhymed, lol. It was remarkable indeed. Terrance made another mental note.... he'd have to take care of the Renae situation sooner than later.

He took up his phone and texted back his Chauffeur, Jacob, who was trying to keep his clairvoyant friends happy. "I am on my way over; how are they doing?' a couple of seconds passed "boss, nothing has changed. They want out of here and driven back to their San Francisco homes.' Terrance needed these women. He was in desperate need of advice and help, texting back, 'let's meet in the lobby in five minutes.'

Terrance stepped from the stairwell, trying not to run into any chatty employees, and hopped into his waiting Golf cart, which he'd parked a mere hour earlier. He drove through the misty air towards the three-story building that housed his specialists and Team Leaders. He had the Presidential Suite, checking the time on his phone. He still had enough time, maybe? He entered the lobby and saw the massive figure of his Bodyguard/ Chauffeur… Jacob walked toward him.

"Jacob, give me an update…." "I'm glad you're here to take them off my hands, Terrance. I did what you asked of me and went to their Fortune Telling business in the Castro district. You knew they have expanded and now have three…." "Jacob, get to the point…." "Uh, well, I contacted Reena and asked her to have her mother, Vadoma, ready to travel with me to Napa. I told her it was an emergency like you said, sir. Reena went off on me yelling… said her mother had just turned 101 years old, and she didn't care if it was you, Terrance, who needed her. She was going nowhere!" Terrance stomped his foot, looking up at Jacob, "man, dude, get to the fricken point. You texted me that… ah, you wanted to speak with me before I went upstairs and met with Vadoma…." "Yeah, well, you have the entire family tree upstairs in your Presidential Suite, and they're crazy, I mean lunatics, mumbling and speaking in tongues. They had me disable your smoke alarms. Whew, Shit, I don't know how or what you're going to do with them… it's your business boss." Terrance tossed his hands up "who's upstairs, Jacob?" "Well, you got Great, Great Grandma, Great Grandma, Grandma. Then mother and daughter, yeah, no shit, the whole fricken tribe is upstairs…." He looked at his phone screen and declared, "Vadoma, 101 years old. Reena is 77 years old, Cilyanka is 57 years old, Cinderella is 37 years old, and Briya is 19 years old. Briya is the mother of little Charity, whom she left with her father, luckily, or you'd have like, uhm, six generations, I believe. I mean to tell you theirs five women up there, howling and chanting like Wolves. Hollywood has nothing on this group. It's like they're doing a Séance."

Terrance shakes his head up and down. "All right, I'll have to deal with it, I was hoping for you to be able to just bring Vadoma and maybe her daughter Roma, but it's okay. You did good, Jacob...." "Oh, boss, I'm sure the Feds were on my ass via a chopper and a few vehicles. I tried to lose them, but you know that's impossible with their satellite tracking cameras." "No worries, why don't you hit the gym? I'll be at least an hour or so." "Sure, boss... ah, that's right, I did what you asked of me, and before escorting them out of the Limo, I hit the blocker, so no one is wiser. No one knows they're here but you and I." Terrance failed to acknowledge him as he stepped into the elevator, put his key into a slot, and went to his private suite to visit with a bloodline of people who had been family friends for hundreds of years and generations. It had been said to him by his Grandfather that they'd been associated as far back as the 11th century in Persia.

He muses about the label... 'GYPSY' is the operative word that defines this group of ostracized people. The reference to being a gypsy nowadays can be stigmatizing. They were often banished from societies across the world. They supposedly first came to light back in Northern India, dating to the 10th century. Like vagabonds traveling in wagon trains and by horseback, they stuck together and formed villages. Gypsies have always been noted for their psychic abilities and their uncanny knowledge of things to come, like seers or clairvoyants. Gypsies were thought of back in America's history as Witchlike.... they were heralded as a people steeped in Rituals in magic and are known to be acclaimed practitioners of the arcane arts and folk magic throughout the world. He remembered reading somewhere that the famous Nostradamus and Edgar Cayce had Gypsies in their family trees. He'd also heard that the term 'Evil Eye' originated from the world of Gypsies…

The last time he visited Vadoma was a couple of months ago. It was her that predicted he'd meet with the long-believed deceased Valerie Amaya when he visited England to break ground on an NIA hospital. Vadoma had employed a Crystal Ball and had spread out some Tarot Cards and read them aloud to him. Then she looked down at some 'tea leaves' at the bottom of a glass cup. His parents and relatives still visited with Vadoma, and her daughter Roma, very seldom making any crucial decisions before asking the Gypsies for insight and approval.

Terrance paused at the door, he hadn't met Vadoma's grandchildren before, and this was going to be an experience that he'd need to speed up. The woman liked to chat it up and moved slowly, and then he chuckled… so would I if I ever made it to 101 years old. He slips his card into the slot and handprint on a pad, and his double doors pop open. It was dark inside. He reached over, knowing where the entranceway light switch was, and flipped it up… Nada. I could vaguely hear music playing in the darkness, then smelled the scented incense… and a distinct whiff of Sulfur dioxide from matches and saw the flickering reflections on the ceiling… candles were placed all over the place. In his peripheral vision, he saw the covers of his smoke detectors on his kitchen counter, with batteries sprawled about.

He stepped down into his sunken living room and saw them… realizing it wasn't music but the women chanting and waving their bodies in unison from their knees. He stopped and patted his left breast pocket, ensuring he felt the package he'd brought to Vadoma. After a few more moments, the chanting stopped Vadoma tensed her chin up while her descendants appraised him. "Terrance, I'll forgo the pleasantries, for we're without them this day. Have you turned your phone off?" He shook his head affirmatively and saw his shadow upon his wall do the same thing. She was helped to her feet by Roma, who introduced him to the rest of the aspiring Gypsies. There had to be dozens of candles flickering in and around the spacious living room, and he could make out in the darkness that the drapes had been pulled.

Vadoma started to walk toward his candlelit kitchen area. The women formed a line and, in order of their age, walked over and sat down around his enormous dining room table, leaving a spot at the head of the table for him. He noticed Red and Black placemats with odd Calligraphy and drawn figures placed in front of each of them. A Crystal Ball was in the middle of the table, lit up with an ominous glow. Briya, the youngest, said, "please have a seat. Can you give me the package that Vadoma asked you to bring, Mr. Hallinan?" I gladly did... Briya took it and raised it to her lips and nose, smelling it… this was repeated… the package I'd brought was passed to each of them, who made the same motions until it was placed before Vadoma. She opened the package, and with her left palm held out, Roma gave her two clips. She took the clumps of hair I'd harvested from Kamryn earlier and Wendi, as she'd requested of me.

Roma started to walk around the table, placing Tarot Cards out; the Crystal Ball was clutched and brought closer to Vadoma, but no one spoke. Cilyanka brought from her hip a container, opened it, and placed a Crystal decanter or round-like goblet onto the table beside Vadoma. At the same time, Cinderella began to hum indecipherable words of a different dialogue. Suddenly the five women stopped and simultaneously took their right arm up, crossing their hearts, saying, *'Cross my palm with Silver,' and bowed their heads*

Vadoma had the hairs in separate clips, nodded, and said, "please pour the distilled water into the goblet." Roma took a bottle from her side and filled it two-thirds of the way full.

Briya had taken each bunch of clipped hair and carefully tied a Plain Gold ring onto the ends. They sat back down, and Vadoma rested her elbows on the table, and holding the tip of the hair in both her hands, she suspended the ring above the water low enough so it rested within the rim of the cup. She waited patiently until the ring began to swing gently back and forth. She didn't intentionally move her hands. The natural draw of majestical powers started the ring to sway by itself. As the swings became wider and broader in motion, the ring started to strike the sides of the glass. Counting the pings told Vadoma not only the age of the owner... but the spiritual currents from the pinging hair told her secrets of the tresses. I would later find out the locks of hair told Vadoma a future and of an afterlife associated with the previous owner of the hair strands. At the same time that this was occurring, Roma was hovering over the Crystal ball, her eyes aglow, Cilynka was studying the Tarot Cards, and Briya was reading the Tea Leaves at the bottom of a China glass. Cinderella never stopped speaking in tongues. The orchestrated event continued until both strands of hair were dipped near the water in the Crystal Goblet, pinging with a chiming sound. I sat there entranced, fidgeting about... dying. My bladder was doing its own pinging. I needed to Pee like the proverbial Racehorse... Ugh!

The five women froze as if "<u>Simon Says,</u>" said Freeze and bowed their heads on the table, unmoving, not an utterance espoused. I sat frozen trying to figure out what was happening, but I'd figured while in Rome, do as the Romans, so I put my head on the table as well....

Slowly Vadoma moved, struggling to get up from her perch on the chair. I followed them back to the living room, where they sat silently. The old woman looked up through the flickering candlelight, nodding, "go to the bathroom, 'T.' We have much to discuss." I returned and kneeled down, matching them around the coffee table. "Wendi Feral will not return to being herself. Her alter-ego Sunshine has control of her, and there's another entity that's hovering about in the young lady's cranium. My daughter Rosna has written a list of ingredients for this recipe. You must gather and mix accurately in the amounts allocated for her to be able to fool the entourage that will be visiting her hospital room later this evening. You have to collect all the ingredients and be exact in formulating this potion. If you do so… And can get her to drink this concoction with the dosage that I've recommended, or at worse, give her an injection with the amount prescribed on this note." Vadoma leaned forward as if stalled and then continued slowly and methodically speaking. "Terrance, you must give Wendi three separate doses if you do… you will conquer your goals regarding keeping Wendi within your haunts here at NIA." Rosna reached out and handed me a crisp note with what I needed to put together for my Wendi Feral problem.…

"I asked you 'T' for the hair strands from your niece Kamryn Amaya because of what I'd envisioned the last time I'd had a visit from you. That's when I informed you that you would be reconnecting with your lost niece of 27 years, Valerie Amaya. I hoped that what I read in the Leaves and in the Tarot Cards could be fallible, but alas, their True. I saw some harrowing visions at that time, and I've since discussed some of these vivid and lurid visions with my offspring,… that's sitting before you this afternoon. In order to have the strength and fortitude to navigate within Divine Metaphysics or in the religion of Spiritualism. I have brought them here, and we will try and perform a Séance for the purpose of 'Receiving Messages' from the Spirit Universe." Vadoma moved quicker than I thought she could and reached out, taking Rosna's hand in her left hand and Cilynaka's in her right. I watched the family holding each other's hands on top of my coffee table, happy that I only observed.

Vadoma lowered her skull, her wispy grey hair in a bun, "like had been my habit formed from generations before us, I will repeat specifically some of my favorite life sayings that reflect your identity. I do so before trying to visit the Netherworld on your behalf... 'Life is hard, but it's harder if you're stupid.' 'If you don't take your life... time will.' 'Every moment is another second chance.' 'Our lives are like a candle in the wind.' 'He who has nothing to die for... has nothing to live for.' 'Life is about falling... living is about getting back up.' Life is a plant... that grows out of death...." *A scroll on rice paper is sent... hand to hand, ending in front of me.*

Again a chanting in a low hum had begun rising in volume. The lady's hands began to rise, then once over their heads, their fingers began clawing violently in the air. Then their arms dropped in unison to the tabletop. The frail elder woman ripped her head back and forth, eyes aglow in the candlelight. She bellowed out in a man's voice while the other women rolled their heads upon their shoulders in perfect symmetry. *'Kill the child, kill the child, you must kill this child....' Another voice exits Vadoma's open mouth. It's a woman. 'The child is a Demon, much more powerful and evil, deadlier than Sara and Valeria combined. She's the SUM of all her devious relatives. Kill the Child!' Vadoma is by now foaming from her lips as a male's voice with an Italian accent... barked... 'Her name and Machiavellian demon spirit are already etched in the annals of Hades, the Blessed Evil Incarnate Sonja. Everyone must cheer for Sonja, Hail Sonja, all mighty Sonja!' Vadoma shrieks out, screaming no... a child's crying stops, a pause. Vadoma's countenance went from ghoulish to a trembling smirk, and her tongue slithered out "a babies voice came from her quivering lips 'I'm your Niece Sonja, Uncle Terrence, I love you, please don't hurt me, uncle, my mommy is your favorite niece... Kamryn.'*

I was flabbergasted, umh, overwhelmed, waiting for this Hollywood production to finalize with Vadoma's head spinning in full circles and her spewing vomit like a massive Volcano blowing. But nothing happened. Not even a squirt gun fired saliva; nope, she slowly fell forward. Her head didn't splatter on the table, and nada… just rested now on her arms, just like the rest of her family. I was beyond confused, call it perplexed, Nah, maybe uh yeh, I was bewildered, to say, ah, mumble the least. I have three nieces that have had hysterectomies. How could there be a pregnancy? And why would this baby Sonja speak to me from the Spirit netherworld calling me Uncle? Then it hit me like a box of Wheaties; bang, I had given Vadoma a slice of Kamryn's hair… come to think of it, she hadn't been wearing her sexy Capri's and had been dressing in bagged-out clothing… No Way!…

Roma spoke, and that's when I noticed the five women were changed. They not only had perspired a river's worth of sweat, but they no longer acted alive, like five zombies blinking in my direction. "Terrance," she said, "you do have an understanding of the Psychopaths in the Amryn bloodline, killers that date back B.C.E. Sonja is the compilation of them all. She has supernatural gifts and an I.Q. higher than any manmade chart. Kamryn is carrying this Demon child; you must abort this serial killer in the making. She will be unstoppable if you allow her to propagate. Kill her today, Terrance."

The women stand, and Vadoma is helped to walk over to my sectional couch. "Please have your Chauffeur here to pick us up in a few hours. We need to rest some. Thanks for your donation to our cause." Roma holds up the satchel of money that Jacob had given them. I stood weary and confounded as to what I must do. I said, 'Thank you, ladies.' I stepped out and pushed the button, and rode my elevator to the ground floor…

Rico tried to concentrate and think of any reason that Terrance's Limousine would be tracked to the seedy side of the Castro district in San Francisco. Now the report he'd read three times.... reportedly, an elderly woman was helped into the back of the limo, with four other women joining her. Then they were driven to NIA-U, went into the locked gates, and disappeared. That wasn't the strange bit that befuddled him. It was where the women came from... a Fortune Tellers shop, and their attire was something out of a Halloween shop, like belly dancers with Beads and long dresses, Gypsies. Before they'd picked up this motormouth Doctor, he'd checked out the video and pictures of the women transported across the Golden Gate to Napa.

Rico had problems. To him, what was life without complications, a patient man who'd learned with experience to take each obstacle by itself! At this time, he was mulling over what had gone wrong with the contingent from Wash. D.C., the unsavory powermongers. He'd already secured the Warrants for Sara and Kamryn's DNA from Judge Delaney. The trouble was front and center. All the participants were apprehensive, like walking on Eggshells Rico had the ominous reckoning that they'd discussed this subject matter well before the onset of the video conference... everyone was afraid to open that can of worms, uh, for the public to get wind that DNA may be fallible. It was so unbelievable that the DNA proof collected proved without a shadow of a doubt that Sara had murdered Carl and Bianca Sparks from her prison cell. He was subtly warned to keep a lid on it... they'd told him to soft-peddle it... Wtf did that mean? Ughhhh, that's right, One problem at a time, now to get Wendi moved!... looked across from him, seeing the Professor of Psychology, Doctor Milo, whom he hoped would be able to talk the Feral's into moving their daughter from NIA. The guy had been running nonstop at the mouth. Rico felt lucky he was entranced with his phone temporarily.

Rico wasn't relaxed, although he sat back in a stretch Limousine awaiting the landing of a small jet at Napa Executive airport. Across from him was the clatterbox. The guy hadn't shut up from the instant he'd shook his hand, ash thinking again of the germs the guy incessantly was spraying in his direction. He was pawing at him, wanting to shake hands again and High five him at every achievement he'd broadcasted. The guy was full of himself, an egotist. He acted like he was a fricken God. Rico bounced back to what Ed Feral had said after he'd mentioned fist bumps and weirdly recalled the visit last week at NIA. The inmates would greet one another with Fist bumps that evolved from the '90s in prisons. It used to be the Hammer. That's where they had it right! He'd always despised the gentlemanly tradition of shaking hands. The oh-so-warm, snug handshake needed to go the way of the Dinosaur. Too many little men tried to squeeze your hand as hard as they could to show how macho they weren't. Some men positioned their hands lobbying for a better positional grip eyeballing their prey's hand so… fricken ridiculous. Such was the man who sat nearby. Umh, where was a set of earplugs when I needed them "so Rico, how do you want me to play it?" Asks Professor Milo for the third time! The guy must have early-onset dementia… Rico didn't bother in answering him this time but relented when he asked a fourth time three minutes later.

<u>Professor Milo was driving Rico crazy, but he had to get a handle on the situation.</u>

Firmly he said, "Professor, this isn't a game here. Like I've said at least three times, this is personal…_" Then he regressed, knowing he needed blabbermouth on his side "excuse me, those were words wrongly chosen. Let me rephrase or paraphrase what our aims are, uhm, what we want to achieve in our visit to NIA's Psychiatry hospital. We want to take Wendi out of NIA, and you're going to help convince her parents that you have the perfect solution....." "Yes, you're correct. I get it now. Aah, no worries. I can handle it, but....." Rico was beside himself like going crazy. Why the hell is this man asking these repetitive questions... geez man, we've been over it all in-depth?

Rico had his staff do the necessary due diligence, and they'd chosen this Professor Milo. Milo had just opened his mental health facility and had hired a group of Psychologists that were starved for patients to be incarcerated at his new clinic. They were trying to manipulate the Federal Government to land the Federal inmates that were considered mentally handicapped and unable to stand trial for their crimes. Milo's goal was to undermine all other mental institutions but primarily wanted to take down the mightiest of them all and take precedence over NIA. Milo and his group of investors wanted all the referrals from the State and Federal courts. It was all strategy sneaking in the back door and schmoozing the FBI, the District Attorneys... AUSAs, and Judges. They played their cards to the hilt, and their applications for inclusion were waved right through, and heck, they were successful. They had built a brand-spanking new large-scale institution for the incarceration of the infirm. Rico wondered how many hands were greased by Milo and his lobbying group of investors. They wanted to be big players and were willing to jump the hurdles...

Rico pretended to be listening to his voicemail, staring at the guy. Yeh, Milo was a piece of work parlaying his academics with a business entrepreneur concept specifically to win one major coup to steal the infamous Wendi Feral away from the monstrosity installation called NIA. He believed this notoriety would bring them more high-level patients. Rico sighed. What was the saying? Oh, 'the enemies of my enemy are my friends' ugh, an ancient proverb, umh, something like that, he didn't like this Weasel of a man. *But hey, his group of investors was against NIA… which made them ok in his book.*

"Professor, our goals are unified. Otherwise, you wouldn't be in this Limo… coincidently, your company is in the process of breaking ground on an additional mental detainment center which is a nice way to say the building is another detention center, ugh, a prison for the custody of…." "Wait for a second, Rico; I take exception that there is any ulterior…." "Relax, Milo. I'm aware that it would be a colorful Peacock feather in your hat if you could corral Wendi Feral…." "Oh, for goodness sake, Agent Captor, I have no hidden agenda. Wendi will be an outpatient client. We haven't any motives…." Rico puts his hand up aggressively, stops wasting his breath, and sits up straight, pointing to the chauffeur. "There they are… the Feral's are getting off that plane drive closer. Let me text them!" He Rolls his shoulders towards Milo "no more business jargon from here on out, only respectful conversations, and you better be compassionate toward Ed and Barbara. They are my friends; do you hear me?" "Well, of course, I do… I'm sitting less than five feet away, and you're raising your voice rather rudely. It's disturbing that we've gotten off on the wrong foot. This wasn't my intention. Nor yours, I assume. I'll be nothing except professional and will do as I suspect you want, and that is to advise the Feral's that it would be in the best interest of Wendi to transfer their daughter to my, um, our new hospital!"

"Professor, you said we got off on the wrong foot. Well, sir, that's the only foot you made available. I begrudgingly took my good friend's advice, Doctor Shauna Roble. I asked her for a list of Psychiatric hospitals. Yours simply was on the list. I do indeed want Wendi out of the claws of NIA, but you're not to ply uh… no pressure whatsoever. We will offer the option to her parents with all your selected propaganda and substantiated success stories. Remember Wendi's parents have a power of attorney, and even if Wendi has become accustomed to her environment ahh, acclimated, and conditioned with NIA's procedures, which may lead to her not wanting to budge from NIA, ueah, they can still sign her out of the facility. You know, starting over somewhere else can be hard on a person. You might need to convince Wendi because she has friends at the NIA hospital and may not want to move to your facility. I guess I'm grasping for wilting straws. Yes, it would be good to get her out of there."

<u>Ed and Barbara Feral,</u>

The Limo lurches to a stop. The Chauffeur got out, opening the suicide doors of the Lincoln Town Car. Rico hurries out, feeling like they're his parents. He has known them for decades. They embraced tightly in a 3-way hug. "Oh Rico, it is such a breath of minty air to see you and hold your handsome face. I have missed you, hon!" declares Barbara. "Barbara, yes, three months is way too long. I've missed you and Ed immensely. At least we stayed in touch." Ed pipes in, "yeah, texting is what you consider staying in touch. Huh, it's amazing that the youngest generation can carry on a real conversation nowadays when they get together in person... with all these fan-dangled gadgets. Rico, don't get upset, but I'm not shaking hands..." he holds out a fist they bump with a smile. "Yeah, after you did this fist bump thing Rico the last time we were together, um. Coincidently, Ma... uh, Barbara here was reading a Dear Abby topic about germs and shaking hands. I guess the inmates and athletes got this one right, huh?" Rico grinned broadly while Barbara held her tiny fist up "can't help but say you read my mind, Ed. I was thinking about the same thing earlier when I was at this high-level conference at the Fed Building with other participants doing the video conference thing. Some of the conference goers were stealth-like, not meant to be seen or heard, you know, the type... Washington D.C. Bureaucrats. Anyways a bunch of big-wigs flew in and attended the meeting in person. All wanted to shake hands and touch my palms. I almost got the heebie-jeebies, not that I've become a germaphobe, but I got all their germs and, of course, had to deal with the macho men trying to prove how strong they were 'playing the Grip Game' done with that, but yah know old habits die slowly."

Rico pointed at the open doors to the limo, grasping Barbara's arm "come on, let me help you in... let us chat while my Chauffeur rounds up your luggage." That's when the Feral's noticed the tall drink of water, a thin, angular-featured man dressed in a 3-piece suit with a matching tie. "Please meet Professor Milo! Uhm... I thought it would be prudent to have another opinion of how Wendi's therapy is progressing at NIA." Rico nods "let me introduce you to a world-renowned Forensic Psychologist. I'll let Doctor Milo tout his resume and describe his many accomplishments in the fields of his expertise... I also have a pamphlet for you to peruse, showing how technically advanced his new treatment facility is... also included are the contracts for the admittance of your daughter to innovative therapies."

Milo bows, bending forward slowly "greetings, Mr. and Mrs. Feral," somewhat reluctantly, he awkwardly raised his fist up for his first ever 'fist bump.' "Nice to meet you, and I'm looking forward to getting to know your daughter!" The Feral's nodded their appreciation toward Milo. Ed looks at Rico and shakes his head "nothing against you, Professor, but we're plumb tired and worn out with all these Forensic Scientist's mumbo-jumbo. We don't need a five-syllable diagnosis and analysis, um, and words about innovative psychotherapy. We plain and simply want our Wendi back, so please be straightforward with us, Sir."

It was dark outside, but Rico thought Milo was glowing Red in the face "sure will keep it straight, umh, short and concise, Mr. and Ms. Feral. Thank you." They piled in the

Lima, and down the road, they went towards NIA. Milo hadn't lost his tongue on another roll as the floodlights appeared in the not-so-far distance. They'd be at the gates in under five minutes. Rico was overly optimistic with Milo and the Feral's in agreement that they could have Wendi out of NIA and in Milo's clinic in less than 72 hours, and that's at the max.

<u>Terrance pondered on what Vadoma had told him about Kamryn being pregnant!</u>

Terrance thought back to <u>earlier in the day,</u> his time with Kamryn at what he'd witnessed when she was reunited with Valerie. He was purely overjoyed and floated on Cloud 9… blissfully. He faced amused stares and embarrassed grins. Even the two guards on the walkway tipped their hats. "Skip to my Lou' was a hit. He snorted out loud with a cackle. Vadoma had said Kam was pregnant with a demon child. He'd have to have that substantiated disbelieving Vadoma for the first time in his life. He thought… he better prepare himself, for now, there were bigger fish to fry. He'd taken the back entrance up seven flights of stairs to his suite feeling empowered, a quick rinse and wash out in less than 7 minutes. Still dripping wet, he chased down his phone, paranoid, and felt he'd missed a chime-chirp or buzz but no calls or texts. He quickly changed into another amazing Brown and Black Emporio Armani suit when the phone alerted him of an incoming email. Sat on the edge of his King bed. 'Professor Milo will be accompanying Rico and the Feral's tonight. 'Fk Milo, <u>another arch enemy Milo….'</u>

Terrance had to rule this gathering with finesse, needing Wendi back from the abyss.

Ruminating back three years plus with intense vehemence furor, akh animus, he was struck down by his own board by three lousy votes advocating an NIA Assassination. Terrance had advocated a hit on Doctor Milo, and.... Ugh, was denied! My last statement to the Board of Directors and silent partners worldwide 'you will come to regret this refusal of what I believe we should do and rue this day. Mark my Words!' Terrance took a last look in the mirror. His exterior self was cool and refreshed. His triple mixed cologne brought the olfactory senses alive gosh loved to collect Cologne from all over the globe, quite addicted, turning with a smile... and speaking into a mirror. 'Counselor, do you want to cross-exam the witness'... No? This wasn't a battle in Federal Court. It was much worse than that, for sure problematic, even symbolic. He would disallow Rico any leniency, as was his confident nature. His defense was impenetrable. Doctor Milo and Rico's treachery will be met head-on. They think they can bring Wendi's parents to my NIA and run roughshod over me. Yeah, got another thing coming, boys!' After confirming it was the infamous Doctor Milo, Terrance played coy with Liz and Renae, trying to get their unbiased assessment of the Psychologist. Ditto!

He had the distinct displeasure of meeting the Weasel years back when Milo returned from his European tour. The guy was an egocentric Pimple.... he despised the fella from first impression onward. It wasn't his new venture in San Mateo or Half Moon Bay, alas, not his venture capitalist henchmen who are investing in the new age Mental Hospital. No, it was the goon himself, a sinister Reptile who was trying to lure Wendi over two his psychotherapy unit.... yep a problem.

Oh, crap, he closes in on the mirror, stops, opens a drawer for a small handheld magnifying mirror, a pair of tweezers leaning in, gotcha holding up the Renegade white hair that was part of his left eyebrow. Nice, am I vain? Well, Hellyeah, what's the alternative? Checks the phone had to move faster down three flights to visit Liz and Wendi at one of the private emergency rooms hoping that Liz had Sara do a makeover of Wendi's self-inflicted bruised face and fingernail scratches. Wendi had to look perfect for the upcoming visit. Sara was so talented an artist, umh, well, it was really Ame that was the artist within her skull using their body's mechanics, a suprema undaunting professional makeup artiste. Yup... Sara was called in to manufacture her magic.

<u>Earlier in the afternoon... Sara watched in revulsion at Kamryn and Valerie's reunion.</u>

Sara stood on the path mere yards from their joyous reunion... If she needed any more validation that she was heartless, it was confirmed. Feeling morbidly disgusted, she tasted vomit and felt truly sick, coming to grips with her sister's shout... 'come on, Sara, it's been 27 years since we were all together. Come here!' Sara would rather stick her arm in a woodchipper didn't walk. No, she ran the other way with convoluted emotions. Sara screamed wildly. 'Ugh, what's wrong with me? Fk!'... Valerie and Kamryn stopped hugging and watched Sara take off like a Bat into Hell... Banshee howled, sprinting down the path away from them towards the largest pond on NIA's property in the direction of the mental hospital.

They stare at Sara... stupefied. Kam opened her mouth "bejesus, that was gnarly sister, what tragic behavior" Val went from sullen to full-on giggles contagiously. Kam joined in "have you ever seen something like that... crap? That girl needs to be committed in an insane asylum," they fell about, laughing even harder. After they recovered, Val held out her right hand. "Come on, Kammy Bear, let's go for a stroll and chat. I've missed you the most of anyone alive I love you, my sister, Kamryn." Kam sniffles "this is the closest to 7th Heaven for me, sis. I've dreamed of seeing you, little sister, for years. I'd cry myself asleep when you were stolen, ugh, abducted from daycare. I was in the car with daddy and mommy. That was the most awful day of my life. I dropped into a shell and couldn't even go to school. I was afraid I'd be the next abducted. Unh don't mind telling you I had many therapeutic sessions with psychiatrists and counselors; my home life was altered forever. Mom and dad stopped talking. It wasn't very good, uh uh, it was Awful. Sara was shipped off again to Papa. It was a horrible time for us, but you, OmGod... You poor girl."

They walked unhurriedly, holding hands. Val kept her composure, not allowing herself to be baited into describing her physical and mental abuse from that horrific life-changing event. Kam continued to cogitate out loud, "Grand Papa tried to help as much as he could. Did you know mom and dad almost got divorced..." "Whoa now," Val stalls turning around to face her "please, let's leave all that negativity for much later. Can we enjoy ourselves again?" Kam openly cried out, "oh yes," they hugged and embraced for a long time, kissed each other's cheeks, and said Zilch the rest of the walk, only smiling.

Sara was still running away.... at breakneck speed, attracting Correctional Officers.... Golf carts with guards and others came out of the woodwork to join the chase. The turrets had long barrels extended from the guard towers. Everyone was on 'Blast' hypervigilant this wasn't an isolated incident. Sara had many of these episodes here on the prison grounds she'd nearly drowned herself a couple of years ago in the same pond where she finally collapsed.... next to.

Clarity finally, hyperventilation subsided. She had to stop. Guards were whistling, yelling, and converging on her Déjà vu. Ugh, her hip vibrated. It was Liz... Sara, still out of breath, said, "uhh, Doctor Hon… Honcho I,…I, I've been running, I'd run uuh running exercising…." "Stop right there, Sara, on your knees, hands behind your back"… five guards had her penned in.

She just sat down and held the phone up with the speaker on and Liz's voice echoing … that by itself warned the guards that she had special rights from NIA management phones were taboo for most, and Sara was an inmate. If you wanted to keep your job, you looked the other way, still out of breath from her spontaneous running temper. "Doctor Honcho, the guards have me surrounded thinking I'm having a moment ugh episode, you're on speaker…." "Listen, this is Doctor Liz Honcho. Leave Sara alone. Don't harass her for running, Sara. I need you in room 311. Which correction officer is nearby?" "LT. Falk is here." "Lieutenant, can you please open Sara's Salon for her?" "yes, ma'am Doctor…" "okay, thanks. I need you to hasten this, Sara. We need a makeover complete on Wendi Feral, including her fingers and toenails painted. I want her to look like she'd just stepped out of a beauty salon. It's super important that you have her ready, uh, presentable by 3:15 pm. Terrance and I are counting on you, dear!" "I will not let you down," she jumped up and pushed and "let's move LT." she followed Falk, who consequently commandeered a Golf cart, and off they rolled on a short quest. She wondered what had happened to Wendi and why it was an emergency… oh well, she'd find out soon enough!

Jax was upset that Wendi was drugged, worrying that Rico would take her from NIA.

"Why would you allow Liz to drug her up, Terrance? What the hell? Isn't it an experimental mixture of drugs?…" "Yes, Jax, I know, but we're desperate. You know Rico is on his way here to take her…." "Sure, I got Walter tracking him for us, and Shen is at your beckoning call…." "All right, Jax will keep you in the loop. Gotta get back to the emergency room and see how the Wendi makeover is going!" "Yeah, most importantly, she's got to regain consciousness, boss! If she doesn't act normal and speak up demanding that her parents leave her here at NIA…." "I know Jax, your speaking with the choir…." They parted, going in different directions.

<u>Wendi is in the emergency room, unconscious.</u>

Terrance pushes the swinging door open and sees Sara hovering over Wendi catches Liz's expression, "how's it going? Are we going to make it? Has she regained consciousness? Damn, we have under 25 minutes will have to get her out of prison and over to the outpatient hospital, and that will take 15 minutes by itself." Sara answered, "I'm close," her face three inches from Wendi's. The bruise was in disguise so was the used to be Purple eyelid. She was working her magic on her eyelashes suddenly Wendi flinched, startling Sara, whose eyes bugged out. Wendi subtly shook her face and winked! 'No.' Sara turned to them… "she's still unconscious, but she might be waking up just moved for the first time since I've been applying her makeup. Hey Uncle, what will you do if she's in this Zombie state when Rico shows up?" Terrance's phone jangles. He peered down… dammit and stepped back out of Wendi's room, "I'll be right back."

Terrance re-enters the room to see Sara leaning over Wendi, a brush in her left hand. Liz looked at a chart with one eye and the other on a beeping flashing monitor. Sara was kind of morose and felt indignant, reflecting back, watching the mellifluous rhythm of a past life, 'hers'… sort of resentful. She guessed she was jealous at the exuberance between her sisters Valerie and Kamryn, bouncing on their tippy-toes, gyrating like they were once again seven years old. She understood. Ahh, heck, Val was kidnapped, thought to be dead long ago, death certificate sealed and delivered. A minuscule part of her wanted to feel overjoyed for the reunion, but rationale took preeminent control. Sara detested the total act wishing not to have been present sickening, uahhh! She now stood applying her trade to Wendi's body but couldn't let go of what she'd experienced only hours ago! She hated seeing Valerie and Kamryn hugging and loving one another… again.

"How is she, Sara?" "Uncle Terrance, she's flinched several times but isn't cogent…." Terrance said nothing, deferring to Liz with a nod, then spoke anyways, "her doctor here thought it was prudent to not only give Wendi a syringe full of our new chemical compound psychotherapeutic drug but also force-fed an Elephant tablet of the same down her throat why don't you ask her what to do now?" He declared in a sarcastic voice. His disgruntled demeanor and scowl were unsettling to Sara, who inputs twerking her chin up at Liz. "Don't you sometimes shoot an adrenalin hypodermic in the patients to wake them up?" Liz was ruffling, wringing her hands together and oddly zoned out, cadaverously pallid when Sara thought, shit, she's the one who needs a freakin makeover. Liz's lusterless countenance remained speechless, obviously analyzing something intently.

Sara exported… "hey Liz, why don't you give me five quick minutes on your face? You could use a fast touch-up. You're as pale as Casper the unhappy ghost!" she busts up over her cute play-on-words and chortles. "That's pretty good, Sara. Ahh, Casper, now that would be a good name for a Black man," as Shon grinned up at her from behind, one of the team leaders for the NIA Militia showing bright White teeth. 'Shon Peterson,' trainer facilitator, his Brown features amused by the Casper anecdote. He jokes, "Sara, my first-born girl or boy I'll name Casper, thanks," as he raises his fist for a mutual bump! From the side of the room, no humor exists within Liz nor Terrance, who says, approaching Wendi's gurney, "Shon call the guard tower at the gate tell them to delay Rico and his entourage until we inform them to permit them in…" "but sir

ueh Terrance that's the in-out patient parking lots what...."
"I know, but they still have to be allowed past gate number
One. I don't care. Shon, your resourceful... figure something
out to stall them."

Terrance looked down at the prone sleeping body before
him. "Shon, stall for at a minimum of 15 extra minutes..." "I'll
see what I can do, boss" he slides out the NIA walkie-talkie
and crosses the floor out the door, leaving Liz still petrified.
She finally broke her silence "remember, what we gave her is
a new formula that our scientists refined on test subjects. I
recall hearing them say something about not mixing other
Pharmaceuticals with this new drug."

Sara was finishing up on Wendi's fingernail polish with her
patented specialty 'Cat's Eye' application. Sara
uncharacteristically yelped, "well, Hell, get the Scientist
director on the phone, Liz, and explain the circumstances
willya shit, we can't just sit here and dawdle muddled in
despair!" Terrance stared over at his niece. This was one of the
reasons he adored Sara, who was a no-nonsense gal. All
business, she'd get it done and move on. He added: "yes,
excellent idea. What else are you thinking, Sara?" "well, we
need to get this damn gurney out of this prison hospital and
over to the outpatient building soon as possible right Uncle?"
With perfect timing, Shon pop's his head in. "So boss, you're
not goin to like this" the three of them gape over at him,
expecting the worse they went through the gates three minutes
ago in a Limousine." Terrance slides his palm up over his
nose, then up past his forehead expels a giant low grumble in
apparent agony "now what?"

Shon lowered his head and then resiliently stood erect,
feeling the pressure of being one of NIA's leaders. Says,
"Terrance let me go over there and think up a diversionary
plan, run a screen like in football." 'T' wobbles his noggin
taking in his trusted friend, "do whatever you can. Shon will
be there 15 minutes late, so around 8:30, keep them in the

lobby. Don't let them get on the elevator and go to Wendi's room...." "Okay, boss, I'll make it work. I'm calling the front desk and letting the guard know to keep Rico and his group in the waiting room for now." No one noticed Liz, who had her back turned, speaking on the phone, a forefinger in her open ear, concentrating on whoever was talking, pacing back and forth by Wendi's side. 'She was having an episode, so I double-dosed her, unh yes ugh no gave her both the needle and pill uhhh, ah, no at once the same time.' She paused and then read off Wendi's vitals. 'Have you no remedies developed?' Liz taps end and lowers her phone with four eyes upon her.

"Scientist Greg Walters is on his way from downstairs, racing up here. He will be here shortly and is bringing an antidote to reverse the effects of the drugs." She rolls her eyes at Terrance, "so you gave Greg a formula from your Gypsy Queen...." Grimacing, "you should have left it in Greg's hands, Terrance. This isn't a fricken curse or some make-believe Black Magic. He's the lead inventor, the Scientist who has been producing astounding results with these new Pharmaceuticals." Not a sweating type of male, Terrance felt he was losing the skirmish. The Old Spice deodorant was in a retreating pattern, being flanked by body odor. "Liz, desperate situations call for desperate measures, your Greg... scientist hasn't developed any type of antidote, and despite your inappropriate words towards my 'what did you call them' uhm Gypsies, yeah, they've never failed me before, so yes I gave him the 'Witches brew um concoction to mix and put together'... to bring Wendi out of her fugue. You got any better ideas?"

Rico's impatience boiling over stopped in the lobby.

Rico's entourage was in the lobby waiting for the elevator to the 5th floor, where Wendi's room was. After a long time trying to get clearance for Doctor Milo to visit with Wendi Feral, finally, the approval was appropriated. You could feel the tension vaporizing in the atmosphere. They felt in control of the situation, having a plan in place to move Wendi. The Feral's new advocate, Doctor Milo, fidgeted with his slender fingers adjusting his tie. Suddenly a loud wailing siren sounded. The blaring horns seemed to catch the staff stunned, more surprised than others in the lobby. They all moved in a non-panic and orderly fashion. A Fire Alarm, 'everybody out!' The guards and security officers escorted the staff and all visitors out the triple doors into the parking lot.

<u>Will Wendi wake up?</u>

<u>Scientist Greg Walters enters</u> the room and takes a stinging look from Terrance. The grimness of the situation was substantial. He wore triple bi-focal glasses, and his nose sloped over a sunken reservoir. His eyes were too distorted to describe the color, bald as a Bat with floppy ears dressed in the prototypical Lab technician garb. In full-on white clothing, including his overcoat. Liz was instantly exponentially more nervous, contemplating that this fellow hadn't been seen out of his offices in months. The dude seldom left NIA, checking the computer time cards he'd been on site 17 of the last 19 days. He was a homely hot mess, probably still a virgin, and all of 45 years old.

He carried with him an 1870s leather haversack, ahh, Doctors bag that you'd see in one of Clint Eastwood's Westerns. He was muttering something unsnapping, his overcoat and mumbling, "so I will have to… oh no, counteract the…" He stops and pulls out an iPad, tapping in a sequence… Terrance had enough never seen this guy who was on his payroll before. He'd sent the remedy to bring Wendi out of her coma that he'd received from Vadoma with Jax. "Doctor Walters, just give her the antidote… didn't Jax give you the formula… shit, do something. Give her a shot of adrenalin. We haven't time for guesswork here!" Condensation made of stress and sweat found the precipice, lodge as a whole droplet fell from the

Doctor's nose. He was faster than he looked, shutting the iPad's scream away as the water hit the floor.

"Mr. Hallinan, Sir, I, unh, we never formulated an antidote, pardon me, but the truth is we have an unlimited number of uhh schizophrenic patients, ah, inmates with mental disorders to test our formulas on. We're looking for positive results, after which I was going to advocate the start of manufacturing an antidote, Sir. Please remember that this is only Phase 1. We're in the clinical trial testing phase… uhh unh, so please let me analyze what the best approach may be…." Terrance lost it. Temper flared like a hot rocket vehemently laced torpedoed directed at Liz…. Sara sat on the tile floor, her face covered, knees up. "OmDevil…" she muttered. Liz shook her winterized face. "Oh fk, what have I done?"

Terrance's Red face closed in on Greg "if you don't bring Wendi back out of this stupor, ugh fngne, you will be receiving a triple dose of your shit before you leave this room." As the swinging doors opened, Terrance had a moment prior to losing it and hit his alert button on his waist… two burly guards stood now in the room "wait outside. I'll let you know when I need you!" he said.

Terrance had given Jax the unique concoction from Vadoma to hand over to Greg and make sure he didn't waver and followed the instructions to the Tee. "Where is the antidote I gave you, Greg?…." Now even more disheveled but kept his composure. Takes the slip of paper with the necessary ingredients… "Please, Liz, write this down along with the numerical value of parts and milliliters 1 Lexapro, ½ Lithium, 3 Belladonna, 1/3 Datura Stramonium, 1 Xanax, 2 Risperdal ¼ Nightshade Flower, and three parts Seroquel." Sara peered up from her palms, knees bent against a wall. "Wtf, Greg? Are you some kind of a Warlock Sorcerer dude, or what? This isn't witchcraft. You're the one that's Insane, the Frankenstein of NIA. Dude, you're a scary little jerk! Ugh, Belladonna and Nightshade are straight out of medieval times!" Greg shook his head remorsefully, stuck Vadoma's concoction into Wendi's I.V., and yelped, "I hope this doesn't kill her... this formula is deadly, in my opinion. It's like...."

Wendi instantly electrifies the room by only turning her Lil head in the direction of Sara, who in a flash is up by her side rubbing her arm, her extended eyelashes fluttered cheeks puffed up with more color the only sound in the room were the chirping monitors attached to her body. "Am I pretty now, Sara?" the sociopath ugh, unemotional Sara almost tumbled over, losing it ahh, regaining her poise. "Wendi, you're a Plum beautiful woman. I only enhanced your outward beauty to match your inner magnificence self unh," rubbing her right shoulder and gazing into her Greenish eyes, "from the Damsel in distress to a waking gorgeous beauty how ya feelin girl?"

"Not sure, kinda dazed and yet not confused been laying here dormant, well aware of all that was occurring around me, sort of like being up in the corner of the room near the ceiling. Unh, fully conscious ahh OBE experience like whoa never mind all that I suppose you better get this gurney moving if I'm going to see my mother and father and sell them this story that Terrance wants to be sold!" Terrance nearly tore his cheeks grinning shouted loudly then caught himself clapped "let's go folks" the guards ran in Liz was disconnecting the I.V. Sara was applying lotion, and a haze with a small sprayer over the I.V. punctures. She was adding a dab of superglue to stop the slight blood loss. Terrance reached over and kissed Wendi's cheek "welcome back, Wendi!" out the doors they went. Scientist Greg Walters and Sara had a stare-off. She smelled herself... ugh, body odor from her earlier frenzied frantic running, shower time, and mumbled, 'good luck, Wendi, you're a Princess!'

Greg was wiping his face with a paper napkin. Terrance brushes past him "you're a lucky bastard. Get back to your cave!" *Terrance next.... texts, 'Show, what's up?' 'Fire Alarm, lol,' Terrance grins and sends a* 😊 *face back, 'going in the back*

Wendi brought her hands up, amazed at how awesome her nails looked, feeling invigorated as if she'd been resting for a decade… wide awake now energized like she'd downed 16 ounces of Red Bull in one gulp the elevator doors open and down the hallway, they rolled. Nurses and doctors were going in all directions. Pulling up alongside them was Brock Dane being pushed along. He twisted in his wheelchair "hey Wendi, looks like I got first place locked in," while his pusher went by. Oh, he then says. "Lacie is on your ass. That's the first Fire Alarm that I've ever experienced here. Hope to see you soon, Wendi."

Wendi's gurney slowed; she turned into her room at the NIA outpatient hospital where she'd resided for months and saw FBI Agent Lacie Link going into the room across the hall. It had been a while since seeing Brock and Lacie, the former lovers and FBI partners. What a fiasco that story from the past was, thought Wendi.

Liz stated, "we've got to get you out of that gurney before they arrive. Terrance leaned down inches from the stopped bed "am I speaking to Sunshine or Wendi?" she didn't answer. Neither of them did, only motioned to Liz to help her up, "I'm woozy and dizzy. I need to use the restroom." Liz grabbed her Pink and White Nike shoes from her closet and put them on her little feet, loosely tying the laces.

Terrance on one side, Liz on the other, helping balance her equilibrium which was off kilter. Shon bursts in, "boss, there in the elevator, not happy campers. Rico was heard mentioning something about a conspiracy theory." Terrance nodded. "Okay, thanks, Shon. Great job. Everyone out except Liz and I." The nurse and others exit. Terrance spun around in a louder voice, "Wendi or Sunshine, answer me, dammit" Her blonde-styled hair swiveled while a wink unsettled him as she disappeared into the restroom.

Liz caught the look scratching her head and raising her diminutive shoulders. Aah, who knows "it's too late, Terrance. Either way, we're stuck with whichever entity is in control of her body and mind!" he interrupts. "She is vital, the most important piece in the puzzle crucial in the NIA missions, especially the planned excursion next month in Seattle. We can't lose her to Doctor Milo. Ughhhh, Liz, we just cannot!"

With a rapid knocking on Wendi's door, Rico's Hawkish glare scopes inside. He swings it wide open. Entering were Barbara and Ed Feral. Professor Milo, alongside… Following up the rear was FBI Agent extraordinaire Rico Captor. Terrance slid, gliding closer to the Feral's. He and Barbara had previously a warm relationship, not friends although, but close despite Rico's annoyance and constant meddling undermining and degrading NIA's medical and treatment programs. Notwithstanding Rico being the reason Wendi was admitted here, along with his friends Lacie Link and Brock Dame! Terrance always countered Rico's latest negative barbs by forwarding Barbara another picture of awards bestowed on the premier Neurology center on the West Coast. 'He didn't stretch it by claiming falsehoods….'

He reaches out to her, "Barbara, it is so nice to see you again. What a surprise had no idea you and Ed were making a trip down here… wished you could have given me notice. It's been too long." She falls into an unintrusive hugging embrace, staring up into his eyes. "I'm not happy, Terrance, and neither is Ed from what Rico has informed us of… where is she, uuuh, my Daughter? You had her outside at your NIA games, not in therapy. She hasn't returned any of our calls, and no correspondence at all. Ed and I are told that she's in treatment every time we call… that's a blatant lie. I've seen pictures of her. What's going on here? Rico has stopped by here a half dozen times, and Wendi hasn't been here. What are we paying NIA for? Where's Wendi?" Terrance releases her and extends his hand to Ed. "Wendi is in the bathroom. Hey Ed, how was the trip?..." Ed held up his fist, smiling. "I stopped doing the handshaking thing a couple of months back. It's a germ thing fist bumps are my new thing," as they bounce knuckles. Rico asks, "is there something wrong?...." "Why would you think that?...." "I don't know a Fire Alarm exercise at 8:30 pm. Kind of strange, I asked an employee, ahh, staff member who told me it was the first one ever!" Terrance raised his eyebrows "well then, it's about time. Wouldn't you say fires and emergencies can happen at any time? It's disturbing that...." "This is Professor Milo. I believe you've met him before," Terrance leered up at the Doctor. "Tell me, Milo, are you here to spy on us to steal trade secrets to visualize how a top-notch facility should ardently be pursued and replicated by your startup? I hear you're trying to duplicate what we do here in Napa in San Mateo, unah; feel free to call on us. We can send some consultants over to aid you for a price… you're going to need it…." Milo angrily steps forward, opening his jaws deliberately. The bathroom door finally opens. First, Wendi's head peaks out. 'Like a soundproof room, not a squeak or breath could be heard… Nope!

-47-

Long time brothers from other mothers.

Jaybird sat across from one of his oldest, truest bros.... Jax Foul was chewing on the last of a ham, egg, and cheese bagel. It was 5:15 am. "Byrd, how sure are we that the three suspects are guilty of spying on us, unah, our facility? You know it's a death sentence, brother..." "Just as it should be, Jax, we were infiltrated up in Montana a couple of years back. My militia had caught seven infiltrators from the Government agencies, uh, spooks. We led the seven off our properties and into the abyss. I don't take kindly to spies. They're like Rats. I realize, pal, and so do you. It is right in front of you, the evidence proves it out, and by the way, you're like the 7-star General here at NIA. You decide… what's the penalty for Treason… brother!"

They share a smile, seven stars inside joke, "Okay, give me the rest of today, Jaybird. I will consult with Terrance per the norm. Needless to say, nothing can occur here at our facilities until he signs off. Did you get the reports from …." "Jax, a thorough analysis by Sandi and Rocky is on our One Drive, and also check out the interesting tidbit added by Shon on the message board." "Thanks, bro. I'll get back to you when we have a game plan intact, all right?" "Yeah, that's all we can do for now, I guess, till you get together with the Big Kahuna. Oh, how did the meeting with Wendi and Rico go? You know she's irreplaceable, bro heck, all our strategies on the upcoming Seattle trip revolves around her…." "I know I'm waiting just like you. Terrance isn't speaking about it… not going to bug him. Recently he has seemed intensely preoccupied. I'm going to let him come to me on that sensitive subject matter. If he has something to say, he'll say it." "Bird, you'll be the second to know after me," they fist bump… Gone!

<u>Rico, Wendi's parents, Doctor Milo… Wendi, Terrance, and Liz are in her hospital room.</u>

After the salutations and greetings, a strange vibe of uneasiness hovered. Liz tried to remember when the tension in the ambiance was so intense, like a 'Live Wire' thinking of an oldie but goodie song by 'AC-DC.' Wendi had peeked her head out, then re-shut the restroom door. It hit her as odd, Wendi's quick glance into the room making her anxious and awkwardly nervous. Terrance tightened his jaw with furrowed brows, and angst rolled from his eyes, scanning everyone in the room. Each person has different ways of handling stress. What got Liz's funny bone during this episode was Rico, Doctor Milo on one side of the room, her and Terrance on the other, and Ed & Barbara Feral sort of in the middle like... Wrestle Mania. With Wendi's hospital suite being the roped-off ring.

A few moments had passed, "I guess I should check on her," said Wendi's mom... Liz was closer and nodded, "let me knock on the door...." Before her knuckles hit the door, it opened. Terrance was a Veteran, his trade being a high-end Litigator who dealt with Life-or-Death sentences on a regular basis in both Federal and State courts couldn't recollect the last time he'd been this strained. It was the fear of the unknown that if Sunshine exhibited her newfangled dislike for Wendi's parents and hadn't shown any improvement or control of her split personality, the Feral's would sign the release papers. Wendi would be gone. He hadn't any legal options to retain her to keep her at NIA, and it was driving him nuts. He was a man that needed control. He could envision this whole setting going to Hell in a Hand Basket. Odds were that Rico and Milo would take custody of Wendi Feral. Unbeknownst to Sunshine, her life would change for the worse she'd become precisely what Milo needed and wanted a celebrity Patient to show off for the opening of his new facility. And a drugged-out Zombie.

Wendi walks out to a hush, stares straight at Rico then, in sequence, her mother and father. The Hawk-faced man in a fancy suit bobs his head, and then she turns her eyes towards Terrance, who is next to Liz. No one breathed, it seemed. She took three steps and did a pirouette holding her hand up for applause, mouths agape like she was deranged. "Did someone die here? huh mother, its morgue quiet heck, you haven't visited me in 93 days...." Her mother pounced, rushing to her with arms out wide. "Wendi...Oh, Wendi, it's you, baby OmGod thank the Heavens Ed, it's our Wendi!" Ed tentatively approaches her, never a fan of Sunshine, "pumpkin, is it you, babydoll?" She cuddles up to her parents like years in the past. A familiarity is silently spoken... a family reunion begins. Letting their emotions flow, both mom and her sobbing, Liz smiled happily and said to herself so much for all the work that Sara had done for Wendi's makeover.

Rico stood stoically as she looked over at him. Wendi knew what Rico was thinking, having the measuring attitude and disposition of a weary investigative FBI Agent. Yep, he was unsure and paranoid because of the last five visits, Sunshine was in charge and full-on Rude she made it abundantly clear Wendi was dead, ugh, gone forever. He recalls her last words spoken to him by the gorgeous woman before him 'Rico, get the fk out of my face and my room. Wendi is history. Get used to it, asshole! Don't come around here no more!' She howled into a hilarious jig. Hey, Rico, listen to that song with the same fricken words by Tom Petty... 'Don't come around here no more....!' Rico was nothing if not a stubborn entity and would never stop trying to find and free his former lover and best friend 'Love a powerful drug the most powerful...' "Rico, are you just going to stand there honey? Really?"

Rico fearfully exhaled. Wendi pushed her parents gently back, but Rico didn't embrace her standing his arms outstretched, holding her shoulders in front of him, profoundly entranced in her eyes switched his hands to Wendi's cheeks, now pulling her face up-leans in for a subtle kiss... just a single kiss one kiss. That was all he needed. Rico bent down and felt strangely lightheaded, and instantly the long-suffering hardened man melted. His heart pitter-pattered. "Oh Wendi, oh Wendi, I've missed you. I love you...." Rico, in his mind, was all alone, no audience in the room. Rico didn't care anymore, not going to live a lie, no more....

She jumped up like she'd done dozens of times when they'd dated, her hands and arms around his neck, her dress at his waist, legs wrapped around his hips. Rico held her and embraced her tightly. Wendi held him and whispered in his ear, "I told you I'd return to you, Babe. I'd win the battle with Sunshine, and you'd know it when I kissed you." She'd nibbled on his lower lip and sucked on it ever so slightly. He closed his eyes, feeling an intense warmth encapsulate his entire being. "It's me. I love you, Rico, Darlin." He twirled her around their faces Red, hot glowing Love flowered again "get me out of here, Rico, let's go to dinner and dancing, please, oh please, it's not too late." Wendi's whisper was all he needed. He suddenly realized he'd been lost in the moment. Mom had her palm covering her mouth, dad grinning, head bobbing yes Terrance relaxed his expression like no big deal, Liz's mouth was still open, and Professor Milo genuinely was displaying a glowering grimace.

Rico put her down again she 'jumping beamed' over to mom. "I love you, mommy. Can we visit in the morning" zah, she giggled. "Of course, baby, I love you too. I can't tell you how much I enjoy your smile and happiness. It's fabulous to see you in such great spirits, daughter." "Daddy, will it be cool with you too? I love you and have missed you. I'm going out to dinner with Rico! Okay, is that fine with you, papa?" He smirks widely, eyes watering, and kisses her forehead. "Absolutely; I love you too, Pumpkin." Terrance was next in the lineup. She winked "thank you for having faith in me, Mr. Halliann." He pulled back a blush "hey, what happened to Terrance? Why so formal? you two have fun," he had his wallet out "you choose any one of my Wineries. Your dinner and night out is on me. Here's an unlimited gift card!" "Umh to kind Terrance, thanks," said a shocked Rico more for the way he gladly accepted the gift card. Wendi snuck up and leaned in for a quick sideways hug. Liz stepped forward "girly, come on in the bathroom, let me fix up your makeup...." Knock, knock. Terrance grinned "no worries... I texted Kamryn. She's here to prep you up, Wendi."

Kam walks in with her little case hanging from her shoulder. "Excuse me, lady, into the bathroom you go." She took Wendi's hand, and the door closed! Rico wasn't prepared for that. He had a Warrant for Kamryn's DNA sitting on his desk at his office. He leaned back. Muttered silently; no, this isn't the time… uh, unh, nothing was going to break and ruin this loving spell that's come over this room. "Terrance, gosh, Kamryn sure is the spitting image of Sara. It's mind-blowing…." Terrance only nodded at him and didn't respond. Wendi's parents were dizzily happy and exhausted instantaneously from the stress and worry and airplane flights from Portland. They went towards Terrance and Liz. She grabs Liz's arm. "I want to thank you both for bringing our Wendi back to us!"

No one seemed to notice the invisible Professor Milo sitting in a chair against a wall. Rico caught Ed's glance and thought oh shit, Milo, ugh damn. "I'm sorry, Professor, for your wasted time. Let me pay for the Uber!" Meanwhile, Terrance was still lost in time and felt a cold flash from his scapula to his sacrum, ice-cold shivers. Ugh, unh, what was it, the eye wink by Wendi? Ahh, weird, huh? Never has she given him a wink. Was he overanalyzing a good thing, a saving grace, unh, nothing it meant zilch, relax, admonishing his suspicious paranoia? Everything was going beyond his highest expectations.

He's witnessed the manifestation ugh the atmospheric change in all the people in Wendi's room, including himself. Rico was smiling amongst the parents… muses, man oh man, talk about a 360-degree U-Turn, going from absolute hate and disdain to looking now at the inhabitants of the room, excluding Milo. The power of Love had won once again. Whew, Terrance was incredibly enthused.

Rico's mood, hem… hell… his everything had been altered. His goal would have been attainable if Sunshine and not Wendi had greeted them. They'd be signing her out and arranging for her to enter Milo's treatment facility. Having arranged this meeting with definite ulterior motives, he'd emphasized the importance of the Feral's flying down. Had met with the dull, drab Milo, all for the move of Wendi from NIA. It was like a miracle. Rico couldn't just let it go feeling awestruck. This was the last thing he'd thought would happen, especially since it had been weeks since Wendi was able to break the spell that Sunshine maintained over her mind. He was blown away that Wendi would reappear. Um, what was the saying 'Don't look a gift Horse in the Mouth' but heck, suspicion reigned!

Terrance was zipping along… neurons and synapses firing across his hippocampus with bonified possibilities, an enigma of sorts Rico from a mortal enemy hostile and furiously contemptuous to aligned now in his camp. Maybe an ally, not ever even in a wet dream Juxtaposition unreal nuclear opaque the vulgar Anti-NIA FBI Agent… Ironically stepping across the line to meet him halfway, he took the gift card from him with a smile and a pat on his back. Terrance wavered. No, don't jump to conclusions. He warned himself Rico would never be a friend.

Still, it was the way he was wired; Rico had Sara/Kara Salon and home under surveillance, his S.F. downtown Law building under scrutiny. Jacob, his chauffeur, had spotted a tail, and they'd scanned several vehicles, including the Limo, and located G.P.S. tracking devices underneath not only his cars but Liz's and Renae's also in the mix was the recording of phone calls of them condoned um allowed by a Warrant from Judge Delaney. Terrance's contacts within the Federal Courthouse alerted him that a special Grand Jury was going to convene soon. It wasn't only Sara under investigation. Nope, NIA-U, his training facility, was in jeopardy also. His informant didn't have any specific information as of yet, but she was working on it. So far, no word-for-word verbatim reports and no recordings could she locate. Rico and his investigators had turned over enough stones. They had to of gleaned some substantial wrongdoings by his NIA faction to intimate that he was prepared to approach the Grand Jury for indictments.

The U.S. Government was indisputably interested in what the three infiltrators, traitors, uh spies had learned from their espionage of his training facility. This was incubated by the prick standing in front of him. It was the snake that slithered perhaps five feet away. The spies on his property stemmed from the insistence by Rico that something was happening behind NIA's fences. Rico was a mortal enemy, no matter how he played it this evening. This was but a mini reprieve; Terrance would go on the offensive soon.

Terrance was cognizant now that the Feds were aware of his satellite militias sprouting up in nearly every U.S. sector, now strongholds in 13 states. NIA was expanding with its graduates moving into homegrown militias. They were being formed and populated like indigenous plants germinating the minds of young people, the ways of freedom leeching systemically into their pores, giving the youth a purpose and a cause that was being instilled within our belief system that they make their own. These young soldiers were aligned with likewise goals and aspirations. NIA's militias were propagating and thriving. Rico's spies would be squelched. The quandary was how to bring Rico off this crusade to destroy NIA and personally Sara, and yours truly.... this was where he was left perplexed.

Terrance blasted back to the current situation inside Wendi's suite 'the group was still animated,' chitchatting between Rico and the Feral's... seemed all positive. Liz had made her move to dissect the Aquiline-nosed Doctor Milo. Sara and Wendi were prissing in the bathroom with giggles and laughter radiating from the open door. Terrance broke off again, recalling Rico's heavy demeanor change, cynically skeptical based negativity when Sara appeared. Of course, the fool didn't realize that it wasn't Kamryn who was in with his girlfriend. He laughed internally, keeping a relaxed face lol. Sara had walked into the room to help repair Wendi's happy tear-stained face makeup. Rico had been transparent and appeared shocked to see her remembering the words the prick had said in the interview room 'he was going to bring Kamryn in for a DNA screening and interview.' Kam was on the 'top of his list' ugh, one of the bones he wanted to chew, yes, something like that. Well, metaphorically thinking, it would be a tremendous relief to have the dogmatic Rico off his tail.

Again thinking how stunned he was when he'd offered the gift cards to Wendi for them to use, Rico hadn't waved them off. In essence, it was like a peace offering, monies not bribe-like, but there was Give and Take! Hell, Terrance wondered if Wendi could harness this enemy and bring him to heel... freakin Love was the most potent drug of all. He wondered if he would ever feel that all-encompassing euphoric endorphin secreted ecstatic emotion again, a body, mind, and spirit high. Never, he was too cold and calculating long-lost blissful was just that ... Lost!

Then in the next moment, like on stage, the audience's ovation waiting, the curtains/door opened, and out came the vibrant, delicious Wendi prancing about, eyes abound on her well-proportioned figure, a change of clothes yum! Energy popped off of her like a circuit breaker. Rico froze... his magnetized eyes departed the parents, no doubt mesmerized. His dimples sprung to his skin's surface. It was just her he saw extending his left hand "shall we, sweetheart..." "we shall, my handsome man, yes we shall!"

Terrance scrutinized each and every turn. Rico never looked back at Sara. They both said their goodbyes to the parents. Dad... said to have my daughter back before curfew but only laughed in jest. Being an outpatient hospital, there wouldn't be any restraints. The door closed strangely. No one seemed to notice when or where Professor Milo had left too. Liz was carrying on with Sara. It was decided hurriedly that Rico and Wendi would take Rico's limo that had dropped Wendi's parents and Doctor Milo off at the outpatient hospital. Rico and Wendi would definitely enjoy themselves at one of his all-time favorite establishments on the outskirts of Napa, in the small enclave of Yountville. 'The French Laundry' was in his top three of the fabulous Chateaus he enjoyed. It was a sublimely relaxing experience, a prime bed, and breakfast retreat /restaurant combination. It was world-renowned, and Terrance was a silent partner owning over 71% of the business...

He beckoned Jacob up to Wendi's hospital room that could double as a Suite and told him to drive Wendi's parents in the limo to one of his other investments, 'Auberge du Soleil,' to dine and spend the night. They said their goodbyes Barbara and Ed looked worn out and might not even make it through dinner, but oh well, Terrance purred a sigh. The door closed, then there were three left sitting close around a round table in Wendi's room. Was it a miracle this new scientific chemical solution, the injection, and the Horse tablet choked down Sunshine's throat? Ugh, how could this night end any better? Exhilaration floated over them. He still heard Sunshine's echoes, blatantly unmovable, determined resolve. Her control was all disintegrated ...or was it?

Terrance elbows on the table, rubbing his scalp "well, have you two ever seen a transformation such as that in your lives? Heck, you're both around schitzo's all the time." He cackled, looking directly at Sara. Who snorted "well, of course," taking her left index finger and touching her forehead "would you like to converse with Ame, Dee, or Al" they laughed. "Right, that's true, Sara, but you are the pilot, the Captain. Your well versed and in control of your diverse entities. I dare say in the realm of personality disorders, your on-call swift change of personalities is extremely rare," expounds Liz.

Terrance shakes his head "you know I was getting used to Sunshine's cut-and-dry personality, umh, to the point disposition crazy but assertive," he peers at Sara. "Well, my unsweetened niece, whatcha think of the Sunshine to Wendi metamorphosis? Did it seem real, or was she playing us with everyone else?" Liz smirked. Sara slapped his arm "unsweetened, huh? I'm unsweetened, Uncle, cuz I'm already sweet enough... lol."

Sara's face morphs as she raises her crinkled nose and sneers at them, leaving a lopsided frown, "Liz, are the heart defibrillators nearby?" she haphazardly shows a crooked jaw grinding at him with furrowed brows. This disturbed him somewhat. "I'm 101 % serious, no jokes. This isn't a playing around moment, Sara. What's your assessment of the dramatic change from Sunshine to Wendi, damnit!" Her silence was a wounding confirmation, loudly speaking volumes nothing was said until it was... Sara volunteers. "I truly didn't spend much time with Wendi, as you know, Uncle. When I was locked up here, I never hung out with her. She was busy with other things and people, always over at the training facilities, and didn't hang out on the prison grounds much. She was never in my chair when I was allowed out in my salon studio. With that being said, I've got to know Sunshine at least as much as her ambivert personality did allow penetration. She was, umh is, a no-nonsense gal seriously motivated to take Wendi's resolve and abolish her from...." "Wait, you were alone with her in the bathroom before any of us saw the performance. What did she act like? Come on... you were up close doing her makeup."

"The Wendi show dramatic act evidently fooled Rico and her parents, and for sure they knew her better than anyone else alive with the possible exception of her estranged brother Mark Feral or Jax Foul." Terrance was examining his cuticle's... fingernails, not a nervous, neurotic individual but tired of Sara's ambivalence "damnit get to the point woman!..." "Oh Uncle, relax geez, it's all good right now...." "I'm not concerned with right now. Well, I am shit, so is she putting on an act...." Liz interjects, "listen, the two of you. I'm the person who spent hours upon hours with Wendi/Sunshine being her clinical psychiatrist heck, during counseling sessions and therapies, we've spent much alone time, and that was Wendi. I'm certain of it, and I should know!"

Sara flipped up her left hand in the air "okay, all right, I'll shut up, no problemo...." "No, speak up," ordered Terrance "please!" She rolled her shoulders and peered over at Liz "how many makeovers have I applied to your face, with manicures, pedicures at my salon?" Liz blinks, confused "umh, dozens, I suppose...." "Precisely Liz, a makeup artist has to get up close and personal with their clients. We nearly need to meld with those who we're transforming. It's not the basic skill one would receive at a typical beautician's hands. I'm in a class of superior artists' talent that's only intrinsic in the Hollywood Elites in my trade!..." "Well, for fks sake, just answer the freaking question, niece!"

Sara raised her eyebrows and pounced, "When I was in the restroom with Wendi, I had to start back to basics. Her tears had smeared her waterproof mascara and blush. Actually, her rubbing-wiping tears of Joy from her face did the damage. Mind you, Wendi is so beautiful. All I do to her is enhance her sensual features. You see, I work with eyes first and spend a lot of my time on eyelashes, brows, and crinkled corners of eyelids. I'm less than 7 inches from those eyes, for sure. I'm concentrating, unflinching, unblinking, what I saw was two people looking back at me. Sunshine controlled the left eye, and Wendi the right eye. It was scary even for me. The evil eye dared me to be quiet, watching me... Her pupil expanding, weary yet in charge. 'That Eye' shot ice-cold chills down my spine, warning me of danger if looks could decapitate you. Uhm, even the pigmentation was darker. Wendi's eyes are translucent, a Greenish blend of Hazel speckles and even a Sea Blue on the outer parts; mesmerizingly hypnotic, her eyes, one of her unique attributes, are drop-dead gorgeous. Point blank, I saw Sunshine watching from the left eye, observing, ready to pounce Lion-like! and sweet Wendi in the right eye smiling."

Silence pervades the room. All that could be heard was a ticking clock on the wall across from them. After a long spurt, Liz finally utters, "if one injection and Horse tablet have brought Wendi to the surface, maybe another dose will finish the job?" Terrance was lost in a mine shaft. Ahh, Sara replied, "am I wrong? but it's Sunshine that's more vital to NIA's missions and objectives. It's her hardcore attitude, and the never say die to take no prisoners, girl. She is proactive and intuitive, the survivor tough as nails. She communicates with animals just like her counterpart, sweet innocent Wendi. This separation was documented in her autobiography titled 'Feral Eyes,' a New York best seller. We've all read that non-fiction masterpiece, right?" They both nod in the affirmative "sure, yeah, that book came out after Jax imploded the Cuban Mafia. That's when Rico met Wendi... Wasn't it in Tennessee?" "Yes, Rico and the FBI had signed a subcontracting agreement with Sandi and Wendi's company 'Feral Feedback,'" answered Terrance.

Sara continued reciting what she'd learned about Wendi's life, "When little Wendi was tossed into the Gorilla exhibit at the San Francisco Zoo and rescued by Rocco the Gorilla, the manifestation began the exchange of life-saving oxygen eye contact by Rocco, which brought back the life in infant baby Wendi at like ahh wasn't she only 18 months old? This caused a split in her spirit and her personality. Every one of you professionals classifies Wendi as a Schizophrenic. I'm not one of them. Liz... Wendi wasn't born with a genetic disorder, with zero cases in her family tree. It was injury-related, possibly a lack of oxygen to her brain. Sunshine became her invisible imaginary friend and savior because of necessity. She helped Wendi partition her newfound ability to understand animals to relate to and speak with them. This was where Sunshine developed and became her alter ego and was manifested into being."... Ugh, shaking her head, "that's my 11 cents anyways!"

Terrance and Liz caught the subtle change in the dialogue... intonations, and verbiage with octaves that they heard. They were well aware Sara wasn't speaking or thinkin. Nope, Liz proclaimed, "thank you, Anne, very well structured and thought out, you could have my job. I'm well aware of your Academic Achievements, young lady. I wish Sara would let you out more often. I'd sure like to pick your brain, Anne!" She stared back at her, gleaming "that goes both ways, Doctor Honcho. I do enjoy intellectual sparring if the combatants are worthy." Anne grinned her always lopsided smile "and Liz, you are worthy of my attention!" Terrance and Liz returned her expression, then Anne spoke last, "aren't either of you curious as to what happened to Doctor ahh Professor Milo?"

-48-

Jacob escorts Wendi's parents to their hotel.

Jacob had the trunk open and was loading their luggage, which was left in a locked room on the first floor of the outpatient hospital by Rico's Limo driver. Ed and Barbara Feral are watching, ensuring Jacob gets all their belongings. She was leaning on Ed, wavering and tired... she admitted it had to be an emotional draw, along with her adjustment to not taking as many pharmaceuticals. Jacob holds the door open as Ed hands him a card from his boss Terrance.

Jacob and the Feral's were acquainted, not friends but certainly more than cordial... 'thank you,' said Barbara. She held onto her husband's forearm. His other hand covers hers as they sit back in the Leather recliners while Jacob fires up the Limo, staring into the strobe lights flashing from her eyes "what did you think of her performance...?" "Barb, she was always the lead actress in Drama class"... Yep!

<u>**Rico was in 7th Heaven.**</u>

He was captivated and spellbound at her sparkling vivaciousness, so alive was his spirit he could dwell on nothing else than coital bliss being deep inside of her, loving her yum this was the woman he desired to love to hold forever beyond eternity. If there were reincarnation, his carnal desires would perpetually live on for generations! They clang goblets of red wine, a subtle Blackberry blend called T-Rex. According to the exquisite waiter, a favorite of Terrance's, the entrée was superb, scrumptious, and displayed magnificently. The conversation was never strained, forced, or coerced... with natural pauses for reflection, reliving past experiences they'd shared. They were having a grand time laughing and snorting chortles, both animated in adoration. Wendi sat prim and proper, belying her true whims. She'd be just as happy at a campsite firepit in the woods below the stars. It was him that made her feel like a Princess and Goddess. Look at him, a ruggedly handsome Goliath of a human specimen, muscles and tender, gentle to feverishly aggressive, insatiably erotic what he would do to her had whetted her appetite along with her luscious crevice.

The waiter approached with the dessert menu. Rico looked at her. She shook no, then wobbled yes; he took affirmative action, "no, thank you. Can you bring the bill, please!" "Oh, sir, I was informed there wasn't a cost. I'm well taken care of by Mr. Halliman. He slipped out an envelope. Here are key cards to our master suite. Actually, the King and Queen penthouse is a glorious space ahh. There's another couple of bottles of your favorite selection of wine by the Hot tub and a full bar, sir. Is there anything else I can do for you both to ensure your evening to be most satisfying?" The waiter grinned broadly and slipped a crystal plate with two large chocolate Strawberries onto the table.

Rico sucked in a noticeably large breath "well, this is fun, thank you," Wendi added "do you have a comment card? You have been splendid, Lyle; a real treat, thank you.... " Lyle scampers happily away, then back with a folded card and a pen 'thank you,' *he said with wide brilliant White incisors bowed, swiveling away from their table.*

They are infatuated with touch; he helps her put on the small half jacket taking her hand in his, walking under the pure guise of enchantment and centuries-old lust, that is, until their ear canals are filled with music... swing dancing music. She turns him toward the direction of the sound, squeezing his palm. Off they go to the ballroom for a few scintillating close dances, rubbing sensual skin, fondling points of thirsty titillation just under their clothes. They Enjoyed the heightened foreplay and mischievousness out on the open dance floor. Was oblivious to scintillating voyeurs watching them dirty dance, thoroughly lubricated, anticipating inevitable climaxes of body and mind. Finally panting, they step off the parquet dance floor. She licked her lips, and he clutched her tightly... blindly unobservant of the onlookers, fiery heat seeking relief. They engage in a long-lasting Frenchy, kissing with deep tongue swirls. He readjusts his well-endowed and engorged member. They pull up to the long curling bar and order two glasses of T-Rex. Rico slides his wallet out. The bartender says, "all's good here, sir" his immediate thought was that they were being followed. He mused for a second, then fell back into her spell, "I love you, Rico..." "I love you too. Let's get out of here, sweetheart cum on..." she subtly shook her head... "not yet, babe. I've waited too long to have you to myself... soon enough, I will have all of you inside me, Rico."

"My lady, would you care to dance again?" she gazed up into his glow "well, yes, my Lord" with a quirky crinkled nose and a grinning smirk on her face, he took a Triple take. Her left eye tweaked and snapped at him. Ugh, an odd sensation, like someone else was watching him. He shuttered and took THEM to the dance floor. Nothing was going to ruin this evening, uhhh... Nada?

<u>**Doctor Milo's Awakening.**</u>

Terrance, Liz, and Sara were enjoying nightcaps while ruminating on how amazed each of them was… that the evening had turned out to be copacetically appeasing. They were waiting for a video-call get-together with Jax after his meeting with the security forces at NIA adjourned. A few minutes passed by… and Jax appeared on a screen. Terrance waited until the rest of the security team had shuffled out, asking, "what's the status on Professor Milo? We may have to rethink how we deal with him. What do you think, Jax?" "So updates, you know we caught him sniffing around the Neurology laboratories and detained him as you demanded. Strangely we'd let our guards down. Doctor Milo had snuck out of the room when you were saying your goodbyes to Wendi's parents. By the way, I received confirmation that Jacob had not only dropped Wendi's parents at the hotel of your choice but had tucked them in. He had escorted them to their room. They were totally spent and too tired to enjoy the splendid dinner you'd arranged. Update on our other detail… We followed Wendi and Rico in his rented limo to your winery for dinner. That's where they remain, currently spinning around on that magnificent dance floor as we speak. Sadly, no one seemed to notice that Milo slinked out of the gathering…." "Yeah, we know Milo had ulterior motives for wanting to take her from us, but we didn't know the guy would go snooping around NIA. He deserves to be taught a lesson, Jax! Tell me, what's up? how…" "Boss, let me finish…."

"Shou contacted me, and I got in touch with our head of security. Your handpicked hiring of Walter paid dividends immediately. I like the guy… Walter promptly escorted Doctor Milo to the lobby, where he placed him against his will in a private room. Sadly, Milo got a little too rambunctious and was duct taped to a chair." Terrance smiled widely. Jax continued with a nod of acknowledgment, "I called your number One bodyguard, Angel, to drive from the City in one of our mockup Uber cars to pick up ole Milo. Meanwhile, Walter did his part, questioning him as to why he was caught in one of our labs taking pictures of files and trying to access our VPN structures. Milo struggled against our security team, then he was stripped of all clothing and probed for the missing memory stick. Um, I'm getting ahead of myself… I forgot to tell you he had the external case of a one-gig memory card in his front pocket, but we couldn't find the card, so they had to do an invasive search of his body!"

Laughing, Sara slapped Liz on her thigh, and Terrance grinning, sipped his totty and humorously cackled, "hopefully, they used gloves," crowing, "this is good ok, yah got me. Where did you find the memory card?" Jax shook his noggin, grinning "you won't believe it, boss; it was in one of our mainframes when he was busted he couldn't retrieve it. So we have it now, Walter parodied calling an Uber for Milo, and Angel picked him up in the fake Uber. Milo ordered Angel to drive him back to his San Mateo home, Angel offering him a bottle of water which was obviously resealed. Its contents had a strong sedative. Milo passed out, and Angel drove him to the lowly crime-riddled section in San Francisco, the Tenderloin kicking him out of the vehicle!"

Terrance displayed a smirking Pumpkin smile. "You, of course, kept tabs on him. Heck, that was a while ago. Why am I just being informed of this?…" "You didn't ask, man. You've been too preoccupied, umh, boss, we're keeping tabs on him for shits and giggles. You can access the live feed… video of him lying in a fetal position." Howls of laughter by the group. Jax nodded and continued with a wry smirk, "Milo was again stripped of his clothing, robbed, and beaten left in the gutter by a Chinese market." "That served him right, but Jax, you're going to ensure he ends up at his residence in the morning?" "Sure thing, that's the program. Oh, if he causes any trouble, like calling the authorities, we have pictures and a video of him breaking into our Labs and trying to steal information. We will also inform him it's in his best interests to remain mum, and the icing on the cake will be when he's shown the montage of pictures and videos of his escapades in the Tenderloin area. Don't think he will be a problem from here on out, boss!"

<u>Workout at NIA's training facilities.</u>

The evening wasn't so blissful back at the facility against a wall on exercise bikes churning on their custom racecourses. Shon, Jax on the left and Jaybird, and Rocky on the right Sandie on her bike faced the guys as they all peddled away, not winded in the least. Headphones and earbuds bobbing in unison. This was what they did, exercise and brainwave. The guys gave their undivided attention to Sandi. Another one of their informal meeting places was inside this soundproof cardio room. Sandi's torquing leg pressure increased as she climbed the road up through the French Alps. She simulated being in the Tour de France race, currently in 7th position; smiling up at her was Shon, who was in the same race he was currently peddling in 5th position.

She spoke between inhalations, "I've been able to isolate the broadcast area. The scrambled signal was detected in one of our dorms, specifically # 66. Running a proof check of our video audio surveillance, we found all participants were in the field or in classes all, except two that is who appeared on the screen leaving the lavatory. Her name is Taif Rahmani, a transfer student from Saudi Arabia, one of our affiliations in the desert." Jax asked before Sandi could continue, who showed annoyance raising her brows "whom is she communicating with? Have we been able to break the...." "Jax, if you could wait until I finish my report, kindly be patient." He displayed a flummoxed satirical grimace, then acquiesced with a portly grin "sure thing, umh sorry, Sandi," as he rose up off the seat and powered his legs even faster.

Shou interrupts, "whoa, looks like your falling behind, girl. You're now in 9th place." Saudi clenches her teeth and puts the pedal to the medal, not in the least amused "all right, boys, let me finish here. We haven't been able to break the code and have no idea who her contacts are. I have a select group scanning Taif's videos since she was introduced and passed our initial screening process. Sofie over in the Admin building is also preparing a report detailing her admittance into our program software. We'll soon enough have her background and family connections, and if she's one of the three moles we...." "What do you mean if... Saudi crap! The girl is busted for linking up with an outside source. What the fk...." "Jaybird, I swear you guys are so impatient spur-of-the-moment I'd hate to get you in bed. Your probably the 2-minute up Chuck version of dudes. Ugh 'wham bam done, no thankyou ma'am!" She smirked wide-eyed and stuck her tongue out. Yep, guys started laughing, then the rebuttals started right back at her for challenging their Macho ego's manhood until Rocky blurted out, "can we stay on topic here? I'm actually Taif's trainer. She's been recruited by one of our noted experts. She's an outstanding student and is close to the top of her class...." "Rocky, I betcha you weren't aware that Taif has put in a 'leave of absence' notice wanting to visit a brother in San Jose and do the Santa Cruz tourist trip. Her application is on my desk and on our NIA Hot mail site. It's under her personal NIA page. Sofie alerted me of this," says Saudi as she retakes 7th place.

Shou fell back to the 6th slot. She decided to spew some banter out, chastising Shou, "hey, black men aren't known as road racers, unh, on bikes, that is." Sneering quickly, he retorted, "well, either are Albino's!" she yelled Touché matching Smirk... 'smiles and smirks' Yep!... Rocky was slightly irritated, "come on now, hey, let's stay focused on Taif. If she is one of the Fed's spies, we will certainly let her show her true colors and follow her to where she leads us. We should all ask ourselves if she is connected to the other two spooks?"

Jax, barely sweating, chirps, "I have a meeting with the boss later tonight. I will inform him of the facts about Taif and will plan from there… now. Our second suspect is far more bothersome. Sandi, will you please proceed with the overview." Her eyes left Jax's. The heat in the air-conditioned room had expanded somberly. They peddled harder. Could it be one of their officers, the nucleus of NIA's military, that has gone to the other side? Before entering that mess, Shon deliberated, "the third suspect has a long line of military officers in his lineage, even predating World War 1. Nothing he has done has created suspicions. It was a look one afternoon he gave when we were showing a technique used in the field, a simple but effective torture chokehold. I had him checked out thoroughly again by Sofie. Some volatile info was returned," Jax jumped in, "then Sofie and our Admin staff are to blame. They're not vetting the new recruits meticulously enough…." "Hell, this starts at the top," says Jaybird. "All participants must run through the grinder… ahh, fine tooth comb. It's like we're getting lackadaisical to the point of being negligent. Perhaps we must have another ritualistic execution like we did to some of the other weak Benedict Arnolds…." "Jax slugs down some water from his bottle. "I'll set it up, Jay. Not a bad idea. I'll run it by Terrance when I speak with him this afternoon."

Shon waited patiently, peddling frantically now nose-to-nose front wheels aligned with Sandi, now sweating, and breathing harder, continuing. "Sofie's crew did an outstanding job after I asked her to concentrate on Jimmy Massery. Remember, his relatives for generations were gung-ho, from Uncles to Nephews, all joining the armed forces. Sofie… after a more extensive scrutiny on Jimmy. Everything still checked out, then hidden in the archives, she found a term paper he wrote while in the 11th grade at a Naval base in Germany, a well-renowned high school. The premise was much allied with pacifism and nonviolence of how the USA should have restraints on how they dealt with dissidents and nonconformists. He spent some of his thesis on the marches during the 1960s, the Vietnam era, and peace movements. He was against violence even when considered necessary it's all under his.... newly formed file. Also, I might add that he voted against the death penalty!" Simultaneously their heads went right to the left... Ugh!

The racers nearly missed a stroke. Shon went on, "Jimmy was in the foreground of a group out of U.C. Berkeley was even detained, not arrested for a sit-in on the campus for the recent Black Lives Matter movement." He looked at his colleagues and friends "yeah, I'm Black, but all lives matter. It wasn't a bad thing that Jimmy was getting involved in this movement. Still, certainly, he was the least aggressive of my trainees. It's a concern we can't take lightly. He could be some kind of pacifist or radical whom Rico and the Feds could sway; he could be a Rat snitch, at least one of the three." Shon went on to say, "and fellows, I'm in 5th place" peddling grinning. "It's not the type of person I want to have to count on when the shit hits the fan...." "Bro, we should discharge him either way," exclaimed Rocky. 'I agree,' hummed the rest to the bicyclists; Sandi growled, "okay, Jimmy will be history. The question really is would he meet the necessary adjudications to feel the Death Penalty that he voted against?"

"Okay, that brings us to the last suspect. Damn, I should have invited our team leader Asia Wei..." said Sandi. "No, nah, leave her on the parallel bars," laughed Shon. Rocky barked, "Oh yeah, our predominate master gymnast. You wanna talk about serious cardio that Asian would blow us out here? Did you ever watch her doing calisthenics, with ridiculous workouts, and acrobatics? She's the dope, the bomb, and she won't go out with me..." They cackle; Sandi wiggles her head, "her team of gymnasts has been essential in many of our expeditions anyways. Her native Northern Chinese language, or Mandarin, has come in handy, especially when dealing with the Chinese criminal enterprises such as the Tongs and Triads...." Shan interrupted, "Okay, Sandi, but we're still waiting. Who does Asia think is working for the FBI?" Sandi pumps the pedals even harder and says, "A member of Asia's team, I will forward all of you her last correspondence; let's brainwave later!"

<u>Brock and Lucie.</u>

Brock was visiting Lucie. It was a daily ritual. It seemed lately they'd re-bonded. She reciprocated at night only by going to see him when they weren't spent from the day-to-day activities. Their therapists also aligned the pool times, and they started exercising together at 5:45 am... seven days a week. It was a full day for the former lovers and fiancés. Still, much love existed.

Lucie was now 71% better in every feasible way. Her body had been broken a 3-story headlong leap from a balcony to escape Sara, who was firing a pistol at her. She was brain-dead/paralyzed. It was the classic tale of Humpty Dumpty, who was broken, and her pieces couldn't be put back together. Whoa, not so.... it had been an excruciating and painful recovery thus far. The mental and physical torture was far from over... although she was able to move on her own now. She suffered flat on her back on a gurney for seven months and another eight months being locked down in a wheelchair... engineering movement by blowing in a tube. Now she could speak in syllables, stammering and slurring her words, and had the occasional twitch and nerve blurbs. Lucie Link was an FBI Agent with a flawless record and pages of achievements. Her awards and certificates proved how she'd achieved stardom within the FBI. She was one-half of the premier tandem of Brock Dawe and her. The dynamic duo was at the top of the food chain. The last assignment they worked on was the 'Sara the Vipress serial killer case.'

Lucie's parents were by her side from the start of this horrific time, faithful God-fearing people who wouldn't give up on her. Nor did the Federal Government, who fitted the bill at no cost when Mr. and Mrs. Link filed and signed the applications for the experimental grants for Stem Cell therapy replacement marrow regeneration. Scientists at NIA were afforded any and all requests monies didn't matter for Brock and Lucie. The only body part of Lucie that wasn't affected by the fall to the pavement was her eyes. Her parents and Brock were there. When she wiggled her baby finger, tears flowed across their eight eyes. There was a glimmer of hope which grew into a beacon, then a floodlight. Human bodies are nothing if not resilient Lucie was a walking phenomenon by itself.

Today was 1/23/2020. Now she could swim 300 yards without much pain and exercise with light weights and cables for an hour. Then could walk on the treadmill for another 35 minutes. Discarding the wheelchair… then the walker, next then came the cane. Lucie was already a candidate for the cover of 'The Stem Cell Journal,' a walking breathing marvel. Each second of her recovery was recorded and videotaped.

Lucie still had a disconnect with her motor skills. To be precise, the connections to her fingers and toes, and Lucie still couldn't move a finger on demand. Her hands clenched, grasped made a fist, and spasmodically shook frustratingly and at times uncontrollably. Her speech impediment was improving. She no longer slurred as much. The impairment of her memory bothered Lucie Link the most. She sat across from Brock, playing Checkers for two reasons one, she wanted to win. Secondly, it was excellent therapy for her… willing her brain to control her fingers just to push a checker piece into a Red or Black square. It was a win-win. Brock purposely wouldn't help her. The worst part of the Checker match was when she had to jump Brock's pieces or King herself. Despite her knocking the board over pieces at times flying to the carpet, Brock only smiled and reset the game. He had epitomized the word patience… she would stare at the hunk of handsomeness, realizing he and she were to be married in less than three months before the attack by Sara.

Little did the former betrothed know that Sara was nearby, close to where they were engaged in the Checker match. Sitting together was Sara and Terrance alongside Liz. They were three floors directly above the checker players. Sara had vowed to end Brock's life and was in a daily panic, worrying and stressed out that she had to kill him before his memory returned. She hadn't figured out how to go about this endeavor because impeding her were the 2 U.S. Marshals on duty 24/7 protection details the former FBI Agents were under guard. Sara knew it was a mandatory task, and while she was at it, she'd flush all Lucie's hope of continuing her Rehab.

<u>Lucie had amnesia and suffered horribly, wanting to remember her life.</u>

Lucie was thinking back, trying to put her memories in order. The photo albums filled to overflowing her Mother brought to her. Brock used to read article after article before she could even focus on them. He would sleep by her side after her injury. He persistently still did work on the Sara investigation with unrelenting vehemence and vengeance to charge and arrest her for the 39 murders associated with the serial killing spree. He dreamed of proving she was the murderer. Sara was the only suspect in the killings. Unfortunately, his colleagues at the FBI couldn't locate her

DNA at the scenes of the executions. Not a single molecule of succinct evidence led to a tangible link to her. Sara was convicted of the attempted murder of Lucie Link and received only a 15-year sentence. But the case against her for the serial killings still lingered. For months Brock spent every spare moment by her side. He'd, in fact, arrested Sara and testified in Federal Court in Sacramento on the witness stand. Sara's Uncle cross-examined him, Mr. Terrance Hallinan unh, who ironically was the CEO Chairman of the board of the very outpatient hospital where they played Checkers now. You can't make this shit up! Nonfiction is way more bizarre than fiction…Yup!

Lucie still couldn't align her facial muscles. Her smiles were ghoulish, lips constantly pursed, but oh, she was, to him… beauty model material. Brock kept telling her… he loved her and adored her spunky, lively spirit. She wanted him and desired him. They'd flirt with their eyes and familiarize themselves with their former relationship, detailed with pictures on his phone. He's showed her them dancing, bike riding, picnics, a vacation to South Lake Tahoe, Hot balloon rides, boating, and their weekly visits to shooting ranges. He, at times, would watch her grin when he slid some risqué pictures of them mostly naked on a King-sized bed, then full frontals all nude. He snapped her on a five-shot blast getting out of a hot tub. He'd waited till appropriate times, showing her videos of their lustful sexiness in various lovemaking positions. He'd tell her when she was a bit down and depressed, holding her body near to him. 'Hey Lace, check out some of our soft porn. They'd taken pictures with videos on several occasions. She watched him smiling to himself. She'd act slightly embarrassed. He said no, it was your idea, not mine, and he'd said no way!" she said, 'yes way, and oh, BTW,' grinning… by the way, he'd never let her forget this fact. Unh, he told her she was the seducer' he played hard to get, still suffering from his broken marriage. They had sat beside each other for literally hundreds of hours, laughing, conversing, and nurturing who they were… and are now… partners for years. They collectively had the number One arrest record for the FBI in the state of California.

Rico was conscious that each move they made was documented, and neither of them could use the restroom without the U.S. Marshal in accompaniment. There was always a female and male Marshal in attendance, and the roving cameras were on a constant surveil. Lacie reached longingly for him. He swiveled out of the chair, moving like an athlete. She stands, and he steps into her. She wished they could get away and leave the NIA outpatient hospital and go to a private hotel. She wanted to make love to him and feel him. One… she purred subtly. She lovingly leans into Brock and puckers her lips up towards his face. Lacie stares into his Studly eyes and then reacts, "who are you?" Shoving him away a glitch… the only memories she had of them were pictures and videos.

NIA's Octopus arms reached across the planet, searching for the very best Neuroscientists.

NIA imported the latest innovative research from the Swiss Federal Institute of Technology Lausanne(EPFL), specifically Neuroscientist Claudia Kathe… Brock and Lacie were tested with 'epidural electrical stimulation techniques,' whereas a surgically implanted neurotransmitter stimulated their spinal cord along with seven weeks of intensive neurorehabilitation that involved a robotic support system assisting them while they ambulated and moved in various positions and directions.

Lacie didn't remember that Brock himself had recovered from being paralyzed and wheelchair-bound. His EEG had shown no brain activity whatsoever. His left-right hemispheric waves were unlit. He nearly drowned and was murdered by the same Psychopath that had attacked her. Sara, the venomous, guilty assailant. He and Lucie underwent the same procedures and many Stem Cell Therapies. He was in the treatment regimen a mere nine months after her neurologists and surgeons had pioneered an experimental set of innovative surgeries, mostly noninvasive, luckily. He wasn't broken like her. His recovery was the thing of legends; Brock Dame was at 93% of his former self. If there were another word that emphasized or raised the bar on a person's Recovery, it would be renamed and coined with Brock's picture allying with it. He smiled at what his best bro Rico had said, 'Brock, my friend, there should be a saying throughout time about your recovery, <u>'Oh, he or she did a 'BrockDame Recovery'</u> for you're a fricken remarkable man bent on determination and fortitude. He checked himself in a mirror... soon he'd surpass the shape he was in before the Sara mishap!

He worked out like a maniac and wouldn't be happy till he beat all his personal records that he'd mastered back at the FBI Games before his near-death experience at the hands of Sara. He kept this information to himself. No one knew the truth except Sara, and his time would come to fruition then he'd attack. No one understood, nor could anyone, the reason he was maniacal at his rehabilitation was the reoccurring images of what Sara did to him. He'd capture Sara, and slowly he'd slice and chop pieces off of her body, cauterizing the wounds from her missing appendages, keeping her alive for months of Torture... Yummy! He gritted his Canines unh, shortly; Brock would have his bare hands around her throat. The game he played ... his malingering, ahh, faking that he'd lost all his memories of what had happened to him on the houseboat... No, never would he forget what she did to him on Shasta Lake. His show of memory loss was solely for her benefit. For now, the end game would come soon enough.... Yesss!

<u>**Rico Captor and Brock Dune.**</u>

Lately, Doctor Liz Honcho had been asking him if he'd be interested in enrolling in NIA-U and working out at the training facility. She had said he'd find the curriculum at NIA invigorating. His Bro Rico was adamantly against anything to do with NIA, which seemed odd because this is where he and Lucie were hospitalized, and if he didn't trust this establishment, then why was he here? When he'd asked Rico about this…. all he ever got was that it's the number one-rated Neurological Hospital in the USA, with the latest cutting-edge treatments. Still, he'd consistently reiterated that there's something wrong with NIA!

Brock replayed in his secure mind many of his best friend's meanderings. Rico had indicated that there was an ongoing probe into NIA's training facilities and even confided in him a while back that it would be nice to have another set of eyes on the ground. Rico described his suspicions and concerns, including the last two Agents that he had assigned the task of infiltrating NIA's University, who ended up dying in bizarre accidents which now were ruled homicides on the hush. Rico finally elaborated on this subject when he pressed him for more information. They were walking the grounds around the park on a trail by one of the largest ponds on NIA's property. 'Okay, Brock, here you go…. speaking about my two Agents who met their demise and were killed in queer accidents, one in Costa Rico and the other in Hawaii. These were not accidents. They were assassinated, uh, executed. Despite this, we remain optimistic and remain steadfast and have re-fortified our position. Currently, we have three other informants inside the program still living on-site. We have new evidence of a conspiracy against our Government. They are training soldiers for their expanding militias across North America!'

Brock shakes his head, thinking back on his best friend's animated soliloquy, kisses Lacie's cheek, "you win," and puts the Checkerboard game up. She asks, "can we walk around the park by the fountains under the stars" he replies. "Sure can," his large hand takes her petite one "come on, let's put on something warmer, sweetheart!" He still feels the soothing melodic sound of Lacie's voice, a combination of a little girls mixing with authoritarian overtones, and chuckles silently. What an odd description, huh?

Helping her into a Cashmere sweater and placing a fun beanie on her head thinks back at what Rico has learned thus far about the facility next door, which was over a mile square of land. Brock had been to War in battles on two tours in the Middle East and was a Special Ops. Marksman Seal Team leader with 57 confirmed kills, attaching another possible 13 to his number. Like he'd told his friend more times than he could count, Rico, what's wrong with a 2-year degree in Physical Education? This was what NIA-U, the private school, was accredited for and was renowned for many of the graduates who went on to win in gladiator contests. The last five winners of Ninja Warrior came from NIA.

Sure, Rico had broken out the maps satellite images of farms, ranches encampments with moderate-sized airplane hangar buildings on properties. The civilian troops of these militias were only multiplying, and now the camps could be found all over the continental USA. They were labeled militias. The argument between the War Veteran/ FBI Agent and the Director of the FBI, who were lifelong pals, was redundantly the same. He'd played Devil's advocate. 'Rico, so what your saying is the training facility is operated like a CIA preparation center, a kill squad. Not a University for learning much other than warfare, and inside the three monumental buildings, many areas are restricted and off-limits to the enrolled students without the proper credentials and classification ratings. A student is limited to a fraction of the classrooms. They are like the CIA, using Retinal scanners, fingerprint pads, facial recognition, and a variable of codes like, unah, well, like a covert military installation. The difference is this is a private institution?' 'Yeah, Brock, that sums up much of what we know....' They walked in silence around the pond, and then Brock felt compelled to continue the NIA-U subject.

Not wanting to bicker or cause strife, he felt because his bro had a serious dislike for Terrance and the way that the mental prison was run procedurally, thinking Rico had closed off his mind to what NIA excelled in. Brock decided he'd reverse back to the similarities to the CIA, allying with his first concerns. He decided to strike first, wanting to understand more of how his former best man thought. 'So what, some of the facility is off limits? This was the same it was for us and all soldiers and staff. In fact, at several military schools, only the senior officers had access to certain areas, so what does this prove?... It's far from illegal, brother!'

Rico was undeterred and then would explain the fact that NIA-U was nearly impossible to get into. Armed guards manned the gates. The entire complex and the facilities were heavily restrictive and unah secretive, and a larger-than-average number of participants never graduated or made it through the rigorous strengthening and aerobic classes. Then add in the weapons training and hand-to-hand combat. To pass the grade, it's like you have to navigate an Olympic obstacle course. Mentally they break you down, and the classrooms are filled with teachings ah lessons about all the significant battles throughout history. Well, even before Jesus Christ was born, at the beginning of time. They practice war games setting up specific battle classics, including the likes of Caesar, Alexander the Great, Hannibal ahh, Napoleon, Genghis Khan, and even the Crusaders of Medieval times, aligning all of this with the philosophies of war. They work on a brainwashing program.' He paused while Brock had thought to himself man, my bro is obsessed with and Hated NIA.

He continued 'the professors are called team leaders. Hell, every week, there are major injuries, some serious, all maintained in-house at their own hospitals. Ugh, it's like signing your life away, Brock!' My rebuttal was, using Rico's own words, 'okay, NIA-U restricts many prospective students indiscriminately. The University chooses who will attend by scrutinizing each applicate from their childhood forward, family history, and grades, and their achievements. Maybe 15% of applicants are accepted and awarded grants, so please explain to me how that differs from trying to get into Princeton or Yale. Ahh, Harvard or Stanford, it's not!...' 'you don't get it do you? There's something sinister...' 'Wait, let me finish what I was going to say, Rico... Those Universities I just mentioned have a moderate drop-out percentage. Not all freshmen make it to graduation. Compare this to special force programs training, huh? A class of 750 start Navy Seal classes, and what 25 graduate? The same can be said regarding entering training programs to graduate to any of the global elite forces. Yeah, a small percentage of maybe 7%, make it as Army Rangers.... Delta Force and Green Berets on and on, tell me, what's illegal about this or wrong? Don't we want or desire the cream of the crop? Rico, as far as injuries go, you and I watched them fall like flies at even basic training. I have heard that NIA has some truly innovative obstacle courses. Some are built to challenge a student's physical endurance and mental fortitude. You have to concede this point to me, right Bro...' Rico grimaced, shaking his head affirmatively, then always retorting... But...!

But there was no denying his third point of contention. It was his meat and potatoes with gravy, conclusion, his preeminent winning argument, the nitty-gritty, if you will. 'All right, uuh, why develop an armed civilian force on American soil? That's what the Armed forces and the National Guard are for, correct?' Then served up the dessert 'why were two of our Agents killed? Who is funding this billion-dollar military insurgent machine? Why is the NIA organization more secretive than the old KGB or MI-6? truth, Mossad, our CIA? Lastly, why are they expanding around the globe?' 'Rico, again, there's nothing illegal with educating and training student participants under the guise of a 2-year program and a degree in physical education. If the graduates are setting up mini affiliates across the country for additional training or for comradery, there's nothing wrong with that. There breaking no laws!'

One thing can be said about my pal he was relentless and held his temper with the best of them. I thought it was time to move on to the next subject, but no Rico disagreed 'the two FBI Agents that died under suspicious situations were labeled accidents. The Medical Examiner changed the Death Certificates to Homicides. This, by far, bothers me, as it should all of us... now my two agents are part of the glutton of unsolved murders. Remember, I was the one to assign them to this undercover investigation. He frowned; his face contorted with a grimacing scowl. I stepped back, feeling empathy 'okay, I'm all for closure and all in with you and would like to get involved in the investigation Rico but wait, though, nothing is leading back to NIA being culpable, right?'

At this juncture in our redundant debate, Rico always adds, 'well, we have a description of Shon Peterson being in Costa Rico near where the Zipline business operated.' 'Umh, I'd say there are plenty of Black Costa Ricans who may look like many African Americans again, so what, where's the Beef dude?' We then walked in silence around the mini lake, lost in our thoughts with NIA at the forefront for me, without their Neurological center. I'd not be walking, and Lucie would be breathing from tubes. I held some appreciation um gratitude and felt blessed to be saved because of their expertise and skills of the... 'A few other points for you to mull over, Brock, who is funding the militia camps? We haven't an idea? Is it illegal funds...' 'Bro, this is beyond my expertise. NIA is a conglomerate, a public company on the world's stock exchanges governed by our own S.E.C. They play by all the rules. In fact, as I mentioned dozens of times, not in vain. Just observe what NIA's Stem cell therapy hospital has cultivated with Lucie and me. It has been nothing if not miraculous!"

This is when Rico bows his head in resignation 'of course your correct, my friend. I suppose that division of the conglomerate called NIA is a blessing for many human beings around the globe, true, but listen, when NIA slips up, I'm going to be there!' We'd smiled in unison that last get-together only yesterday when Rico agreed that it might be an excellent idea for me to try and enroll in NIA-U, and that was what I was going to do!

Rico waved goodbye to his friend, mulling over the reasons he'd not informed him of what they suspected of Sara, that she'd somehow escaped NIA and gone on another killing spree this he kept under wraps until there was more clarity. <u>But Rico was unaware of the history that Brock and Sara shared, and Brock would keep that as it is, maybe until after he shredded the psychopath.</u>

Lucie and I strolled hand in hand, the pretty Mallard Ducks flipping wings washing, and swimming in the overflowing fountains. I prayed openly with Laci at a concrete bench, "please, for the miracles to exponentially grow and for Lucie's memories to return." Her parents had only the week before told him that Lucie had told them word verbatim, umh, being very descriptive to the Tee about a vacation they took to Rosarito Beach in Mexico. She told them about them going Horseback riding on the beach and visiting the site of the Blockbuster Movie Titanic. She surprised the parents by remembering what they ate on a dinner cruise on the Pacific Ocean. There was a real plausible feeling of palpable excitement... which radiated from their hearts.

49

<u>Sisters Valerie and Kamryn with some alone time.</u>

On a blustery windy day, rain fell. The skies above Napa were curiously purple and blackish, quite the contrary to the sisters who were visiting for the 5th consecutive afternoon. It was a late lunch in a crowded pavilion near the outdoor arena where the Track and Field contests were going on at that very moment.

Valerie was highly candid when it came to any subject not only outspoken but considered herself open-minded to the max and was fully engaged, wanting to very much bond with her elder sister Kamryn, true they had been apart a better part of 27 years, but in just a few short days there could be no mistaking the same blood pumped through each other's veins.

They had to set parameters, one of which was a dark topic that immediately caused strife. There would be no discussions about their other sister Sara. She was off-topic. Val had warned Kam that we don't talk behind each other's backs unless it was something we'd say to their faces or had stated before. Don't slander each other we're the last of the bloodline. There would be no more Amaya's. <u>In the past five days,</u> they'd experienced both spectrums at maximum limits, from severe craziness and outright hate to the exhilarated peaks of love!

It didn't take Kam long to realize there was no more baby Val not as she remembered. Of course, she guffawed. She was but five years old the last time they'd been together. Sadly, Valerie was cursed just like Sara and many of their deceased family members. Val had at least 2 or 3 sides to her, uhm, personality changes. She was like a triple-edged sword thinking back to that first afternoon when she and Uncle Terrance were goofing off. Skipping to my Lou's.... fun stuff, that's when she'd seen Valerie for the first time since when she was but a child. Val and the witch Sara were off to one side of the path by the pond. The reunion with Valerie that day was fantastic… until it became toxic. Out of the blue, the very next day, I visited with Val… literally unexpected, like a flash flood, she jumped me!

They were happy having a small breakfast, and everything seemed fine, until… a couple of hours later, in Valerie's flat, umh studio apartment, that she was awarded by their Uncle. He'd intimated that Val would be a team leader at NIA, which had her thrilled to death. Ah, maybe that was a bad choice of words…Death. Kam made an almost fatal mistake, ah, fatal not in mortality, call it umh, lethal in the dissolution of sisters. *Suddenly Val's face twisted in a flurry. Val threw her wine cooler against the living room wall and told her to get the fk out of there now. Her eyes were Wolf-like in a rage, growling. I bolted towards the door, yelling, " You're just as crazy as Sara," and reached for the door. I opened it and took one last peek at her expecting her to be near my back. Ahh, what I saw caused me to hit the Emergency Brakes and stop!*

She was on her knees convulsing, shaking her palms on her head tightly grasped, shouting no… NO, ugh, no, in a man's voice. My sister Valerie was sick, and the family curse lived on. I ran to the bathroom, wet a washcloth, unafraid, galloped to her side, and bent down to soothe her. She pounced, tossing her Red eyes up, growling. Her scary, twisted, and distorted face glared at me. She didn't resemble my sister. Her teeth clashed, then clenched, and blood squirted from her lips. Then a guttural howl from deep down in the pits of her stomach… bang, she went from her knees to standing in a flash. Calmly I repeated baby 'Val, umh baby Val, I'm Kammy. Aah, Kammy, please, baby, please relax.' Her left hand flinched an open switchblade knife… a 7-inch steel blade extended. My hands went up my feet went back. I screamed at Valerie Amaya. 'I'm your sister Kamryn Amaya Stop!' I turned to run away, finding my back flat up against a wall. Val quickly flips underhanded the knife throwing it at me. It zinged past my right ear sticking in the drywall, not an inch away from my death.

'Oh, Kammy,' suddenly the alien blitzed towards her in a wanting embrace. Kam shrunk into her off the wall. Remembering their mother and the resemblance in Valerie's eyes, glad the episode ugh spell was over for now. Realizing next time, and there would always be a next time... she may not be as lucky, and fate may finish her, she wiped the drizzling sweat from her forehead.

Kam checked the clock on the wall biting her upper lip, thinking how crazy this was. They enjoyed wine coolers and chatting about Europe less than an hour ago. Valerie described the fascinating museums and architecture throughout Europe; she'd been to Buckingham Palace and had a flat for several years in London. Val giggled and brought up this English chap that was hot on her, describing his flirtations and gifts to her, ugh, presents galore. He'd taken her to the best restaurants and clubs for dancing and cavorting. She said, 'here, let me show you a picture of the man. His name was 'Sir Oliver. Shoot,' she grimaced, 'it went all sideways from there.' I said, 'do you remember that Oliver was the same name as my, um, our baby brother's middle name, your older brother Val, Kenny....' She raised her head peculiarly as if she heard something in the attic, but there was no attic. I sat back on the couch, said zilch. Just observing her, my skin in a weird shiver, I soldiered on, 'Val, do you remember anything about our brother?'

Val had put her phone down, entranced wide-eyed her expression had changed to an odd inquisitive statuesque glare her mouth was slightly ajar. 'No, I don't remember a thing about him other than his baby pictures on the walls all over the house.' So here's what I told her 'Kenny had Colic. He was a sick baby boy, always crying and whining, but as he got older, he got much better Sara, and I were almost seven years old when it happened. He was nearly three years old, and you were practically two.' Valerie sat at the edge of the sofa. Her legs crossed, listening at attention.

'It was a gorgeous bright sunny day, and our father had to work only until noon. Uhm, at noon, we were having a barbeque family fun day. Daddy had bought a grand Doughboy pool. It was the best. I used to hold you in my arms while you giggled and kicked your chubby short legs. You loved our swimming pool, Val!' I drank some of my wine cooler, watching her do the same.

'The day in question, I wasn't at the family BBQ, unfortunately; otherwise, things may have ended up differently. I have regretted it ever since. Anyways I was at a sleepover with one of my best friends. I was going to show up in the afternoon for dinner, so at our house were mom Sara, Ken, and you.... Valerie. How the story was relayed to me and told to me hundreds of times, uhm, again, I wish I was there, Val. Maybe I could have saved our brother.' Valerie seemed instantly intense. Her impatience became obvious. 'Ken, get to the point, please. What happened to my older brother?...' 'You really don't remember, do you?' she shook her head no. 'Okay, this is the most popular version of what happened. Mom had started the barbeque and was sunning herself on a lounge chair and dipping into the water when she got too hot. Sara was diving into the water, swimming, and playing with baby brother Kenny and mom had you out by the pool in your Lil car carrier, keeping you in the shade. When it got hotter, she put you in the house into your crib, where you fell asleep. Mother brought your crib close to the screen door, which looked out on the pool and was the entrance to our living room. That way, Sara and mother could hear you cry out when you woke up. And give you a bottle of formula for lunch.' I recall pausing at that time, having an odd premonition of caustic vibes like what was I doing? We'd made a pact not to discuss any damaging family secrets. And here I was, breaking that pact, being egged on by the person who'd made me promise to only discuss happy family times...

But I soldiered on, for there wasn't a way that she'd allow me to say, ahh, forget it. She was wide-eyed and crunching down on my every syllable. "Valerie, this is from the Police reports that I was able to read after mom died of Breast Cancer. The reports were in her jewelry box. I still have them, by the way. Anyways, one report I'd read had stated that *Mr. Amaya was attending the barbeque, cooking ribs and hamburgers up on the deck overlooking the pool. The youngest child Valerie Amaya a 2-year-old, started to wail, crying loudly from her crib by the patio door. Mr. Amaya went running to check on her. The small boy Kenny was in the family pool and was upright inside a floating device… like a saucer with a weighted bottom. It had a seat in it and was rated… for 25 pounds more than the boy's weight, so he was floating around the pool. He started crying, probably because his younger sister was wailing. Watching him in the pool was his older sister Sara who was seven years old, who claimed she was playing with him in the pool, trying to get him to stop crying.*

This was when it all turned murky. We've interviewed the young girl Sara Amaya numerous times, and her story remains oddly the same ahhhh… why oddly? Well, many child Psychologists have suggested and professed that children in Sara's age bracket in stressful situations will normally tell erratic semblances with different variances of what had occurred, not Sara. However, when interviewing her, it was like a recording… it was almost word for word the same interview, and the transcripts were nearly identical. Another conundrum was that Sara never shed a tear and didn't seem upset, possibly in shock, but in my opinion, she acted suspiciously.

This is a follow-up on case # 711757. "T Tanner Rink" badge number '928' was the first on the scene. After the paramedics arrived, Mr. and Ms. Amaya were beyond distraught and terror-filled. Ms. Amaya had to be sedated and given Oxygen. Mr. Amaya had rushed home after receiving the emergency call. He couldn't and wouldn't believe his son had drowned and fought to take the deceased boy in his arms. He had to be restrained multiple times. He went berserk with screams and tears.

The Coroner has ruled the death an accidental drowning, but some unsettling information has come forth. Sara has been a regular patient at an outpatient treatment center for mentally challenged children. She has been seen by a total of seven psychiatrists and is currently on medications.

The infant named Valerie refused her bottle and wouldn't stop her incessant howls of agony like she was in pain. We took her from her crib while other female officers attended to the infant. I sought out the only witness to see what had happened in the pool. Sara sat by herself as if she were self-medicated, eating a raw hamburger blood fell from her chin, and she seemed to be in an induced state of shock at first reckoning. Her eyes were focused on the Doughboy pool or into space, sort of unfocused. I waved my hand across her vision, and she smiled and asked, 'why are you doing that?" Sara showed no emotions whatsoever. Zombie-like, well, that's my subjective opinion. Other than that first smile, she continued to chew the raw meat. I said, 'give me that.... it's uncooked.' She did it without comment. So I put it back on the cold grill. I asked her, 'Sara' can you tell me what happened to your little brother? How his upright raft had overturned, I added that according to the manufacturer, it would take a pressure of over 25 pounds to turn over the inflatable child's safety raft. I looked at her non-expression. She didn't reply or make a comment. I.... again proceeded to explain to her once again.

'Sara, it would take 25 pounds of pressure to turn it over. If you added the weight of a child, it would be much more difficult to flip over or spill over.' I implored the 7-year-old to answer me and give me a response. But she still didn't meet my eyes, just entranced into the swimming pool, unmoving and non-responsive. 'Sara, please tell me what you saw.' Before she spoke, a Social Worker from the County who worked with CPS, the child protective service agency, showed up and took the child Sara temporarily. Later I joined them back near the pool's edge. Ms. Fields, who had a degree in Child Psychology, was on Sara's left rubbing the child's hair. I sat next to her with a radio-shack recorder and my notepad.

Ms. Fields asked Sara again what caused Ken to be turned upside down. Sara turned not to her but found my eyes. She said, 'Baby sister started to scream like a snake had chomped on her. I saw my mommy run over to the patio sliding door, and my brother started whining. Ugh, I didn't pay any attention because he was spoiled rotten and always whined and cried all the time. I climbed the stairs to check on the Barbeque. It was smokin. It wasn't long till I turned around. My baby brother had finally shut up. That's when I saw the round bottom of his innertube up above the pool's water. I knew that Kenny's head had to be under the water. He was strapped into the seat. I jumped into the water to save him. It was hard for me to turn the tube back up. When I did, my brother had a still Blueish look. His eyes were open wide, not blinking. I knew he was dead then not hurtin anymore, no reasons to cry no more.'

Ms. Fields and I would consult about this interview and listen to the tape dozens of times. We'd lost count of how many times… that Sara was asked in various ways. <u>So aren't you sad for your little brother? Don't you see how your mother and father are so upset? Why aren't you upset, Sara?</u> The small girl returned Ms. Fields' glare and ominously said, 'Like a Fairy Tale, in the end, everyone lives happily ever after. Baby Kenny no longer had to cry. He was happy now!' I stopped writing the report. The Social worker said Sara must be in shock and that all humans don't react the same way to trauma at the scenes of horrific accidents or cataclysmic earthquakes, um, hurricanes. Some people haul off, laughing hysterically at the mayhem, chaos, and torn bodies. Mentally they lose control of the present tense and are lost between consciousness and subconscious states of being protected by their amygdala. Human brains fall into a default mode. Perhaps Sara is in shock. That would explain her attitude and disposition.'

The little blonde girl seemed to listen to Ms. Fields' words, looked at her and me, then smiled briefly. "Yep, I'm in shock and getting hot. I think I'll jump into the pool, excuse me!" We watched seven-year-old Sara smirk and do a cannonball into their doughboy pool.

Addendum > 3 weeks after the accidental drowning of Kenneth Amaya, Sara remains unchanged and ambivalently apathetic towards the loss of her brother. She has been characterized as a Sociopath currently under psychiatric care. The girl seems to have no feelings. I, for one, consider this incident not an accidental drowning. We have created a mock-up and placed a doll weighing the same as Ken Amaya having several test subjects try to turn the innertube over. There was no way to flip the tube upside down without considerable physical force. There was no way the boy's tube could have flipped over; naturally had to be human manipulation even waves of someone jumping in the water next to the floating raft didn't come close to turning the innertube over.

IMHO, in my humble opinion, which apparently counts for nothing, the Death certificate should be modified from accidental drowning to death by homicide. I have attempted numerous times to have this case reopened but have faced roadblocks. The Coroner absolutely is adamant Kenny died by accidental causes.

Valerie remained perched on her couch, nearly falling at the edge of a cushion, a bewildered look that crawled worm-like to an expression of contentment *'so Kam, there wasn't anything conclusive I get where you're going with this story that some indicators might sway us to believe that Sara might be a Monster to the 6th degree, but she's innocent in the murder of our brother it's all mere speculation is although I can concur with your assumptions. Yes, Sara, like me, is a Psychopathic killer...... '* She squeezed her left forearm, saying, 'one day. I'll fill you in, umh, we can talk about the justifications that I had... for the acts that I'm guilty of.' A few moments passed by, then she said, 'so why the pale face Kam? We can't assume Sara Killed our brother we.....' This was when Val went ballistic. I only said, 'Val, it's a mistake me being here. I need to leave now.' 'You're going nowhere bitch' was the next words shouted toward me. If you're reading my journal and paying attention. This was when she attacked me, nearly impaling me with her switchblade knife.

Suffice it to say. I didn't leave her apartment because Val wasn't having it. She demanded I sit back down. 'Kam, you don't start something and not finish it....' I replied, 'you spoke in a male voice. Val, who was that?' 'I'm sure your aware we have demons in our bloodline... shut-up Kam, I am who I need to be. Now let's finish this conversation. Go grab another wine cooler out of the refrigerator for us.'

I did as she ordered and decided to throw caution into the storm. 'Valerie, like you... I stopped thinking about Kenny's demise. As the decades unfurled, our brother's death drifted further from my frontal cortex. I seldom thought of the horrific day that instantly changed our whole family's dynamics. After that day, Sara was extricated or exiled was shipped to Grandad to Papa's house to live. She was only allowed to visit when both mom and dad were home.' Valerie took a big gulp of the Strawberry cooler 'you've forgotten I was a tiny baby girl, just two years old I must have blocked the incident out. Tell me something, sis, how much do you remember from when you were two years old?' I gave her a lopsided smile 'you got me on that. The first memory I had was when I was maybe three years old. Anyways we, ahh, our family tried to give Sara the benefit of the doubt.'

So yes, I had an agenda which was that I wanted Val to stop communicating with Sara and bond with me, sure I was jealous of their newfound relationship, but also I felt the need to warn her that our evil sister had zero taboos she'd go after either of us in a heartbeat if it benefited her warped mindset. 'Val, we have so much catching up to do. Here's just a crumb um food for thought Sara and I grew up apart. I was sent to New York to our Aunts, and she remained with Papa, and yet we stayed in touch and spoke on the phone. Even though we grew up and flourished over three thousand miles apart, I'd say we talked at a minimum of about 2 or 3 times a week. I was busy working at Schwab in New York City at the stock exchange, and Sara had her Psychiatric treatment center opened in San Rafael,

California. Sara also had parlayed her business shrewdness and wisdom and had three successful Real Estate offices in California. Once all the notoriety hit the media, and she was arrested by the Feds accused of being a serial killer, I put in for a transfer from my firm… Charles Schwab. I worked as an investment broker, moved to San Francisco, and was awarded an upper management position in their main office on Market Street.' She stood up 'excuse me, gotta pee. These wine coolers are going right through me.'

Valerie returned with two more drinks. I waited impatiently 'let me fast forward, Val. I was here for Sara during her long battle in court, our Uncle, and her attorney. I'd see her nearly every day and didn't miss one day of the 11-month trial. I supported her despite the hatred spewed by not only the relatives of her victims but by the media. I hadn't any allies except our Uncle. Since Sara and I are identical twins, I even changed my hair color to brunette and almost got a Tattoo collar around my neck to separate our look…' 'Wow, I bet it got sort of hairy here, sis. It must have been a stressful time…' 'That's true, it was horrendous, um, after Sara was convicted and placed here at NIA, I visited her when I could, sometimes once a week. As you have learned from Uncle, she pulled a 'Mission Impossible' escaping from NIA by switching, uh, swapping me out in her place. Sara drugged me, and I awoke in her cell…' 'Yeah, I heard of her plot. It was simply brilliant. I mean to say it should be on Netflix or Hulu, maybe even a series. A spectacular mastermind is our sister…' 'Umh, you seem like you're condoning her vile act like your proud ahh…' 'Come on, Kammy, yuh have to give it to her if you stepped away and saw the plot from a distance she played every card with adroitness using the guard Carl and…' 'Yup, she just murdered Carl and his wife Bianca real brilliant let's move on Val.' 'No reason for the sarcasm, sister; it is what it was!' Val showed me a grinning tooth display.

'Val, this is no joke. I implore you not to get close to the vile creature. She'll reel you in, then stab you in the back. She's a Viper, ugh, snake. She's got three prominent personalities. The only one I like is her Ame. She is an artist with the skills to make a decent living. She sold paintings and worked over on the pier at Fisherman's Wharf as a professional talent. You ought to see how fast she can draw a caricature in chalk of you… simply a fricken amazing talent. Ame has several degrees from the finest Universities in America, is no fool, and is the brains inside of Sara.' Val nods 'yes, I've seen some of her charcoal drawings. Ame is the Cat's meow when it comes to freehand drawings, heck, all types of paintings, your right, but while we're visiting memory lane, Kam, what's that got to do with our brother? Isn't that where your long story began?' I feared how Valerie might react when I told her about Ame's drawings but soldiered on. Yeah, I'd opened my big mouth, and she wouldn't let me change the subject without completion.

I wasn't annoyed actually was enjoying myself learning about how my younger sister was straight to the point. A no-nonsense gal how she rationalized what I was trying to communicate to her… Val was obviously an intelligent woman with an analytical thought process and very hardheaded muh. This was my first impression of our first time sitting together and talking. So after malingering around the subject, I started back up. 'Yes, so picture this pun included Sara was locked up for years in prison cells with nothing but time to connive and think uhm, analyze plan, and scam. Sara escaped into her entities Ame, Don, and Al, but the alter ego that maintained priority and significant conscious time was Ame.

While I was caged in her cell, I read dozens of Sara's manuscripts. She'd demanded that Ame draw a chronological time frame of events in their life with colored pictures detailing all positive fun times she'd experienced on some extra-large sketch paper. Then draw and paint the opposite of her experiences, describing negatives in her life in picture form. Ann used Charcoal, chalk, and even Magic Markers in some memorable scenes. She also used Acrylics and Oil'

'Sorry Kam, so far I don't hear a pun?...' 'unh, maybe I used the wrong word, perhaps anyways I woke up in her cell drugged out after a few days trying to reconcile what had happened to me. I sat at Sara's table, opened one of the Art folders, and started turning the pages. Remember, Sara... and I am 7 minutes apart. I, of course, could relate to every drawn scene of our childhood back... I was there beside her most of the time. Each picture drawn by Ann brought me back in time and place. The lucidity of her talented art was stupendous, and the details were astonishingly accurate right down to veins in the eyes of her characters.' 'Kamryn, I enjoy your articulations and descriptive words and the horde of adjectives... why can't you just spit it out... get to the point. Your...' 'Because I'm like replaying it all for the first time, Valerie. I mean, telling you what you want to know is heartbreaking and deviously inspired all at the same time!' Val sits back. 'Go ahead, Kam, it's your story. Tell it as you have to.' I frowned, dropping my memory back to <u>That Day.</u>

'I still could feel the empty hollow, hopeless reality that encompassed my breathing soul back in the claustrophobic cell in solitary confinement. The walls shrank into me. My ribs could barely expand, my lungs closed down, and I was hyperventilating, frozen in fear in paranoia. I cowered, crawling under my steel cot. After a while, I had no idea how I survived that episode like a smokescreen dilating my vision. I found myself back with the Art portfolio in my hands, flipping pictures over. I came to the pool pictures and the precise time of Kenny's drowning. Ann had it all drawn out. I wasn't in any picture because I wasn't there. I was at a sleepover at my best friend's house, Nicole's. It was her birthday slumber party. Uh, my scalp tingled. I remembered feeling trepidation. This was a revelation for me. I slowed down and took

in every detail.' Valerie waved her hands in a rolling motion… like come on out with it, stop stalling!*

'Val, please listen to me,' she nodded, taking another gulp. 'Um, first, I counted seven drawings of the corrosive catastrophe, then I mentally backed up to the first picture. That revealed daddy, about to head off to work for a few hours. The picture was of dad kissing mom and helping her start the barbeque. Then he hugged and kissed Sara and Kenny and picked you up… Valerie, the drawing showed daddy snuggling up to you and kissing and pinching your cute nose. All smiles in this sequence. The next drawing was of our brother's expanded face. She had made it super pouty with snot streaming from his nostrils, and he was sneering and snarling in that picture. The next shot was of him floating and strapped into the raft, and mommy was putting on suntan lotion beside the smoking barbeque.'

'The following drawing in a moving graphic sequence showed our mother running to the sliding glass door screen to see you, Valerie, you were screaming. Anne provided a three-dimensional view… Sara was shown looking back at Kenny eerily with a fiercely ugly furious teeth-clenching grin. And her larger-than-life eyes peered into him with purely insidious evil. I couldn't break my eyes from how she'd morphed. Her sinister stare matched her next motions, with her two hands outstretched, grabbing Kenny's floating baby seat. The last picture showed our brother's feet kicking… his head underwater, and her laughingly raising her chin. Sara brings her right hand to her lips, kissing it and blowing oxygen toward Kenny's still feet. It was her final kiss goodbye to our brother.'

Grief-stricken, Valerie's countenance had mutated. She was no longer my sister. Quickly I stood up and walked backwards slowly towards the exit door of her apartment. I kept my cool, already having dealt with at least one demonic side of my younger sister, thinking maybe she was disbelieving... of what I'd said. I repeated, 'the stacks of drawings are still locked in Sara's cell, proof in the pudding. Val, all this time, we gave Sara the benefit of the doubt. It was her that....' Val tossed her head like a Horse whinnying exorcist shocked by an electric current... she leaped forward. Reptile quick grabbed my legs, throwing me with enormous strength and rage over the coffee table, then stalking me again, tossing me like a rag doll over the sofa. I didn't bounce, laying still... now terrified, Val was like a wild Wildebeest!

Stranger than fiction, Val dropped off of me, her lips trembling, pupils enlarged just stopped moving as if she'd gone dormant. Ahh, catatonic, I bolted out of her apartment... momma didn't raise no fool. I exited stage left as fast as my short legs could carry me. Whew, that was fricken scary, for Real!

Later that afternoon, I was leaving the gym wanting to get with my Uncle Terrance and finally leave this God-forsaken place 'NIA' in the dust. In an on-campus library, I found a corner seat sat down with a book, crossed my legs, and reveled in the beauty outside the large window in front of me. The largest body of water on NIA's property glistened in the sun's rays. It was a picturesque panoramic view.... the gorgeous pristine lake with waterfowl floating over the rolling waves.... Drifted off with Valerie on my mind. I closed my eyes and nodded 'needless to say. I learned a necessary lesson....' about what not to communicate with Val. Surely it would be prudent of me never to discuss any traumatic subject matter regarding Sara again. Val was a touch-off balance and had to set limits. Strangely her escapades and stories of her atrocious killing spree across the pond, uh, different continents were okay for her to extrapolate on. She was even-keeled while going into morbid details about how she took vengeance, um, retribution on the couple who'd abducted her.... Valerie could calmly act as if like she was at a diner, nonchalantly asking for a cup of coffee, describing her decapitating her enemies with a skill-saw, with zero emotions.

Val was ruthless and calculating. She was a predator. Better to stay on her good side; no, maybe it was better for me to get away from her and Sara and NIA! ... <u>Now that I had a reason to live... grinning hugely remembered seeing my beautiful daughter coming from my womb five days ago. 'Sonia' was a beautiful baby girl with shaggy blond hair right out of the Gate!</u>

If Val and I were going to continue nurturing our relationship... I'd have to place barriers up with stringent guidelines, yet I believed at this time we'd grow closer and be able to bridge taboo subjects when our trust was built up. Like the analogy of rungs on a ladder, we started on rung # 1. If we could reduce stressful conversation, build up trust add levels of familiarity, I was confident we'd climb the rungs of sisterly love, but she had to stay away from Sara!_ Yep!

Speaking of a segue into sisterly love, our Uncle was looking forward to the first time in 27 years having Val and his favorite Niece, me, lol, join him for dinner. He was having his Chef put together a Surf and Turf, um, a five-course meal, oh yeah, yummy. Terrance had sent a group text to all three of our cellphones along with a corny video of long ago when we three were super young kids, smh, so old school. I texted back that I would attend the dinner if Sara didn't. I made it crystal clear don't expect me if Sara was going to show up! I would not be around the freak; I'd rather starve to death than sit next to that viper. Sara, luckily, declined the invitation. A little later, Val and I video-chatted. That's when Valerie made a reference to my maternity-like baggy clothes.... Saying what's up, girl? With the way you dress yourself up, it's like you're a Vagabond. Why don't you wear something more formfitting you got the body for it. She displayed partial despair when we talked about the dinner engagement. She said she worried about me, but then I broke the news that Sara wouldn't join us

It was around 7 pm. I'll never forget the date, January 23rd. I was walking by myself as I did most of the time. I was not at the NIA prison, allowed now to live on the grounds of the NIA-U training facility, nevertheless under lock and key. Guards manned the two gates into the property, and the entrances were... umh, let me describe it so that you will understand my dilemma of trying to escape with my baby. So, if hypothetically, you wanted to exit the grounds... you'd pull your vehicle up to the first set of gates to be scrutinized, you know, your license, NIA badge, etc. You're okayed, then pull into the middle cordoned-off area between the entrance and exit gates. That's when the canines are brought over to your vehicle, sort of like entering the United States from Mexico. Except that NIA had manufactured an innovative enormous saucer-like scanner... ah, think of it as a giant magnet that rotates over your car from above on levers. Oh, kind of like a garage door opener flowing over you or like maybe entering a car wash. Anyways I'm spending too much time on this description. The vehicle is literally X-rayed right down to the treads on the tires. After this passes inspection, the last gate is opened, and you either enter NIA or exit NIA. There, do you get it? I looked down at my old school notebook and saw that I'd taken two total pages to write this.... Unhhh...

Yep, so I was stuck; for now, my intuition or paranoia told me there was something in the Air, I couldn't put my finger on it as of yet, but people, ah, the staff seemed to be ultra-vigilant, like on guard. I'd tried to call Liz to tell her I was having shooting pains in my abdomen and worried about my pregnancy. Besides the doctor, she was the only human alive who knew of my predicament other than Rocky... who was one of my impregnator's best friends. I wanted to see Brock Danne and let him know he would be a daddy for the first time in his life. Last I saw him. He was in a wheelchair on one of the docks at NIA. He was drooling and could barely lift his chin up. Rocky had told me weeks before that Brock was making unbelievable improvements.

The best guess from the OBGYN at NIA was that I was now about seven months pregnant. At first, I felt it was weird that an OB/GYN would be employed at a prison; Liz had filled in those blanks for me. At NIA, there were approximately 1,300 females incarcerated in the mental institution and around 1,700 males. Of course, they were kept separated most of the time, but that wasn't the problem. Predominantly the Correction Officers were of the male persuasion and were the sperm donors of the mentally despondent baby carriers. Thus to keep everything in-house, NIA had its own Abortion clinic.

I strolled over from the main library on the grounds toward the cafeteria and heard my name 'Kamryn, Kam....' I spun around to see a magnanimous grin. It was the wildly handsome Rocky. He was standing on one of those new-wave scooters "hey there, how are you doing? Geesh, it's been, uhm, for weeks since I've seen you. Where have you been hiding?" He reached over, and we hugged. He instantly jumped back "whoa, now!" "Yeah, the baby bump has grown, and because it's my first pregnancy, the baby has dropped, so the doctor told me that I was around three to five weeks from delivery of Brock's baby girl!" His feet left the ground, and he clapped simultaneously "it's a girl. Omg, no one knows still, but Doctor Honcho?" "Yes, you and Liz are the only ones well, except for Doctor Kathy Wei. I was afraid that they'd force me into an abortion...." "Sshhh, Kam, so if you don't mind me asking, what's the plan?" A sharp static sound blasted from Rocky's hip. He turned and said, "hold up, excuse me for a sec," stepped to the side, and I heard the correspondence.... 'Breaker Rocky yuh gotta copy'... over 'Yes, Shun go ahead'... over 'Rocky, Terrance is up in arms about that FBI Agent Rico Captor visiting tonight with Wendi's parents, and wants to have me stall them at the gate, do you have any idea of how we can do that?... over' 'Wait Shun, so when does Rico supposed to be here?'... over. 'Around 8 pm at the outpatient hospital, and Wendi isn't Wendi bro, she's her alter ego Sunshine, Terrance and Liz are acting crazy, and they have her sedated down in the emergency wing... over' 'Wow, okay, let's hook up I'm on my way out of the training facility will meet you in the lobby of the outpatient hospital in 25 minutes.... over. '10-4.... over.'

Rocky swiveled, knowing I'd heard their conversation, but said nothing of it other than I got to get going, checking me up and down again. "Kam, you are the most beautiful pregnant woman I've ever seen," grinning largely. I reached out my hand to slap him playfully, but he'd made me feel so good inside that I had to smile. "Oh, your such a flirt, aren't you?" He shook his head, "if it weren't so cold and windy, everyone would be able to see that big belly of yours..." he laughed. I tugged my Peacoat tight. I replied, "yea, I'm always in thick baggy coats and sweaters if it were summertime, I'd been busted months ago, but as the doctor said, with my petite frame, I wouldn't put on much weight. I last weighed a whopping 147 pounds." He spun a crinkled smirk at me and said and heck, what are you 4 foot 15 inches tall, uhm short!" He got me. I started to giggle "no, mister, for your information, I'm barely 5-foot-one inch tall and was around 115 pounds pre-Prego...!"

Rocky hugged me again "don't worry, I will meet with Liz and your baby, um, Brock and your baby... wait, did you say, girl, baby girl?" I snugly quirked my nose up, smiling "yep, her name, I've not decided. Doctor Kathy Wei did an ultrasound, and I got to see the little girl inside me. It was super exciting and scary at the same time, and I wish Brock could have been there. Hey, hold up. I have a picture of the baby girl. Since you're going to the outpatient hospital where Wendi and Brock are, can you please show him and speak with him, Rocky!" I saw immediate apprehension gruffly appear on his face, then it vanished. "Of course I can, Kamryn." I pulled out the envelope from my bitty purse and handed it to him, watching him tuck it away carefully in his vest pocket. He hugged me once again, reached over, kicked the kickstand, and glided away on his scooter.

Water breaks.

I didn't make it far; doubled up in pain, I fell forward, shifting my body so as not to fall directly on the baby and my belly, hitting my left side and screaming out in agony. In seconds I was surrounded. People came out of the woodwork, and only one of them did I know. Rocky must have heard my wailing cries; he waved his arms and shouted, 'get me a Golf Cart....' Someone had yelled, 'I called 911, the paramedics are on the way.' I barely heard Rocky's muffled voice say I got to get a hold of Doctor Honcho. The last sensation I'd had was wetness from my uterus. I was soaking wet. With no one to consult with and my first pregnancy, I'd read that my amniotic sac had to of ruptured and amniotic fluid was what I was feeling. For some reason, I blacked out, perhaps it was stress, or maybe I was sick?

Sometime later, I awoke to a scary petrifying site. I laid on a gurney flat on my back, machines were beeping, and to my left was the incubus evil creature herself, Renae, who ordered Nurse Williams to stab me with the poison hypodermic needle inside Sara's cell. Her intent was to either to kill me or zombify me. Either way, I whirled around, screeched, and shrieked out in panic. A snug feeling of impairment struck me. My shoulder was pinned to the gurney, and his face closed on me. It was Rocky who slowly bent down and whispered, "darling Kamryn, it's all going to be okay, I'm here, and nothing is going to happen to you and your baby...." I burst out sobbing loudly. He held my head and rubbed my hair, and I began contractions again. They were coming on stronger. Renae said where is Doctor Wei at. A nurse from the foot of my gurney said, 'her cervix is dilated to about 6 centimeters. She is in the active stage of labor....'

Rocky held my right hand tight as I bucked up, yelling in painful exhilaration. I could faintly hear someone say Doctor Wei is on her way... Then Renae said too late... sweating like inside a steam room, gasping for fresh oxygen, feeling like my innards were being eviscerated and ripped out of my vagina. Ah, the pain was gloriously mind-altering. Thinking only a masochist could enjoy this experience.

There were five of us in the hospital room, and then there were Six, a yielding high-pitched squealing of... could it be giggles, uhm, laughter? I knew her name before I saw her damp blonde curls of hair... Sonja. Next, an odd scream and a nurse fell to her knees, spasmodically twitching. 'I, I I ahhhh can't believe it...' the nurse had bitten part of her lower lip off. Blood poured down her chin and onto her white outfit. She shouted, 'I was just shocked, like a 220 volt of electricity just shot through me, when I cut the umbilical cord...' Sonja was cackling, laughing, and peeing simultaneously.

Within seconds Sonja was no longer awake, her eyes shut down, and she'd stopped gesticulating, bam, like she'd been shot with a sleeping dart. It was... sleepy time. She was wrapped up and taken from the room to be weighed and checked out. The room went vacant, and Rocky peered down at me... "whew, girl, I've never been part of something like that; I've killed all kinds of people but never been a part of a life beginning that was fricken awesome, dude...." "Dude," I muttered. He clutched me tightly, leaning over me; "listen up, I don't know how or what Terrance will think about this. For now, this is our secret...." "Secret Rocky, no, this is no secret anymore. Renae and the nurses, this will be news across...." "Ssshh, I am going to handle that. Now get some rest, Kamryn."

I awoke later in a single hospital room, and baby Sonja was inside a crib on my right side. I gingerly reached up and took her chart that was on a clipboard... I knew Sonja was about two months premature, but she was a big baby anyways. She weighed 7lb and 11oz and was 25 7/8 inches long. She didn't make a murmur as I picked her up and held her tight against my bosom. When she awoke, I'd breastfed her in silence, and she dug into me, purring like a kitty cat. I was a mommy... yep. 😊.

A while back, I was given a private phone that was only connected to Liz, Terrance, and my sister Valerie. I tried in vain to get Liz on the phone a dozen times, if not once. I texted her to call me... I didn't dare text that I'd had my baby. I was now slogged down with paranoia. It wasn't a help to my disposition at what Rocky had said before leaving my gurney side. 'I have squelched my talk from the nurses, and Renae will most certainly be silent concerning baby Sonja. She will be in to speak with you soon. Liz and Terrance are unavailable and are dealing with the Rico visit and with an unconscious Wendi Feral. I think it prudent that we, uhm, you speak with Liz now that your healthy baby girl is here. There is no fear of your uncle or the NIA wanting to abort it. Relax, Kam...' He stared longingly at me, then at the wrapped-up baby. 'Here, hold Sonja and give her a snuggle before you leave... umh, will you be Sonja's God Father?' He smiled 'well, I'd be honored, of course...' he held her up and cuddled carefully into her. 'One question Kam where'd you come up with her name Sonja? I mean, don't get me wrong, I like it. It kind of sounds exotic or maybe like from Russia or....' 'Rocky, I have no idea, had never thought of that name, can't recall where I'd heard it before, but when she arrived, a feeling came over me like she whispered, my name is Sonja!'

<u>**Renae snarled, thinking of how she'd pay back Liz and Terrance... Sonja!**</u>

The bastard had played the evil conspiring game with Ron, her husband, betting on him stabbing her with the hypo-needle. Terrance hadn't a clue that he was what do you call it a "Grand Uncle?" No... a great uncle, well, that he wasn't. If she'd have her druthers, she'd kidnap this baby. A payback for him putting her daughter Candice under his microscope and tracking her in Colorado, threatening both Ron and her that if they didn't stay in line, Candice wouldn't make it to her University of Colorado graduation. Ole Terrance thinks his nieces are suckers, but nope, he's got another fricken thing coming. He's screwed with the wrong momma bear! Now how do I get this bratty baby out of NIA?

Renae pushes open the swinging door to see Sonja nursing away... sneering at the niece of Terrance... "Hey there, how are my favorite patients doing this evening?" "We're just fine, and I want to thank you for all you did for Sonja and me! Where's Doctor Wei? Isn't she going to..." "Oh, there's no need. Your baby is perfect, and you'll be up on your feet in no time. I bet you're strolling the yard by tomorrow morning." Before she took Sonja, who was once again sleeping, she said... "Listen, I realize we have some unpleasant history. Please, I'm not asking for your forgiveness, but only your understanding of what happened. It is true that I was going to have you injected by Nurse Williams. But I didn't want to, Kamryn. I hadn't any choice, for your evil twin sister Sara was blackmailing me. She promised me she'd kill my daughter and husband if I didn't. Sara, I shouldn't have ever got involved with her, but it's over now, honey, even if you don't think so. You can trust me to keep Sonja a secret until you've decided to let everyone know about her birth. The nurses will be quiet after Rocky read them the riot act, that I can guarantee you of. So what do you say about us having a truce and a restart?"... I only nodded affirmative, showed my willingness to let bygones be gone, and handed Sonja over to her.

Renae reached out, peering into Sonja's sleeping face. Startled, Sonja blinked open her left eye…. "Hey, I'll be damned, Kamryn. I believe your baby just Winked at me!" Kam laughed "no, Renae, she's snoring. I'm suddenly starving and cannot get a hold of Liz. That's what I want to talk to you about…." "Oh, no worries. I have a dinner tray on the way for you, my dear. Listen, Rocky has filled me in on what's happening, and I must say you're a brave and strong young lady. To have concealed your pregnancy from your uncle was probably a lifesaver for Sonja. You were correct in your assumption, and you'd most likely been forced into having an abortion." The doors swung open, and in came a cart, the aroma of food wafers, into the room.

<u>Seven nights later, Terrance planned an icebreaker for his nieces. Conniving was Terrance's second nature.</u>

Terrance kicked his feet up on his ottoman and relaxed with a cold Cranberry juice drink. He'd questioned his decision several times and was done. Kaput, he was over all the animus and bullshit jealousies and immature renderings. His nieces would have to get along and work together. Recalling the video chat with Sara, who had declined his dinner invitation, which wouldn't do, and he made it clear she was expected to arrive at his 7th-floor suite at the top of NIA's Surgical center. He was fully aware that his intervention plan was mandatory if be was ever going to have his three nieces get along harmoniously. He didn't divulge his ulterior motives but suffice it to say he needed them to comingle respectfully to work together cohesively. This was his goal, and Jax was going to play the mediator. Jax listened to Terrance and chuckled. "Aah, what could be more terrifyingly ironic? The three sisters were signed up for the next semester at NIA-U. They would be in some of the same classrooms sparring in the ring against one another, martial arts training hand-to-hand combat with a full seven days concentrating on obstacle courses. This was going to be a blast to watch. Terrance, you sure know how to keep things interesting around here!"

He listened as Jax went over it again with amusement, nearly giggling. The three sisters start the core curriculum on the same day. They will no doubt be in classes together and share the same locker rooms either they could handle it maturely, or they'd fail. None of the three were failures... nor quitters, unh. Quite the opposite, indeed. They were going to be navigating stressful times in the next 24 months. February 1st, 2018, is the date for the new recruits to be on-site. Graduation of the 2-year degree in 'Physical Education and Well Being' is on February 1st, 2020. However, you could graduate early on September 1st, 2019, but that would be an exceptional accomplishment and rarely done. In some extraordinary cases, participants can graduate early at the 19-month date if they were phenomenal athletes with mental acuity to match... in synch. To date, only the Team Leaders at NIA have incredulously attained this early graduation goal date!

Jax picks up the sisters Valerie and Kamryn for the dinner engagement with Terrance.

Jax and Valerie, and Kamryn 4-wheeling.

One thing was for certain the verbiage never slackened. It was continuous banter, laughter, and fun. The sisters had met hours after the traumatic tussle, with Valerie throwing the switchblade knife into the drywall an inch from Kamryn's right ear. They'd left all that in the abyss, making a pact not to discuss any toxic topics anymore, hugged and, like water off of a Duck's back, let the confrontation go. They were strung tight and getting more snug Kam and Val's relationship was now on the other side of awkwardness. They waited at the exit of # 3 Hangar for Jax to wheel up in his magnificent Hummer. He would escort them from the training facility to the Razor-wired prison compound to Terrance's immaculate, spacious 7th-floor suite for a scrumptious dining experience with no conflicts of contrasting personalities... Yes!

Jax yanked the 4-wheel drive monster under the awning with a masculine Honk. They were aware chivalry was dead, at least this time. Val steps into the passenger seat, seeing Jax for the first time since the finals of the NIA Games Championships, where he gave out the winning medals of Gold, Silver, and Bronze. He comfortably acknowledged her with a pleasant headshake. Kam bounced into the back seat. He said, "ladies, you look fantastic wish the weather outside was in collusion, and we'll pull up to the Porte Cochere; hopefully, the wind isn't blowing sideways, and you girls don't get soaked!"

Val looked below his scarred face seeing his attire, dressed like a Hollywood Don Mafiosi right down to the Red kerchief in the left top pocket of his dark Blue blazer, wow the dude was in a 3-piece suit, "well, I'll be my… my Mr. Jax Foul I dare say you look mighty fine yourself my man you clean up well." His controlled, austere demeanor ricocheted across his dimples and then vanished. She could tell he thoroughly enjoyed the compliment as he donned his Dark Derby Hat "well, thank you, madam!" All giggled.

Jax flipped up the volume, and the music thumped on the surround sound… Valerie instantly drifted into a daydream she'd experienced the day before, feeling heated attraction for Jax.… 'we as humans believe we don't or can't pick whom we fall in love with like traditional love, ah spontaneous combustion, like an Arrow from Cupid. Even today, in 2018, many females are told and sold into marriage in not-so-special situations or circumstances. Sometimes rarely, over time, in these forced couplings, there is a bond of love. Perhaps it's there because of respect, loyalty, children, or fondness over time unh, familiarity rare is it that when in an arranged marriage, they actually 'Fall in Love' or truly are 'In Love' a difference 'In Passion' it's like lukewarm vs. boiling lust.'

'Val was lost in this narrative, letting her mind drift and meander further.… dissecting this magnetic attraction for Jax Foul. Lord knows he's not a debonair handsome one got more scars, bullet holes, amputations than a Crash site dummy.' But he brought her attentive level higher than all the handsome G.Q. types or the rugged men she'd entertained with her lusciousness. Yep, no questions existed… Valerie was into painful satisfaction of the insidious kinds. It would be likewise with Mr. Studly Foul. Yes, she would seduce the war hero, National hero social media star of several all-time viral editions. He was real. She needed to believe that this could be the beginning of love, then laughed out loud.

Kamryn was in constant flux.... worrying about her newborn baby Sonja.... but was told by Renae to relax. She was going to take care of Sonja. Renae lastly told her to have fun, don't worry, sweetie. Kam looks on from the back seat pondering, like, Wtf? Is there something flirtatious going on in the front seat? Wow, Jax was a character, and the President, unh, leader of NIA-U, nicknamed the General of the physical regimental divisions, uh, whatever that meant. But Jax was not the least bit on the desirable side, not even for a one-night sling. She always wondered why it was called a one-night stand. They'd be not much standing, maybe drunk swaying or on the bed screwing, no, not standing. Unh, perhaps she misconstrued the meaning of... one-night stand... grinning into a morphed sideways quirky smile.... trying to see herself in the rearview mirror... knowing she was a cutie pie. Suddenly her butt flipped up off the backseat... as the Hummer thrashed through the flowing water puddles. She watched Val scoot over closer to Jax and slapped him on his back, both grinning like Newlyweds. It was weird how they seemed to stare into each other's eyes.

Jax checked the clock, smirked as per usual ahead of it, and said, "put your seat belts on, ladies. I'm going to take us on the scenic route, some 4-wheel drive obstacle courses for an appetizer." Then he roared hella loud, "Buckle up, Girls!" my sister simpered, and we buckled up. I spirited out a weak "no, we only have 15 minutes to get...." "Nah, Kam, Terrance is backed up about 30 minutes on a conference call out of the country. We're not due to the main building for 45 minutes, so let's turn the music up. How about heavy metal or some heavy bass-thumping Hip-Hop Rap?"

Kam didn't have to take a second glance to see Val was enjoying this impromptu macho twist. She yelled, "giddy-up then!" Jax broke off. That's Cowboy jargon. Then we hit the first huge mound and went airborne "holy shit... hold on!" I screamed.

<u>Doctor Liz Honcho was nearly in a panic, worrying about Wendi.</u>

Inside one of Liz's offices, she'd just finished reading some of the reports about what other inmates had experienced after the same medicine that was administered to Wendi was tested on them.

Liz solemnly listened to Renae, explaining some unsetfling, disturbing information about the test results of other inmates with personality disorders being dispensed the exact dosage Liz had forced on Sunshine. Liz stood to the side, listening, her mouth covered in fright, then interrupted Renae. "It's been a week since we've given Wendi/Sunshine the new combination of Psychotherapeutic designer drugs developed on-site Wthell Wendi seems fine. What was the average time that these side effects took place?"

"Liz, as you are well aware of... Wendi was our first patient that received a double dose. Uhm." She shuffles through her screen "ahh, seven nights ago, the five test subjects were given the same dosage as Wendi, and four days ago, two of them started babbling incoherently gibberish with incomprehensible run-on sentences. Two others had different reactions. They have stopped communicating or even reacting to verbal commands. Catatonic state of being, hey, listen here." Renae continues to read from the proprietary iPad spreadsheet a company issuance, "they're not even capable of feeding themselves. We should be...." Liz grimaces "this is not my fault; I'm not going to have my head on the platter.

Terrance was there. He screwed up too…." "Wait, Renae, didn't you say there were five test subjects?"

Coincidently, Terrance called like he had ESP… Liz picked up the video call and added Renae to the screen, "so I'm all ears. What are the results? Hey there Renae?" She joins her, scrunching into the screen. 'Liz fills him in, brings him up to speed, and then says, Renae, take it from there!' Renae stops and sips some warm bottled water looking at the file. "Oh, here it is. The 5th inmate that was dosed with the same formula is better than okay. She is non-stop energized and focused. We've allowed her out of her Cell block under guard. Her test scores from when she arrived have increased by 37% on the same exams she's taken at yearly intervals. Also, she's much stronger in physical assessments, unh medically, her vitals are improved…" Liz offers "well, last I had a conversation with Wendi, she'd just returned from a concert in San Francisco with Rico. She couldn't be better. I surely hope…" pauses. "How many females are in the five test subjects?" asks Terrance. "Let's see, three of the five were male…." "All right, I get it, but were the five test subjects injected with the same syringes solution and simultaneously fed the fricken Horse tablet, as Liz did to Wendi over a week ago… Renae?"

Renae leans over her iPad, and Liz peers over her shoulder, worried. "I don't see how that would matter. Terrance, wait a sec. No, eh, all five were given a double dose via injection." Terrance says, "there's maybe our saving grace. Also, let us not forget that we humans look the same on the outside or at least similar, but on the inside, our brains, minds, internal systems, glands, and secretions of hormones are never the same. Even in virtual identical twins, there are differences so far, so good Wendi is better than all right. Stop the panic and negativity until we have reasons to act that way. Where's the optimism? All is well thus far. Yes, thanks, Renae, for your analysis and update on the test subjects. Well done, keep Liz and me up to speed…" He puts his hands together in a steeple form "ladies, let's remain optimistic that Wendi will be all right!" Terrance bows his head. Listen, it was about a week ago, and we were panicking over Wendi being able to fool her parents and Rico. The injection you gave her with the horse tablet worked magic for us. Wendi has been keeping Rico out of our hair, she's been a savior, and besides that, I heard from her the other day, and the girl is having a blast with the guy. Let's leave it alone until Wendi has one of the severe side effects that you both have been describing to me. Make sure that your Greg… uh, Scientist puts together more of that formula I gave him from Vadoma just in case everything goes to hell in a handbasket, and we can make sure that Wendi gets another dose. I have to go. I have a dinner gathering I can't miss. Let's reconvene on this tomorrow and see if either one of you can interview Wendi before then."

<u>Terrance had a big surprise for the sisters.</u>

Terrance had just concluded a meeting with his upper management staff in the medical department with interactions from other affiliates in Eastern Europe while his niece Sara was on a personal mission to check out what her sister Kamryn had been up to in her cell after she'd swapped her out. Terrance still didn't have confirmation from Sara that she'd attend the planned dinner gathering with her sisters and Jax. But Terrance knew it was a certainty. He couldn't remember the last time his purposeful manipulations had Failed 😒.

<u>Sara hadn't been back to her old prison cell in months. Lol, well, ever since she'd escaped.</u>

In another area in the Max security section, Sara was allowed back into her old cell, escorted by Shem, who stood guard at the steel door. Sara was looking ominously at a life she'd thought history, staring at what Kam had laid out on the table 'why am I surprised Kam went through all my portfolios and case files? Heck, I set her up to do so.' Then she spies an 8 X 11 composition notebook ah, not hers picks it up and reads what was written on the front cover 'I'm Kamryn Amaya, not Sara Amaya' she opens to the first page, headlined, and underlined with a Black magic marker 'Proof Vindication.' Sara flips through several pages and then comes to another headline 'Ame's drawings prove Sara was a killer at a young age.' Squeezes the notebook, scanning Kam's words and format, the bitch had the numbers of the paintings and descriptions of what they depicted. Ughhhh, stopped at the five sequenced paintings, graphically displaying her first murder of crybaby Ken, her brother. Banging on the cell door opening, it was Shon. "Hey girl, yuh got that dinner trip with your sisters and Uncle? I was told to ensure you're on time, so we have to roll...." Annoyed, she barked back non-aggressively, "Okay, let me grab a few things" she tucked the composition book under her arm and followed him down the hall.

50

Wendi dropped unconscious, entering an elevator.

Wendi is once again in a familiar setting lying on her back in her hospital suite across the hall from Brock and Lucie. She'd had an episode falling across the threshold of an elevator at NIA's outpatient hospital. Liz was listening via conference call with the medical staff, with Renae at her side debating Wendi's diagnosis. She finally had heard enough and interrupted their banter of frustration, "okay, let's stay with the facts and act accordingly. It's like Wendi suddenly is having fits of syncope. This is the third time she's fallen unconscious in the last few days. Can you give her another EEG let's get a third opinion! Our in-house Neurologists had come to the exact same conclusion umh since they're on my staff here hate to say it could be a case of collusion. Let's send Wendi's EEGs out to other renowned Neurologists. Send the first one taken when she arrived at NIA. I want to take this a step at a time. I want results ASAP... email me when this is done, and C.C. Renae." Liz pushes the end of the conference call and turns towards Renae, who nods at Liz. "Before we alert Terrance, we need to neutralize a lot of the data.... he will over-exaggerate this.... and blow it up out of proportion. The man freakin frets like a worrywart. L.." "Liz, there are two sides to that. Suppose he finds out we have been holding back on him, especially concerning his precious Wendi/Sunshine. In that case, our Asses will be in a world of hurt!" Liz stares up at the rotating cameras "sshhh, don't talk so loud, woman," whispers, "I'll take the heat, umh responsibility. Here's what we need to do go back in the archives. I also want to include all her earlier records from her childhood. I want every EEG ever taken of Wendi, starting from the anomaly that occurred at the San Francisco Zoo when she nearly drowned and when Sunshine arrived on the scene, invading Wendi's brain as a little girl. We can't leave a stone unspun."

They walk together towards the cafeteria to get some breakfast finding a table off in a corner with a selection of pastries and fruit Liz was putting some Vanilla creamer into her steaming coffee with her left hand stirring with her right, whispering anxiously. "We are aware of the stark contrasts between Wendi's EEG when she's in control of her brain... and Sunshine's EEG when she is controlling her mind and body. It's like night and day, right? Even a layman could see the difference. All they would have to do is look at the left and right hemispheres on the brain scans. Sunshine is left-brained, aka... methodical and analytical. In general, the left hemisphere or side of the brain is responsible for language and speech. Because of this, it has been referred to as the Dominant hemisphere. Wendi is right-brained, aah more creative, and artistic, their opposites."

Renae chomps down on her Egg sandwich, "true same as in her limbic system, her amygdala, which regulates emotions, is opposite when Sunshine is in control of her personality. In the brain scans, we can see a stark difference between Wendi and Sunshine. When stimulated by showing pictures of war or natural disasters, Wendi displays empathy, quite the opposite of Sunshine, who shows extremely aggressive behaviors when watching violence or movie scenes of battles. The disparity is as obvious as black and white, with her brain flashing Neurons & Synapses in nearly exact patterns and the same sequences. We can't deny it, yes a glaring difference indeed, Liz...." "I'm a believer like you. With her brain scans, we can determine who is in charge of her human shell. Hey, ush, maybe better than fingerprints. <u>No one's brain waves are ever identical or matching. Neurologists commonly refer to this phenomena as Brainprints!</u>"

After a bathroom run, Liz, still engrossed in their discovery, see's Renae on her phone sitting at their table "you know, girl, we are supposed to lock those in our lockers while in custody areas....." They Smiled, for this was one of the many rules that countless employees didn't follow. Liz stared at her iPad screen. "X-rays, MRIs, and EEGs are objective views... and are accurate. We can see the subtle nuances ush changes in her past exams. If you take Wendi's exam yesterday and compare it to when her personality was Sunshine's 37 days ago..." "Liz, I was there when you showed our head of Neurology the scans when you Blacked out the names on both the scanned charts of Wendi and Sunshine and asked her if she saw any similarities what were her precise words? 'These brain scans are like comparing Salt and Pepper' docile and empathetic versus aggressive and apathetic." Liz slams down the empty cup of coffee "yeah, I screwed up. It's frightening, and we can be sure that the double dose of our Psychotherapy drug was the cause. The character we have known as Wendi or Sunshine is now an Alien, uah, entirely a different creature! She's no longer Wendi or Sunshine. Who the hell is she?"

"What are you trying to say?..." blinks Renae. "I think it's rather plain and simple. Uh, I just said it, ahh Rico and her parents, um, all of us maybe are in the process of getting to know the 3rd identity in Wendi's brain, one that can access the traits and feelings of Wendi's loving nature at the same time lurking on the other side within striking zones is Sunshine's hard-ass attitude cut and dry and ruthless self unh its mindboggling! As I said, we need to send photocopies of her brain scans across the globe. We need to...." "Enough, okay, I get it. The more eyes and analysis, the better, but maybe this is a waste of time, at least to me, sweet little 5' 1" Wendi is back; I was joking with her before the tests yesterday. It was the same girl we were laughing at about things that had happened long ago. She's got me fooled. That's all that I'm saying! But yes, we'd better be safe than grilled by Terrance. You can count on me. I'll get right on it this morning, Liz!"

<u>Twenty-five minutes later, at the inmate hospital, Renae, Kamryn, and Sonja.</u>

Liz went one way and Renae quickly the other, checked her phone she'd be late. Kamryn was due to nurse.... feed her tiny baby Sonja; Kamryn's face lit up when she held and nurtured her baby. Renae had three nurses around the clock, keeping an eye on the baby. Renae knew she had to figure out a way to get Sonja out of NIA. But since her fiasco at the San Francisco airport, causing Terrance's wrath and raising his ire toward her.... she was being scrutinized like she wasn't to be trusted. She sneered, 'ole Terrance and NIA have another thing coming, I'll snatch up his offspring, and he'd be at my beckoning call. Renae had so many plans but felt confused about which way to move. So she decided to hunker down and hold her cards till she could formulate a proper plan. She jumps off the Golf cart, seeing Kamryn waiting.

"Renae, is it true? I can't stop thinking about what you said to me. I have been avoiding Liz like the plague...." "Yes honey, it's true, all true, and don't you worry, you're pretty head... the nurses watching Sonja will stay quiet; thus far, not a word has been spread about your baby." "What about Doctor Wei, and how about?..." "Sshhh, Rocky has handled that!" "Why hasn't he come to see me? It's been over a week?" "He and I spoke only this morning, Kam. He believes that it's best that we keep your baby safe and not let anyone know of Sonja!" "What, Renae, didn't Rocky tell Brock about his baby? I don't like this. It scares me. I want to meet with Brock and....." "No, Kam, at the risk of my life and my daughter Candice who's in College in Colorado and has been threatened by your uncle, I'm dead serious. We must keep this on the down low!" Renae clutched Kam's shoulder and said, "there are cameras everywhere. Let's enter the stairwell. I have to show you something, and then you'll understand why the story I've embellished to Liz about you having a miscarriage has to be believed and not countered. It's life or death for your baby... I threatened Doctor Wei explaining to her that if she wanted to keep her job here, she'd better play ball with me! Doctor Wei had a face-to-face with Liz and told her about your miscarriage, and believe it or not... Doctor Wei said that Liz had grinned and laughed and was heard singing a tune, walking away..." They close the steel door looking up flights of stairs, "here, Kam, you need to see this; Rocky printed this out from NIA's private encrypted server, it's amazing... check the time stamp on the missive, Terrance somehow knew the name of your baby, before she was born. Before you mentioned her name to me or even thought of the name Sonja!" "Wow, that's impossible. I hadn't an idea of what I'd call my daughter until after she was born...." Kamryn read the subject matter in an email from a person named 'Vadoma' to Uncle Terrance…'Sonja is the Devil incarnate; you must kill the child! 🌐'

<u>**Terrance was strangely energized and apprehensively anxious, and equally optimistic.**</u>

He sat on his tiled seat, the multiple sprayers flushing his skin with cleansing stings. He reduced the intensity and let the shower steam up. Terrance did much thinking and analyzing in water. If it wasn't a hot tub or swimming pool, it was in his two-person shower. He was in his Presidential Suite at NIA and had terrific plans for the evening… He'd have his three nieces together for dinner tonight. He reflected back as the heated mist clouded the glass enclosure. 'Surprised that he'd not had a heart attack traversing what he'd experienced in only the last few months.' Where'd it all start? Oh, yea… that's right when NIA's stock price went into the toilet when pressure surely didn't make diamonds. He'd had to put off the secondary offering and slow down his expansion of NIA hospitals in Europe.

The Doctor Garza debacle and the wrongful death litigation for correction officer Bruce Glades, his company being investigated by the Feds. He'd dealt with too many subpoenas and warrants to count. On top of that, his former employee, Doctor Garza, was spying on NIA, whom he had brutally arrested for stealing drugs from his in-house pharmacy, which was now being temporarily regulated by Rico's squad of delinquents.

He took a sponge and wiped his face. Then my niece Kamryn had proven to him she'd been swapped out by Sara, who subsequently murdered another correction officer at NIA… Carl Sparks, but wait, let's not forget the 31% drop in NIA's stock when the allegations of sexual assault hit the newswires... when Carl was charged with sexually assaulting Sara. She, in cold blood, kills Carl and his lovely wife, Bianca. If that weren't enough, the news then hit me like a sledgehammer, with the FBI certain that she'd used the same poison that she'd used on her killing spree. Killing the fricken attorney... I had the New York Times investigative reporter up my ass, Rico Captor, and his sidekick Doctor Shanon Roble wanted DNA and to interview Sara, who wasn't on site... Then I discover that one of my employees, Renae... is deep in cahoots with Sara and has colluded with her and against NIA. The shit list goes on and on...

<u>Vadoma, my family's Gypsy Mystic... informed me months ago that my niece Valerie Amaya was alive and that I'd hook up with her when I cut the tape for my first expansion of NIA in England! That wasn't so bad, but when she told me that Sara was a girl scout angel compared to Valerie, meaning she put the word KILL in Killer. Had triple the slayings of my dear psychopath niece Sara.</u> Ugh... My net worth has tumbled along with the stock price of NIA from a high of $277.11 to just this morning $77.57 since the onslaught of terminal news hit the news wire. An ole CNBC Analyst, Jim Cramer, took the proverbial Stake and hammered it in my chest with his annoying repetitive words Sell... SELL, sell... Let's not forget the pressure Rico Captor constantly leveraged on my head... wanting to take Wendi from NIA. My worldly investors and associates were uptight, revolting against me at every turn, wanting to Oust me as the CEO of NIA. Terrance growled then cackled, and heck, 'that's not all the bad shit that hit the fan in the last months, just the tip of icebergs.'

Terrance stood up, turned the heat down on his shower nozzles, and decided he'd better shave; his nubs were jutting out too far... He then itched a thought that he couldn't work around in his mind. Vadoma had called him a few weeks ago and said it was mandatory that they get together... Demanded to see him. He had Jacob pick her up. She'd brought her fricken family with her… the news she'd told him. Had miffed him with an odd and unsettling proclamation concerning the past visit by Rico with Wendi Feral. But Vadoma seemed off base on that prediction. Then she'd mentioned this hateful evil baby named Sonja… Wtf, Sonja? Where the hell did Vadoma come up with that? Heck, the old woman is ancient and had just turned 101 years old. Who's to say dementia hasn't set in? His nieces couldn't get pregnant as far as he was told they'd had hysterectomies to prevent spreading their demented bloodline. But he'd recently visited the three of them, and… he stared down at his belly. 'I'm more pregnant than either of the three… lol. He and his family believed… all that Vadoma would profess. Vadoma came from a long line of Seers and in Terrance's history with the woman, Vadoma had never misled him… ugh hadn't professed anything that hadn't come to fruition! The elder woman was a Seer with paranormal skills, a Clairvoyant, but hey, even Nostradamus screwed up 🌑… Terrance steps out of his shower enclosure feeling as if leaving a Confessional booth, invigorated and ready to Start A-new!

<u>Terrance meets with Sara to preplan dinner topics.</u>

Terrance texts Sara, 'where you at?' she texts back….'check out your cameras… heading to your place now, seeya soon 🌑!' Instead of him smiling, he's cautiously pessimistic because, for the first time, his nieces will be together with him since pre-puberty two of the three are confirmed, psychopaths. He had always been confused with sweet apprehensive Kauryn; how'd she come through the bloodline unscathed? He'd put off the catered dinner for 45 min. to finish up with Liz and Renae. The conference with his medical board of directors lasted longer than he'd expected.

Terrance… wanted to have time to engage in a pre-dinner meeting with Sara, now happy as he saw her exit the elevator down the hall. He greets her while Sara stares up into his eyes… then turns and stops, "hey, Uncle." She puts out her right hand grasping his they walk to his luxurious suite without speaking. "Would you like a drink before your sisters and Jax arrive?" "No, just a bottle of water will do, thanks, unh. I hope you do understand that Kam and I will never see eye to eye, and ain't no way we will ever be close. It's an impossibility she and I are complete opposites that don't attract like... fire and ice or, better, Acid vs. Alkaline heck, we could come up with a dozen or more different parallels, Uncle!"

Terrance grabs her favorite mineral water Perrier from France. He ambles back to his wet bar, pouring a stiff Club Soda and Tahoe Blue Vodka, mulling over her comparisons. "Yes, so true, but hey, your 37 years old twin blonde beauties with the same figures. There's a blend to be found, a combination, if you will... Sugar and Salt, like call you two Salty Taffy." lol laughing, she joins in, "ugh, not bad, Uncle...." He "I'm counting on you, Sara, to make the first 2nd and 3rd attempts at reconciliation. After all, we know you stuck her ass here at NIA, put her in your freakin prison cell, and put her through almost mortal hell! She's still kinda living in the same world you deposited her in... dammit, niece. Kam wants out of here like yesterday, and you were there and heard what Rico wants...." "Oh sure, you're correct. I swapped places with dear perfect sweet, unassuming sickening sister Kamryn tried to steal her Fiancé Brock Dame, who arrested me with his skank, FBI partner Lucie Link. Then I failed horribly at killing the bastard who has more lives than a rabid Cat; look... Uncle. I was living in Kam's house, opened up Kam's Salon under her name, threatened her, drugged her, shaved her body bald, and restrained her in a wheelchair hell. What's the fkn problem? If you were her, wouldn't you want to be friends?" Sara jumped up, slapping her thighs and howling hysterically. He just scowled annoyingly, with no humor in his mind.

By the time she was riotously on her knees laughing at her own words, Sara was drooling, hacking, trying to catch her breath, muttering, "ain't that a song 'Why can't we be Friends' rolling on the couch "unh I could be a comedian...." Coughing, spitting, leaving some last giggles. Then she looked over at the now somber Terrance, who said nothing... yet she had never seen the expression he conveyed toward her. Ughhhh, angst sliced and molded over his features. Terrance didn't laugh nor even smile while watching his demented niece. She jumped up off the couch and said, "what, that wasn't fkn funny," lol, tweaking her face in a ghoulish stare and sticking her tongue out. Terrance choked on his own saliva, trying to hold back laughter, and losing... splashes some of his drink on his Armani Suite. "Aah, alright shit, I guess after that monologue, I get your point. It will be futile trying to reconcile you both... okay." He coughed, "with all that being said, try to be pleasant and non-combative, even friendly... for me. I know you don't give a Rat's ass...." "No, that's where everyone is wrong, the Scientists, all the wannabe psyches. I've had hundreds of sit-downs and laydowns with these supposedly educated fools. They don't get it and never will. None are close to my level of intellect, and no, I'm not a Narcissist!"

He waited for her to continue she didn't, so he prompted her raising his palms up "ok, I'll bite. What are the professionals missing?" "Uncle, I could enter this subject matter ahh topic and still be just getting warmed up in the first hour. If you truly want to hear my points of view, let's schedule a day for us. Uh, suffice it to say that all, ughhhh, a super quick synopsis... sociopaths/psychopaths are not made from the same cloth as your so-called professionals have believed for centuries. It's always about clinically categorizing, labeling stereotyping patients into their fragmented charts, graphs, and algorithms. For these so-entitled Doctors, it is essential to take their patient's interviews and counseling sessions and isolate them into a type of mental disorder. It's all about the diagnosis. Yeah, in my way of thinking, it's the doctors that are mentally deficient." Terrance slyly spied his Grandfather clock across the room. In less than 13 minutes, the rest of the dinner party would start arriving, continuing to listen to her ramble on aimlessly.

"Uncle, are you paying attention here? I've read the bogus diagnosis I'm 'delusionally paranoid Bi-Polar hyperactive, a sociopath... psychopath, hyper, manic-anxiety-laden... attention deficit ah Autism... schizophrenic oh, that's right, don't use that word schizophrenia. Nope, it must be politically correct. Now it's, um, 'Dissociative Identity Disorder' there are literally dozens of acronyms describing mental maladies the professional Quacks must believe this falsehood... in their cluttered and disheveled minds, for it, all must compute. Yeah, sure, it's not a fricken broken arm... Everyone ah patient falls into a category that's so wrong on so many levels. Um, isolate my illness with subjective nonsense, Uncle. The stigmas projected upon typical patients are enormously harmful then comes loads of prescriptions from the mighty capitalistic business of Pharmaceuticals. Oh, she's a 'manic depressant' let's look at the chart. What drugs can I give her? Umh, which prescriptions would benefit her the best and give me the most kickbacks... lol." Terrance nodded, thinking his niece wasn't lying. She was on one of her patented rants.

"If you're not Crazy when you visit one of these Shrinks, your nutty as a fruitcake by the time you're into the first trimester of their drug regimen, yah no, Uncle. Many times these drugs are dispensed because of the incentives parlayed by the drug manufacturers themselves. It's total bullshit; I have lived around schizophrenics side by side here at your NIA. We're not like, uhm, none of us are the same, not 2 Peas in a pod. Certain similarities exist. It's not like a Smallpox virus. Get the anti-virus shot; Walla, your cured or exempt from the virus, nope. You see, we're all treated the same, but none of us is the same inside; no, so drug us into Zombie land. Oh, Lookie there, Sara is doing the Thorazine shuffle. She's getting better. The treatment is working. She's a docile wart on a Hog. Good job, Doctor!"

"What wart on a Hog, Sara shit, come on, I get it and agree it's all about money...." She was up now, pouring a stiff drink into a cocktail glass. "Don't be naive, Terrance. Professionals can manufacture plastic hearts, knees, and robotic artificial limbs... organ transplants, Uncle. Try that with the human brain. Believe me, Frankenstein physicians have been trying in basements and dungeons all over this planet for centuries experimenting on human casualties. Have they figured out how to transplant a human brain yet? Duh!" We clinked glasses and took a sip, and no arguments could be found. My niece was correct. "Now, how do you want me to handle this Kamryn situation? I'm all ears. By the way, for the record, you're wrong to assume I don't love Kamryn, and heck, I just met Valerie. The jury is out on that one, but despite what you or the good doctors believe, it would bother me some if she no longer lived. Put it this way. If you lined up two guilty parties that needed to be executed, one was Kam, the other Renae. I'd kill Renae first, see, so I care more than you think!" cackling.

Terrance only shook his head, figuring they now had seven minutes to game plan the dinner gathering... and objectives. "Sara, I have to have your talent on our team. You're a once-in-a-generation talent, a Savant when it comes to multiple facets, including disguises, and you are a supreme makeup artist. Your unrivaled 'Anne' she's an artist of Hollywood material. Your other entities 'Al' is an unmatched ventriloquist. His abilities are remarkable; being able to throw his voice and his intonations and altering octaves, he can replicate even quirky accents... Al is simply a must to work for us here at NIA. We have so many noteworthy goals, and lastly, 'Donny,' ugh," Terrance grins on, "I still haven't figured that dude out," snickering.

She pushes him playfully "oh, Don or Donny is my sensual lover, Uncle, a dream guy. He knows just where to touch, squeeze, and bite me. He's awesome. He also does double duty. He's Anne's secretary. Oh yeah, he's a dreamboat, subservient in the methods that please me... and is like a symphony instructor. Donny works in Sara's orchestra, so that's about it," she giggles. "Yep, ah, there's so much more to me, uncle... and Donny knows my ins and outs.

They swivel their eyes to the monitors watching Jax, Valerie, and Kamryn walk up the hall. He says, "game time, let's make this transition. Sara, come on, your slick enough to reign in your sister Kam. I'm counting on you, niece!" "Okay, Uncle damn okay enough."

<u>Sara opens the door of Terrance's suite to greet Jax and her sisters for a dinner party lol.</u>

Sara opens the door like the hostess of the mostess, smiling, "hello there, Mr. Jax Foal," a sideways impromptu embrace. "Hey there, sister Valerie, good evening,.... ok hi there, my special twin, I'm sure happy that you could all make it, and you're okay. Kam, I was worried about you when you had that episode the other day. Glad it was only Diabetes...."

Kamryn frowns, backing quickly up, in shock, not wanting to put on a show.... In a low monotone and in control of her temper. "I will make my way back to my room. I no longer have an appetite. You fricken freak, you should be caged in a zoo. You're not supposed to be here. This is a setup, and Oh.... so wrong Wtf I will not...."

Terrance was in her face in a split second, taking her by the arm "come on in, relax; I'll get you a drink, please, for me, if not for anyone else. Please, Kam, give this a chance...." Kam tries to jerk free. "Please leave me alone; you lied to me! I would never have come here if the freak was going to be here. I made that clear to you, Uncle. That bitch drugged me, violated my body, stripped me naked, and shaved me bald. She stole my freedom and left me here in her place! I believe proof will come out that she tried to kill my fiancé Brock Dame. I used to defend her and didn't miss a single day of her 11-month trial. I no longer believe she's innocent of all those murders. In my mind, she's as guilty as Sin! There isn't anyone that's eviler than Sara. Now get out of my way. I don't want to spend another fricken second here! I want out of NIA tonight, Terrance!"

Valerie reaches over and takes Kamryn's hand. "Please, honey, please just sit next to Jax and me. Let's try and at least enjoy dinner, okay, Kammy?" "No..." "Terrance whispers in her ear, dragging her close "you listen here, young lady, you're going to get through this... Sara wasn't going to show up. I didn't lie to you. She just popped up here at my door. Kamryn, if you want out of NIA so badly, then you must stay here tonight through dinner. Then I promise we will devise a plan to get you back to your life on the streets... okay? Now please do this...." Kam bounced from him, displaying squinted eyes, a solid scowl, with her nose curling up, saying zilch ducks past Sara, fantasizing she had a handy dagger that she could impale the witch with!

Sara caught Terrance's expression of approval; thus far, she was handling the intense first moments rather coolly. With a blink, they made their way to the living room for some pre-dinner articulations. Kam leans on the bar looking away, seething. Jax and Valerie were still hyped about jumping jumbo dirt mounds in the mud and pouring rain. Kam gulps a shot of Crown Royal and pours another "oh crap, do you remember almost tipping over? We were titter tottering my butt left the seat so many times...." "We nearly went nose first cartwheeling shit. I never knew four-wheeling was so much fun!" Val's hoarse voice clearly needed a drink. Jax was beaming "yeah, the Hummer took us for one of these Monster Truck rides. Hey, Val, grab me a beer!"

At the door was Terrance's staff. His Butler and servers, and bartender sauntered into the room. Ready at their beckoning call. The five of them sat down, four of whom were finished. Kam was furious, about to bolt. Ugh, even for her Uncle, she didn't believe she could remain in the room with her wicked sinister twin. She knew her uncle loved her, but that wasn't enough for him. Always for Terrance, what came first wasn't his family. No, what was most important… first and foremost in his heart and mind, was and always would be NIA…

Weighing heaviest on her soul and heart was her child, daughter Sonja. She had to get her baby out of this hellhole safely. The information that Rocky was able to glean from the encrypted NIA server was of utmost concern and worry. It was an obscure email with her name in the subject line. Rocky had run a search with 'Kam' and Kamryn in the proprietary network server and found an email in Terrance's semi-private inbox. She had read the printed-out email that Renae handed her, and then Renae took it back and shredded it. 'Terrance, I've tried many times to reach you. It's imperative that we get together. I hate to be dramatic, but it's a life-or-death matter. A baby is coming into this world from Hades. Her name is Sonja. We must eradicate this child at all costs. Please contact me at once. Vadoma… Please, Terrance, I am willing to visit you at NIA if you can't make it to my San Francisco business.'

Kamryn remembered her skin crawling with tingles. How did this Vadoma know her baby's name before she had decided to name her Sonja? Beyond that, though, where'd the name come from? It was spontaneous and natural. The baby's name popped up the second she popped out! Kamryn had to play it cool, contemplating how she would gauge her next moves. Renae had said it was impossible to get Sonja out of NIA unless she left in one of the VIP's vehicles. That meant there were only three people who could get her child out of

NIA, and they were Jax Foal, Terrance, or Doctor Liz Houcks, who weren't inspected at the exit gates of the NIA facilities.

Back to the current quandary, should she leave this dinner party, for she was scammed by Terrance and Sara? At least, this was her assumption. But if she did leave, how would that affect her getting a gate pass out of this hellhole and back to her life… where she was exceedingly happy. How to get on the outside of NIA was her dilemma. Therefore she coolly decided to suffer through this necessity, not look at the slimy Lizard. They were seated in luxurious reclining rocking chairs facing one another. An odd sitting arrangement, thought Kam. Then she peered around at the long spectacular, hardwood dining room table. Then conceded an excellent choice of furniture, for she had her own space. In front of each of them was a wooden deluxe TV tray unit custom made, no doubt… with drink holder compartments. They were waited on like royalty, of course, by NIA standards. That's precisely what they were and are.

Jax was usually not a talkative individual. A man who listens and observes, although he went on a tirade about when he let Valerie drive the Hummer. "Valerie missed 3rd gear, and that's when the Hummer rolled up and over like a crooked somersault and back up on the four wheels." He described grinning wildly; she remembered the moment when the three of them fist-bumped. He said, "man, oh man, Terrance, you'd need earplugs. The girls were screaming from the bottom of their lungs, and I thought they would pee all over my leather seats! Their red and pink puffy cheeks looked like they'd bust." He wasn't exaggerating; I still felt the energetic fun and action while he replayed some of the maddling jumps and our ride.

"Whoa, wow, it seems that Uncle Terrance and I surely missed out on some awesome fun 4-wheeling. I wanna go next time," teases Sara with a twinkle in her eye directed at Kam. "Tell me, Jax. I wasn't aware we had a 4-wheel Monster Truck course… where?" Jax looked awkwardly at Terrance "well, boss, I kinda tore up the Moto Cross track, our training course for dirt bikes, Quads, no worries though, when the weather clears, I'll get the crew out there with the Bobcats.... Backhoes and Bulldozers, I'll make the track better than new. It was a blast, however, listening to your nieces scream bloody murder!"

"Since Sara and I were into more mundane tasks, perhaps you could show us this 4-wheel drive um excursion." Terrance points to a grey and brown Tablet. Jax was busy chewing voraciously on a jumbo Shrimp dipped in spicy cocktail sauce with a squirt of Lemon and a dab of Horsey Radish. "For sure, boss. Why didn't I think about that? We have onboard cameras, and maybe the surveillance cameras around the training facility got some good video even through the squall." He was smirking, holding up another Shrimp "after I have a few more of these. Ahh, yum, you sure know how to eat up here. It's rare I'm invited up to the penthouse Terrance." Smiles all around, except for Kam.

Terrance, amused, running his tongue over his front teeth, "we will have to change that, Jax, most definitely. I know it's always business with us. By the way, you look really suave nice suit, guy!..." "Thanks, boss, saw one like it from an old wanted poster from the Mob days 'Pretty boy Floyd' um," the girls beat him to the punch. Openly laughing loudly, Sara exclaims, nearly choking, "you ain't no pretty boy, Jax" more laughter as Jax bent his head down and then found Val's eyes searching for his.

After the appetizers were devoured, Jax went through the security codes and the closed-circuit network locating the cameras that projected over the dirt racetrack. Then, he pulled the internal videos from the Hummer, which were uploaded onto his VPN and projected on an 8-foot screen in front of the group. He backed up the recording, and there was the Hummer with oversized tires, a rollbar, and a super lift kit. He pushed enter on the keyboard. When the Hummer was at the starting line, the rain sprayed at angles. The halides from the floodlights showed bright mud already caked and kicked up on the running boards. He turned and looked at them. With open amusement nodded "get ready for a replay, girls…." he clicked play. "I'll play the outside view first, then the onboard cameras!"

Throughout the playing of the videos, the atmosphere and ambiance rotated into complete uproarious hilarity, smiles, cursing, shrieks, and shouts OmGod's they were howling, "did you see that?" aah Val yells. "We could be on one of those Bigfoot shows…." "Shit, look at Val. She's crawling over Jax, falling squealing fun fun stuff," yelps Kam. The Hummer stops momentarily, and we watch the inside cameras "that's when I took over driving howls," Val. "Oh fk," Terrance was slapping the inside of his thigh, freaking delighted even Sara let loose with a howl. It was like the three riders relived these memories in real time and enjoyed it even more since they were safe and warm, sipping their totties. A cozy fire was blasting through a log of Oak. No doubt, as they watched the replay of the ride only an hour before, it was major league hilarious, fun stuff to the max. Who knew you could have such a blast in the mud… loving the flinging dirt and the 4-wheeling. Terrance and Sara's eyes were wide open, aligning with their mouths… relating vicariously through the rider's wild expressions. It was sure a hit and just what this gathering needed to break the mounting tensions.

Terrance's "Wait staff" had texted him that the main entrees were ready a few minutes after the mud fest replayed. He said with a sigh, "wow, how do yah follow that up? All right, dinner is ready. Please join me at the table." What was weird to all was that the Cherry hardwood table had placards with names for seating like a conference meeting. At each head of the table were the men. On Jax's left was Valerie to Terrance's left, arranged strangely were the chairs for Kamryn and Sara. Kam thought all other chairs were removed, odd and uncomfortable, 'uh, like being forced to eat Green Peas as a child!'

Everyone took their seats except Kam, who was miffed that this arrangement wasn't respectful of her feelings nor warranted. The last person she wanted next to her was her evil twin. "So, whose wise-ass idea was this?" No longer a shy, timid lady after the debacles inside of NIA. Sara instantly threw her hand up high and wiggled her fingers "the idea was all mine, sister dear. Even Uncle didn't know about it; just a gesture on my behalf to try and mend a few of our broken feathers, unh, broken-winged relationship. I'm sorry if I inadvertently offended you!" A silence fell over the group... A 'Sonata by Pavarotti,' 'Ave Maria, ' playing over the surround sound speakers, no one uttered a syllable.

Sara then slowly stood up, turning her hands on her hips. Kam snatches up her chair and proceeds around the table, now next to Val. No worries, yet Terrance caught the vibes seeing Kam clutch her purse, knowing his niece was about to scamper away. "Kam, please sit down, okay? This is a family dinner, my fine nieces all in one place together again. Please, let's make peace for just this evening!" "Kammy, put your purse back by your chair and join us" she frowned at Val but did so and hung her purse on the high back chair. She angrily wrung her hands nervously "ok, I'm sorry that was rude of me, unh, maybe!" Jax responded, "well... if that's all settled, I'm starving. Give me a shovel" the rest of them accepted his peace offering. For now, crisis management accentuated just maybe end the end a positive outcome that most wished for.

The delicious cuisine of Mediterranean dishes kept mouths moving, tongues swishing, licking lips yum, and no desire to waste time when your largest orifice was being satiated. Aah, the satisfied clanking of wine glasses with a one-barreled beer bottle Jax's. Delicious food.... very seldom did any of the five even make eye contact other to telepathically say, "this is fanfantastic hey, you're going to leave me some of that…." The bowls on the table were quickly losing their contents as arms reached out for thirds.

Nearer to the conclusion than the beginning, Terrance wiped his jaw "we'll have after-dinner drinks and dessert in the library, umh, den. I have a few announcements to make and discuss with you all. I look forward to your interactions. Enjoy Salute." Wine glasses raised, tapping Jax's beer mug. "Oh, save some room for dessert will enjoy a superb blend of pastries, German Chocolate cake, and varieties of Cheesecake and my fav. Carrot Cake ala mode."

Only Jax replied, "heck, I'm already stuffed. This is the best…." Terrance interrupts, "after dinner drinks, we'll let our stomachs rest," contentedness table-wide. A while later, they retired to the library, more of an intimate, cozy space furnished with old English-styled woodwork, shelves of books like in a library to the ceiling, and even an old-school rolling ladder. The mood was reserved, sitting in a large encompassing circle with reading lamps and small tables were the five of them. A bartender stood accommodatingly by the wet bar area, arranging shot glasses and some fine Port wine. Other liquors were in purview, like the books they were climbing the walls, so many bottles of alcohol umh uncountable. In a Humidor where some of the world's finest cigars were…. Terrance had selected one of his favorites and took a toke.

He stood "all right, folks. I hope we can convince Sara to indulge us… come on, Sara, it will be fun. You'll enjoy it too; let Al out to give us a short performance; niece, show us some of that talent that's hidden within ventriloquism. It's such a rare talent; please come on now, Sara… what's it going to hurt?" Sara didn't answer him, but his Hawkish eyes never left her face. Finally, she got up with two fingers wiggling, miming them at Terrance, beckoning him to come here and follow her for a private talk.

Terrance follows her out of the library. Val asked inquisitively, "hey, what's going on? No private conversations. I thought we were

Sara takes his hand abruptly.... "hey, by the way, I might be off base. Tag me out if Jax and sis Val don't seem to have the hots for each other I mean, ogles grins some pandering touchy feelie stuff, hah...." "I don't think so, Sara, Jax isn't a good-looking man, and your sister is the bomb. He's one big cut-up scar and missing pieces of his body, I really think...." "Terrance, um, uncle, you men just don't get it at times. I think you believe there are standards or rules for attraction. Sure, for both sexes, it's the look that draws the first impression, but what flows the magic is endorphins aligned with enhancing pheromones. It's always about what's under the skin. First, I'm telling you I'm uncomfortable letting Al out...." "Hey, you two do you need some help out there?" asks Val.

Sara ignores Val's question and continues, "Uncle will discuss my philosophy about attractions in budding relationships later. Listen, I'm a bit uncomfortable haven't practiced Al in months. I've stifled away Ventriloquistic acts and literally have shunned that form of my inner-selves, I think..." He gently grabs her shoulder and winks with his nose snarled up "please, we all know you called Liz pretending to be me ugh.... An excellent rendition of me.... and hey, how about the attorney you killed? How'd you get him to meet you, girl? Don't play flim games with me," he chuckled. She stuck her tongue out, licking her upper lip "okay, I'm busted, Uncle. You win; oh, by the way, umh..... Do you ever lose?" He smiled wide ass "just let it flow; roll with it, Sara. You're a chip off of Papa's back. You're a show-stopper, Star. Come on..." smiling, and they drop back down into the sunken library. Hearing first, then saw rain splatter against the huge bay windows and the blazing fire in an uproar keeping the area comfy.

the night," looking at Terrance. "I'm as intrigued to hear your announcements as everyone else is. I'm sure that's the real motivation for why we're all here together." Sara bows her head toward the group and excuses herself quickly. "I'll be back.... I need to warm up my vocal cords." Stepping out of sight and going to the nearest restroom to blow her nose of phlegm and hack and clear her throat. She looked for and found some Hydrogen Peroxide mixed some in a small cup of water, then gargled. This was the habit taught to her by Papa, her loving Grandfather who was a World-renowned showman unk ventriloquist. Papa traveled overseas and was invited to Buckingham Palace. He was the ultimate showstopper, but where he made his fortune was on the Las Vegas strip. His name was on the Billboards lit up in the sky. He'd perform at Caesars Casino and the Wynn casino, and there wasn't a top-notch casino that he didn't headline in Vegas. He was there at the top. He was a headliner and performed all over the planet. You could name the most prominent venues, and Grand-Pa had been there. He dazzled hundreds of thousands and had taught the genetically gifted Al all he knew when it came to the art of throwing your voice, a skill 95% of ventriloquists can't achieve. Al was the best Papa had said, and they even did shows together a few times in Vegas. Papa had said to Al that he had the skills to supersede him.

Papa, she remembered, took her in after she killed her brother. Although he nor anyone at the time knew it, Sara drowned the brat. Papa had said that he believed she, ugh, Al, could be a grade better than him with practice. I loved papa, but one day, he forced me to have to Kill him too. That was a genuine pity. Um, that's the only murder I think might bother me a tiny bit. I think I miss him. He loved me with all his heart. I was the most special of his grandchildren. He would always compliment me. Oh well, life doesn't go on sometimes.

Sara took some deep breaths and did some stretches. She had pulled her blonde hair back into a black net.... taken some black mascara, outlined her eyebrows, took a pair of brown contacts out *of her bitty purse, and put them in. Next, she attached his uh… Al's form-fitting mustache, rechecking herself in the mirror. I'm as ready as I'll ever be she pranced out and made her way down the three stairs into the library where the conversation and mood had eased, going mute once she raised her arms to get their attention.*

<u>Al… the Master Ventriloquist bowed his head…</u> 🐢

Terrance was clinking glasses with Jax and saw Sara/Al approaching the library's steps, standing, rolling his hands "and now, ladies and gentlemen, it gives me great distinct pleasure to introduce to you the one and only Ventriloquist extraordinaire Mr. Al Amaya!" Sara bowed, then pretended to curtsy… their three heads, in unison, turned swiftly to where Sara had entered the sunken room. The sound of a Train, ahh, I mean a real train chugging down the track right towards them, then a train whistle. The four were totally shocked, then no sound.

Next, Sara leaped down the three steps and stood in between the four of them. On her left were Val and Jax. To the right, Kam and Terrance. They had moved the coffee table from in front of them. Sara had their attention as they were sitting on the edges of their seats. "Okay, everyone, close your eyes, no peaking," a very faint buzzing sound is heard in the air, coming closer and closer. Al attacked Jax right behind his left mangled ear. The sound of a huge Bumblebee… he wildly jumped, slapping at the Bee. All laughed, and Jax said, "oh shit, that felt real" the group now sat tense. They collectively were trying to catch Sara's lips moving and wondering whom she'd pick on next and what she would do next.

Sara/Al was tutored by Papa and practiced throwing her voice as a child for years. Then locked in confinement in prison, she refined and upped her game. Al was a savant-like genius. Al then stares at Kamryn, a 'Roar of a Lion,' a fierce growling rumble. Valerie leaps out of her chair, tumbling on the floor, kicking, and screaming, "Oh Fk!" Proving that Al could look at a person and throw his voice at another behind his back, pausing while Val and Kam were laughing hysterically, if not nervously, a culpable fear of the unknown grasped the group Jax was cleaning up the spilled Gin and Tonic that Val had toppled over.

It wasn't hard to calculate that Sara had gone after Jax and Val leaving only her and Uncle. Kamryn was on point, thinking she had to be next. So far, a Railroad train... a Bumble Bee now a Lion's roar scared Valerie. *Using Terrance's voice,* Al says, "all right folks, for this part of the show, will you please set your drinks down? We wouldn't want to stain your fine duds!" Strangely the group stared at Terrance, not Sara... Their mouths open in Awe and disbelief at the flawless delivery. Terrance stood clapping. "I had to check my lips, making sure it wasn't me talking," laughs fill the room. Still, Kam was uneasy.

Terrance had planned this entertainment earlier and had inherited all of Papa's performance props from Vegas after he was poisoned and died, another unsolved murder. Papa's famous props had been in a storage room down below in the basement of one of his properties in Pacific Heights, San Francisco. He'd shuffled through the hordes of props and belongings of Papa. He'd found two puppets, a boy, and a girl, with large round heads. The girl had long Blonde pigtails like Sara and Kam used to wear as children. The puppet's eyes and brows mouths would move, engineered by the hand that held them. The boy was dark-haired with the same facial features moving. Terrance had them hidden for now!

They obeyed and placed their glasses on solid foundations. Al stood sideways to them and finished Terrance's voiceover. Kam shook her noggin and started to clap, then they all did, joining Terrance, just truly astonished, unh, flabbergasted, still perched on the edge of their seats. Al then looked up, as did the group taking a couple of steps backward, fiendishly lowering a smirk at them. Then it happened, oh fk, a 35-shot fusillade bombarding them, a blasting sound of AK-47 bullets ricocheting off the furniture, bullets flying and zinging across the library right at the group. This was Real. Ugh. In less than 3 seconds, Jax had his Glock in one hand and his 45-caliber pistol in the other. Valerie had a 7-inch throwing knife in her right and a taser in her left. Terrance had slid his custom 2-shot Derringer from his right sleeve. They were ducking, bobbing the bullets which continued to be fired, then falling over each other and on top of poor Kamryn, who dived for cover then hysterically lost their oxygen, choking and gasping… "Omigod Kam… yelled, this shit is dangerous!"

Sara gleamed smugly with pride, thanking Papa and her inner beings for such inherited talent! She held up her hands as her audience put their weapons away in another well-known voice, "Mr. Jax Foul, well, I'll be… your supposed to check your weapons at the door, bad boy… Bad Boy!" <u>Almost simultaneously, they shouted, 'Liz, umh, Doctor Honcho, which was Liz's voice was perfectly done…' smiling,</u> Jax said with an awkward grin. "I never leave home without them, sorry!" they cackle. Kamryn shook her head and declared, "wow, I'm really impressed you're crazy gifted and brilliant. I'm really enjoying myself, sister. It's been so long since I've laughed so hard that my tummy is cramped. I used to remember you impersonating the cartoons and TV commercials driving daddy nuts or the morning alarm clocks. Mommy would get oh so angry with you, Sara…." "Umh, Kamryn, I definitely was a pain in the ass, a naughty kid for sure…." "Sara, how many times were you suspended from Daycare for letting AI cause trouble mimicking the teacher and other students…?" Suddenly, they heard banging and knocking on the door, then it became louder and more aggressive. Terrance jumps up… "who the hell ah, could that be at this time?" Looking up at the door monitor, which is vacant. Shaking his creased-cheeked smile and pointing at his niece, "nice one, Sara," she flashes a dimple… Yep!

Terrance knew his suite was soundproofed, now wondered if his decision to do so was a good idea. If, for some fricken reason, there really was a shootout in his suite, no one would come to his aid or even Hear it.

In a quick blitz of words, Al started singing the song 'You can't touch this' by MC Hammer, then imitating President Trump, next Rico, and Wendi, and then added in Sylvester Stallone and Kevin Costner, and a few… other actors that everyone knew. She lastly did some requests such as Dog barks, Cat meows, squealing tires, and a creaking door opening slowly that was so freakin authentic they had Al do it three times. A horn honks. She was wounding down when Terrance pounced up, standing, grabbed a big bag from behind his Rocking chair brought it to his lap. "I've got a real surprise tonight and pulls… out each puppet."

The four of them spun around to the sound of a gasp watching Sara/Al bend her head in a bow nostalgically. Kamryn saw her sister and knew at once…. The Puppets were Grand Papa's most precious belongings. They were him, oh how Papa adored the Puppet acts. Memories flooded back sentimental heartfelt feelings overwhelmed her/him. An unknown element, the emotionless Sara/Al/Ame/Don, became human, their heart on their sleeves. Don, in a fraction of a millisecond, nearly teared up…. <u>What occurred next was Titanic… on her feet. Kamryn instantly by her side.</u>

Grasping Sara's head was her identical twin Kamryn, the only one of the four that understood what Papa's Puppet shows meant to Sara. Her visceral haunting heart sensed remembrance of times when innocence still existed within her sister, when Papa would put on Puppet shows at their birthday parties and on special occasions with some of their friends. They begged Papa to come to their kindergarten class and bring the Puppets. Of course, the blonde pigtailed puppet was Kamryn and Sara.

No tears fell from her eyes, and her face was dry, but the change in the room's ambiance could be felt. Don said in a wavering sensitive voice, "thank you, Uncle Halliman, for bringing back those memories." Terrance hadn't heard Don's voice in years, acknowledged by saying, "you're welcome, Donny. He hopped up and pulled the Mahogany rocking chair to the middle of the group as Don walked into him for a hug, reached down, and greeted the puppets, saying hello in a baby voice. 'Hi, Jill... Donny takes her in his right hand, then says, hello there, Jack' to the boy puppet.

Sara/Al sits and rocks back, reveling, ruminating on past times, holding the puppets on each thigh, and starting the mind-boggling interactive action. Sara's mouth didn't quiver. Her throat didn't retract or fluctuate. She calmly looked at each of them as if she were just another audience member, arguably the world's premier ventriloquist and Gold Medalist. She was a phenomenon all by their-selves.

A person could try to describe the skill set or reality visualized audibly and physically in all phases and forms when the Puppets came alive. It was one of those heralded events 'that you had to have been there to feel how succinct the puppet act lived.' It was like two children sitting on a lap, and the dialogue was entrancing. Jack and Jill took the audience away. The puppets were having a conversation verbalizing in quaint endearing voices, making jokes and sarcastic quips, chastising Val and Jax and the others on such skits that hit home. Jill mumbled, "looks like it's love at first sight, just like Jack and me." Singing the nursery rhyme 'Jack and Jill went up the hill' referring to the blushing Val and Jax. Laughter, hooting, and hollering mixed in with knee-slapping, the group was laughed out, throats raspy and stomachs clenched like they'd finished 503 sit-ups, then they howled for some more... Yep! Al... finally took Jill, and Jack, to the finale. The puppets kissed and embraced, bowing to their audience with each one standing in Awe. The four bowed, cheered, clapped, and embraced Sara/Al afterward. Even Kam had dethawed.... ice had broken, umh, melting. Perhaps there were new beginnings, or perhaps not?

Terrance beckoned them to follow him to the dining room, where a dessert display was laid across the table. Jax yelped "geez, boss, there's no way for us to dent these desserts," patting his swollen abdomen. "I'm going to have to put in three hours of cardio just to break even." Others didn't pay attention and just started shoveling.

Later, sugar high squished, "it's time for a couple of announcements." At the same time, the last fork touched a plate. Terrance tapped his wine glass with a Silver sterling spoon "attention, you all, it's something I will admit to dreaming about happening. Having my three nieces back together is fantastic and totally exhilarating for me. The icing on the cake is for them to join our NIA Team. I never could imagine three sisters together. Valerie appears out of nowhere. We haven't a clue as to what fate has in store for each of us! Who's to know? But we must be prepared for anything. I truly hope the three of you find each other's hearts again and are rekindled and joyously reunited. Here are the division leaders who have chosen to guide our newest recruits. Sandi will have Kamryn as a newbie, Valerie will be under Wendi's scrutiny, and Sara will study and train under Asia's tutelage. You three will begin your 2-year tenure on Feb. 1st, 2018. I, for one, am excited and proud that I have three beautiful and talented Nieces that will graduate and become leaders for Our.... NIA!"

Terrance hesitated, seeing the wild eyes of his relatives, "Jax, do you have anything to add.... being our fearless leader and super tyrant at NIA...." He smiled teasingly "thanks, Terrance, and yes, I have been called worse names than a tyrant. I want first to thank you, Terrance, for inviting me to this evening's superb cuisine, which is only matched by all of your company. I don't usually enjoy myself like I have tonight. You are all amazing to me. Nothing can top Sara's astonishing entertainment. I will only add hey, you three ladies, your Uncle has you set up to be teacher's pets. Let me warn you that being Mr. Terrance Halinan's nieces will not be advantageous; instead or in fact, you three will be counted on setting good examples. It would be best if you were proactive, steady performers, for everyone's eyes will be on you. I look forward to seeing your progress. I'm thoroughly pleased to have you on our team. Please feel free to seek me out if I can be of any aid. Also, be aware that there is a chain of command!"

Jax's words met three nods, then Terrance retook the floor, "Currently, we're scheduling our first action for the 2018 graduating team, which will involve NIA standouts in only a few weeks. We call them fondly 'Mission Impossible's.' Typically, according to necessity, we are averaging between 5 and 7 yearly assignments. Our chosen militia participants are contingent on the needs and skills we deem necessary per… mission." Jax added, "it wouldn't be odd for one of you to be chosen, or for that matter, or all three of you could be included in the next mission impossible. It will depend on how you progress and whose squads we… the team leaders, choose you to join. I will determine the participants. With your Uncle Terrance overseeing this process, our next operation was to be on Feb. 14th… Valentine's Day. Aah, because of circumstances not under our control, we've had to extend the implementation dates of a mission to Seattle. We must deal with a planned penetration by another faction, ughhhh, trying to leverage our gambling operations throughout the Northwest." Jax sighed "well, I'm done with that rah, rah bit boss. Do you have anything else to add?" Terrance purposely took a look at his wristwatch. "I have a meeting at the Federal Courthouse at 8 am in San Francisco tomorrow, so let's finish this evening with our last bit of business regarding freedoms… logistics, and collaborations." The sisters eyed one another friendly like, at least that was their non-competitive appearance, but each one of them had their agendas, and to them, that's all that mattered!

Terrance sipped some Orange Liqueur, his favorite Grand Marnier... "First, Val, I'd like to have you on-site, full-time. You have a Suite on the top floor reserved for team leaders. I'm well aware it doesn't compare with your luxuriant opulent, unh, shall we call it an Estate in Pacific Heights in the city. I'm not asking you not to leave the facility grounds. Still, please spend most of your time here at NIA... not to extort you or to add leverage to this request against your freedom, but I have reasons for my demand. I am certain that your analytical calculating brain will conclude that what I'm advocating is about your own self-preservation. I've had visits to my law firm in the last three weeks from MI-5, Scotland Yard, a few Mossad Agents, unh, and Inspectors wanting interviews with you. Apparently, they seem to believe they will have enough evidence, uh, proof, to have you taken from us and back across the pond filing for extradition to face upcoming indictments... for several homicides in various cities in Europe."

Terrance deliberately waited for a response from anyone, nada, then slowly sipped, "we all have met the prick FBI Rico Captor who is courting our Wendi Feral. Ugh, anyways, he is also on board with these law enforcement agencies abroad. And has a team of his Agents on your case and has happily joined the investigation of you, my dear niece Valerie." She lowered her head, met his, and started rotating her face to the others, not happy Uncle was throwing this gauntlet down for all to hear. Valerie would be much more comfortable in a private setting, one on one with her uncle. Then conceded this was who Uncle Terrance was, at least when dealing with his nieces. He was the boss, and the guy didn't budge or cut them a break. It was a cut-and-dry scenario. Val realized that, most likely amongst his trusted personnel, everyone was privy to her supposed exploits. Valerie then came clean to herself while partitioning her uncle's spiel. It was only Jax that she cared about knowing, and heck, he already was in the know. Smiling inside her skin… hey, she would have killed the predators all over again. <u>It is what it was.</u> "Val, I hope you concur with my concerns for your well-being. You're one of the reasons for my 8 am Fed meeting in San Francisco!"

"Uncle, there's no need to be concerned. It's a witch hunt, but alas, I shall remain here and only leave after you and I discuss my needs. You will maintain my properties like you had intimated before…" "yes, absolutely," he states resoundingly! Terrance walks closer to Kam. "Now I realize before I open my mouth, there isn't going to be any way possible to mitigate your emotional upheaval and disillusionment on what you've endured… or enhance your good-natured disposition knowing just what you want from me, um, without pointing fingers and ending this fine warm enjoyable evening on a negative." Kam looks around at everyone. "Kamryn, each of us in this room is fully aware you've been locked up undeservedly." Sara looks down with a necessary guilty countenance, "Agent Rico Captor and the Feds are out to bring you in to take DNA samples and to interview you. Your twin here has been accused of three more homicides… our once employee Carl Sparks and his wife Bianca and attorney Pat Hanley Jr." Kam nods and doesn't seek Sara's gaze. "Kam, it's essential that you invoke your Miranda Rights to have an attorney present which will be yours truly… don't say a word other than plead the fifth. The word from the Federal Courthouse is that Rico has obtained a Warrant, so he will be able to get your DNA." Terrance looks around at their faces, happy to see them concentrating, and continues to zoom into Kam. "At the same time, you were incarcerated in Sara's place. You know Sara opened a Beauty Salon in San Rafael named 'Kam's Salon and Day Spa.' It's currently being managed by Crystal, one of my staff. I implore you to live or spend most of your time here at NIA at the facility. You will have a fine Suite to call your own. I know this isn't what you would like to do, but I must stress to you the importance of doing exactly this until Rico completes this investigation!"

Jax steps into the conversation "we are in the process of evicting one of Valerie's neighbors and moving her to another apartment, so this will be your furnished domicile. Kim, you can drive out the gates once your Uncle lines up your gate pass to check on your Victorian Villa in Marin County and Rico's investigation cools. Please be cogent that you are under surveillance by the Feds and enrolled in a 2-year physical education course here with requirements for weekly and mandatory classes...." "I want you living here," interrupts Terrance.

Under her epidermis, she's screaming ecstatically joyously, having been in solitary confinement, beaten, chained, shackled, even gagged, imprisoned, disrespected, and physically molested by a female guard. She had to fight to defend herself. Geez, what hell she'd survived? She'd been drugged into oblivion, humiliated beyond repair, dignity shattered, devoured in a fugue, almost lost her sanity, and finally, unh, freedom. The proof was overpowering, and yet she was dissed at every move.

Now it was out in the open that Sara had switched places, all conceded... the truth, the overwhelming vindication, was mind-altering. Calmly, she said, "Uncle, I already volunteered and signed up to be in the 2-year program. If you look back at all my academic achievements, I've always finished what I'd started. I will no question abide by all the rules, and I look forward to visiting the Salon that Sara has opened, and yes, I'll spend most of my waking time on site. Thank you." A brief hug is felt between Uncle and Niece.

"This leads me to you, Sara, and you already know where this is going. After Rico's visit a while back, you realize that Medical Examiner Doctor Rable and he are hot on your tracks. We cannot afford for you to be stopped and picked up! Or mistaken by the Feds to be Kam and be tested for the new DNA, um, now that Scientists have discovered innovative techniques to differentiate between identical twins, triplets, and so on. NIA and all we've accomplished and stand for or what we may endeavor to do would be destroyed, and that's not even touching a minute fraction of the financial losses if you're implicated in any crime outside of this facility. If the FBI can prove you culpable, yuh might as well flush NIA down the toilet!" Sara held up a stop hand "enough, Terrance, I'm not deaf, dumb, or blind. I could have read the writing on the prison Cell wall long ago. Still, I ask for incentives for conciliatory appeasements, a give and take what's fair is fair, and that is for sis Kam to have her freedom. It was dastardly shameful, appallingly wrong, and selfish, ugh, unforgivable what I did to her! I get that and own it. I will never be able to make it right, for it was wrong! But I still request ah ask for some leniency and freedom. I'd like to be able to leave NIA...." "Sara, there can't be two of you outside the prison. Tell you what, I'll take you out in the Limo every now and again, ah quite often, and when or after the Rico investigation concludes, you can work out with Kam to use her gate pass while she stays here! Ok?"

Kam interrupts, "Sara, I'm not averse to doing so. We can work together. Heck, it's better than being confined to your Cell. At least you will have a dorm room, um, suite to share with me...." Turnabout is fair play as Terrance re-interrupts, "yes, regarding living arrangements, you will have your same Cell but the use of their suites if your sisters agree!" Val and Kam smirk "well, of course," expresses Val. "That is unless I plan some hanky-panky," Terrance declares, "it appears all is settled for now! Oh... I have had meetings with the correction officers assigned to your wing. There will not be anyone spreading rumors about your movements, and they are all team members of NIA. It will not be like it was when you attempted to work out at NIA-U before... no one will cause you any discomfort, Sara, and if someone does... see Jax, he'll immediately handle it!"

They all embrace. Sara only said, "ok, I guess I'll head over to my Cell then...." "Oh no, you don't. Your sleeping at my place" smiled Val. Jax walked out into the hall. "Let's roll, girls." The three sisters strut satiated and content as adults for the first time since infanthood with engorged tummies of Lionesses. Terrance watched the four of them walk away. He was satisfied. Could this planned dinner... gone any better? Amazed that there wasn't a Catfight, he conceded yes, Sara was dead-on putting on a sensational act. Most certainly, something was brewing in her conniving mind. She was heating up body language subtleties, motions unspoken, but what? She was correct... a definite attraction between Jax and Val, not at all opposites internally but definitely external opposites. Attracted, he grinned, maybe that's backward, lol he was freakin burned out, exhausted, forget it, so tired he wasn't making sense to himself. A quick dip in the hot tub with the rain falling, then collapse on the Kings bed... Yup!

Jax glanced at the time. Almost midnight, he was thrilled at being invited, having one of the best times he could remember. The sisters were quiet as he parked under an awning "hey Val, you offered Kam to stay at your place. Have you forgotten Sara hasn't a place to lay her head yet unless I drive all the way back to the custody yard?" Valerie smirked with a devious grin on her cheeks. "Jax, well then, let me propose I let my sisters share my apartment, and you come with me and sleep at my place in San Francisco?" "Yeah, sis, that's what I'm talking about," snickered Sara. Jax felt a sudden warmness hit his skin, "unh, Val, yah got a point... Okay, that'll work," Val handed the keys to Kam. "I've deactivated the alarm system for you two. Seeya... in the morning!" Yup!

Terrance was depleted of anxiety, a temporary reprieve and assuaged of much of the tenuousness before his three nieces had got together for the first time for a dinner gathering. Terrance hadn't felt this close to being happy in months... although he still weighed an idea that Jax and he had pondered... let Sara pretend to be Kamryn and let Rico serve his warrant for her DNA... which would match the DNA that he'd obtained on his last visit with Sara here at NIA. That would prove that the innovative mitochondrial and splitting of the circular chromosomes found in the cytoplasm could be faulty. If Rico was told that the DNA from Sara and Kam matched, then the FBI didn't have a case. For Sara and Kam didn't share a tampon... Yup!

-51-

<u>Jax and Terrance fondly recall the grand dinner gathering.</u>

The Limousine banked following the curvature of the onramp Hwy 101 South on a Monday morning. It was 6:19 am staring up from the laptop. It was just a touch overcast. The Sun would threaten to battle the rainclouds today. Terrance had flashed back to last night several times, heck, many times. After Jax and his three nieces had left his suite, he thought he'd fall asleep in minutes, but that wasn't the case! He was wired, even after drinking various forms of alcohol, and couldn't shut down his brain. He was worn out and, instead of making some espresso in his limo, had asked Jacob to stop and get him a quadruple shot Americano at Starbucks. He wiggled his head with a smirk... couldn't recall heartily laughing so out of control he would have to watch the replay from his surveillance cameras in every room except for the 2 ½ bathrooms lost again in the comedy of the evening. Oh shit, when Sara pulled the automatic machine gun, firing rounds ricocheting through the library, Jax's face... his expression and look was utterly monstrously anger-driven in attack mode. No Fear displayed a weapon in each hand.

He answers one of his cell phones, stopping the vibration. "I was just thinking about you, Jax...." "Yeah, it was an awesome majestic night indeed. I want to emphasize how much I appreciate the invite, boss. That was a blast, a near-perfect evening...." "You're welcome. Since when are you the socialite you normally are hermit like I'm...." "Actually, it's the first time I accepted an invitation in I don't know how long, hey you ever read poems? I was this morning and..." "WTHeck has gotten into you, Jax man oh man, I might need to have your head examined... maybe some of the old school stuff like Thorazine is what you need" he snorted, then left a cackle... for Jax to hear. "Surely, boss, you'd not want to see me do the famous Thorazine shuffle. Isn't your favorite actor Jack Nicholson doing that shuffle after his lobotomy in that fanfantastic movie 'One flew over the Coo-coo Nest!' you...." they both chuckled "what's up, why the call?" "I know you're heading into the City, but I have some interesting news. In all sincerity, I've witnessed this for the first time in my military-civilian career. I ran it by our Egghead Technicians. They were also flabbergasted!"

"Ok, Jax, I'll bite. Whatcha got?..." "I wished you would have waited until today before sending Sara's audio recordings imitating your voice and Liz's...." "Why, what's the difference?" "Cuz you knew me, I couldn't rest. I'm like a Pitbull when I get a bone to pick. Damn, I spent most of the night cross-referencing the voices ran and overlaid with our voice recognition software programs. Check this out!" "I'm all ears. Getcha on speaker phone."

"This is astounding. Sara didn't miss a beat of her rhythms, octaves, speech patterns, highs, and lows; twangs and accents were dead-on. I even made a comparison on an Oscilloscope. The cadences are as authentic as if you and Liz spoke. Miraculously the technicians have never seen such collaborating analysis, and I've never seen it either. All humans have slightly different ranges of tones. We need AI for this next mission, boss. She will be able to get our team past the voice recognition obstacles we have been sweating. This is huge...what we can achieve via verbal commands from cell phones is unmeasurable. All we need to do is get her a tape of the voices she needs to imitate, and we're fine Golden boss... she'll be able to get us into the compound. I'm going to text her some more with your permission!"

"Jax, thanks for the uplifting report. Sara is definitely going to be an asset. If she called me pretending to be you, I'd be entirely fooled without any suspicion. We know she can be devious. We ought to consider a code number or name before exchanging classified information. I'll check in when I leave the Feds. Do us a favor and have Sara at our high-level meeting this afternoon regarding that mission, and yes, do some further due diligence." "Sure thing, boss ah... hey, I want first to tell you not to worry about what I'm going to say...." "Whoa, now that sounds like another confession from a guilty client. What's going on, Jax? What could have happened since last night's get-together?" "Terrance, after the dinner party, instead of having Sara return to her cell, Valerie invited the sisters to stay at her place at NIA-U, and we left Napa and spent the night in the city at Val's Pacific Heights home. And might I say she's got it going on? What a magnificent property. We had fun... have you been there? She's got an indoor shooting range. We shot an assortment of her custom bow & arrows and Crossbows. I hope you're not pissed off, boss!"

Terrance shook his head and sipped his Americana, staring at the Golden Gate bridge. Jacob was maneuvering the limo through congested traffic. "Jax, I'm glad you and my niece are getting on well, but didn't we decide she was to stay on-site? You know Rico, and the Feds, along with Inspectors from Europe, are investigating her and...." I know boss, but she needed things from her home, and besides, she offered to be company for me and help with the surveillance of Wendi later this morning. Slam and Jaybird are outside the hotel Rico, and Wendi stayed in last night; they're off the clock at 9 am." Okay, afterward, I want the young lady back on NIA grounds, and why don't you delegate someone else for the mundane task of watching Wendi?" "I will, and Good luck today with the Feds!"

<u>Rico and Wendi.</u>

Wendi was feeling much better since her syncope bout and the testing at NIA. She smiled inside her skin and grinned on the outside, staring at him. Rico was smitten once again. It had been a furious whirlwind week and a half. He and Wendi were inseparable. He brushed his teeth gazing in the hotel room's mirror, rousing some past recollections. His investigation of NIA had continued without him. He hadn't taken any vacation days in years or ever since Wendi, and he had traveled to the Trinity National Forest a couple of years before. It was supposed to be an FBI safehouse for rest and relaxation, that was until the Mexican mafia showed up. It was the most fun he'd had in a decade. Wendi and he had spent days on Trinity Lake skiing, wakeboarding, and swimming in the cool water.

Although Rico was a dedicated workaholic without a life... he grinned, uhm, since Wendi had broken out of her fugue and had control of her alter-ego, Sunshine, again. Rico paused that thought, eliciting some self-retrospection... admitted it wasn't that he didn't like Sunshine. No, he did, but it was Wendi's sweeter side he loved. Gosh, he felt alive. He was rejuvenated and wanted to take her away to the Caribbean for an Island getaway for two weeks.

Wendi and he had many shared investigations over the years, with her being a subcontractor for the FBI. Wendi and her partner Sandi had a business called 'Feral Feedback,' On a whim, he'd talked his superiors at the FBI into hiring her team of animals. Heck, despite the FBI denying that we used paranormal individuals in desperate cases, the FBI director Tanya Finn was distressed and disheartened. The serial kidnapper of children had been on a rampage for 25 months and counting. We were at a loss for clues and reached out to Feral Feedback. As 'Paul Harvey' would say, 'and now you know the rest of the story.' Without Wendi's assistance, we wouldn't have solved that horrendous case. That was just the beginning of their working relationship. The most notorious and successful investigations that Wendi had worked with him were the Ocala National Forest Pandemic and the Cuban Mafia's exploitation of children in porn-laden sex slave rings, that one involved Jax Foul.

Since Wendi was three years old, and now she is 37, Wendi has helped Law Enforcement with unsolved crimes of violence. She was now a veteran of her 7th sense, and she would avoid the eyes of all animals, for once a Cat or a Bird, or a Racoon caught her eyes, they'd be mesmerized. Could you imagine what it would be like to be able to read animals' thoughts? Besides mind-blowing, it would be time-consuming Rico and Wendi had poured a foundation over the years, a rule of thumb that while out and about to ensure they wouldn't be bothered by animals, the only eyes she was going to look into was his!

Her late husband and avid gambler David had leveraged Wendi's value for millions until Rico discovered the plot. He was broken from his reflections. She squeezed his hand ever so slightly, walking through a beautiful part of Golden Gate Park the Bay was full of sailboats. Alcatraz was in the distance, and frisbees were being tossed about. People were out, having fun flying an uncountable number of kites in the bright Blue, cloudless sky. Music played from every angle, and a yummy aroma came from a barbecue nearby. The screams of fun... children playing on slides and swings, vendors on the sidewalk peddling their wares, a mild pleasant afternoon, the Golden Gate Bridge loomed above to the Northwest, a picturesque day indeed. Wow, and the weather prognosticators had predicted rain... Uh!

They were dressed leisurely in sandals and shorts. He had a colorful Tommy Bahama shirt she had a slight Cashmere sweater "honey, how about we get an ice cream?" "That sounds fab, okay" they strolled to the three-wheeled cart getting in a line they congregated. Rico said, "I'll have a fudge sickle. Wendi added I'd like a Neapolitan ice cream sandwich, please!" he grabbed a couple of paper napkins. Off they went. He said, "wow, I was lucky that the guy had change for a C-note, um, hundred-dollar bill!... Hey, there's an open bench. Let's snag it quickly, finish our ice creams, and do some people-watching," exclaims Rico. She says nothing as she lets him lead her to the bench 'besides perhaps New York City's Central Park, there's not a more diverse crowd of humans than in San Francisco. Just look at the groups out there. You'd swear the hippies of the 60's never left and were still in vogue!'

Rico suddenly noticed the reticence "hey lover, what's up? Did a Cat catch your tongue? You haven't said a word since we got the ice cream?" "Oh ah, I'm just enjoying mine" as she takes a paper towel and puts the wrapper inside, he peers down at her gorgeous face, her hair of blonde in a bun. He'd always been a brunette kinda man "why that look, babe...?" "Oh honey, it's just that I broke one of our Golden Rules, that's all. Let's forget it, okay?" A low baritone chortled, "yeah, sure, you say now to forget it to a Detective. You broke a rule and just forget it, duh now ya gotta tell me what's up, Ms. Feral?" Smiling at her with undaunting love, "nuuh honey, it's best left unsaid. We've discussed this a hundred times, if not once! We have our afternoon cruise going to Sausalito for an early dinner. I'm not going to ruin or spoil that!"

He stood up, taking her wrapper "stay here, let me throw these in the waste basket" she watched his fluid, sexy strut seeing his fabulous glutes naked not hours ago. Yum, what a hunk of virility. He satisfied me mentally and physically, and we're working on the spiritual bit. She couldn't help but grin, "that's my girl. I saw that smile. What's up? Listen, we don't have to go on the dinner cruise. I'm just as happy to be with you anywhere, k?" She decided to put her reservations aside. Unfortunately, he wasn't sitting back by her side. "Ok, woman, what has you so darn preoccupied? What's bugging you? I've seen that loveable scowl before, maybe a dozen times. We go back a decade plus, so cop to it!" "Cop to it," she cackled "what a parallel, no babe, it's my fault I had the option. Could have stopped when I approached the target, yah eh, I shouldn't have broken weak and tunnel-visioned into those damn eyes!"

Rico squeezed her left thigh "what target? Whatcha talking about? Um, no, you shouldn't have what?" surprising her, he snorted into a short snicker. "Okay, now what, Wendi, the guy? Aah, the ice cream guy is a serial killer, right, nah, or a gangster?" His face showed total amusement with overwhelming love. She slapped down on his left thigh a hard thwack "no, smart ass, he's only a counterfeiter, and you have three twenties that are fake out of the four he gave you back in change, ha-Ha ha!" Wendi then explodes in laughter, "no biggie, let's go" if he were a casser, he would have yelped out some expletives… "what?" he loudly barked, "no way!" He pulls his wallet out. She says, "nope, just forget it, boy, let's roll. Not going to…" "stop a second, sweetie, let me examine these."

"These are good, and even the paper is passably correct. I…" "So I was wrong. Come on, let's get a Crab cocktail appetizer at the wharf…." "No, Wendi," he spins her to face him and puts a fat kiss onto her supple lips, moans "yum, tell me please, what do you know?" "No, Rico…" "yes, Wendi," he clutched her wrist "please, I will not let it ruin our day, I promise!" She slinks back and cowers, then abruptly stands tall, all 5'1... inches, gawking up at him "you promise?" "Yes, I've told you I have never broken a promise before, so spill the beans now; let's walk... you talk."

"All right, but come on, let's go towards Fisherman's Wharf." After about 35 feet, she had muttered not a word....

patience was not one of his most commendable assets. "Wendi!" "fine," she waved her hand at the rows of vendors. Some had flags blowing in the relentless cool wind. He almost steps on her Crocs with his sandals "oh, I see... the two birds." "Yep, Rico, two Lovebirds, uhm, Parakeets so in love swinging on the wooden dowel. Um, Abby, I couldn't resist her stare." "Come on, Wendi..." "No, that's the pretty female's name. I wouldn't be making that up," she gives him an elbowed snort.

Pointing, "there are Abby's owners, a husband-wife team, and brother-in-law who are up on the sidewalk with all the other vendors. They're part of an organization that filters counterfeit money, mostly to tourists. Abby told me that Tariq Aziza was the Uncle who was in charge. He was the boss. They

have a printing publishing business on Market Street." "Wendi, are you kidding me? Pulling my thumb, that little bird told you all that while we ordered ice cream, please?" "Nope, I just made it all up. Come on," he jerked her hand to a stop, "now all right, all right, I believe you. We still have some time before the dinner cruise. You said his wife and..." "Damnit Rico, all I want is a Crab cocktail. Please don't start a freakin investigation. I'll tell you, sometimes my big mouth ruins everything. Shoulda kept it closed...." "Wendi, you can't just expect me...." "Yes, but there's a horde of vendors. I don't know which one the wife works at," taking his arm. "I'll just go back and ask Abby... honey, I don't want this to ruin our afternoon... damnit!"

Rico and her step around the ice cream line pretending to admire the Parakeets. Wendi puts her finger between the cage opening. Abby had second thoughts suddenly, saying as she... pecked away at a Sunflower kernel, "I shouldn't have told you anything. Forget it. Ralph is pissed off at me... her mate fluffed his wing out, brutally knocking Abby upside down. Abby still clinging to the wooden dowel, Ralph chirped "my girl is a birdbrain listen we want no trouble here ma'am." Abby answered Wendi's question without ruffling her feathers... upside down. "The wife is selling leather goods wearing a silk skirt and a Purple and Black blouse..." "thanks Abby and you, Ralph, be nice!"

They walked up the steep hill towards a portable cart and lean-to. Rico checked and had only two large denominations left in his wallet, one fifty and a last hundred-dollar bill. They started browsing over all the leather products, belts, hats, fanny packs, wallets, and some colorful purses. Rico was on one side of the display checking out cell phone holders near the gloves and vests. Wendi was perusing the leather skirts and jackets, stopping by a pair of Brown boots. Soon enough, the owner spied them after settling another transaction. Wendi held a small pocketbook purse. The price was a whopping $55.00 for authentic Buffalo Hide.

Rico started the bartering process "can we have it for 30 dollars... cash, no taxes?" the wife flashed annoyance, shook her head negatively... walked away to another customer. Wendi looked up at him with an Owl slick smirk and whispered, "way to go, slick" he furrowed his manicured brows, blinked, and pursued the mischievous vendor. Holding out the bait that gave the woman a triple take a one-hundred-dollar bill, "here, how about $35.00, no taxes. Come on, please, my lady wants this?" The squat, unknown-figured woman with purple eyeliner showed sharp teeth, her silk skirt un-formfitting her long black braids with colored beads dangling a Gypsy look. Rico took a closer look. She was a handsome lady.

"The best I can do is 35 dollars plus tax Uncle Sam's taxes. We would be shut down if we didn't pay our taxes, sir!" Without waiting for his reply impatiently snatched up his wagging hundred-dollar bill and casually strolled toward the cash register. Omigod, that's when the other bird cage appeared hanging above just to her left. Rico whispered, "oh crap, not again," staring at Wendi; he got an elbow in return. The cash register opened, and the drawer lifted. He watched her take three twenties from underneath, then the rest of his change out of the top drawer.

Wendi watched her grab a bag "no bag, thank you" they walked away holding hands again with a swagger that displayed a cocky success. Waiting for the Trolly, he compares the twenty-dollar bills again but still can't see the proof. He texted one of his Agents that worked the area to meet him at Fisherman's Wharf inside Scoma's restaurant at the Bar by the bay. Suspense eating at him again, squeezing her wrist "what do I have to do? prompt you every time, come on…?" "What the heck, why the attitude, dude…?" "What did the other birds have to say, dammit?" "Oh, you wouldn't want to know. I can assure you of that….." "Stop it try me," she bent her chin down then posed "fine the female birdie said to me, lifting her feathered arm at you. 'Wow,' you could have done much better than him." He cackled loudly and returned an elbow into her back, gently… "Touché babe now come on willya?"

Wendi felt like having some fun and giggled with a swirl, dimples popping. "Yep, that's what she said to start with. The male bird nodded affirmatively while cleaning her feathers. Um, ok, neither one of the birds were the chatterbox type, not talkative. I had to pry it out of 'em. I'd caught them in a scuffle fighting over a French fry from McDonald's….." "Sshh, stop it. Why all the humor, no horse-crap girl, geez come on, I'm serious," he snorted, "bullshit," then fell into a laugh. "No, I'm dead serious. A customer snuck one into their cage. It was a war over the fry," she giggled. "your way too serious, dude. Ok, lighten up. Not much did I learn? Yes, counterfeit money below the top drawer, and the woman was mean to them, sometimes leaving a dark covered sheet over them way past noontime."

They boarded the Trolly standing on the outward step holding the chrome bars, bells ringing, jangling… fun stuff. Oh, how she enjoyed the City. Wendi was ecstatic to be the prime entity again and be in control of herself… on occasions, she was a recluse. At times of stress, Sunshine had taken complete control. It's not that she didn't adore and Love Sunshine, who now lurked close to the surface of her optic nerve, cornea, um, the retina of her left iris. Not backing away, only observant, scared because there wasn't any conversation with her inner self. Sunshine was angry that much was clear but too bad she was only her invisible guardian. This was her life. It was time for her to be happy; her inner clock was ticking. She still wanted to be a mommy and a wife again and marry Rico. Strangely she felt an oddity lurking within this unfamiliar feeling that weirdly caused her not to think she was alone with Sunshine, as if someone else was stalking her. Ever since the injection by Doctor Liz Honcho and her jamming the Horse tablet down her throat, she'd felt like something had changed. Whatever psychotherapeutic drugs she'd been forced to consume had somehow altered who she was…

At Scoma's, a couple of plump Agents had shown up. I'd told Rico I didn't want to be involved. He had agreed it would take hours to convince the Agents that I spoke with the Parakeets. Even with all the global publicity and the sensational trial of Jex Foul, most people considered me a con artist and a fake.

Coincidently her phone rumbled, and it was the infamous man himself. "Hey Wendi, how's it rollin'" she filled him in, then he said, "I'm glad you got a hold of me and left me the message to call you; I've missed speaking with you. We have to brainwave that upcoming situation on the subject of your brother Mark. There have been some changes. Has Rico broached the NIA investigation and mentioned anything about Sara, Kamryn, or the moles he's placed at our facility? As you well know, there are three rogue spies!"

"No, Jax, we have guidelines and parameters set forth we leave our personal business, and that includes anything that happens at NIA at the curb. As you are aware, this is the only way we're copacetic, and way before you ask me, you can tell Terrance I will not be a double spy for him or anyone else. We fight like Cats and Dogs when NIA is brought up. That has been the norm for years now. Jax, you realize I truly love this man!" "Ah, that's no secret, girl, but he's Terrance's arch-enemy who has started a Federal Investigation and called for the Grand Jury to convene. Hey, not only is NIA-U being scrutinized, but so are...." "I know, but that's not my problem. I am a trustworthy advocate for all that NIA stands for...." "But we must squelch stop this investigation whatever it takes, woman...." "I can say this he purposely missed a scheduled meeting with the Federal Judge Delaney. He's kind of preoccupied with me, Jax. He loves me too, and behind that rough and tumble exterior, he's grateful for the NIA hospitals and their amazing medical techniques and innovations. You ought to hear him animatedly rev up about NIA's Neurology division, primarily the Stem cell hospital. Rico raves about the recovery of his best buddies Brock Dame and Lacie Link, both, as you know, touted FBI Agents. I mean... hold on, he's staring at me with some local Agents. Let me step away and walk up the deck a bit further."

She listened but felt she wasn't the only entity on the live wire, "all right, fair enough, but without you on board, our Saint Patties party will be hampered. You are irreplaceable, and you have a new class of enrollees starting on February 1st. You're not going to shirk your commitments, are you, Wendi...." "Nothing has changed. I'm a team leader and will not let you and Terrance down. Think about it wouldn't it be a superlative feather Peacock style to add Mr. Rico Captor to our team!" Jax hacked, coughing quickly, rebuffing that notion "your insane, Wendi. There's no way Mr. goody-2 shoes is going to join our subversive group. He only wants to sink us. We haven't a clue as to why. Look, Wendi, he has you back, and Sunshine is relegated back in the shadows." "Your right. Maybe I am insane. I know, but it's not a bad thing… right one can wish for the positives."

After a long pause, he said, "I miss your company. You know you're my best friend and partner," she didn't pause. "Jax, I love you, and as you're well aware, so does my alter ego. She's madder than a witch; Sunshine literally adores you…." "How are you feeling? I was supposed to keep this on the down-low ah hushed, but the new medication that you were injected with has caused serious sickness in others with the same oral and intravenous applications. We're worried about you!" "Jax, I have had some side effects, no doubt, feeling queasy at times, I also have this odd feeling every so often that someone is watching me ugh from within, but anyways I love you like the brother I didn't have. I'll see you later. Rico's fine ass is approaching me, Chow!…" "k Chow girl." Jax felt a little guilty because he thought he knew exactly who Wendi referred to as…. someone watching her…but he would be dead Wrong. Valerie sat alongside him in the NIA Mercedes tinted window van and had her in view at Scoma's on a pier. They watched as FBI Agents joined Rico at the restaurant in the Fisherman's Wharf area in San Francisco. Now they saw Rico waving his arms toward her. But others were watching.…

<u>Terrance almost fell down the last step out of the courthouse, preoccupied with contemplating how it could have gone any better.</u>

Jacob pulled the limousine to the curb, opening Terrance's door swiftly. "How'd it go, boss?" "much better than expected. I'm almost ready to pinch myself; thanks for asking," he grinned. Jacob had the Limo's doors open. Terrance ducked inside. "Back to the NIA-U facility, please...." "Yes, sir," said Jacob with a flare... musing, 'Things must be good if Terrance was in a good mood leaving the Federal Courthouse.' Terrance reached into the mini refrigerator, grabbed an egg salad sandwich, selected some tomato juice, and sat back, replaying the messages he'd missed in the three hours plus he'd dealt with the inquiries about his niece Valerie. Strangely the Feds didn't grill him about Sara and the DNA warrants for Kamryn. Biting into the sandwich, well, maybe this rekindled relationship... uhm, Rico and Wendi's re-bonding may prove beneficial!

The fifth message on his private cellphone had him anxious it was Vadoma... 'Terrance, please call me, it's rather important, thanks...' 'Rather important hmm.' He said to himself... what the heck. It had been a good morning thus far; he'd wait until after lunch. He mused about Jax and Val. Were they hooking up? How crazy would that be? Jax isn't pretty, and my niece could have any man. A chime sounded. He took the last bite of his sandwich and drank the tomato juice down, accidentally dribbling a drop onto his suit vest. Wiped his face, "hello, Vadoma, how are you doing today?" "Not good, Terrance." As was their common theme, he clicked his video conference line, and she peered at him from his 23-inch screen attached to the limo's back wall.

Vadoma was sitting in a highbacked rocking chair, Briya, her great-granddaughter, stood in the background, and Charity, Briya's daughter, was also on the screen. "What's so darn important, Vadoma? Everything is going just peachy today. Gosh, I hope you're not goin to rain on my parade...." He laughed at his play on words because it was supposed to rain a little later this afternoon. She cleared her throat and sipped her customary Tea, "I had another disturbing vision this morning and spoke to your mother and father only an hour ago." Terrance sat up straight, 'wondered what could be so important to involve his parents?' Heck, they were in the Bahamas at one of their beach houses the last he spoke to them. They were going to cruise the Caribbean on their Yacht. Vadoma didn't squander words, a right-to-the-point gal of 101 years old. "Why didn't you administer the remedy I gave you for Ms. Wendi Feral?" Feeling a bit off-kilter and cynical of the lady's powers of soothsaying, "I gave Doctor Walters your formula, and Wendi was injected once, haven't added the other three injections you advocated because Wendi has some severe side effects... Vadoma!" There was a long pause, and Terrance felt compelled to add that Wendi popped up from the gurney and seemed to be okay. She'd recovered from what Liz had injected her thanks to your tincture and...."

Vadoma didn't speak, sipping her cup of tea and looking at Briya, who took a tea kettle and refilled it. Terrance was uneasy, looking intently at the old woman, remembering Liz injecting Wendi and shoving the horse tablet down her throat. The last report of other tested inmates receiving the same medications proved worrisome, and some inmates were adversely affected, coma-bound, and in straitjackets. But as of the previous report from Jax, Wendi was just fine. "Terrance, my family... and yours go back well before the first Tsar of Russia 'Ivan the Terrible' we have been tied to the hip for centuries. I'm not here to waste what breaths I have left. You failed to follow my explicit instructions... Wendi is now, no longer Wendi, nor is she her alter-ego Sunshine. The caustic mixture of your Psychotropic experimental drugs has partitioned her dominant personality. Soon if something isn't done, her third entity will compartmentalize Wendi and Sunshine. 'Judea' has now entered the fray… you're familiar with the history of 'Judas?'… Terrance!"

Terrance was now alert, "I have her under surveillance, and one of my people just communicated with her. She's fine, Vadoma… What would you have me do?" "Inject the formula I gave you at our last meeting at once…again. I can't see the future, it's cloudy, and this is worrisome, Terrance." "Okay, I'll work on this, and thank you." The frail woman holds her cup up, leaning forward, "I am not finished; Sonja lives. I made it clear you must eliminate the evil spirit and entity before it grows." Terrance has had enough and calmly barks back, "Vadoma, you said that one of my nieces was pregnant and going to give birth to this sinister child, Sonja… it's not that I didn't listen to you. My nieces are not pregnant. In fact, they can't…." Vadoma hacks, reaching for her throat. "I cannot see the future, which bodes ill luck, and certainly means I will meet my demise soon. At our last meeting, I could envision her evil spirit, that she'd become the worse serial killer of all time in our world. Excluding Hitler, Stalin, and Chairman Mao."

Terrance watched as Vadoma slowly placed her cup on a placeholder. She rolled her head and stared up. "Sonja is here; I feel her intensity. You have to kill her, Terrance, and cremate her malevolent wicked body and soul… she's being hidden and cared for. I will not be of this earth much longer. Sonja is alive and living underneath your thumb, your niece…. Ahh… Vadoma clutches her throat. Her eyes roll up White, then her fists pound on her withered chest. She keels forward into Briya's arms…

<u>**Jaybird and Sandi had returned to NIA from their task of surveilling Wendi, leaving that assignment to Jax and Valerie.**</u>

Jaybird and Sandi had just completed their 3-mile run around the track. Smiling with sweat glistening, she shouted, "seeya in the pool" they went their separate ways to the locker rooms. He was mightily attracted to the sensual Albino beauty, such a wildly confident woman, a fine addition to the growing formidable NIA teams. He grabbed some shampoo and soap, a beach towel, and some Teva's water slippers, made his way to the shower, and saw his iPhone flashing Blue. Should he or shouldn't he.... no he'd check it later.

Later it was while flexing in a mirror, looking at his reflection, seeing his dark hair and tanned skin and deep Blue Ocean eyes, trimmed beard, and high cheekbones. He grinned and rubbed his Roman nose... handsome, he decided, as he had for decades in his prime, he had just turned 41 years old. He could do 17 pull-ups, the same number of chin-ups, and 55 dips with 45 pounds belted to his waist, consecutively following that up with pushups jumping jacks into burpees, barely breaking a sweat. With one glance at his phone's screen, Sweat continued to boil up. What could be wrong? The code flashed originated from his militia in Montana. His cellphone was secure, but he'd have to scan it before contacting Helena's central compound. He put it out of his mind wiping his brow and sucking down the rest of the bottled water on the prowl for some Albino meat. Ahh, kind of crude, he thought, um, prowl for some fun with a beautiful and enchanting lady, Sandi, ahh... much better!

Jaybird sat dressed, leaving his swim trunks hanging in his locker and opting for his casual attire with a deep blue Polo shirt which he knew accentuated his mesmerizing eyes... yep! Sandi saw him at once... a frown started forming from lane #

3. She swam up "where are you off to, mister!" he grimaced. "Umh, sorry, we can get together for dinner as we planned too, and I look forward to some dancing and…" "What's up, Jay? We had this entire afternoon planned. What about our Ziplining? I …" "The central office in Helena, Montana, sent me an alert. I must have some additional news on ex-bro Mark Feral. I'm going to the secure room guess I'll have to do the raincheck thing with you… for this afternoon. Still, as I intimated, dinner will…" she flipped on her back to start a lap of backstroke. She said as waves started up, "it's not the first time you pulled the raincheck bit on me. This time I hope it doesn't bounce!"

He took her fascinatingly proportioned, sleek, muscled body into his loins. Deep sigh, Lord knows, "You're down for dinner tonight, beautiful, um… correct?" Sandi flipped her feet overhead and reversed somersaulted back from the pool's edge. "Jay, it's a yes I'll be ready by 6:15," she kicks off, leaving him a kittenish scowl with gentle, fluid motions and a foreplayed splash; under the water, she vanished.

Jaybird checked the time on his phone. It was 1:37 pm. He'd be at dinner with the scrumptious Sandi in less than five hours. The anticipation of her touch…. swelling his heart and love muscle slightly, with expectation. He went to handle the militia thing and mused aloud, 'how could I allow Wendi's brother Mark, a proven adversary, to depart to the enemy? They were buddies, and he bought the story hook, line, and sinker years back after getting out of Federal Prison. He was arrested along with his lifelong pal Jax Ford on his property in Plant City, Florida. They were in a mini battle with the Cuban Mafia when some Federal Agents met their demise. He'd met Mark Feral after his release; the guy showed up at one of his militia functions. Mark was an outlaw and had absconded from parole from San Quentin; he also was on the FBI's top twenty wanted list. In the beginning, Mark was welcomed with open arms by his compatriots. Let's face it Mark was a charming snake. Well, thought Jaybird, that was until the truth came out about his obsession to kill his sister Wendi Feral. We, um, my leaders in the Montana Militia, sent him packing. Being a resourceful guy, he'd started up his own militia. Right outside of the city limits of Helena, Montana, we'd been adversaries ever since. According to Mark... Wendi had a long pattern of informing the police and the authorities about his criminal deeds dating back to when he wasn't even a teenager. He was sent to Juvenile hall, and his road to San Quentin was being paved. Because of Wendi, not only did he end up there, but so did his best friends, Joe and Tank. A little more than a year ago, Mark was accused of shooting Wendi in the head while she was driving on a highway up North. That was the reason why Wendi was admitted to the NIA Neurology outpatient hospital, besides the Sunshine personality disorder that Wendi's parents wanted delved into by the professionals at NIA. Rico had made his main objective to capture Mark dead or alive, the former being his wish.

If you wanted to start up a subversive militia, there wasn't a better State to start with other than Montana. Mark was highly efficient and had an innate quality to manipulate weak-minded people. His followers wore blinders, and he was sort of like an evangelist the guy could put on a show, eloquently persuasive. His militia had grown exponentially, and now he had base encampments in Utah and Nevada. At last guess, there were over eleven thousand followers on Mark's heels. Mark was a former bro and was slick, hiding like a Possum until he had gone to the dark side... no loyalty remained. Mark would rather commit appalling crimes, and he's become a daunting and fearsome foe. He only refined his acumen while doing stints in San Quentin and Soledad prisons and some Federal time. Jail for him and his cronies was like recruitment centers. He had 'Skinheads, the Aryan brotherhood, heck... he had gangs of revolutionists to pick from in Prisons. His old grudge against his sister and Jaybird's colleague Wendi was old news. The dude couldn't let it go and wanted Wendi Dead! Ugh.

Jaybird rushed out of the gymnasium, thinking he was jumping to conclusions. It might not be about Mark Feral could be anything, but the ominous code that he'd seen on his phone had taken precedence over any optimism and peripheral thoughts. He had just hopped off the Golf cart when he heard his name yelled loudly. "Byrd Dawg, whatcha doing later this afternoon? Shea and I are taking the quads up into the mountains for a ride. Maybe bag us a seven-pointer. There are some major racks out there, some humongous Bucks aah, nothing like Alaska, but hey Jay, why don't you…." "Thanks, Rocky, but I've got plans this evening. You and Shea have a good time and be safe… good luck! Oh, remember you guys… we have that conference meeting with Terrance and Jax in about three hours. Is that still on?"

"Yeah, I've not heard otherwise seeya there, bro." "Hey, thanks for the invite. Maybe give me a raincheck next time I can make it, Rock!" Rocky rolled his shoulders aggressively, simultaneously finding Jay's eyes "not the raincheck thing. Dontcha know your credit stinks; ask anyone?" they laughed, bumping fists. A few moments later, Jay opens the door after inputting his fingerprints on a screen and peering into a retinal scanner disappearing from the somber blue-grey sky.

Renae and Liz are brain-waving about Wendi's Psychotropic treatments.

Meanwhile, Liz was listening to Renae, who had left the outpatient Neurology Director minutes earlier. Wendi/Sunshine's brain scans were the topic of focus. "Liz, to sum it up, they called it an anomaly" "anomaly, my sweet ass, that's their way of saying they are flm clueless!" Renae stood by the door "should I go back and press them?" "no… I'll call them, thanks. Even you and I can see the stark differences between the scans. Terrance will not be happy with the anomaly bullshit!"

"I thought not, also. Liz, hey, Ron and I are throwing a potluck dinner for the 5-year-old whom that drunk-driving neighbor ran over. Can you join us tomorrow nite…?" "Um, yes, you can count on me, and I'll even hit Terrance up for a fat donation for little Lacy. How is she doing?" "They just pulled her off life support she's maintaining on her own were all cautiously optimistic." "That's great news. Tell Ron, hello, I'll ask Terrance when he returns from the city. Hopefully, it went well…." "Why don't you text him and possibly chat with him before the big Pow-Wow this afternoon!" "Sure, um, okay."

'No rest for the wicked…' Terrance in his Limousine has more crap hit the fan.

Terrance, far from resting in the back of the Limo, heading back to Napa. The abrupt ending of the call with Vadoma had him on edge. But now more Toxic news had slammed him sideways, his employees, trouble uh…. Sofie and Nadia damnit… He thought about the stock market and how the latest news if exported out of his private network, would further drive a wedge into the upward momentum he was trying to invoke by manipulating investment bankers to raise their guidance on NIA and publish 'Strong Buy ratings' NIA's stock, had been in the toilet and was just starting to recover!

Man, he needed a vacation, like yesterday. He had constantly communicated via FaceTime with Sofie from the Administration department at NIA-U. She was currently taking a tongue-lashing, not the type she enjoyed. "Sofie, it matters not what you do in your spare time, but you must acknowledge that if that statement were to be true, we wouldn't be having this conversation, correct?" "Uh, yes, sir, Mr. Halfinan, I take full responsibility for Nadia and my miscalculations. I'm also well aware of the employment disclaimer contracts I signed regarding proper etiquette being lawful and respectable. I'm sincerely sorry."

He hacked, clearing his voice derisively, looking at her sullen face, "have you read the Napa Valley Register or the Sonoma Index... Tribune?" "No sir, I don't read the newspapers. They're kind of obsolete. In fact, I don't know anyone that..." "never mind that. Have you read the local news, Sofie, online?" "yes, sir, on my phone, and I must say it's wildly embarrassing, immorally untrue, blatantly slanderous, Mr. Halfinan. I wonder if you could have someone from your law practice file a lawsuit. Someone told me you have 35 or more lawyers ah attorneys working for you!"

He let her ramble on… knowing why he'd hired her; it was a favor for a partner. Her Russian lineage goes back to the Grand Duchy of Moscow before 1377. He muses she's been a productive asset, loyal, no-nonsense, and not any trouble, but this was legendarily problematic. Otherwise, Terrance would have one of his upper managers deal with it. Now he'd have to call the NIA affiliates in Moscow. Favors always seemed to come back to bite him and haunt him. She was still carrying on, "no, it's so horrible, sir. How American media can exaggerate and sensationalize the untruths, it's not like that in Mother Russia. They'd be chopped off at the knees. We have to do something. They also dragged Nadia through the meat-grinding chipper, too, sir!"

Terrance was working on three devices while she was uselessly defending herself. He had his laptop open, tapped, and flipped to the next page of her Bio. 7 ½ years with us, Damn Sofie! He glanced to his left to read the latest headlines on his iPad, the 3rd page of the article. The headline… 'NIA has once again had a negative impact on our fine city of Napa.

NIA Employees arrested for DUI… drunk and disorderly! Lewd Promiscuous nudity with sexual aberrant perversions using foreign instruments!"

Terrance quickly turned the FaceTime screen over and held his nose tight, trying not to cackle. This was awful, the epitome of negative press, but it wasn't such a surprise in his twisted mind. With his warped contrarian way of thinking thought it great fun, then regained composure back to the terrified makeup-stained cheeks. "Sofie, let me see Nadia" she passed her phone over to her the video came back into focus. "What do you have to say for yourself, Nadia?" it was apparent to him that she was spent… like severely hungover. Her milk-white complexion was now in splotches. Her Romanian cream face was blanched, a straight mess with streaks of mascara running down her face. "I'm ah um eh so sorry sir please sir you think my Papa will find out… you not tell him?" "I've bonded you out of Napa County Jail. I'll have a Limo drop you at the gates of NIA-U. Listen, you're old enough what…?" He quickly scans their bios. "You're both 27 years old, you know not to go out on the town and get fricken wasted… you're suspended as of now. My staff and I will decide what sanctions to impose or how we will proceed. What you're guilty of is cause enough for termination. You're both confined to your dorm rooms, with no further contact with each other," he ruefully sneers at them.

Sofie wasn't done. "Mr. Hallinan, in America, aren't we innocent till proven guilty, sir….?" "No, it's quite the opposite, but don't let me get into my personal feelings, Sofie. Unlike Russia, the Napa police department uses pocket cams with audio. Since my office will take up your defense, the five videos the police filmed of you two in compromising positions will be sent to our email addresses." He watches the girls do the hand-to-the-face cover-ups looking at the screen as if shock slapped them silly… brazen guilt exposed with shameful embarrassment, blushing Sofie mumbles. "Aah, sir, did you say holding up five tiny digits, there are five cam's videos of us?"

With his thumb pressing on his veins, Terrance kept his face tight and squeezed his wrist. He was recording the fright on the young girl's torn-back faces. They were hungover, still drunk, unslept unkept leftovers. He maintained his composure with a final pinch of his skin. Laughing subsided within; he'd had to admit it something was wrong with him. He was actually enjoying this reprimand. Ugh, with respite, went silent and sighed. Nadia and Sofie were sitting on a bench outside of the jail, being watched by a Deputy. Neither of them was allowed to drive, and surprisingly they were let out of the drunk tank even though they still had B.A.C, which was still over 1.1. They were tested an hour ago and were still blowing into a tester over the legal limits. They'd still be in the drunk tank if it weren't for his influence.

Finally decided to lighten up the scenario "it's all speculation conjecture, all hearsay," Nadia asked, "well sir, what's hearsay?" Terrance kicks his feet up, leaving the slider down for his Chauffeur Jacob to enjoy. The banter was a thrilling change of pace; Terrance hits mute... as Jacob rips out a howl, "sshh" scolds him, "be quiet," adding some snickering of his own, unmutes the call. "Nadia, hearsay is like unproven... like someone or a group claim to witness something that's unsubstantiated. It's not factual yet. But the five videos can mean that there were five police officers at the scene or perhaps fewer, and the video was taken by dash cams. Ugh, what is indisputable is Sofie had a B.A.C. of 2.1, and you 2.3 totally inebriated 0.8 is the legal limit, girls."

The girls are rapidly becoming Redder, blushing as Terrance piles it on! "We can assume that if five videos were taken, at least two police cars had pulled up, maybe three without you two being aware that they were even there, totally oblivious cuz you were busy being intimate and soused... uh drunk. The preliminary police reports state that your SUV Ford

Expedition was half on the road and half on the soft shoulder. You had your music at full volume, the German heavy Metal band 'Rammstein' blaring out of the four doors, which the reports say were flung open you both were explicitly naked. Nadia had a ball gag in her mouth and a choker chain around her neck. You girls were on your knees on the back bench seat. Sofie, you were seen with a Horsey whip in one hand and a strap-on dildo...." <u>"Halt, no halt ugh alto stop sir they have this on video OmGod oh no!"</u> Jacob covers his face with his jacket lifting the glass slider voluntarily, pounding the steering wheels, tears dropping rapidly, mumbling "This funny as shit!"

Terrance again hit mute and flipped the phone over, for he was uncontrollably laughing almost 35 seconds later. He looked back at the Guillotine stares, "I'm afraid that's about all I have for you two. For now, do either of you remember aah, or let me rephrase, unh, redirect that question? What do you recall from last night?" Jacob rolls back down the slider saying, "11 minutes to NIA, sir."

Sofie was in a muted babytalk voice, "uh sir, I guess we're fired. I don't...." Nadia interrupted, "Unh, no, it was my birthday. I love it at NIA-U. If it matters, I won the archery Gold medal over Ivanka at the NIA Games, I promise...." Sofie breaks in being the coy dominant one with another play "I feel like you Americans say... like death warmed over a skillet like me and Nadia maybe was drugged you know plenty of townsfolk's were buying us drinks this is crazy that we got caught doing that perversion sir, uh wonder where all that paraphernalia came from, ugh...." Terrance was genuinely beginning to admire Sofie. She might have a future. She had lips, big lips well, he snickered inside. Well, I will wait for the videos.... lol.

"Sofie, don't worry when Jax received the call last night at 3:15 am, he requested blood tests. Terrance pointed to their arms... bandages. See, we'll know if you were drugged. I want you two to go back to your dorms and get some rest. Okay, again, you're not to leave your rooms...." Nadia hesitates, then speaks, "Oh, for Christ's sake, is anyone else going to find out? I mean other workers at our offices, unh, at NIA, we need to keep this a real secret, sir, right...?" "No, Nadia, absolutely not!" she was relieved that Terrance had reassured her. "Ahh, people can't find out. That would be so terrible. How could we work with...!" Terrance wobbles his head in the negative, "Oh, I'm relieved. Thanks if this were to get it out...." Nadia pauses.

"Nadia, you asked if I would keep this a secret. What did I say to you? You're not understanding this situation, girl, shit think... we don't live in the Dark Ages. Unh, gosh, your brains are still swimming in alcohol. How the Hell can this be a secret?" Nadia jumps in "sir, you said, 'no, absolutely not,' right?" "Exactly, thank you. No, your porn show will not be kept a secret. It will be mandatory viewing for every prospective participating student. I haven't thought up a caption or heading, um, not even a title, maybe ash, 'This is not acceptable at NIA-U!' no, girls, I'm sure my staff will come up with the appropriate heading for your educational videos."

Their heads drop non-fake tears boil up and bubble out. The phone slips from Sofie's grip, and Terrance pushes end. Jacob drove through the gates "hey boss, Dontcha think you were a little rough on them? I caught a glimpse of their pathetic embarrassed expressions...." "Yes and no, surely it was a break from the monotony, but what they did was irresponsibly dangerous, illegal. They were lucky that the cops pulled up at 3:15 am could have been a couple of drunks with shotguns!" his words wafered in the air between them. "I suppose your correct, boss. You're not going to send them packing, are you?" "No, in fact, I might reward them!" it was Jacob's turn to blanch with perplexed confusion. He recovered as he parked and got out to get to Terrance's door. "Hey, boss, you will get me a copy of these videos, right?"

Terrance smirked and left him with a swirl, no answer to Jacob's overt yearnings 'damn,' he muttered, I'll find them on YouTube or somewhere online, maybe PornHub, umh, or OnlyFans; their sex show will be out there. Sofie and Nadia are hot bitches. What they need is a real man stud saw his reflection in the mirror flexed... Yep! His cell phone rang as he put the Limousine in gear. "Jacob, don't forget the girl's SUV was towed to our outpatient parking lot. No use paying any more tow fees than necessary...." "Yes, boss, I'll take care of it. I might need to contact Sofie since she probably has the keys. Didn't you say the vehicle was under her name?" Terrance smiled. "No, I didn't... you must be back here to pick me up by 7:15 pm, Jacob. Go pick up Nadia and Sofie!" "Yes, sir, boss!" he grinned. The boss is fkn way cool.

<u>Hours later... Terrance was mulling over Rico and Wendi's relationship.</u>

Terrance's next stop was to visit Liz at the low classification prison unit's medical dept. His main concern was the multiple EEGs that Wendi endured the day before and how she felt physically and mentally. Was she experiencing any side effects from the new-wave designer drugs that Liz forced upon her? He didn't call Wendi, for he knew precisely where she was.... Wendi was with Rico in the city, enjoying the break in the weather. His trackers were on the ball with video and pictures loaded to his burner phone, and Jax and Valerie were watching the odd couple. His stomach felt cramped, and he had to release a pent-up fart. Ooh, I have to hit the restroom. That one was stinky. 😷*

Resting on his throne, he mused how Wonderful.... the only word that could describe the dual circumstances exponentially paying dividends involving Wendi and Rico's renewed love affair. The re-invigorated bond of their intimate loving relationship might be just what the doctor ordered for NIA. There was nothing that* *influenced or controlled a human's mind than the obsessive emotions of silly love. Nada, love consumed the entire spirit like falling rocks on one's head… falling in love was straight up dumb! Rico had opted out of the Federal Court proceedings delaying his summons and inquiry by the Grand Jury. This morning couldn't have gone better, nmh, other than if the Feds dropped the Sara killings… and DNA squabble. But at least it was on the back burner. For now, thank the Devil for love.*

<u>Terrance hadn't heard if Vadoma was okay, but he'd ensure Wendi got her potion.</u>

Terrance pops his head into the laboratory, Liz says. "Yesterday's blood tests are right here," pointing to the screen, he replies, "it's all mumbo-jumbo, not my forte. What am I looking at?" "Okay, the bottom line is this Terrance the shot and Horse tablet's chemical compounds residual concentration is still quite strong. I have conferred with our Scientists and Neurology Division, and since this formula is experimental, it's better to ride on the edge of caution. A wait-and-see diagnosis is all we're left with," expounds Liz. She then opens the can of worms slightly. Terrance, we have Wendi's brain scans from as far back as when she had that accident at the S.F. Zoo when she was barely 18 months old. We also have the EEGs of when Wendi was five years old, dating back to when Sunshine arrived on the scene. None of the scans are similar to what you're looking at now…. we're concerned that the drugs had altered how her brain functions in either of her personalities…." "Fk Liz, what the Hell are you trying to warm around? Are you saying there's a third personality inside Wendi's head?…" "Nah, Terrance, don't get all worked up yet. It's only guesswork for now…." "you better have this under control, woman!" Shivers went up and down his spine, stopping at his sacrum. Vadoma's words were haunting him. Liz, where is Doctor Walters and that formula that he was supposed to...." "Terrance, what? Don't you recall Wendi came out of her fugue; she didn't need an additional shot of that witchcraft from your Gypsy woman!" "Liz, I want that mixture ready for a needle. We'll still inject Wendi and follow the protocol I gave you!" "But Terrance, she's already dealing with this newfangled messed up experimental psychotropic batch; another injection could do irreparable harm." "Do it, Liz!" He walks away, lost in thought, down the hall.

Terrance checks out for a second, leaning back in his comfortable chair in his office overlooking the lush NIA fields. After a millisecond catnap, he pulled his phone out and reread Barbara's text from last week when Jacob delivered the Feral's to the airport to fly back home. 'Hey, Terrance, sorry for doubting NIA. I'm not casting stones, but Rico was unyielding and adamant that our precious daughter was sinking further into her own fugue. Per our contractual agreement, she will remain at your facility until July 11th. Food for thought, though, from Ed and my perspective Wendi is not transmitting or conveying to Ed and me to be Sunshine, but Wendi isn't herself either. Something worries us, but we can't put our fingers on it. Please keep us abreast of any changes, take care. Hope to hear from you and your staff regularly as always... yours, Barbara 🌐 *.'*

He pushed the intercom to Liz, "I want you to read this from Wendi's mom," forwarding the text to Liz's phone, "but first, how did everything go at Ron and Renae's potluck dinner last night for the 5-year-old girl? How much money was raised for her medical expenses? Does NIA need to add to the contributions? I heard the baby girl was breathing on her own. She was still not out of the woods in a coma. Still, tell me?" Liz was holding her mouth open in surprise "umh, I think you are confused, or I sent the wrong information to you. The potluck dinner is for tonight, Terrance. It hasn't happened yet. Yes,

Lacy is breathing on her own, though...." Terrance shakes his head. "I'm just fatigued, so much on my mind, sorry...." "No worries, but her parents asked if NIA might consider allowing Lacy to transfer to our Neurology Hospital. The caveat is they have zero insurance and no monies...." "I will approach the board at NIA. Until then, why don't you go ahead and start the necessary paperwork to move Lacy to our hospital?" "Oh my, Terrance, that's so generous beyond what we expected," she wanted to reach out and hug him through the phone. He wasn't finished "what's going on with the drunk neighbor that ran the little girl down in her yard?" "Terrance, the woman that ran her over, is still in the county jail. They're waiting to see if Lacy survives. She doesn't have a bond yet.... And other charges are pending."

He slams his fist into his palm "she should be prosecuted to the fullest, uh, no excuse for her to be driving drunk. What was it... her third DUI in the last three months? I don't get it. Why didn't the prosecutor insist on her having one of those blowers that detect alcohol on her steering wheel that is attached to her ignition and prevents it from starting? Oh well, hell, keep me posted... Ttylater."

<u>Liz, for the fourth time, tries to get Renae on her phone and then hits the loudspeakers that echo across the NIA properties. Five minutes later, she's checking out the cameras.</u>

Liz picks up her phone. "Sorry, Liz, I'm at the clinic...." "Renae, what's up with you, woman? What have you been so preoccupied with lately at the hospital clinic? It's like you're living over there now. What's so important over there?" Renae rocks little Sonja in her arms, remembering how her daughter Candice used to love the sun's rays coming through the window. "Liz, I'm on my way. I have been checking on some of our past patients, is all." "Okay, we have problems. I've tried to get Greg, um, Doctor Walters on his phone. Terrance wants him to go ahead and mix up another batch of that concoction that he was given for Wendi!" "I'll check at his office for him; seeya in a little over an hour, Liz." Renae turned and hit the intercom for one of the nurses she'd assigned to take care of Sonja to let her know she was leaving. She kissed Sonja on her forehead... the baby looked at her nonblinking. Renae strangely thought at that moment, odd, I've never heard Sonja even whimper, never has she cried. Huh!

<u>Sofie and Nadia are in recovery mode.</u>

Sofie had taken three showers, drained a gallon of water down her esophagus and still felt buzzed, and then tried to eat some buttered toast. This caused a vomiting attack, followed by diarrhea and Raw Anus Syndrome or 'R.A.S.' She couldn't believe her B.A.C. was so high last night, wondering how her G.F. lover Nadia was feeling. She was hesitant to even look at her phone. The barrage of Emojis had hit her cellphone. It was like nothing in this world was private anymore fk who didn't know about this calamity? She didn't dare open her other social media accounts. At last count, the most popular Emoji was the 'Laugh out loud' yellow face with a wide-ass smile and tears falling um streaming downward, eyes squinted coincidently like hers.

She hated this felt like never leaving her dorm room, sick to her stomach, and everything else within her anatomy. Texts of the Red Devils, all the various smiley faces, girls on girls with matching words of innuendos, she'd received many Rolling Stone Tongue pictures. People were assholes! She ducks her head down below the curtains peeking out towards the baseball diamond infield outside her building. Yep! she was on exhibit. Why not stick Nadia and her in a see-through glass cage on a rotisserie grille or parade us around the NIA's grounds like we were on exhibit?

Sure enough, there were seven people in a group, standing outside her apartment, one pointing upwards to her dorm room. All she wanted to do was disappear. Not a suicidal candidate, she believed, but now rethought and scrutinized that belief. She had to hide from all people. A tingling paranoia grasped her, staring into her tiny kitchen at her knives in the wood block. Bothering her more than she wanted to admit. Nadia, Wtf was up with her? She hadn't answered the phone all day, ahh damnit, maybe one more shower. She and Nadia had a mandatory appointment later this afternoon, which meant they would probably be terminated. Fired, 'Nadia, oh, I love that woman.' The looks Nadia gave her with utter disdain were voraciously cannibalizing her heart. 'No, please, I love her. I can't lose her, please God no…' gazed in the mirror 'gosh, we're so screwed!' The Freight Train migraine echoed in the tunnel between her ears.

<u>Terrance is putting out fires.</u>

Terrance cruised down the stairwell from one of his offices after hearing over his walkie-talkie that there was another death on the grounds of NIA. He jaunts over to the triple-gated maximum-security side of the prison. Another damn suicide on one of the three ground floors, the basement, called the dungeon by some guards and staff. This was where the most dangerous of the criminally insane were housed, and many referred to the maximum facility below ground as the Tomb or torture chambers. Inmates were dealt with swiftly for transgressions against the staff or fellow prisoners. <u>Terrance does a quick scan of the suicide victim's records… she hadn't any visitors in over 13 years and had no outgoing mail nor correspondence with the outside world. Her phone account hadn't been accessed in years. No one would miss her… he ordered her body cremated on-site. Even though her death was</u>

suspicions, there wouldn't be an investigation; he had other issues to deal with.

Terrance's mind reverberated on what the old lady had said. Sonja was alive under his thumb! His niece had given birth to an evil spirit; what a trip… Sometimes this Hocus-Pocus spoken by the Gypsy family unnerved him. He was raised never to doubt the words of Vadoma. His parents and relatives had counted on the Gypsy as if she preached the gospel… it was too bizarre. However, he realized it had been a long time since he'd received a wrong 'Reading' from Vadoma. He'd reminded himself to have Walter, his head of security, put together a video footprint for each of his nieces. He knew NIA had over three thousand cameras filming 24/7. He parks the Golf cart seeing Rocky pull up in his Jeep. Terrance hops in, "how's it going, boss…?" "It's going. Can you drop me by the cafeteria? That's the last place I saw Kamryn on our cameras." "Sure, hey, how'd it go at the Federal building?" Terrance rolled his shoulders, very well, my friend, much better than I believed possible." "That's good, ughhhh, I've given much thought, Sir, about what I'm going to advocate." "I'm listening, Rocky. Please don't call me Sir; we're on a first-name basis; please go ahead." Rocky nodded "unh, Brock Dame, as you know, is one of Rico's best friends. He's been prodding me to get with the NIA-U board and to allow Brock to enroll in our next semester…." "What, Rocky, you're joking? Why would he want a two-year degree at our university? The only reason would be to spy on us." Rocky grinned and patted Terrance on the shoulder, "yes, that's what I'm counting on. We allow Brock to see and observe precisely what we want him to report… back to the Feds. Let's face it, they've already planted three spies, and we have their names. This isn't going to stop, unh, I mean Rico's suspicions, so let's let his best friend feed him information that we…." "Yes, wow, that's brilliant. I'll bring that up at our next board meeting. Not bad, uh, not bad at all, Rocky." Terrance hopped out of the

Jeep and strolled over to his Golf Cart with the intention of finding Kamryn. She hadn't answered his texts.

Terrance sucked on his lower lip, mulling over what Rocky had said. Knowing that Rocky and Brock were also very close friends and had worked for the FBI on many cases together. It is clear that Rocky was naïve about how Brock could singlehandedly destroy NIA, or maybe he thought he could run some form of interference. Brock was someone who could push NIA off the proverbial cliff into bankruptcy, and that would be the ultimate financial ramifications. What would follow, no doubt, would be dozens of Federal Indictments. If Brock recovers his memory from when his niece Sara tried to murder him on Lake Shasta... Oh, why is life so fricken chaotic, yeah, Brock has amnesia, and the best Neurologists and Psychologists have stated that his EEG shows areas within his brain are dead, brain damage? But Brock could place Sara on his parent's houseboat and prove that his Fiancé... Kamryn was switched out... damn the list of negatives is infinite. The best conclusion of the Brock Dame saga was his terminal demise, but he was under 24/7 guard by two U.S. Marshals. Problems, problems without remedies. Ughhhh!

<u>Another Mandatory meeting of NIA's leaders in the War room.</u>

"Okay, it would appear we're in the majority, voting in the three latest Team Members to our NIA Squad. I must say, speaking for myself, this is an exciting graduating class... NIA-U is churning out top-of-the-line participants. Even the average finishing times of our obstacle courses have bettered by 3% overall." *Jax grinned, "and now we know what is coming...." Staring out at the original Team Leaders. He paused for effect.*

Jax faintly simpers, "that brings us to the last matter at hand; it was a couple of nights ago... No, let me rephrase. The incident occurred in the early morning hours; the first filming of the debacle was around 3:15 am. I suppose proper etiquette is dismissed when we discuss this next topic.... our own Sofie and Nadia, the dynamic duo, were arrested." He muttered not another syllable, weird amused facial alterations with sighs, a moan or three... head wobbles with Terrance rolling his eyes, articulating. "I'm sure all of you have caught or heard the gossip that their shameful behavior has gone Viral. Now streaming across many social media sites picked up by Youporn.com, short movie clips from five different angles our girls filmed in compromising action-based positions. Sofie had, I believe, a 2.1 and Nadia 2.3 B.A.C. or something close to that. Needless to say, they were Wasted!"

Jax took the baton "Sofie, of course, is our Administration Department Manager of seven plus years, and we all witnessed," Jax stopped, beamed at the NIA leaders, and nodded. "My team won in the Archery competition, Nadia taking the Gold Medal. They apparently have an affinity for female genitalia, primarily each other's," more smiles. "I've spoken to our fearless leader..." turning his eyes towards Terrance, "Mr. 'T' has been dealing with the two lovers and has offered several options, which are as follows we send Sofie and Nadia packing back to Lithuania and Romania, or we sanction them by restricting them taking away their gate passes for a year. Terrance and I have discussed another alternative we believe can teach these two outrageous lovers a lesson and be used advantageously for our recruits. Since Nadia and Sofie are into productions of exhibitionism, we could order them to go on our stages and have them perform for us here at NIA... if they refuse, we can send them packing."

"Instantly, five of the seven in attendance howled, slapping the tops of their tables... and laughing wildly, teeth shining, dimples flashing "well, Hellyeah shouts Shon. Why not? I'm down for that!" Terrance holds up the stop sign palm "all kidding aside, they made the newspapers and social media sites, and worst yet, a Napa police officer went entrepreneur on us trying to market the videos illegally to several porn sites. We tried to put a halt to that, but it's out there on some rogue sites. NIA's reputation is further dragged through the cesspool, now down significantly in stock price." He checked his phone, seeing his stock accounts down another 5% today, with NIA being the largest loser of his diversified investments. Terrance then added, "the incident had found legs on National news with Joe Kernan and his sidekick David Faber on CNBC, who hid their faces with files chuckling and cackling." It was hilarious as laughter could be heard from a few NIA members who'd watched CNBC earlier in the day. "It wasn't funny for me, nor shouldn't be to any of you. Their immoral acts affect all of your retirement funds. Ugh!" He recants his last words.... "the girl's sexual acts weren't immoral. What made them so was that they committed them right out in the open. Like most of you, I don't care what sexual proclivities we enjoy, but we should keep them private. Their drunken escapade has already cost us thousands of dollars as of today. Let me also remind you that money isn't everything. It's our reputation that matters most."

The foolish humor was natural given the circumstances, but commonsense bared credence. Terrance continued, "we're all shareholders in NIA stock. Your monies and bonuses have been reduced by an additional 7.3% as of the stock markets close today." Moans and negative body language were on display. "Not so funny. Investment bankers, hedge funds, Mutual funds, you name it... the investment community and world soured on us. Many have invested in our vision here at NIA. Our secondary offering is now permanently spoiled and shelved. This latest catastrophe leaves many in the investment community seething. My phones have been blown up from the CEOs of Goldman Sachs to J.P. Morgan, to name just a few of the incensed individuals. If you'd like, I'll forward some of the calls, texts, and tweets to you…. nope, not fkn funny!"

Now, absolutely no humor resided within the chambers, the smiles flipped upside down, sitting tensely edging to the end of seats, Jax taps a key on his iPad. They all looked up to see them sitting on the 1st floor in the lobby, their heads held by their hands, looking like well-done 'Rigor mortis cadavers.' Yes, it was Sofie and Nadia waiting to be called into the meeting. Jax took the impetus "well, are we ready to grill the girls? Should I have them escorted down?" Terrance sighs "shouldn't we have a plan or decide their fates prior to bringing them in…" Jax is rather amused, "I thought we had decided to, um, humiliate them by having them perform reenactments like a 'Take 2' sequel, but this time they're going to be completely sober." Everyone looked seriously somber…. Terrance says, "Okay, send them down here!"

Moments later, the two girls stood before the panel, both with loose-fitting sweat outfits, their tiny frames…. are hidden beneath. They acted timid and really scared to death, lips on Sofie quivering. Nadia kept looking down at her toes, frightened and way out of their comfort zones. Jax allows a grimace to impart his face and grabs the microphone. "I won't bother in pleasantries, girls…" both uttered yes sirs "we're sorry OmGod we…." "Sshhh, you've left us very few options of which first, evict you, ugh, send you back to your homelands. Second, retain your services with sanctions levied against you. We've weighed some punishments such as 'loss of pay… fines or take away your gate passes or thirdly, you could both put on a reenactment of your porn exhibition for our staff and select cadets. We're thinking maybe a separate showing in our main Theater on stage. We can even have your Ford Expedition pulled up on the stage for you… If you choose the first or third choice, your punishment will be decided today… I'll allow you to confer with each other." Jax waved his arm, pointing to an alcove at the back of the spacious room.

Nadia was Redder than blood. Sofie wavered and lost her balance, her face blanched ghost-like. Nadia stood perplexed, staring into space, then focused on her lover stepping into a corner of the room. They whispered, "what I don't understand… unh like we're going to ah…." Sofie breathed, "they want us to repeat the performance like what we watched us do on the internet, have sex live in front of hundreds of people, Nadia," espousing Sofie, totally exasperated.

Terrance finally temporarily stopped the pain and suffering "you go back to your dorms and think about it. You have 48 hours to make a decision. When you do… contact Jax via his office number. Is that understood?" They shook heads and were escorted out of the room.

When they left, the fun went with them. Terrance finalized the reprimand, "all right. We've had our fun… with them. Still, let us further their embarrassment and have them speak to all our recruits at the inaugural ceremonies in the first week of February. We will display their dirty deeds on the screens around the amphitheater, and they will formulate at least 700 words each to describe what you don't do while attending NIA's 2-year program. Of course, like many of our new students, we are 'LGBTQIA+…' friendly, so no disrespect to anyone. We believe in Live and Let Die!" 🌐

<u>Terrance finally locates Kamryn…</u>

Kamryn had left the inmate hospital only 25 minutes after seeing Uncle's last text. He wanted to meet with her to discuss something, probably about how the pre-Grand Jury meeting at the Federal building in San Francisco had gone. Kamryn had nursed and cuddled her gorgeous baby, leaving Sonja with one of House's trusted nurses. She grabbed a ham and cheese sandwich at the cafeteria, knowing that Terrance would find her with all of the roving cameras watching every move. She wondered how long she could keep Sonja a secret. The cameras had her coming and going from the inmate hospital.

Terrance was walking in, she out, and he put out his hands "let's take a stroll, niece, no skipping this time." She wiped her face and swallowed her last bite with grueling trepidation. "We need to develop a plan today" "a plan. I'm all ears, uncle..." "This isn't a one-way conversation, Kam. I will let you in on some information I was privy to because of our contacts inside the San Francisco Fed Building. A few of the FBI's upperclassmen and women are on our payroll." She paused to say something, then didn't... better to let him play his opening move out. They walked together to a waiting Golf cart. "I also spoke with the AUSA and Judge that signed the warrants for Rico's DNA testing here at NIA for your sister, the same Judge Delaney that found enough circumstantial evidence to agree that a Grand Jury was warranted." "Pardon me, uncle. Please be cognizant that I'm an innocent victim.... Sara, I will never forgive.... I despise every centimeter of that rotten bitch. I was to be married to Brock Dame.... she's ruined my life. But Hey, that's okay right uncle?" "Kam, I understand how you feel, there's no reason to pile on more sarcasm. I..." "No, you don't. How can you pretend to understand how I feel.... if you believe that, then you're as insane as many of them...." "Such, this is counterproductive. I'm going to get you out of here, niece. Let's work together for a common goal, all right?"

Terrance and Kam sat alongside each other in the moving cart in silence... Kamryn mused over how she could get Sonja out of this Fort Knox prison. Terrance decided that no matter how ridiculous it would sound, he'd have to address this baby Sonja conundrum that Vadoma had claimed lived under his thumb. He'd contact the person who knew the inner nuances better than anyone else, Doctor Liz Honcho, who had her finger on the pulse of NIA. He again checked Kamryn out... no way the girl could have been pregnant. Just like her sisters, they were slim and trim. Vadoona had made a mistake, but hey, he'd still have to complete his due diligence.

Kamryn was finally done with being the person who'd dealt with the brunt of FBI Agent Rico Captors' investigation into all of unh… Sara's killings of the attorney, the correction officer, and his wife. Why was any of this her problem? I mean, come on, huh? "Uncle, shouldn't Sara be part of this conversation too?" "Yeah, uhh, yes, it would save me the time of explaining it twice. I suppose if you're comfortable discussing this narrative with her present, we know this is her fault, culpable to the max unh, 9th degree…." Kam didn't respond, only texted Sara, who immediately texted back lick-itty-split, looking up at him. "She's at Val's apartment and waiting on us now." They drove by a fruit orchard underneath a Pecan grove, swerving around the sprinkler nozzles. He stopped the Golf cart. They got out by a spring-fed creek "come on. We have a little time. Let's walk to one of my favorite places. I want you to know this. I'm ashamed I haven't taken you to the side, Kamryn. Please let me try to convey to you how much my heart went out to you and for you. Since you proved that Sara had diabolically escaped leaving you here in her place in our prison, the strength and fortitude you had to sustain while you were ridiculed, laughed at, humiliated, degraded even beaten is beyond my comprehension. You are an amazing young lady. I'm so impressed with your resolve and inner strength, so proud to call you my Favorite Niece!"

Kam stops in the path by the brook steps in front of him, now holding both his palms, focusing upward, her tears exposed. "Kamryn, I'm sorry, so damn sorry to have hung up on you when you called my law office dozens of times, sorry to have disbelieved you. I'm encouraged that there are people on this earth with your constitution… of unrelenting superpower. I love you; don't you ever question that or how proud I am to call you my family, um Niece, I owe you many apologies which could never ever be enough just want…" "oh Uncle L…." "No,

Kam, I don't expect you to forgive me at my beckoning call. No, when you have recovered as much as you feel you can, that's the time for us to have another Uncle... Niece, chat, um, talk about all that's happened to you... on your terms about whatever subject matter you want to discuss. You're a blessing, and you're not a psychopathic killer like your sisters are!" He pulled her in for a gratifying embrace; then, they soldiered on.... hand in hand.

They cruised along. It was just after lunchtime, and the sky was cloudy, but the sun was giving it the College try, and it seemed it would break through. Teasingly did so a few times, bringing an incredible feeling of warmth. He hoped where he was driving to wouldn't result in a jolt of coldness and that the sisters could be cordial like they were at the end of the dinner party last night. He parked outside of Val's apartment on-site. It would be just the three of them. Val was with Jax in San Francisco, surveilling Wendi Feral and Rico. Terrance had spun the same web storyline of the S.F. Fed trip earlier in the day to his chauffeur Jacob, feeling it had been adequately rehearsed. He was preparing himself for this semi-confrontation with the sisters.

Sara met them at the door, and they coolly entered. Kam and Sara nodded at one another. It was like the night before hadn't happened. The sisters were getting along then. He needed another ice-breaker but hadn't one. Knowing their bond was shredded, he waved his hand, and they sat around a coffee table. "I must say, nieces. You would have been proud of how I'd faced down Forensic Pathologist Shanon Roble, who made it clear as windowpane ahh glass that the Pubic hair found in Carl's throat and teeth had your DNA.... Sara. The odds were astronomical otherwise. Sara interjected, "but hair analysis has been notoriously fallible...." Terrance nodded with agreement, "yes, which I presented to the panel. For instance," Terrance held up his iPhone. "In case law... 'The state of Wisconsin used flawed microscopic hair comparisons calling it evidence to convict innocent people. At least 13 individuals were sent to prisons, and errors of up to 89% were made in Federal cases across the USA.' So, girls, I won this small battle regarding hair fibers used as evidence proving hair analysis is futile analogous, and controversial... about the same as the lie-detector tests." Sara grimaced and then seemed to relax a bit.

"But Doctor Rohle then hammered the nail in flat and buried it along with us. The period blood on the Tampon string was yours, Sara. We can't dispute it. The labs confirmed it from Rico's DNA samples on his visit here... it couldn't be Kam's. This is new technology. The nucleus of this discovery is found in the Plasma of your blood. Irrefutable evidence that the DNA of identical babies can now be isolated. This is a fact now proven from Germany to China and for certain here in our country. This puts you at the scene of the homicides. Doctor Rohle vehemently argued this to my face and the panel. I stood there in a face-off with the Judge and AUSA, along with other officials. I raised my hands, chuckling, I told them.... what your saying is physically impossible. Sara doesn't have the keys to the prison gates, her Cell, or any other doors. In fact, I said, look at this time-stamped video. I showed them a video of Kamryn in your cell at the precise time that you, Sara, were at Carl and Bianca's home. My investigative team had parlayed the neighbor's closed circuit video's timing coinciding with the double murder with exact time prints, which gave us the precise time of your executions."

Sara ghoulishly smirked "that was awesome, Uncle, but how did you discount my DNA? Um, blood, isn't that enough proof to hang any man or woman? I mean, it's far from circumstantial, right?" "Correct, Sara, our only defense isn't to argue the test results. We lose that argument; we call it absurd and impossible!" "Oh, all right, Unc, but...." "So I steadfastly and sarcastically said, what did Sara do teleport over, or was this an OBD out-of-body experience? You bring these charges forth, and all of you will be laughingstocks across the globe. How the hell could Sara have committed the crimes and, oh, throw in the poisoning of the attorney? It's not I that will be laughing so hard that I might die of lack of oxygen. It will be in the tabloid's… social media. It will be on every TV and cell phone, and news channel. You will set back Forensics for decades thinking of just the one headline, 'Sara, the Vipress Serial Killer, escapes NIA Prison to kill again then returns to her Cell for dinner!" Even Kamryn giggled… "that was a good one, uncle!" Turned a half frown at Sara.

Sara was thoroughly enjoying herself, contrary to her sister's countenance. Kam was disgusted not showing it, however. "Sara, I see you are gloating, but you put us on a slippery slope with your suntan. Forensic Pathologist Shanon Rable had wrested control back from me and asked how did Sara get a suntan locked in solitary confinement? I replied, looking at each female in the Judge's chamber with me. Doctor Rable, AUSA Beckwitch, and Judge Delaney… <u>'Sara had a bottle of 'spray on tan' or lotion in her belongings. It's available from the prison's commissary.'</u>

Then a Court Clerk handed each participant at this Grand Jury panel meeting a thin folder. I wasn't prepared for the near 'CheckMate' trap… on three sheets of 8 X 11 paper in bold type print were the results of the scientific analysis. It was a 'hair follicle, combined with blood tests that proved no artificial chemicals.' No tanning solutions systemically entered Sara's epidermis or bloodstream. She was tanned by the Nuclear reactor in the sky, in other words, The Sun!" "Well, shit, uncle, dammit, they got us…." yelped Sara.

Terrance was on a roll, shaking his noggin… "The Judge then asked me, "what's your explanation for this irregularity?" Sara folded her arms together over her breasts like waiting for a punch line at a comedy club. Kam said, "so how'd you get out of that one?" I said, "well, obviously, I can't refute the blood tests, girls. So I played it off like one of my employees had to be guilty. I told the judge that it had to be an in-house problem. Perhaps a few of our Correctional Officers allowed Sara out in the sunshine or recreation yard against the orders in place. That's my best guess." Terrance smiled, matching his nieces smirks, "then I finished off with this final statement. Believe me. I will most definitely get answers for you all on this matter. On top of that, I will satisfy my own curiosity… thanks for the information!"

Sara bows her head at Kamryn. "I'm sorry, Uncle, to have caused so much strife and trouble, and Kam, again, I'm so apologetic. Gosh, I screwed up. There's nothing I can…." "Thanks, sister, I know, so where do we go from here?" Terrance says, "Wait, I'm not finished with the Feds. The Judge agreed and signed a warrant and deemed it necessary to collect new DNA from Kamryn to eliminate her from the homicides. Also, NIA is to comply with all demands of releasing the time stamp videos of you in your prison cell and all NIA gates for the three days, starting before the killings and after. Strangely she granted Rico, who was absent, the time stamps for the period when the attorney was murdered, so no, we're not out of the woods. The last thing the Judge intimated is that this is highly suspicious. She is determined to have answers wanting further case studies on the new DNA technology tests proving that you, Sara, could only be the one who committed the crimes!"

This toned down the exuberance. Sara hopped up, got the pitcher of iced tea, and refilled their glasses. Terrance rolled on "here's an idea. I'll run it by both of you. Kamryn… Jax will have your gate passes activated tomorrow. I want you to drive to your Tiburon home. You will be followed by the FBI, Rico's agents, uhm, his surveillance team. After a while, go to your salon that Sara opened while you were in her prison cell and get in touch with the manager Crystal who works silently part-time for NIA. Also, while there, I want you to rent out your workstation, go into Sara's office, and we need you to get anything that would be incriminating out of the Salon." Anything whatsoever that could implicate Sara, we need to be a step ahead of Rico. I'm surprised he's not tried to get a search warrant for your salon thus far. It's only a matter of time. We know he's got Agents watching the shopping center and has pulled videos from adjoining businesses already!"

Sara sat silent, realizing that she'd left a horde of compromising proof in her office at her salon. She decided to try and vindicate these errors, "Uncle. I'm sorry to have to tell you this... I never had time to take the poison spray or weapons back to my storage in the city. Remember I had that acerbic confrontation with Renae on that stormy night, and the next day we met at the Federal Courthouse. Terrance, right after that, I went to your law office for our first meeting since my swapping out of Kamryn. You captured Renae that night, and then I agreed with you to come here to NIA with you and do the interview with Rico. I've been here ever since... So how can I be held responsible for all the incriminating evidence I left at my salon? *Terrance shook his head while Kamryn sipped the tea after watching Sara and her uncle do the same, not wanting any more of Sara's poison elixir... uh, laced tea.*

"Sara, you don't have to make excuses. We can't go backward, um, well, only to learn what we must do. This isn't a fault-based discussion. We have to be proactive, my niece. I understand the circumstances that you have defended yourself under. Let's move on... Sara, I want you to make a list of what your sister needs to get out of the salon, along with where to find the stuff... and give the combination of your two safes in your office to Kamryn." "Uncle, we have Crystal managing the salon. Why don't you have her handle this problem?" "Because she's not a team member here at NIA, she has awesome skills in managing small businesses with the experience necessary to keep the salon in the black. Crystal is not in the know and will remain oblivious to our inner core. She's a great asset but not qualified to be privy at what we're about here."

Kamryn was now on the edge of the couch, not paying attention well, only peripherally. She was more enchanted and excited about her gate pass. 'Oh, yes, I'm going to get my baby out of here...' Sara proactively declared, "Sure, ok, Uncle, there's a ton to keep Kam busy. Certainly, we have to get that evidence out of the salon, I agree. It would help if she could video chat with me when she is at the salon. What do you think of that idea?..." "Great idea; we will do so on our private network." Kam nodded in agreement, sort of excited that she'd finally be free at last from the armpit of her life thus far, wondering if she had the 'Lips' to make the move and escape permanently from California with her baby.

"Kam, I have been informed that Doctor Roble will be in the morgue at San Rafael General Hospital between 1 pm and 5 pm tomorrow. She is speaking to a bunch of third-year students who aspire to be in Forensics. We will surprise her together. I'll pick you up at the salon at about 4 pm. This will stop the interview that Rico wants to have with you. Lucky for us, Rico and Wendi will be together hours away on a camping trip at Half Moon Bay!" Kam rolled her eyes "wow, Wendi is such a freakin asset, huh?" Terrance smirked, "love is so magical; changes all dynamics" he didn't linger on those words. "Clever uncle, so I will provide Dr. Roble DNA hair follicles and a swab or whatever she wants, and if she has any other things up her sleeve, we will deal with it, I assume." "Yes, Kam, this takes Rico out of the equation. You can spend the night at your Victorian home tomorrow night. Then I want you back here at 9 am, okay?" Kam is delighted but doesn't act overly excited, with Sara's eyes and feelings gauging her expressions. "You got it, uncle."

Sara rolls out a puzzled stare, "so we're going to give this Roble autopsy; woman doctor Kamryn's DNA isn't that going to prove that she wasn't the killer? Where does that leave us? I don't get it. Wouldn't it be better to have Kamryn disappear?" Terrance frowned, "this is the better of two evils. We don't want Rico interviewing your sister… right. Let me repeat this the Fed's had old DNA collected from Kam when they were investigating you, Sara. They used this in comparison, and it already proves their assumptions are true. They merely want new DNA for these newly discovered innovative tests…. To alleviate any of this, we could send Kamryn to Siberia. Still, I believe this is a new Scientific experimental way of extracting Plasma to test identical twins. It's in its infancy and might not be accredited for years. It wouldn't be prudent for them to do anything without substantiated evidence of you leaving NIA Sara. They will not open the huge can of worms that DNA could be fallible or even in the realm of possibilities that DNA proof could be tainted." Sara bends her head down…. "Okay, uncle, I'll trust your judgment…." "I have to roll… girls, give me a hug." He bid Sara goodbye, but Kam clung to him, and out the door they went.

He was thinking of the ensuing fire he'd have to extinguish… texting Jaybird, hoping that he'd be at his place. Due there in less than nine minutes. Kamryn clapped her hands together, "Uncle, where are you? I was speaking to you…." "Uhm, sorry honey, I was preoccupied…." "When do I meet with Jax and get the gate pass to go to Sara's salon and my home? I don't have Jax's contact information." "Oh honey, no worries. He will get with you when he returns from Fisherman's Wharf with your sister Valerie; their surveillance shift of Wendi and Rico is over at 5 pm." He hops into the Golf cart after hugging Kam again. Kam felt like skipping away in joy and decided to beeline back to her precious baby Sonja. Terrance was nearly giddy with 'optimism growing, hoping that positive momentum would continue overwhelming negatives,' but will it survive Jaybird's revelations? His tone was weary, ahh, his voicemail, that is. Before he knocked, the familiar voice was heard, "come on in, Terrance. I have a pitcher of Sun tea on the deck, ice, and a couple of glasses umh, been thinking over this latest news. The situation is quite disturbing." 🌐

<u>Wendi's brother Mark Feral reenters the fray.</u>

"Jay, couldn't this have waited for our team meeting later this afternoon…?" "Surely could of boss, I suppose, if I didn't think I should be leaving soon for Montana to stem the bleeding." This got Terrance's attention, and he poured some tea without ice "tell me what's happening; you're worrying me!" he scowled and clenched his teeth… fists tight. "Mark Feral has gone rogue. It was bad enough that his mercenary ass had joined C.I.N. that was 19 months back and old news. I realize how appalling and detrimental this may sound… his betrayal yesterday put him on the top of our hit list! He recruited 11 of my officers, and 79 soldiers have joined his organization from our original militia. Uh, and on top of that, the 11 senior officers were all graduates from NIA-U, and 57 of the 79 soldiers he's pilfering… came from our private army."

Terrance stands, wavering a touch, and leans out over the railing, turning back to Jay, deep in thought. "Must have been mighty significant powerful incentives to lose those Officers. What did he bait them with? How could he have…" "Yes, it's almost 1/5 of the entire legion based at the Herzog camp in Montana. But my main hierarchy remains intact… like I've said a hundred times if stricken once, what a horrible mistake I made allowing him to get close to me. I should never have allowed him to join us. I take full responsibility for giving him a civilian division South of Boise, Idaho. Why would I'd give him control over…" "Jaybird, that's like crying over spilled milk. I'm worried, umh, we can't afford to have any more deserters. When mutiny begins, we must circle the Wagons and pull everyone in closer to our leaders. Remember lessons of the past… over the annals of history. Mutiny is easily justified and proliferated by humans for predominantly self-survival or monetary gains and is often formed by strong,

*manipulating individuals and then followed by weak minds. A...
contagion begins, and that mindset is propagated and gains
leverage. It exacerbates because this world is full of Sheep and
followers whom powerful personas can manipulate. Mark Feral is
an Evangelist with death and destruction as his mantra. His God,
his objectives are sovereignty, money, and prestige." "Terrance, I
couldn't have called the kettle Blacker than you. Uhm, your dead-
on, Terrance!"*

Jay sneers as he flips on the screen hanging on the wall of
his deck. He's a man that's usually calm under fire, a Veteran
with tons of experience and bloodshed. His indoctrination was
with a Delta Force he commanded, missions to clandestinely
disperse... 'Kill teams in the Middle East.' "Here are some
satellite images from 49 minutes ago. This is the little city um
town of Elko, Nevada. What you're looking at is a C.I.N.
installation center. Now watch the monitor, Terrance." He
rolls a trackball, and the images slow, then he enlarges...
zooms in on some large box trucks, several semi-trucks with
40-foot trailers attached. Jay quickly passed them by with a
flick of his wrist and then expanded the video to show a two-
lane entrance into the C.I.N. installation center. Jay paused it
on a blurry Black and Silver Jeep Gladiator. It was the leader
of the pack. He points out, "there's the bastard, our mortal
enemy." He rolls the trackball, zooming into the tanned dark
features of the driver, which was Mark Feral smoking a fat
cigar.

Terrance states, "from a legal perspective, Mark hasn't
committed a real crime against us. It isn't like you had a
noncompete contract signed, right? The men that left with him
weren't under contract. Their free agents sort of like sports
athletes. They go where the sun shines on their asses best it's
not about loyalty anymore with the latest generations. Umh,
team players are hard to come by nowadays!" "True, Terrance,
those trucks you see are mostly owner-operated... not the
personal property of Mark's group of radicals. He is

undoubtedly a cut-throat bastard, but I'm more concerned that
he will try to use my pipeline business associates. Remember
that NIA's network will be compromised, umh, damaged if
he's allowed to run roughshod over...." "Haven't we already
dropped video and leaks to the FBI? I don't get it, Jay. He's
absconded from a seven-year probation obligation after being
paroled from San Quentin...." "Sure, I know he's on the FBI's
most wanted list. Now we have more ammunition for the FBI.
I was wondering, boss, if you'd like to copy some of this video
to your contacts in the Federal Government."

Terrance sips on an ice cube. "I'll run it by the board for
sure we must be careful of how we approach this situation, for
we're in the same business!" Looking back at the monitor, "we
will not feel the brunt of Mark's action like an analogy NIA is
like Giant surfable waves breaking on the beach leaving a tiny
ripple...." "I don't understand your comparison. What?" "Um,
just discombobulated gibberish considering us at NIA, the
giant wave, and Mark's C.I.N. barely a ripple on our ass, my
mind is elsewhere if yah only knew all the shit slapping off the
fan blades that I'm dealing with... Ah, okay, back on point, I
do agree that we must quell the bleeding. We should have
erased Wendi's brother Mark long ago, but tragically it's the
C.I.N. organization that could end life as we know it on
Earth...." "Btw Mark now has been anointed the Northern
Nevada Director of operations. That's what scares me,
Terrance." He flips the satellite images off and turns,
frowning.

"Okay, I understand what you were trying to say.
Remember, we are much larger than C.I.N., but they are also
expanding, and we have seen significant build-ups at their
Topeka, Kansas properties and Sweetwater, Tennessee
installations. C.I.N. unbeknownst to the authorities, um, the
Government isn't privy that Mark's organization is slowly
cannibalizing America like a stealth virus eating us from the
inside out!" "All right, I've seen enough. Why don't you and

Rocky and Shon take one of NIA's jets to Montana tonight and call for an emergency meeting of our prime operators? Find out why we had so many deserters and what was the Golden Nugget that coerced our soldiers and Officers to mutiny. Ah, check our armory's arsenals, bunkers, and warehouses. I want a fully comprehensive inventory assessment completed. It's crucial we stem the losses of our personnel Jay. I don't have to remind you that this is your puppy, your sector, Montana, Idaho, Utah, and Nevada. Find out what's really goin on and report directly to me on our private network!"

Jay rolls his shoulders, pondering, why not approach his yearnings with logic.... "I really could use a female on this quest. You know they can go places we men can't. Uh, I mean, their less threatening can blend in easier than...." "Yeah, I get it. Whom do you want?" "Ah, Sandi will work...." "No, how you figure she'll blend in being an Albino? She will do the opposite, draw attention, and you know Mark hates her guts, absolutely not.... Sandi set Mark up on that sting involving Wendi's deceased husband, David. Let's not forget that... lol." "I understand. I just think I could use her in the peripheral, ok. How about your niece Valerie?" "I don't know. Let me think about it; we have others that will fit the bill."

Jay hadn't given up on Sandi joining him, so with a last-ditch effort, "you know, boss with contact lenses and a wig with makeup, Sandi will blend in just fine; heck, she's...." "What the hell, Jaybird let me guess... are you romancing her? Um, let me think about it!" "We just don't want any more deserters." "Terrance, let's look at this with a positive spin. If we succeed in our ambitious aspirations on March 17th, the deserters that joined the C.I.N. faction at the Elko facility will be eliminated. There will be no survivors. It will be a fatal decision for them... following Mark to their death. We should be back in less than three days. This will not disrupt our participants at NIA-U will put them in the classrooms, labs, and lectures until we get back."

"I want to correct you, Jay. It's not that if we succeed. Nope, we will destroy C.I.N. at Elko. Jaybird, what eats at my craw is that Red-blooded Americans have joined C.I.N., knowing that the acronym denotes 'China, Iran, and North Korea!' See you at the conference, and thanks for the tea, mighty refreshing...." "You got it, and thanks, Terrance, for your leadership" they grasp each other's shoulders and leave with a fist bump. Terrance checked his wristwatch. It was only 2:30 in the afternoon. He felt like he'd done Youmans work already and was still pumped up on his secreting endorphins. He also reminded himself to check in with Shon, the team leader heading up the mission in Seattle... later next week.

-53-

<u>**San Francisco's Fisherman's Wharf... overlooking the Bay.**</u>

Valerie watched Jax from the other side of the tinted window; he was on his phone. Strange that he felt the need to leave NIA's Mercedes surveillance van to make a call. It was a different experience last night. They'd left the dinner party from her uncle's suite at NIA and driven to her palatial Pacific Heights chateau in San Francisco. She'd had fun but not in the way she'd expected. There wasn't any close dancing, no fondling, no kisses... just laughter and intriguing conversations. Down in her basement shooting range, she'd shown Jax some of her unique Bows & Arrows, Crossbows, and her favorite selection of Camo-colored blow dart guns. Valerie had predicted a bout of intimacy. Heck, they were adults... wasn't it obvious to Jax that I wanted to have him ravish my body. I left my sister's at my apartment at NIA and held his hand all the way to the garaged Mercedes van. We listened to music... even sang some old-school songs. Driving along, we had fun and chatted it up. What am I complaining about?

Wendi had just ended the call with Jax because Rico was approaching her from the doors of Scoma's restaurant. Valerie and his job this afternoon were to watch them…. as Rico reached for her hand, and they walked back down the pier, talking. He never liked Rico. It wasn't a competitive thing, he'd told himself dozens of times, but ultimately he'd acquiesced and admitted it as such. He could never compete with the debonair gent that Rico portrayed. But Jax got to know Wendi's other personality, Sunshine. He was close to both of her unique entities. Suddenly there was human movement on Jax's left side, approximately a hundred yards away, where he saw the Seals splashing in the water and making a ruckus. He spun back to the van in a hurry.

<u>Rico and Wendi are on a pier on the other side of Scoma's restaurant.</u>

"I know, sweetie, but give me a few more minutes with my Agents, and we will have some lunch, and the rest of the afternoon we'll…." "Rico, this, unfortunately, will always be us. I should never have told you about the fricken parakeets. It's my fault. Will I ever learn I'm…" Rico touches Wendi's shoulder, "babe. I'm sending a few Agents to the vendors. They will be collecting some more of the counterfeit money, and I am passing the criminal case over to my lead Agent. Just give me a few more minutes…." She waved her hands up "go ahead. I'll be out here. I understand, honey." But Wendi wasn't in a Sunshine kind of mind, nor was she herself; the psychedelic experimental drugs injected and force-fed into her bloodstream had altered her mindset… possibly forever. '<u>Jadex</u>' nodded and pecked Rico on his lips…. he stepped momentarily, gave her a doubletake, and then walked back from whence he came.

Rico nods towards his shadows, subtly acknowledging his extended team… that were always supposed to be in the background. He and Wendi are under constant scrutiny. His agents kept watchful and attentive eyes plastered on them. Rico had ordered three of his team to rotate around the clock; ever since the attack on Wendi and him a few years back in Trinity County, he had arranged protection. He shrugged 'what's going on with her, she's got this weird expression, and her pupils are pinpricks. Even her voice doesn't sound….' His phone vibrates he sees it's from his office "sorry to bother you, Sir, I know you're on a mini vacation…." "Beth, no worries, I'm always available to you; what's up?" "Just wanted to let you know the Judge signed the additional warrants you wanted on the Kamryn and Sara investigation." "Thanks, I'll be back at it on Monday, have a good weekend, Beth, and say hi to your hubby."

Jax grabs the handle and opens the slider to see Valeria, "I mean, talk about amateurs. You see Rico's FBI Agent over there by the Seals barking and carrying on. That's the last place she should be. There's way too much noise coming from over there!" Valeria didn't reply and wasn't paying him any attention. Val was focused on the moonroof periscope contraption, an innovatively designed super binocular hidden from outside views, for it rotated inside the bubbled moon roof on top of the van. "Jax, it seems Rico has more than one Agent surveilling Wendi and him. Here take a look at a couple of guys and the girl on the other side of the dock. Zoom in on what the dude is reading. It's an advertisement for the San Francisco Ferry. It's upside down. They're watching Wendi and Rico too." She slid out of the way, and he rubbed her lower back, "I had fun with you last night, girl…."

<u>Wendi is not feeling herself?</u>

Wendi felt like she was high, oddly not discombobulated like she had been ever since the night when her mom and dad had visited her with that Doctor weirdo Milo. Confusion and fantasies with visual impairments were her themes since being drugged. Every waking second, she watched a kaleidoscope of memories from two opposite personalities and perspectives. She hadn't slept much in the days since her drugging, the movie of her life continuously playing on the screen of her optic nerve. Her last visit to NIA wasn't leaving a fond taste in her craw. Wendi had a bout of syncope and blacked out… without a warning down, she went.

Doctor Liz Honcho was hyped up, it was like she was under the microscope, EEGs, and scans, and her sidekick Renae had intimated that something was wrong with her… Seriously Wrong!… Duh, 'Juden' rolled her head. Ya, Think! The drugs you fed me were more potent than LSD, Psilocybin, and Mescaline combined and then added in other Barbiturates. Juden had company flashing in her left eye, Sunshine, and in her right was the meek and sweet Wendi. She was now in control and would block the invasive couple out! She was the combination of both of her personalities; added together, Juden was singularly in the custody of this body and mind. And she was going to be proactive, aggressive, sensible, and eunuch like… emotionless as if it was ordained and fated. Juden would consult with her triumvirate, rather than shun Wendi and Sunshine she'd connive to utilize their superior mindsets and worldly experience. Since Juden was now the central character her plan was coalesce the applicable values of Sunshine and Wendi to guide her moves. Their triad would be omnipotent.

<u>Jax and Valerie.</u>

"Jax, what do you think? Why would Rico waste four Agents on surveillance of Wendi and him? It doesn't make sense to me?" "I don't know, Val. Check out the reports, and let's look at the videos of the Agents that have been known to surveil Wendi. It could just be another team." It bothered her, so she decided to broach the subject, "hey, you still got something for Wendi? I mean, you two have a history together…." Jax rolled his eyes at her, "well, that's a topic for another time. Let me just say this, you are aware that since Wendi's childhood trauma, she'd developed an invisible friend, Sunshine, who is the protagonist of the two. She'd been hot on me, uhm, attracted to me, Val, and we've been on over a dozen missions for NIA and your uncle. On one occasion, we'd got a bit frisky and almost did it, but I pulled out…um, not literally, I mean I…." "TMI Jax geesh okay I just…." "No, we kissed and fondled but never had sex…" His private line jangled "speak of the devil, it's her…." "Who?" "Wendi, let me step out?" "Why do you have to…." "I think better on my feet." He opened the slider with the phone in hand, mulling over his disclosure and not being entirely truthful. He desired Wendi and always had.

Wendi, 'Judea' looking through comingled eyes, sees a threesome across the way on a dock. One person stood out…. her skin flushed hot; no, it couldn't be. No way the guy was still locked up in San Quentin. She slipped her phone into her palm and, as nonchalantly as possible, started walking down the pier toward Scoma's and where Rico was. "Hello, Wendi…." "Jax, I hope I'm not losing it, but I could swear I just saw Joe Sable, one of my brother's childhood friends…." "What? where Wendi?" "He's across from me on a dock, in a group of three people he…." "Hold on, what? Last I checked, he was incarcerated, uhm, locked up in Quentin with Tank Shaw… we have tabs on your brother Mark's partners. Hold on, let me tap in his name and double-check… give me a few seconds. Instead of texting NIA and someone in his research team, Jax just Googled Joe Sable.

Seconds later.... Jax reads a report that Joe was paroled from San Quentin only last month. "Wendi, get in the restaurant. I'll check it out, and we'll text from here on out!" Valerie popped open the sliding door, "Jax, there is no mention of additional Agents that match the three individuals on the dock."

Jax quickly bounced by her, grabbed the periscope, and zoomed back into the suspicious dock people, "we'll use facial recognition, Val... Wendi said she thought she'd recognized one of Mark's friends over there...." "Mark, uh, Mark, who?" "Mark Feral, her brother, has a vendetta against Wendi. She's the reason he and his pals were locked away in San Quentin. He's tried to kill her countless times."

<u>Joe and Sammy, and Randy are hunting Wendi.</u>

Joe nods at Randy, who turns to Sammy, who takes her satellite phone from her purse and taps a key. Mark Feral answers before the first ring finishes, "Mark, we're not going to be able to abduct her without bloodshed, and you wanted to keep this on the down low. Mark, as Joe has told you, we could have wasted her a dozen times by now." "Sammy, I don't want to have to repeat myself. We will kill her. Most assuredly, she'll meet a slow and painful demise. But again, I've received from the C.I.N. headquarters that NIA is moving against us, and some of Jaybird's militia members have been seen on the outskirts of Elko, Nevada. We need to capture Wendi since she'll have inside information, heck she works with Jax and Terrance on covert missions. We will end the little bitches life soon after interrogating her. Now stop questioning me.... when you have the opportunity, take her, abduct her, and keep her breathing. It's only temporary, darling. I don't care who dies but make sure that Joe puts a bullet in Rico's head. The bastard has chased me across the USA. I want him, dead girl!" Mark shuts down his burner phone, thinking, why didn't his Bro call.... Mark despised talking with Joe's whore.

Jax was busy watching the threesome, he'd checked the van for the directional Phallic listening probe, and it was elsewhere. He thought, whom the hell had taken that out? When the computer banged out an alert. Valerie saw it first and said, "facial recognition has confirmed he is the Joe Sable fellow... Whew, the guy has a serious criminal record. But that's not the only person identified. The woman's name is Samantha Timmons, your right. Their members of C.I.N. Mark Feral's people!"

Jax reaches for his NIA phone and texts Wendi... 'Stay inside Sonna's. Don't alert Rico. Stay calm, and please let me know before you're about to leave the restaurant... you might have to stall by going to the bathroom. I'll let you know.' Jax turned to see Valerie with a pair of binoculars, "what is the FBI Agent doing? The agent is supposed to ensure that Rico and Wendi are safe?" "Jax, she's uh, the agent is looking at her phone right now and seems oblivious to the threesome." "Some security old Rico has; we're going to have to do something, woman." "Well, what are you planning, Jax? I need to call my uncle!" "No, you don't... grab up your Violin case. Let's go...."

Wendi sit's at the bar and orders a coffee, only nodding at Rico, who looks to be finishing up with two of his Agents; she texts her parents. 'Love you bunches, your daughter, and I'm doing fine!' Moments later, dad sends back, 'we love you, Wendi. It was fun seeing you will be down again next week to visit. Mom sends her love 😊.

Jax scans the area and declares, "okay, this is about as close as we can get..." she takes her crossbow out of the case, and sets it up on an empty barrel, takes her scope out, and gauges the distance of her shot. "Jax, why don't you have a sniper weapon in the van?" "Remember, girl… we adlibbed this. We just relieved the NIA team on a whim, for Terry's wife went into labor. So all we have in the van are pistols and automatic weapons. You are correct. We should always have a sniper rifle also in our arsenal. I'll suggest some changes. Nevertheless, your crossbow will have to do." "Jax, despite me being an Olympic Champion, our targets are over 75 yards away. Just like vertical bows, kinetic energy is the name of the game as an arrow follows its trajectory down range. The greater the distance to its target, the more loss of kinetic energy occurs. I'll have to let loose the arrow well above the target…." Jax, a little frustrated at her technical jargon, yelped "can you make the shot, Valerie? Or do you want to see if we can get closer to them somehow?" She fired…

Sammy relays her conversation to the guys; Mark wants her alive… nothing has changed. We could have eviscerated the snitch Rat so many…" a Swishing sound and Randy is knocked off his feet into the air and lands like a Hollywood stuntman act into the waters of the Bay. Sammy screams out and ducks, along with Joe. The FBI Agent lifted her head quickly from her phone's video game, one earplug out, scanning around the restaurant her boss was in. She apparently didn't see anything and went back to play.

Jax sprung up onto his toes. "Yes, nice shot, girl. Wow, that was amazing." "Yep, gotta say impressive that was a 77-yard shot, hit him in the shoulder." Jax has his binoculars leveled "yeah, that should keep the threesome busy; let's get back to the van." He texted Wendi, 'we hit one of them. You guys need to bail right away… don't say a word to Rico. His outside Agent is preoccupied with her phone and doesn't see a thing but her screen. We'll see what Mark's crew wants to do next?' 'Thanks, Jax, you didn't tell me you were out there watching us… huh?' 'oh, Terrance wanted to ensure you were always safe.' Suddenly she is pinched from behind "hey, who are you texting? We're done here. Let's roll, Wendi… we have the rest of the afternoon to enjoy. Come on…" Wendi was about to tell Rico that she wasn't feeling like herself and then realized she wasn't herself.

Sammy and Tank had finally fished Randy from the water; bystanders were out staring at the rescue, wondering if that was what it was… or did some fool fall into the water drunk?

Jax and Valerie maintain a visual on Joe's group while watching Rico and Wendi cruise back toward their hotel room. So far, So good…

<u>Rico and Wendi nixed the boat ride to their favorite Marin County restaurant in Sausalito 'Spinnakers' and decided to drive instead. Wendi was feeling a bit under the weather.</u>

Rico held Wendi leaning her up against her A 8 Audi convertible, a sleek Tigress of a machine he didn't much care for. The show car brought way too much-unwanted attention to his lady. Wendi was enamored with the damn car. The vehicle was three shades of Purple metallic and lacquered to a fine sheen, the thick paint almost wickedly sexy looking. He had to confess; it was a one-of-a-kind sharp attention-getter…. ride.

Like entrapment, it lured him inside, and the A-8 Audi pounced and captured him while he sped over the Golden Gate, enjoying the instant power under his right foot. The sign and tunnel appeared. He punched the accelerator down and whizzed into Marin County. Wendi only gave him a sly wink…. Yay! "Hey babydoll, this car should be illegal, lol. By the way, I'm going to my office. I broke weak and answered Doctor Roble's text," she chuckles. "Come on, babe, where have you not answered her text back, I'll take in a workout at NIA-U umh, were still on for dinner?" "Wendi, you know I'm not a fan of NIA; even if I am happy for their successful treatment plans for you, the specialists at NIA are top-notch in my book. No questions there, but....." She retracted her window and neglected to enter the fray "are we still on for dinner or not?" "No doubt, sweetheart....." "Ok, looking forward to that, ok, and don't fret, I will be an advocate for you honey regarding your wanting to tour the NIA University. Ahh, it's a malignant request on the surface," she quaffed her bottled water. "Sheesh, woman, did you have to use malignant like Melanoma? All I want is for you to ask Mr. God Terrance if he'd allow you to give me a tour of this NIA-U, that's all, huh?"

"God, whoa, you're such a sarcastic dude. That's the first time you used....." "I'm only joking. It's just like the guy puts a new shine on Teflon...he's bulletproof and connected to powermongers like Gorilla Glue. Whenever I seem to corner Terrance or pin him down... grease slick, he slithers away like a testy snake. I mean, it's....." "Testy snake Rico, shit, get with it, dude. If you can't beat them, join the team. The water's fine. NIA has given my life back to me. Ah, Hell, our lives as Lovers and best friends," she winks. "Wendi, I'm going to be taking NIA down. There's ill repute written all over that guy... criminal enterprise equals NIA. "Stop it. I will not keep defending NIA. This is getting old Rico, please, I thought we had a fricken agreement, hell with it, don't talk to me, get where you're going, leave me alone, dude...!" "Wendi, something is wrong with you, woman. I mean, you're not acting like yourself, even your words, like calling me over and over, dude. You're not Sunshine, but you're surely not acting like my Wendi. What gives?"

Judas is smoldering, trying to keep calm but losing focus; better to say nothing. He whizzed by two semi-trucks, silence between them. "Ok, it bothers me, I've witnessed NIA expanding like a plague when Terrance first became CEO, and his group of investors had purchased the NIA mental institution years ago. I didn't like the guy back then. He was always the Defense Attorney for the Stars. The next thing I knew, NIA bought up the properties adjacent to the mental institution. Then came the first outpatient hospitals, then the Stem-cell and Therapy buildings. The business flourished, then they broke ground on that damn private University, and NIA is increasing its footprint into Europe." Judea was thinking about his statements before his redundant ranting about Terrance and NIA, so he questioned who I was and mentioned how I sounded different! She tuned back in, listening as he kept the pressure going... "speaking of the University, I believe we should take some courses and graduate together, you and me, honey. Heck, the more education, the better. I bet you can enroll me in the next semester starting in a few days. Yuh know it never hurts to move the bar higher, more stability in our commitment, you know...." "No, Rico, I disagree; move the bar higher, man. You're not making any sense at all...."

"Why hasn't Brock Dame been accepted into NIA-U? There's something sinister going on...." She derisively snorts with a cocky smirk "whatcha getting at?" "Oh, I feel-yah, you're not about being user-friendly. What do you want me to spell it out, girl?" "Spell it out, Boy...what's it?" "You know exactly what I'm referring to and trying to say. Why can't you work with me here, Wendi? You are tied to the hip with NIA. I saw the pictures of you at the NIA Games, and you have a huge spread with animals and even an aquatic center. Tell me what I don't know about your NIA?...." He sees a CHP and checks the speedometer. It's at 87 mph shit hits the brakes. "You know fool, by hitting the brakes, you show the cop you're guilty... I thought being in Law Enforce...." "Shut up, Wendi... I mean, dammit, I'm sorry, I didn't want to say that...."

Judea was mixed up, and if you were in her sandals, you'd be in the same sort of quandary... barking was Sunshine in her left ear... don't give the prick any information about NIA! And in her right ear was Wendi… stop, don't argue with my Rico. A song took precedence. She turned it up 'Don't Worry Be Happy' sung by 'Bobby McFerrin.'

The song ended as she spotted his Federal building, "oh, Lookie, here were at your office. Better hop out. You're blocking the handicapped parking!" He flexed angrily, furrowed brows, then relaxed. "I will revisit this topic later!" She muttered, "Duh!" He leaned over aggressively, snatched her by the nape of her neck, and powered a salacious lips-parting rush of swirling tongues dancing in unison… she matched his tongue. Tango swished then with a triple peck on his cheek. "Seeya later tonight, Tiger!" said Wendi/'Indea.' He "I'll text you if anything comes up!…" She "likewise, honey." 🖤

…Indea…

She pulls from the curb, feeling anxiously weird like a foreboding reckoning was about to hatch within her skull. A buzzing sensation like Bee's eating her brains, she grits her teeth and, with gutsy fervor and intense full measured spunk, disposed of it. The dashboard rings, his face glaring at her. She facetiously shouted, "Wow, Dog, you miss me already, huh ain't I special um, must be love, or are you in heat, dude?" "Stop it, Wendi, but yes, I miss you just got a text from my lead Agent on our task force I formed at Scoma's while you waited. Your Golden, the ice cream vendor, the Leather goods kiosk, and two other shops were caught passing counterfeit bills, and the Ice cream vendor was followed to his Uncles with stacks of clean cash. You were correct. All fake twenties… I just wanted to thank you for your help in getting those scumbags off the streets… seen enough. We will follow the chain of command and arrest all the counterfeiters simultaneously. I'll be there when we capture the head of the snake and Chop it off, Guillotine style babydoll! Thanks…"

"It's not me to thank. It's the Parakeets and my failure not to make eye contact. I feel like when I pick the brains of pets, um, which, unbeknownst to their owners, are existing snitches, sleuths, um, covert spies right out in the open. Pets are there all the time, watching, listening, and non-threatening. Pet owners, no matter what legal or illegal enterprise they're involved in, don't lock their animals out of the loop, I mean…." "Wendi, this subject is worn out. Have to go Luv yah" … click.

Wendi pumps the brakes, 'uuh-oh-no, not a Freudian slip,' the 'Luv you' crap that's a first… shit. This is getting serious; he'd never said that before. Uh, dash rings again 'damn, it's him again' Nope! "Hey girl, are you going to make this conference this afternoon?…" "Yes, Sir, Jax, and thank you again. I sure am….." "Sir, huh ok, well it's about time you put a Sir out there." Laughter, uhm, you can thank Valerie. She got one of them in the shoulder with an arrow, anyways seeya at the conference; I'll fill you in then." "Good enough, thank her as well…" "I'll save your seat next to me." …click.

_—54—_

<u>Kamryn is blissfully satisfied, her Heart thumping with contentment holding and nursing her baby girl Sonja.</u>

It had been like a whirlwind of highs and lows…. of uplifting then downtrodden sewer-ridden emotions over the last nine months, now near the pinnacle at the top of the mountain. She'd be in heaven once she was on the outside of the Razor wire with her baby Sonja. Her baby Sonja cuddled to her left breast as she rocked her in a comfy chair. Heather was the nurse on duty, telling her explicitly that Sonja was remarkable. Heather was the mother of three babies, and her sister owned a daycare facility in nearby Calistoga, so they had plenty of experience with newborns. Heather's words still hung in the air above the rocking chair, 'Sonja was by far the best baby she'd ever been around. Sonja never cried out nor seemed to want for anything, always even keel. She took to the bottle being able to grasp it right away.' Kamryn had zero experience being a mother. In fact, this was never supposed to happen. She'd thought she could not conceive. Sonja was a miracle, and according to Heather and Renae, she was lightyears ahead of any child either one of them had been around. 😊

It was almost like Sonja was an aphrodisiac… for her internal system. Just seeing her and holding her brought endorphins to rush from her adrenal glands, like an overload of Dopamine. Then a weird conundrum resulted, like being full-on excited and then… subtly relaxed and satisfied. She'd melt emotionally, bonded to the only living human that mattered in her life at this very moment.

Uncle Terrance had betrayed her and kept her locked up in her sister's place, even after knowing this was the case. This afternoon she'd get her first whiff of freedom. Jax was supposed to have a gate pass left at the back exit gates of NIA for her. Sister Sara was a ruthless freak, and if any reason arose that she felt justified enough to attack her, she would, without any qualms, stab a knife in her back. Sara wouldn't hesitate. Valerie was a knockoff of Sara, a PsychoSociopath killer who had jumped her and thrown a knife, barely missing her right ear only days ago. Before locked up, Kamryn was wildly popular and had dozens of friends, with five super close ladies who were going to be in her wedding…when she married Brock Dane. But Kam had dropped off the face of the planet and hadn't nor could contact them for months, for Kam wasn't allowed to phone them from the inmate phones, all was regulated… she was allowed only three phone numbers. Most unsettling was that she'd heard through the rumor mills that Brock Danne, her ex-fiancé, was achieving major strides at recovering from Sara's attempted murder. Kam had heard he was rekindling his relationship with his ex-fiancé Lucie Link, who had lived for months in adjoining rooms at the Stem-cell outpatient hospital. Jealousy reared its smoldering head, and Kam slapped it back down. Sonja was Brock's baby. He was daddy, which might add up to something, and maybe they could make a go at it and have that dream wedding after all!

It was only a matter of time before Terrance got wind of her baby. This couldn't be kept a secret much longer. Just to maneuver over here to visit Sonja was a chore. Kamryn had read the missive saying that her uncle was warned that a baby girl named Sonja would be born and he must abort the baby. This was time-stamped before Kam had even given birth to Sonja and before she'd decided on her name! With the cameras, there was no way of hiding where she went on the NIA grounds; lucky she wasn't being scrutinized. She would follow through with her uncle's orders and go to Sara's Salon and gather any and all incriminating evidence that could be held against her. Kamryn knew that the FBI had a team waiting for either Sara or her to show up and had outstanding warrants for her DNA, and that Rico wanted to conduct an interview with her. She had to be cautious, get the job done, and return to NIA. After understanding how the process worked, leaving the gates, tomorrow she'd devise a plan to conceal little Sonja and escape NIA and disappear from everyone with her baby.

She held Sonja up, and a wide-ass grin shot right back at her... mused gosh, babies without any teeth look somehow like old people without wrinkles but toothless, lol she giggled. Where'd that come from? Something itched inside; yeah, after a month or three of freedom, she'd get word to Rocky to inform Brock that he had fathered a baby girl. Rocky and she had a pact. A promise was made and adjudicated not to let Brock know he was a daddy until he completely recovered from his physical and mental injuries from sister Sara's attack. Like Rocky had told her, despite his physicality coming back, he was mentally weak and on the fringes, and they couldn't afford any setbacks for Brock, so Mum was the word about his daughter until he was better. Once it was considered appropriate, she'd be reunited with her lover and best friend, and if it's in God's plans, we'd be together raising our baby girl and live happily forever like a Fairy Tale.

Kamryn looked down into Sonja's eyes and felt whole. The door wafts open, and standing in front of her…

<u>Doctor Liz Honcho is called to Terrance's office.</u>

Come in, and have a seat, Liz. It's been a chaotic day so far. I hope you will bring me some peaceful resolve; I have a few matters to discuss with you. I…." "Geez, Terrance, what are you wired or something? I haven't even made it in the door, and your pacing like an expectant daddy!" He chortled, musing how close ole Liz was. "I brought you some iced tea, Terrance." "I just had some Sun Tea over at Jaybirds. I'm Ok, thanks."

"If this is about Wendi, I haven't anything that's conclusive. I have feelers out there and have contacted the world's renowned…" "excuse me, Liz, for interrupting you but again, let me ask you did Doctor Greg Walters put together another batch of the elixir that I'd given both of you the recipe of… we need to follow through with two more doses of the concoction according to Vadoma I want the next shot injected into Wendi this afternoon." He raised his palms up "now I know you think she's a modern-day sorcerer or practices Witchcraft. Still, I trust her far more than I do your Greg doctor." "Okay, I'll bite Terrance. What's wrong with Wendi? What is your main concern?" "Jax isn't the only person that has brought this to my attention. Wendi isn't acting like Sunshine or herself. We need her for the next operation. She's an essential cog in the newly formulated team. Jax knows her better than anyone, with the possible exception of Rico Capter. I trust Jax's evaluation of Wendi… Liz. Vadoma had told me verbatim that we'd better give her this antidote or regret it forever. Vadoma said something to me about another entity competing with Sunshine and Wendi of uhm, and I vaguely recalled her saying 'Judas' is in her skull or a Judea."

Liz was a fabulous Poker player and held her Poker face… wily said nothing about the EEGs and scans showing her brain wasn't the same, didn't match her Brainprints, and were not of Wendi nor Sunshine. After all, it was her that injected Wendi, but it wasn't like Terrance wasn't the co-conspirator. Yep, she went above and beyond the proper dosage jamming the Horse tablet down her throat. What the Hell? She folded and told Terrance about the Brainprints, divulged all to him…

By the time she was finished, Terrance was pacing like a Rat in a maze, "so what your saying is Greg can't find any more of the homeopathic herbs needed to make up the rest of the remedy that Vadoma had instructed. I don't get it… if you can't order the crap on Amazon, then go to the country where the plants are indigenous and buy them there. Remember, it's got to be fresh herbs. Just get it done before something bad happens with our Wendi/Sunshine Feral." Okay, she felt relieved to be less burdened with this Wendi enigma, she was about to stand, and he said, "Wait…."

Liz, you're going to think I'm off my Rocker or am one egg shy of a dozen, blown a gasket, gone batty, gone off the deep end, or flipped my lid!" He let a grin escape; she laughed. "Not a bad icebreaker. Okay, you've lightened up this morose conversation." He blurted out, "have you ever heard of a girl named Sonja?" She frowned, shaking her head, no can't say that I have. That's an odd name; why should I have___" "Has a baby been born here at NIA? Umh, has anyone of my nieces had a child?" He cackled. "I just saw them. I knew this is crazy… but tell me, because if anyone here at NIA were privy to this information, it would be you, Liz… has any of my nieces been pregnant." Liz lost it, wigging out, hopped up, and started pacing. Oh crap, she'd kept Kamryn's pregnancy a secret. This could be a serious problem for her. "Liz, you are scaring the shit out of me. I've known you for decades. What's it you are not telling me, woman? Come on. We go way back to our College days. What have you not told me, Liz Marie Honcho?"

"Please sit down, Terrance," she sighs, exhaustively placing her right palm over her heart. "I have something I want to get off my chest." He shook his head, "no, spit it out… have you betrayed me? Wtf is going on right under my thumb… huh?" "Why are you so worked up over a baby, Terrance?" "Sheesh, I didn't think it was such a big deal, and after what you and I had done to your poor innocent niece, I thought it necessary to keep her promise. She made me vow not to tell anyone…." Terrance pounds his fist on the table, knocking Liz's drink over… "Who? What are you saying… promise!" "Relax, man. You're going to have a heart attack. The baby is dead; geez, Kamryn had a miscarriage. She was pregnant with Brock Danne's child…." Terrance juts back out of his seat "Brock's baby, huh?" "Yes, before Sara switched Kam out, Kamryn had conceived with Brock…." "No, I was informed that my nieces had hysterectomies for they wanted not to propagate their tainted bloodline… no more Amaya's."

Liz sits back, letting her blood pressure reduce. "Here, let me get Doctor Wei on the conference line…." "Wait a second, Kamryn didn't look anywhere near being pregnant. How far along? Where is she at? Get her ass over here now!" "Hold up, Terrance, have some compassion and empathy. Don't you believe the girl has gone through enough pain and suffering… wtf what are you? Fricken heartless. Stop… listen to yourself." He raises his head and looks to the ceiling, then wiggles his head shoulder to shoulder, "damn, it's always fricken something. Luckily, I don't have a bleeding ulcer; when did this miscarriage occur? Heck, just last night, Kamryn was at my place for a dinner party. She never looked pregnant…."

"Some women with petite figures don't show until the last trimester or until the baby drops. Kamryn, if you remember, always wore baggy clothes....." "Well, yes, but it's wintertime, and everyone is wearing coats and sweaters, Liz. I mean, how could you tell?"

The room went silent as they listened to Doctor Wei's voicemail pickup... Liz spoke, "Doctor Wei, I need you to call me as soon as you get this call... Terrance wants to hear the details of Kamryn's miscarriage." Terrance pounded his fist into the table... "I'm waiting-woman; tell me how it all unfolded. I thought Kam and I had the kind of relationship that she trusted me, heck, we were only last month skipping down a path by a pond... laughing and having fun." "If it makes you feel any better, I didn't know. In fact, no one did until she had that diabetic stupor, uh, when we discovered she had Diabetes. That's when I saw the baby bump, and the subsequent blood test proved it out. Kamryn kept it her secret. Can you imagine that? The poor child was pregnant ever since she was falsely incarcerated here, and dammit, think about how lucky it is, sad to say. That she lost the baby, can you imagine what the baby would be like after all those chemicals were injected into your niece? I mean, we'd had her pumped full of pharmaceuticals. Some were experimental, Terrance, and would have, in my estimation, harmed the baby!"

Doctor Wei listened to her voicemail for the second time, worried sick, and tried for the third time to get a hold of Renae. Renae was drying off from her second shower of the day. Sick to her stomach, having another bout of premenopausal sweats, and hot flashes that slammed her hard, she felt she was too young to be experiencing these symptoms, only 43 years of age. She'd have to.... despite hating to take any medications, would have to check into what could alleviate this bullcrap. She muttered, 'men had it so fricken easy,' she'd complained to her husband Ron, and he only shrugged, 'that's life.' "Yeah, Ronny, it's life, and I might just take

She checked her phone, missed five calls in the last thirteen minutes, and read a frantic text... 'call me, we have problems.' 'We...' thought Renae, 'how could 'we' have problems?' Hit speed dial. "Hello, Kathy..." "Nice that you could get back to me...." "What the hell is wrong?" "Liz called and wants me in Terrance's office to discuss Kamryn's miscarriage. That's all, Renae. You wanna handle it for me since this is your BABY, pun intended! I wasn't into this conspiracy at all. If you weren't blackmailing me for my frichen affair, I wouldn't have lied. You better take care of this. L..." "Shut the fk up, Doctor Wei. Get a grip, breathe, and get over to my office pronto!" Renae punched... end of the call and phoned Liz. "Hey Liz, just checking in. I'm sure you are aware of the stabbing in the cafeteria this morning. We pronounced one dead at the scene. The other three are getting stitched up." Liz raised her hand and shook it at Terrance... and turned on the speaker of her phone. "Your on-speaker Renae, we're trying to get a hold of Doctor Wei. Terrance has checked the cameras and can't find her as of yet. Remember, a couple of weeks ago, you and I had talked about Kamryn's miscarriage!" "Yeah, so what..." Terrance interrupted, "what happened? I wasn't aware that my niece was pregnant." "All I know is she lost the baby, and it was taken to our cremation chambers." "Okay, thanks, Renae...."

Liz scowled, barking, "Terrance, there have been seven abortions here at NIA in the last three weeks. Kathy has been busy dealing with this in-house problem. If you could meet with the Correction Officers Union again, make this a priority. It would help. The frichen guards need to keep their pants zipped...." "Sssh, I'm calling the head of security. We need to find Doctor Wei." "Yes sir...." "Hi Walter, I want a trace on Kathy Wei can't find her on-site. She was checked in at the

East Gate at 7:11 am. Can you find her?" "No problem, sir, I'm on it; I'll get right back to you."

<u>Rocky and Kamryn</u>

Rocky stood frozen at the door; his eyes were extra wide, matching his grin. "Kamryn, I thought I'd catch you here, girl. Wow, let me hold her...." Kam rocks forward and carefully gives him Sonja, and he swings her around gently, his back to her. "You know we can't keep this a secret from Brock much longer. I feel guilty as sin whenever I see him. Lately, I try to avoid his eyes. I know it's best not to mess with his mental recovery. His psyche is fragile. At least, that's what Doctor Lamen had informed me of yesterday. She's his primary Neurologist and in charge of his treatment programs." "You didn't tell Doctor Lamen about...." "No, are you crazy? I just went around some things in Brock's past about you and your marriage that was planned and asked her if it would be okay to start bringing up the past and some of the caustic events in his life. Doctor Lamen told me Brock was not ready. So in my humble opinion, we should keep Sonja under wraps until a little later, and he's recovered enough to be shocked into fatherhood!" Rocky held her up, and Sonja smirked, creasing her bitty nose up. "God, she is adorable. Wow, Kam, congratulations again. We need to get you and her out of NIA. The rumor is that Jax is working on your gate pass. Can you believe that crap on your uncle's email about this baby being the devil incarnate? Geez? That's what you get when you deal with sorcerers as Terrance does."

Suddenly the room added two more humans, breathing heavily, staring directly at Sonja. Renae with Doctor Wei, stop frozen in place.... over the loudspeakers, 'Doctor Kathy Wei, please pick up the nearest phone and check in with Security now.' These words were heard repeated three times as Kathy ducked into the bathroom doors opening. The only place that didn't have cameras, well, at least that, was the assumed beliefs of NIA's staff.

The security director for NIA… Walter Hale, was replaying Doctor Wei's entrance into NIA's gates from earlier this morning and slowly followed her steps to her office in the main hospital.

Rocky hands Sonja back to Kamryn while Renae, hyped-up, yelped, "we have to get the baby out of here." Rocky's response was serenely espoused, "that's impossible. The gates have the latest Thermal Scans. No one is sneaking Sonja out of the gates. The place to hide her is out of the camera's view. I have yet to figure out where, but one thing is certain Kathy here better have a plan because she's easily tracked to where she is standing…" the announcement again rings over the loud system. "Kathy, I want you to call Walter right now and let him know you are on the way to Terrance's office. You have the Flu and have been in the restroom. We will then have some time to figure out how to approach this situation. Instead of picking up a wall phone, hit him on your cell phone…." Doctor Kathy Wei at once steps into the bathroom and calls Walter.

Rocky reached over and under the end table…clutching a device, "this is a signal blocker, so the security cameras can't pick us up on film. Nor hear what we say. But if Walter does a cross reference looking for sectors in his security grid, he will find out this area is completely blacked off… then he will send one of his employees over here to troubleshoot the problem. We don't have much time." Renae closed her eyes and bent forward, "allow me to tell you two what I've been working on, and please let me know what you think! Rocky, some of the female inmates have the wherewithal to keep their pregnancies private. Their body types sometimes help them with this concealment. One such case happened last month. A three-hundred-pound woman who is serving a life sentence had a child. I was able to take the child from NIA and drop her off at an adoption agency. No questions were asked!" Rocky, puzzled, offered, "so you were able to get a gate pass…" "no, not exactly. There are a couple of gate guards that are advocates of the pro-life movement, whom, are steadfastly adamantly against abortions... I approached them with the picture of the baby girl and told them what my plans were. They turned the other cheeks and let me pass with the baby. Let me remind you, I've been able to do this three times in the last year."

Rocky clapped his hands together "well then, why is Sonja still here, Renae? It's imperative...." "That's just it..." she looked at Kathy, Rocky, and Kam, who was cuddling Sonja. Then slowly opened her mouth with a near smile. "The lead guard at the West gate is out on maternity leave and will not be back until..." checking her phone, "ironically, she comes back on duty this afternoon at 5 pm! I'll get Sonja out of here tonight for you, Kamryn." Kam nearly leaps up. "I should have a gate pass this evening. I am doing my uncle's bidding, cleaning up sister Sara's beauty salon of incriminating evidence, and then I'll meet up with you. Please leave me your contact information, Renae." She grinned back "no question; I'll text you it right away." "Okay, what about me?" asked Kathy. Renae said... "you are going to prance right into Terrance's office and tell him Kam's water broke, and she was rushed to the hospital, and you did all you could do, but the baby was stillborn and had died. You then followed proper protocol and had the baby's remains cremated... done deal, Kathy!"

<u>Back in Liz's office with Doctor Kathy Wei.</u>

Terrance and Liz had listened to Doctor Wei's narrative of what had happened to Kamryn's baby and hadn't any questions. Liz seemed somber. Terrance acted depressed outwardly but was relieved that the baby that Vadoma had predicted to be an evil seed and would turn out to be a worse psychopath and killer than Sara and Valerie was dead and crispy. Actually, he breathed in and tried not to act giddy with contentment. Now off to put other fires out, he spun out of his seat and said to Liz, "we'll discuss your omission of truth later, woman. I got other things to deal with. Keep the fort down and under control, whatever that means… Later!"

<u>Kamryn, her gate pass… Sonja, Brock Dame, and Rocky Blake.</u>

Left alone now with her baby, a sense of anticipation and hope had resonated within her. Holding her baby tightly, she believed she could envision the finish line lifting her spirit and giving her strength was Rocky and Renae. He'd said before he'd left Sonja's room… 'You should have the gate pass by this afternoon.' Since her incarceration in her sister's place, she'd felt stifled, underwater, unable to breathe. Suddenly buoyancy had found its way into her lungs. Soon she would be out of NIA forever. She had the 'ways and means' to be independent… while locked up, her trading accounts had been left dormant. The only stock in the toilet or down was, ironically, NIA. She fondly thought of her career choice: to become a financial consultant and work for Schwab. In the eight-plus months that she was unable to work and make a single trade, luckily, her accounts had gone up a whopping 21 % which was significant.

Kam rubbed Sonja's blonde curls… what a perfect baby girl, rocking her in a chair, dared to dream of their future together. Renae would sneak her out of the NIA gates, and Kam and Sonja would put as much distance from NIA as possible. Kam had unrelenting regret for not being able to share the birth of their newborn daughter … but agreed with Rocky that the time would come to inform Brock Dame that he was a father. Kam held out hope that one day they could and would be reunited. One thing was for sure she'd not be visiting Brock at the NIA Outpatient hospital. She wouldn't step another foot on any land associated with this sinister organization. Nursing Sonja contently, she rocked on, knowing her last interaction with Uncle Terrance and her despicable sisters would be only hours away. She never wanted to see any of them again, no matter how long she lived!

The impetus for Uncle Terrance to allow her the gate pass was mucky in her mind. She couldn't quite grasp the logic of her Uncle. If Rico Captor had a warrant for collecting her DNA, why would he make her available? His words reverberated his truth. 'My favorite niece, we haven't any fear that your DNA will prove that your sister was at the scene of the double slaying. No doubt, let the FBI bring it on.... there isn't a shot in hell that they can make the case against Sara stick. Just the inkling of DNA being faulty would open a can of worms felt across the planet. Can you imagine the News Wires? Sara Amaya breaks out of NIA Prison, murders Carl and Bianca Sparks, then returns for dinner! LMAO.'

Terrance had told her.... 'Relax, we will circumvent Rico, and the Fed's interviewing you for we will go to the hospital like I've told you to visit with Doctor Roble, who is Rico's DNA collector. After you finish the chores, you can go to your Victorian Home and take a few days off. Remember, what is mandatory is that I need you to go and retrieve all the evidence that Sara has left at her office at the business she put in your name. Go to 'Kam's Salon' and clean it up for us, be cognizant that the FBI was keeping the shopping center under surveillance.' Why didn't dear old Uncle send someone else to clean up Sara's mess? He'd said.... 'No worries, they don't have any right to interfere with you other than to ask you to let them take a DNA swab, and they will not do that unless Rico is present. We have Wendi keeping him busy, and besides that.... these DNA tests will take approximately two weeks to be completed if they put a rush on it. Or it may be a quick turnaround in under a week. But niece, you will be back here at NIA by that time; relax. All will be fine…honey.' *That's right ole Uncle; everything would be fine. I would not be coming back to this hellhole again!*

Kam leaned her face downward, seeing her precious sleeping baby. Soon they would be whole. Renae was going to bring Sonja to her Victorian home in Tiburon at 7:30 pm, musing sleepily at how amazing it had been. She'd become so attached to Sonja that it was hard to leave her with the nurse on duty and go about her daily activities. She decided that she hated Uncle Terrance. He wanted to harm her baby. Why? How did he know what she'd name her… the name Sonja had never come up… so many oddities and questions unanswered…

<u>Brock Dame and Rocky Blake.</u>

A whirlwind blew in from the doors being abruptly flung open. Brock Dame stood at the entrance alongside him was Rocky grinning wildly. "I broke weak Kamryn and couldn't keep Sonja from him any longer. I'm sorry." Brock's facial expressions melted before her. He hurried to her side, dropping to his knees. Tears streamed down his cheeks. "Kamryn, Omg Kamryn, oh how I've missed you. I love you, girl. I love you with all my heart." Kamryn had tears cascading off her chin, sobbing happily. "Can I hold our baby?" In heavenly bliss, she open's her arms wide as he took Sonja to his chest in an awe-inspiring heart-melting tingle. Brock swung her around in a pirouette and sat on the tile floor. Brock was Kissing her forehead and pulling back her loosely wrapped baby cover. Sonja started Babbling and Cooing and released her first-ever giggle along with a bowel movement. He laughed. "Gosh, my Kamryn. She's so beautiful like you, ummhh… she's got a poopy diaper. I'm not quite prepared to do my daddy part." He held her out, arms stretched. Kam clutches her and yelps out, "I got it; you might as well watch… you are going to be doing a lot of this. I love you, and Lord knows I've missed you. It's been forever since I've seen you, Brock."

Rocky interrupted, "listen, Kamryn, I don't think you should risk Renae trying to sneak Sonja out through the NIA gates. I've discussed this with Brock. We've come up with another plan if you're daring enough.... Brock and you and Sonja will be airborne in less than 30 minutes." With Brock's hand on her shoulder, Kam was cleaning Sonja's butt up, "I'm listening, and I agree I don't even like leaving Sonja for a second, mind you allowing Renae to take her through the gates...." "Brock was a first-class pilot before his injuries at the hands of your sister Sara. He was an instructor specializing in flying Ultralights." Brock took over the conversation "yes, over at the NIA-U airfields, there are seven Ultralights, and Rocky has a two-seater gassed up and ready to fly. We're getting out of here... babydoll!" She nervously barked out "no way, guys, I'm not getting into one of those flying lawnmowers with our baby!"

After some more convincing... which included a few videos of Brock flying and landing Ultralights back when he was the lead flight instructor. "How will we move about NIA and get past the internal gates to NIA-U and the airfields, Rocky?" "I got that covered." He jumped up from a chair and, swiftly walked over to a window, pulled the curtains open. Dusk was setting up, "is there anything you want to take with you, Kamryn?" She gave Sonja to Brock, reaching out and clutching her mega-purse... "everything I need is here," embracing Brock, who held Sonja, "this is a dream come true...." "Oh no, Kam, don't jinx us," cackled Rocky. "I have my deluxe Golf cart awaiting you, it's not a Chariot or Coach with magnificent Horses, but it'll have to do. The West gate is manned with guards that I'm scheduled to play poker with tonight, and they are pliable. I will get you three out of here and to the airfields next door. Let's roll!"

Next thing she knew, she heard the loud sound of the Ultralight humming past her earphones. Sonja had a cute pair of earmuffs and seemed to be enjoying herself. They were clear to take off. Brock rolled his shoulder and leaned into her kissing her lips gently. He kissed Sonja's forehead, they looked out, and Rocky was smirking and nodding his head, hands up in the air… Thumbs up!

Kamryn was giddy with exhilarating euphoria… She had all she'd ever wanted… Brock, her baby, and a bright unrestrictive future. "Hey, Brock, where are we going to land this lawnmower…" she chortled. *Brock spun her head around, growling, "don't you mean Brockbaby… sister dear… SARA snickered and smiled, blood dripping from her chin, and her ghoulish vulture eyes took her in. Kamryn bolted up from the rocking chair, nearly dropping Sonja to the floor. Kamryn instantly was seething at the Davmare she'd just had. One… I was fricken dreaming…*

Wendi left Rico at the hospital to visit with his friend Doctor Shanon Roble.

Rico, who had been dropped at the San Rafael General hospital by Wendi an hour before. Rico wanted to speak with Doctor Roble and arranged a meeting with her due to her request earlier in the day. He stood at the see-through window and watched her perform a demonstration on several cadavers that lay on gurneys. Students surrounded Shanon; he was behind glass, mulling over what she'd told him, and checked his phone. Where the heck was Wendi at? He'd in vain tried to call her several times and sent her three texts, but she wasn't replying. They had a later dinner date, and he just wanted to hear her voice. He had to admit it. He loved her, dammit. It was nearly 5pm. He tried to call her again to no avail. She was acting weird and kind of off-kilter, unlike Wendi… was usually. He was comfortable communicating with the girl. He shook his head…wow he'd known her for over fifteen years…but hey, the girl was a bit quirky and odd in a good way… anyhow. Rico felt a little disheveled, contemplating how their conversation had ended on a sour note. Rico had a problem with NIA and again, like a broken record, barked vehemently at Wendi…. if they were going to make it, alas, as a couple for life, he'd have to let go of his Angst toward Terrance and NIA! For the third time, he sent Wendi a text. 🐾

Rico returned to reassessing his conversation with Shanon before he had Wendi drop him off. Shanon's advice was usually dead-on. He respected her mind and the way she formulated plans. Still, initially, he'd disagreed with her approach but now was reconsidering everything about this Sara and Kam investigation. There were other contingencies… stroking his analytical mind with the deviously aggressive suggestion by Shanon. He was about to conclude and concede that Shanon was correct. It was time for a gamble. If not for Wendi, he'd already made a move against Terrance and NIA. Rico admitted what ate at him was the way Wendi constantly shielded NIA and would become so agitated when the subject was broached, like either she had something to hide… or ahh ulterior motives to defend NIA. He stopped and closed his eyelids, remembering her facial contortion when he'd asked her, '<u>what were you doing with Kamryn at the Quickdraw competition? Didn't you see Sara, who was supposed to be in lock-up, riding up on the Horse with Terrance…what's really going on in that facility?'</u> She'd slammed the bathroom door in a huff right in his face and took a shower. He'd said to hell with it and left for his office. Nothing else was said on the subject, and the door remained shut.

The question that kept gnawing at him was why discussing anything regarding NIA was Taboo, ugh, toxic for Wendi and him. With my lover's answers always vague and deceptive, she was evasive and illogical to the point of being fallacious when she defended NIA. She must have had ulterior motives! To hell with it Screw it…. I'm taking Shanon's advice throwing caution into the hurricane…. Shanon had said to him staunchly, 'Rico, listen to me please,' grabbing my chin and pulling my face down to her. 'We are at a Stalemate. I know you're moving tentatively in this investigation because of your relationship with Wendi. I can respect that, but this is a certainty that the DNA proves that Sara murdered Carl and Bianca. Microbial DNA attests to the fact that she also killed the attorney. I will stand behind you since this is an unexplored unmitigated innovation separating the DNA of identical twins. I realize there has yet to be any case law or litigation dealing with this newly discovered anomaly in Deoxyribonucleic acid. I will even back you if you decide to put pressure on Kamryn by arresting her. You have the wherewithal to arrest her with a standing warrant on the matching DNA. Let's claim that Kamryn committed the homicides, which were certain that she didn't, but sometimes I believe we have to gamble that Kam knows far more than she's letting on. Remember, we've viewed the video with time stamp proof along with everyone else that Sara was absolutely locked up in NIA. Hence, one of them was the assailant, right? So arrest Kam putting the impetus on her to prove she didn't commit the homicides! Maybe some of the forbidden fruit might find gravity and fall into your palm if you shake the tree hard enough?"

Finally, with relief, he sees Wendi's text, 'hey honey, I'm at the Flatiron Sports Bar enjoying some delicious libations and yummy appetizers. When you are done with 'Sloppy Seconds, ' Y don'tcha join me 🌀?' Rico snarled and texted back, 'I thought you had a precious meeting with your conspirators at NIA... R we still on for dinner?... what are you doing at a bar drinking?... sloppy seconds, geez girl, get a fricken clue. Shanon and I have a special friendship, and that's it.' 'Rico, it's imperative that we speak; not being overly dramatic, uh, but call it a Life-or-Death matter... get your ass over here to the Flatiron Grille. We can have an early dinner, not going to Sausalito this evening with you... things have cum up!'

Shanon had changed out of her working outfit and had spied him... "what are you scowling about, pal?" "Pal hum," they chuckle "uhm, Wendi just texted me that she wants to discuss something important." "So talk with her, Rico... I'm on my way back to Cottonwood. Jason and the kiddos are putting together a late dinner, and we're going bowling." She checks her wristwatch. "I better get going. It's a three-hour drive." Rico was going to ask her to drop him off at the Flatiron but decided to take an Uber and not take up any more of her time. They hugged, and she whisked by him… out of the blue, he had an idea. "Shanon, why don't you drive me to the Flatiron pub and then go to the executive airport? I'll arrange for an FBI chopper to take you up to Cottonwood; you'll be there in less than 45 minutes. Surprise, your family… I will have a car waiting at The Redding airport for you…" he smirked "whatcha think." Shanon nearly jumped into his arms, "yes, oh yes, I wasn't looking forward to that Friday afternoon drive from Marin. Let's do it. Thanks, Rico, you're a Saint…." Yup!

<u>Wendi had to leave the bar stool; the aggravating arguments were ringing in her skull!</u>

Can anyone imagine what it's like to be me? Omg, mused Wendi, she was placed on the outside peripheral of her complicated diversified minds as is plural. Yes, as a child, she'd imagined and developed a strong and unafraid companion. 'Sunshine' was manifested into a living being, an invisible protector and friend to keep her company. According to child psychologists, this wasn't bizarre or truly unnatural… many children who are an only child or have been traumatized find themselves alone within their inner-self. On the outside of her skin, she aesthetically seemed to be normal, like many other people sitting nearby in the lounge, sipping drinks… and watching Soccer matches and other sporting events. She took to staring at her phone's screen and, acting preoccupied with it, had been approached by several men, who wanted to chat, one offered to buy her a drink. She politely declined and said she was waiting for her Fiancé.

If not for her inner chatter, she might be able to think clearly. Wendi traipsed off to the restroom past the pool tables and dart boards. Everyone was priming the pumps; it was 5:37 pm on a Friday. She closed the stall and sat fully clothed on the seat of the commode, her palms clasping her head and covering her ears. She mumbled internally, 'stop it please, enough the both of you, Judea, I agree with Sunshine... you can't trust Rico he is Law Enforcement first. Everything else, including us Second. Enough of this conversation; we will not be telling him anything of the sort!' 'Wendi, I don't think you understand this situation. I no longer need your approval, nor the crass Sunshine's. Your both antiquated litter tossed to the curb.' 'Listen, little missy. I am not crass; I just speak the truth...' 'No, Sunshine, you speak your truths, your selfish and egocentric, wanting to control Wendi, hell you want to be Wendi forever, and you've succeeded....' The loudest voice of the three wasn't in doubt. It was Judea who controlled Wendi's vocal cords located in her larynx at the top of her trachea. Therefore with Judea maintaining 34% of Wendi's brain and thought process, combined with a mortal lock on her voice and words, there was absolutely nothing that Wendi or Sunshine could do to prevent her from divulging sensitive information shared within their skull.

Wendi tried to convince Judea that she would cause irreparable damage to NIA and could cost them their life; NIA's board of directors would eliminate her like a flush of the toilet... Uh, in a heartbeat, if she betrayed the powerful mongers who were connected with the Who's Who of the Leaders who bolstered the highest positions. The ones who made decisions through intergovernmental political forums. Judea knew that NIA was bonded with NATO, and G7 and Terrance had his pulse on the heartbeat of the shot-callers across planet earth.

She stood up and flushed the toilet, and it was done. Judea stepped out, washed her hands, dried them under a hot blower, checked her look of determination in the wall-length mirror, and shoved the bathroom door open. Where the fk was Rico? Ugh, still wasting time with his Doctor friend? 'Sshhh, calm down, Judea; remember your Wendi, and for God's sake, don't act like her alter-ego, Sunshine.' *Judea needed to get this done before the drugged cocktail Liz injected into her body with the new concoction that Terrance had arranged to also stab into her body, ughhhh, metabolized or disintegrated.* What was the shelf life of the drugs that she not only ingested but was still pumping through her veins? Judea didn't know if her control of Wendi was temporary or not. So she must move deliberately and concisely and be steadfast with a purposeful aim to enlighten Rico before it is too Late!

The bartender joked, "I was going to send out a search team for you…." he grinned, winking his eyes… Judea played it off, even though she wasn't into superficiality. "Yeah, it was a difficult extrication," smirking back at him. He popped his fist up for a bump, "you want a refresher there?" "Yes, and could I see a menu? Please, I might be into some appetizers." "No problems. Might I suggest the Buffalo wings or the chili? They're our best sellers." Judea had carefully listened to her voice, trying to imitate sweet soft Wendi's delivery. Still, sadly she was in between Sunshine and that melodic charming slight girl intonation that Wendi verbalized. Remembering what Rico had said while they drove down the 101 freeway… 'that she didn't sound like herself!'

-55-

<u>Shanon drops Rico off at the Flatiron Bar and Grille.</u>

"Shanon… say hi to Jason and the kiddos. Hopefully, I will be able to visit with them one day real soon." Thanks again, Rico, for the helicopter ride home. It saves me a lot of stress driving. The traffic is horrendous on Fridays getting out of town, at least this late. He glanced at her dashboard. It was 5:47 pm when she stopped at the curb. A sideways hug, and he was gone.

After he consulted with his Doctor friend Shawn, he didn't want to be drinking alcohol, having too many things to consider, yea, even though it was a Friday, and the weekend loomed large. Rico was definitely weighing options, knowing they had a dinner engagement and their mini vacation was planned. He and Wendi were going to Halfmoon Bay to rest and relax on the beach. He'd secured a cottage through Airbnb and wouldn't check out till 9 am on Monday. One part of his psyche echoed that he wasn't being responsible. He had the warrants signed for Kamryn's DNA, and his number one in charge of surveillance had Kam's Salon under the microscope, waiting for Kamryn to show up. She'd been AWOL for weeks, and no one at the shop knew where she was. Her cellphone was disconnected, and she'd not been on Social Media since July of last year. Something smelled fishy, but Rico couldn't be bothered with spending time analyzing it. He would be interviewing Kam one day and had a hot tip from one of the beauticians at her shop that Kamryn had a meeting with the Shopping Center's manager over a leasing issue tomorrow morning. Wendi had thrown a wrench in the original plan for a superb dining experience at Spinnakers waterside restaurant in Sausalito. She opted for a dive bar and grille in San Rafael, maybe for a few drinks. Then we could make it to Sausalito, but if not… oh well, he mused… he'd be saving a lot of money lol… ✿

Bells rang out as he pushed open the doors. It was warm and loud inside. He spotted Wendi smiling at once as she paddled a stool with her left hand. Rico looked down at the bar and realized it was the only open stool, thinking Wendi must have had a hard time saving it for him. She popped up, and they embraced with a lips-pressing kiss. "Well, I was getting worried that I'd lost you to my rival. Where is she, and how did you get here?" She was about to use the word Dude, but thought better of it, recalling his admonished tirade about her using that word. He couldn't help but nod and grin, slapping her back gently, "yes, my other girlfriend had to return home to her husband and children, so yep, you're stuck with me, Wendi."

Judea cleared her throat, making a concerted effort to make him notice this hacking sound, then she clutched her throat a little. "Don't tell me you're getting sick, Wendi...." She mocked her sequestered entities, peering out from her eyeballs. "No, it's just my throat like something is itching, and my voice feels raspy and not like what I'm used to hearing." He squeezed her hand... the bartender asked, "and what can I get you, my friend?" "Oh, let me have a glass of your house red wine..." "House wine, she gulped. No way he'll have the same as me." "What are you having?" "Toasted Head Cabernet, of course; it's one of our favorites. Not like we're wine snobs, but why the hell would you order some rot-gut house wine...." "Excuse me there, ma'am, our house wine is...." Judea waved her hand, smiling. He stopped speaking, wiped the bar top in front of Rico, and placed a glass of her preferred wine down. "Have you decided on some appetizers yet?" She peered up at him, "no, I'll let you know... what's your name again? I'm sorry L...." "Benny like the Jets," smiling, "you know the song." They amusingly matched his stare... rolling their eyes at him.

"Wow, ole Benny is a character. What do you want to do about dinner, babe?" She hands him the menu, "check it out... Benny suggested the Buffalo wings and Chili!" "You don't want to have dinner in this joint, do yuh? I mean, I thought we were going to...." She quickly spotted a booth by the front door. The parties were getting up to leave. "Hey, Benny, can we grab that booth over there?" "Sure, I'll have one of my servers clean it for you. Give me a few minutes...." "Oh, can we have a bottle of that Toasted Head and a couple of orders of your Wings with extra Ranch and Blue Cheese dressings and a bowl of chili to share, please?" He smiled "good choices…." "Ok, I guess we're hanging here for a little bit. I have to make some calls, so I'll…." "No, Rico, we need to talk, seriously, have a discussion. That will change everything you have ever thought about NIA." "Huh, what, Wendi? I don't want to argue anymore. I'm sorry I went Postal uh hostile on you about NIA. I know we'd decided not to delve into the NIA subject, umh, and try to keep peace with your strange addiction to…" "Shush now, um Rico…" she saw the table cleared out and ready, clutched his right hand, and dragged him with her. Knowing she needed to maneuver the minefields that NIA represented for him mellowly.

<u>Rico is aroused to an epiphany aligned with NIA's aims.</u>

"Rico, for once in your life, listen to me without interruption and try to have an open mind, pretend you don't despise NIA and…" "Wendi, it's not that I despise NIA. I know Terrance is corrupt and…" "Please… I'm fed up with your wild Goose chase and your preoccupation with Terrance and NIA; you know, I hate to say it. But sometimes I can't help but think one of the reasons you're with me is to pick my skull about NIA, hoping I'd let something slip that would be useful in one of your rueful investigations into NIA uh, as…." "Get a grip, girl L…." "You see Rico. We're already at each other's throats in a mini argument…." He sighed, shook his head, and leaned back in the booth across from her. "Honey, all your negative actions and viciousness towards Terrance and the NIA complexes are out of whack and unfounded. Gosh, talk about hypocritical you're the one that advocated your best friends Brock Dume and Lucie Link to be treated there, and have you forgotten how you politicked my parents." Judea slammed her palm down hard and fast, slapping the table.

Unexpectedly from their side "excuse me… my name is Lila, and I'll be your server…. your food will be up in about five minutes. Is there anything else I can get you?" "Yes, can you bring us two glasses of water…" "Sure…"

Judea waited till the server was out of hearing range. "Give me seven minutes of your time. Promise me that you will not interrupt me, and I will inform you of what you don't understand about the NIA Organization. But I promise you this, if you interrupt me even once, I will not ever broach the subject matter again with you, now small this mandatory, uhm, like declaration over, and let me know if you can glue your mouth shut till I'm completely finished." Rico gawked at the woman that he loved, just wanting to have an enjoyable time with Wendi, tapped his phone, and said, "I have to call my senior agent Tammy Fae that's monitoring Kam's Salon, and then call my office. Then I'm all yours."

By the time Rico returned through the front door, Wendi's paws were messy with wing sauce, and on her chin was… a smudge of chili. He sat down and went right to work on the appetizers. When there was a lull in satiating their hunger, he looked over at her and said, "I've made a tough decision…" pushing his plate aside. He took his right forefinger and said, "I'm zipping my lips shut. I'll listen and not say a word till you're done, Wendi…" then he swiped his forefinger from left to right across his closed lips…. miming glued shut!

Wendi 'Judea' knew right away where she'd start… "Rico, please only nod affirmations or shake your head in the negative. If you need further explanations, don't speak…." His eyes were wide open while he wiped his face for the final time with a cloth napkin. "Are you familiar with the term Black Op's or Black Operations?" One nod… "For the sake of being thorough, let me elaborate on what that term means to NIA and our US Military. Black Ops describes covert, military, or political operations employing measures not generally authorized by normal means. A covert, clandestine operation by a government agency, a military unit, or a paramilitary organization such as NIA. Yes, NIA is a private company that carries out secret black operations that are not attributable to the United States of America. They have teams that engage enemies of the State, here in the contiguous 48 states Hawaii and Alaska and abroad on foreign soil."

His shocked and bewildered expression while chewing on a stirring straw… led to her momentum. "Many times, NIA is called on to rescue captured Americans from enemy forces, to fire off smart bombs, or umh drone attacks associated with assassinations of foreign enemies. Osama Bin Laden comes to mind, but most of their operations involve military leaders you've probably never heard of. NIA was first on the ground in Iraq, taking out Saddam Hussein's hierarchy. The lists go on and on. Rico… if you checked out many of the trainers at NIA-U?"… Juden paused, knowing he'd been up in the helicopter spying with the doctor on the Quickdraw competition and had taken a slew of photos and videos.

"Rico, I believe you've done your due diligence regarding whom you and your friend Doctor Roble had taken pictures of at the Quickdraw contest… and in that case, ask yourself why you did or didn't discover that the Trainers at NIA have… too many accolades to name. A few to mull over are the Congressional Medal of Honors, the Distinguished Service Cross (DSC), the Navy Cross, the Silver Star Medal, and the Purple Hearts… They are the who's Who. Where NIA crosses the line is they employ criminal masterminds, many of whom have been believed to be Insane. NIA can be called a recruitment center and training center of Black Ops that work for the USA." Rico wanted to jump and verbally attack her… realizing that somehow Wendi had known of their helicopter ride over NIA… wondering how she'd had known that he and Shauna had taken a horde of pictures… this was a question he'd place on a back warning burner. Make no mistake. He'd want clarification... Ugh, was NIA surveilling him or Shanon ahhhh?

Judea gulps down some water, "I realize you are disbelieving my words... that would make sense, but I have just broken every rule and oath I've ever made to NIA and our Teams of mercenaries. I will be shunned and neutered from further missions our government will order. My skill base was necessary to carry out and complete countless objectives. Sunshine, my more aggressive side, has worked alongside Jax Foul over a dozen times, and at the instant, she is barking in my ear, spewing vileness, warning me to shut up. But I must finish what I've started!"

What Judea didn't say was that Wendi and Sunshine were squealing mad and screaming from their compartmentalized and partitioned Brain Cells. Rico was displaying an almost humorous expression like 'whatever, disbelieving her words like she was the person... who was insane.' But Judea soldiered on. "Terrance doesn't make a move unless ordered to do so. This information I'm divulging to you isn't known by incoming or outgoing Presidents, nor 95% of government leaders, or for that matter, military advisors. Terrance can't make a move unless the board of directors decides unanimously that NIA is needed. Yes, NIA's elite crews are the equivalent of Hollywood's television shows like 'A Team' or 'Mission Impossible Squads;' we employ the finest warriors this planet has to offer! Each mission is uniquely different. Right, this minute, a Team is up in Seattle... Squelching an illicit organized crime syndicate that deals with human trafficking and gambling."

Judea reached into her purse and pulled out a satellite phone, "I became privy to one of the Prime leaders of the 'Task Force,' ahh that's the name we call the 'Shotcallers' that utilize NIA's skillsets on operations they daresay are critical for the USA. These high-level individuals not only need to be monymous, but they must remain isolated from any of the actions that the NIA Teams commit."

Rico took his wine glass and raised it up with a gruff smirk…. and motioned to Wendi to tap cheers. She did so…. he wasn't smiling, but it would be evident to anyone familiar with him that he was merely amused and didn't believe this fantasy-related Hollywood scheme. Whoever was behind this melodramatic, orchestrated, grandiose histrionics should write a fricken book! Uh, Rico wondered who put her up to this fiction-based bullshit, but he remained quiet. And he couldn't wait to launch into a verbal sparring match with Wendi. How ludicrous is this strait up nonsense? Terrance and NIA worked for the U.S. Government…. Heck, they were on the same team. LMAO! He kept a somber face, drifting and pondering the next thing Wendi could say to make her statements more preposterous; uh, … Terrance could sprout wings and Fly… 🦋. 🦅 Lol.

"I memorized this person's private number, haven't called him, and only spoken to him once before on a covert mission to, uhm, Washington DC. to recover a Russian Diplomats wife and daughter who was captured, umh, kidnapped by our CIA illegally… I know bizarre, but have you heard the name of Five Star General Bill Hullinger?" Rico choked… drooling some red liquid from his lips, and quickly wiped and regained composure. He was well aware of who General Hullinger was. Since Five Star Omar Bradley died in 1981, he was the only Five Star Army General America had. Rico nodded. Judea punched in the code, and moments later on the screen appeared the General, apparently mobile, sitting in the back of a Limo. Wendi slid over in the booth closer to Rico. Now they were touching, and she held the satellite phone's five-inch screen out after shunning the server away from their table. General Bill Hullinger scrunched his eyelids, focusing on her… but said nary a syllable.

"Hello, Sir, do you remember me…." "Yes, I do your Wendi Feral. Where is Terrance Halliman, or Jax Foul, who allowed you to use this encrypted encoded communication line?" "General Sir, I felt compelled to contact you because my Fiancé is close to interfering with NIA's nucleus and could jeopardize our Operation in Elko, Nevada, next month." Rico felt a boiling hot flesh hit his reddening face; Fiancé Wtf? He hadn't proposed to Wendi, and now she was throwing him under the bus for his valid investigations of NIA…. R U Kidding me?

General Bill Hullinger proclaimed… "that upcoming mission is by far the most important endeavor that I've ever been a component of… I recognize you, and we've had our tabs on you, regular updates of what you're up to, Mr. Rico Captor. Congratulations, I wasn't aware that you and Wendi were engaged. It seems that young Ms. Feral has decided to forego proper protocol and contact me unbeknownst to her employers. Circumventing the Chain of Command, there are only three satellite phones that have been allocated to NIA. Who permitted you to use this phone, Wendi?" Rico was shocked into silence, which is not typical for him. Judea replied, "Uhm, Sir. Can I text you a code that should alleviate your concerns, and we can get down to business?" "Well, missy, that is precisely what I'm waiting for." Wendi takes her old school notepad out and texts the alpha-numerical code to General Hullinger, who nods and states, "give me a few seconds…." The screen went blank, and Rico opened his mouth to speak until Wendi pointed her finger at her lips.

The screen reopened, and they saw the General perched up, leaning forward on a bench seat; through the tinted windows in his limousine, they saw the 'White House.' "Please refer to me as BILL I have validated the code and can discuss some mandatory issues with you, Rico. First and Foremost, Rico, you have been a thorn in our sides for a long time…. this vendetta you apparently have against NIA and Terrance Halliman has gone way too far. But I don't want to broach that subject as of now. I want to know if you have heard the name Colonel Ruiz." Rico spoke for the first time in thirteen minutes, "yes, Sir, I have. He is a war hero and was in charge of Guantanamo Bay. He's highly respected." "Yes, that's him... have you heard the acronym C.I.N.?" "Yes, Sir, it stands for China, Iran, and North Korea." "Correct, it's a combined multi-faceted Faction that's Anti-American. Well anti-humanity. Rico, I will not get into the particulars or inner nuances of what C.I.N's objectives are, but I will say this they must be stopped."

Rico reaches over and places his hand over Wendi's. "Rico, suffice it to say Colonel Ruiz is well connected and has his far-outreaching tentacles on the pulse of our armed forces. He has allies at the pinnacle of our government. We have yet to filter out the moles and undercover spies that work for the C.I.N. network. We have vetted some and allowed them to continue their unhealthy ways, against Democracy and our ways of life." Without warning, General Hullinger cackled and then promptly snarled. "I don't want to sound like a damn politician. Let me cut right to the point. Colonel Ruiz and his affiliates are propagating like rodents. He has become aware of what NIA stands for. He has pressed his colleagues in the CIA, FBI, HSA, and ATF, to name a few of the acronyms he's infiltrated and aligned with his Faction. The Colonel's deluded group of adversaries want to end NIA's growing militias....." He stops as another phone rings loudly. The screen went dark, and the sound was muted.

General Bill Hullinger came back online a few moments later with a sense of urgency, and we could hear a machine in the foreground. He reached out, brought a plain piece of old-school paper up, and read a memorandum "Mr. Captor, you must not change your modus operandi. Stay vigilant, proactive, and steadfast in your pursuit of damaging NIA's viability. You're envisioned as an ally to C.I.N.'s goals. We have been able to Vette several of the people you relate with on occasion, such as Judge Carolyn Delaney. She is dirty and a definite ally of Colonel Ruiz's. Her niece is married to his nephew. Your top field Agent Tammy Fae is also part of C.I.N. We have yet to uncover others in your office. Still, I am certain that there are, at a minimum, another three that figure into being compensated for their allegiance to this nefarious group of mercenaries. Wendi's brother Mark Feral who you've personally been chasing across the USA ever since he absconded from parole from San Quentin, has now signed on with this mercenary group of disrupters. Rico, we need to navigate this quandary carefully. With precision, each move we make needs to be quantified and Vetted. Do you understand?"

Rico couldn't hide his shock and astonishment… Lila returned to the table, and all went silent as Judea grabbed the phone and winked at Bill Hullinger. Alone again, she places the phone in its cradle, and they see the General's arms wide open as if waiting for Rico's reply. "Sir, I believe I do. It is shocking that the Judge.…" "Rico, I must go…" we see him place the missive into a shredder at the back of his limo. And he magnifies his face by getting closer to the camera. "Rico, you work for the FBI and our government. I order you to go ahead as if we didn't have this conversation, and you must not waver. You must follow through with your attacks on NIA, for sadly, we don't know who the moles are.… that work for NIA or our FBI. What we are sure of… is that someone close to Terrance is leaking vital information to Colonel Ruiz. The only people you can trust are Wendi Feral and Jax Foal. They are not complicit with our enemies. Do you accept my orders, Rico?" "Of course, Sir, but I was going to arrest Kamryn and serve Warrants on NIA… how can I do that with all of this being.…" "I've told you to continue in what 'They' expect you to do, don't waver. We will speak again later next week. God Bless America…" The Star-Spangled Banner played in the background… Bye-bye now.…

<u>**Rico capped the bottle of Toasted Head Cabernet.**</u>

Rico sat flummoxed. An eleven-minute conversation had spoiled all that his life revolved around. Judea slid the satellite phone back into its pouch and said, "I have been requested to attend a mandatory session at NIA, babe. I'm sorry I cannot go to the beach with you this weekend; besides, it's not beach weather...." She smiled, knowing that he had reserved a cottage for them in the town of Half Moon Bay. He said, "I have a lot to think about. One thing is for certain, uhm, I must not alter my plans as the General had said. Babydoll, can you drop me at the Fed Building? I need to pick up my Jeep. Agent Tammy Fae, geez, I just can't get over it. She's a fricken traitor. Okay, let's plan something after your NIA gathering. Maybe we can get a hotel in Napa?" "Excellent idea. I will secure us a room, honey-bunny... my Fiancé. He picked up his credit card and took her out the doors of the Flatiron grille, spinning her around for an impromptu Frenchy. "I do Love you, my Wendi" Judea didn't reply, only tugged him closer and whispered into his right ear, "when are we getting married, Mr. Captor?

<u>**-56-**</u>

<u>***How life suddenly sunk to new lows for Kamryn!***</u>

Kamryn checked the time on her phone. It was already almost 5 pm. She gave her daughter Sonja a last hug and kiss, handing her to Renae.... "I will see you and Sonja at my home in Tiburon at 7:30." Renae nodded and sternly gave her a half hug. Jax Foul had contacted her, telling her that she had a gate pass to pick up at the Administration building. This had set

Kamryn's heart fluttering. She'd first have to visit with her vile Uncle and play his game. Terrance had changed plans three times and was now back at the starting gate…. He planned to circumvent Rico, trying not only to collect her DNA but not to be able to interview her. Terrance had ordered Kam to say to him, 'speak with my attorney and my Uncle Terrance Hallium.' To make this adjustment palpable, he had asked Jax to request Wendi to keep Rico Captor busy at the Flatiron Grille. Her Uncle and her were going to the San Rafael General Hospital under the guise of willingly giving her DNA to Doctor Shanon Roble…. Rico's sidekick.

Kamryn looked in her rearview mirror as the gates closed behind her. She was driving an NIA company van. Freedom felt anxious as her heart pitter-pattered. She was uneasy and beyond nervous, like afraid…. Why? At times of her torturous time behind the Razor Wire in the prison, she'd thought she would never live to feel this moment. It was here now, but she couldn't wrap her mind around the fact that she was Free!

Kam drove directly to the Salon to start the process of making sure if the FBI ever obtained a search warrant for Kam's Salon…. that, it would be clean of anything that could lead back to NIA or to sister Sara. All that was going to be left at the Salon was to be Exculpatory evidence proving Sara's innocence…

Terrance has his plans altered.

Terrance checked his phone. He had 11 texts. The last was from his niece Kamryn 'hey, Uncle, are we still on for this afternoon's meeting with Doctor Roble at 6 pm? I'm in the Salon office and have communicated with Sara via a secure video conference hookup. I'm in the clean-up process….' Terrance was running way behind and rushed to the elevator. He didn't care if he broke the F.A.A. rules and regulations of not flying helicopters in or out of a Prison complex. Now on the roof, he jumped into the waiting chopper. He texted her back, 'yes, we will meet at 6 pm at the hospital. I had issues, and I'm running late. I will be there as soon as possible!' 'Okay, uncle, I'm working with Sara… no worries, I'll see you there.'

Terrance didn't bother telling his niece that the plans had been changed. His NIA security team had sent him pictures and a message that Doctor Roble had flown out of the Executive airport and wasn't going to be at the hospital to collect Kam's DNA. Terrance was undaunted, and he'd contacted the hospital and spoken with Doctor Roble's assistant, who'd be there to take Kamryn's DNA. He sneered; good luck Rico at interviewing Kamryn or even seeing her. You got a warrant for her DNA we will comply, so… now what?

<u>Rico had been enlightened, confused, and bewildered, uhm, shocked to uncertainty.</u>

<u>Rico wasn't disoriented anymore; it was a shocker sneaking with General Bill Hollinger… Alongside his Wendi Feral. Now fully aware of what he must do. His task was to follow through as if he didn't know that ulterior forces worked against him and his beloved country, the USA.</u>

Rico pulled out his FBI edition phone and called the Agent that was in charge of his surveillance team that watched the shopping center where Kam's Salon was. He felt a sick twinge in his guts as he heard the traitor's voice. "Tammy, I want you to be prepared to serve the DNA Warrant at the Salon and personally hand it to Kamryn Amaya. Tell me, Tammy, What is she doing at the salon?" "Sir, well, she's been inside for approximately 15 minutes, and we can't see inside the salon." "We'll close off the Beauty Salon and shopping center once I give the order. I want you to preserve the scene. Tammy, keep me posted. I'm on my way." "Yes, Sir," she said, rather excited... Rico added with a raised tenor that... "if we find anything incriminating inside the salon, I want her taken directly to the Sacramento County jail. There subcontracted to take Federal prisoners!" "Yes, sir, I'm here awaiting your orders... it will be done!" Rico's strategy was en vogue now that he was out to protect Kamryn and NIA, so any disturbing evidence seized at the Salon would be illegally confiscated, for the Warrant was only for Kamryn's DNA. Hopefully, Tammy would go all Gung-Ho and screw up, taking ownership of anything detrimental towards NIA. He couldn't believe that within a half hour, he was working to preserve and safeguard NIA 🌀

Terrance lands and is off to 'Kam's Salon' to pick up Kamryn.

Jacob had been waiting half the day at the Executive airport. Finally, Terrance's chopper could be seen hovering over the landing strip. He pulled the Limo over to the waiting area. Moments later, Terrance was in the backseat, and they were heading to the Salon to pick up Kamryn and take her to the hospital, where Doctor Robles' assistant would swab Kam's mouth for up-to-date and current DNA.

Kamryn was on her third trip out to her van, which was parked behind the Salon. The only positive other than her being outside of NIA was that she wore gloves. She was thinking, not too intelligent, that Sara had left all this compromising evidence at the Salon. Was it a setup? Sara had time to dispose of all this damaging evidence, so why didn't she? Something smelled putrid. She had an ominous feeling of despair! All she wanted was to meet with Renae and have her daughter in her hands again. Kam emptied the floor safe of all Sara's paraphernalia and now was carrying out the last of it. She had to admit it. She got sick to her stomach when she saw the squirt guns and the bottle of formula, most certainly Sara's poison that killed the attorney.

Rico glanced at his phone's screen. It was Tammy Fae, "hello…." "Sir, Ms. Amaya is carrying items out of the Salon. She's on her third trip out. One of our Agents thought she'd spotted a gun, uh, weapon in her hands." "Tammy, arrest her and serve her the search warrants now!" Rico regrettably was still twenty-five minutes from Kam's Salon, now doubting anything that Tammy told him, but had to play it close to the vest like General Hullinger had ordered him to do!

On her last trip out of the salon, she felt a surge of wariness 'from the corner of her eye.' She noticed quick movements and then squealing tires. She sprinted to the back door, locked it, and struggled to find her cell phone, which was in the salon office.

Then a loud bang and a high-pitched female screaming loudly…. noises erupted like a volcanic blast. The back door gave way to a battering ram. A man shouted, 'get down on the fkn floor now.' She almost made it back to the office door before she was tackled and laid straight out on her face. Her head slammed and bounced off the hardwood, her arms pulled out of joints and cuffed behind her back. "Kamryn Amaya, you're under arrest. You have the right to remain silent…." She was Hogtied inhumanely by the aggressive Agents. Kam didn't fight them nor scream out…. it was only Par for her course. All she worried about was Sonja, and she hoped that Sonja was safe with Renae on their way to her home in Tiburon. Kam kept a level head, knowing that her Uncle would be there soon and she would be exonerated and free to go home.

Rico had his sirens blowing from the external speakers and Red and Blue lights flashing from his dashboard out the front windows of his Jeep Gladiator. His phone rang again. Tammy shouted, "we have weapons, sir, and other paraphernalia…." "Lock Kamryn in the back of your police cruiser Tammy. I'm on my way. ETA eleven minutes!"

Before she could catch her breath, she was tossed face-first onto a backseat. She was caged, her hands bound, and her legs shackled. Kam was in shock, having difficulty breathing, and trying to calm herself, but she was unable to do so.

<u>Terrance, in the back of his Limousine, Jacob was driving him to 'Kam's Salon.'</u>

His briefcase chimed a tune, knowing it was the secure line from NIA. He dug it out "yes…." It's Walter, his breath harried, "The Fed's just raided Kamryn's Beauty Salon. She's been arrested, boss, and…" "Wtf are you talking about, Walter? What the hell…?" "Jacob hit the gas, flooring the accelerator. "Don't get us pulled over, Jacob. Take us on the fastest route to the Salon now!" "Walter, now relax. Tell me exactly what happened?" "I was monitoring the screens and police scanners, and you know we have cameras at the Salon. They just swooped in just like that and took Kam and cuffed her up. She's inside a cop car, don't know anything else." "Is Rico on site?" "No, last we knew, he was with Wendi at a bar." "Walter monitor Cal-Trans highway cameras. They will not do anything with Kamryn until Rico shows up… keep me posted; I'm fifteen minutes off…" "okay, Sir, I will do so…" Click.

<u>Judea drove towards NIA in her Audi.</u>

Wendi… 'Judea…' driving down the seven-mile road ending at NIA. She was singing the song "Old Town Road" sung by 'Lil Nas X' happy thinking she'd made a good contribution at the impromptu conference call moments before. She figuratively stood up for her beliefs and couldn't wait to see Rico and fill him in on some of the possible changes. Knowing it wasn't sure, but it may happen… such as the Board of Directors at NIA was likely going to let his best friend Brock Dane start up classes for the next semester at NIA-U that started on February 1st. Her stomach growled; the chicken wings and chili didn't fill the void. She anticipated a fine dining experience with Rico later at her favorite Hotel in Sausalito. She was driving through the gates of NIA, grinning for all the cameras to see her in her brand-new A-8 Audi, snug and comfy, then all Hell broke out! Answering the call from Terrance, "Wendi, the Fed's arrested Kamryn. I've tried several times to get Rico on the line he doesn't answer...." "Omigod no what all right ngh um let me Geezus Christ sakes uuh okay let me try I...." "I'm only 15 minutes from the Salon Walter said they took her in an SUV. I can't get any clarification from any of my contacts. Please get back to me at once. Call fricken Rico... Wendi shit, all they had was a Warrant for her DNA!" Click.

<u>Back at NIA-U, sisters Valerie and Sara Amaya discover that Kamryn was arrested.</u>

Valerie and Sara had been working out in the cardio gym when the news hit. They separated... Valerie called Jax, who was beside himself in anger, "can we do anything to help Kam? I can't believe this has happened?...." "Meet me outside Hangar three and pack for the night we're leaving for Sacramento. Val, I'm at the pumps filling the Hummer seeya in 15 minutes." Jax had a heavy heart, for he didn't know how he was going to introduce the latest toxic confrontation that her Uncle Terrance had dealt with on the 'E.U.' Unh European union had submitted a request and inquiry for an interview with Valerie Amaya. It was always the first step in the extradition process. Forensic scientists found DNA linking her at the scene of her first homicides. She left relevant DNA evidence when Valerie killed her captor couple in the most horrific and graphic way. Heck, Valerie was barely a teenager ....

<u>Sara's partitioned personalities were Irate screaming in her ears and cranium... Sara meandered toward Valerie's suite, squeaking out loud to the three entities that lived within her skull. Anne was stressed out 'you know that this is going to come back and bite us, Sara. Kam will blabbermouth her ass off and snitch us out. We're in a cesspool of trouble; Kamryn</u>

will discover our fake identification and passport with our itinerary; dammit, Sara, you left all our information in her jewelry box.' Then it was Al's turn who... butted in using his ventriloquist skills with Ken's voice, 'uncle roo, my twisted sister Sara was going to bail and escape NIA and leave us to handle the homicides of the Sparks and Renae's attorney. I have proof...' Donny cried out 'oh my oh no, whimpering, we're going down, babe!' Sara gesticulated her arms wildly and shrieked... her outburst, causing others around her to jump. 'Shut the Fk Up!...' she screamed out loud. Seeing other students at NIA-U eyeballing her, she mimed at her phone holding her hands up to her side and nodding her head as if to say... sorry.

Rico had second thoughts about how to proceed.

He had hung up the phone with Agent Tammy Fae, whom he'd found out wasn't loyal to him or his country. He again, for the umpteenth time, mulled over what General Hullinger had told him and Wendi. He decided to play it differently and picked up his radio attached to the dashboard. Knowing anyone with a police scanner could listen in, and most definitely, he believed Terrance's hooligans were. He uttered the words that would change the direction of this case... 'Breaker TF-6, do you got a copy?... over.' 'Yes, Sir RC-7, Go ahead... over.' 'Take the subject, Ms. Kamryn Amaya, to the Sacramento Jail for booking... over.' 'Sir, we're set up at the Marin County Jail... over.' 'TF-6, take her to Sac County... over.' 'Yes, Sir RC-7... over.'

Rico couldn't wrap his mind around the possibility that he and the arrogant, egotist Terrance Halliman were on the same side. It bothered him more than he'd like to admit. He didn't like the smug asshole. Yes, asshole, nope, not being honest with himself... if he knew he wouldn't get in trouble, he'd follow him, get him alone, beat the brakes off of him, and smash the prick to a Pulp.

<u>**Change of direction.**</u>

Terrance's private line rang again. It was Walter, "Sir, I just recorded a conversation on the Police Scanner. They're going to take Kamryn to Sacramento County Jail for booking." "Thanks, Walter; ensure you get all the video and pictures of what they are taking out of Kam's Salon...." "Terrance, you're not going to believe this one, the cameras in the Salon are still working, and I got all the video of what they are taking out of the office. The fools didn't shut down the camera system, insane as that may sound." "That's crazy, Walter. That was way unprofessional and irresponsible. It's like dealing with Mayberry RFD... keep me posted. I have to go."... Click

He hit the intercom in his Limousine; "Jacob, slow it down and drive us to the Sacramento County Jail. That's where Rico and the Feds are taking Kamryn too." "Wow, wonder why they didn't keep her local, ok? I'll set the GPS and let you know when we will... arrive there, Sir." Terrance once again tried to get the bastard on his private phone, but Rico didn't answer. After the third call, he decided to leave a message.

<u>**Rico found himself in a quandary... confused about which direction to go.**</u>

Rico was on his way to the Sacramento County Jail to interview Kamryn, avoiding the calls of Terrance and others, when he spied Wendi's name on the phone screen. Oddly, he felt apprehension. For he'd played the fool, attacking NIA at every corner, but how would he have known they were on his side, some of the good guys? It sank his mood, but the ball was rolling, and he would follow through as the General had ordered. He'd act as if nothing had changed. He was a stalwart individual, an FBI Agent that was going to nail Terrance and NIA to the wall! Finally answered her call... "Hello, sweetheart, I'm going to be late... not going to be done with this Kamryn booking and interview until later." "Don't you, sweetheart, me, you bastard… why are you arresting Kamryn? That poor girl has been through enough. Are you a maniac? What a cruel… didn't you pay attention to what the General had said?" "Stop it calm down, stop screaming at…." "Where is she? What are you doing? I can't believe…." Rico suddenly pulled the phone from his ear; chills crawled up and down his spine, tingles followed by a spasm, and sweat beaded up… his hands were clammy. "Rico, you have made a dire life-ending miscalculation. You will regret this rebelliousness and crime against NIA and…" "Who are you, who's voice? Uh, you're not Sunshine and definitely not my Wendi. Who the Fk are you?…" Click. Wendi glanced into the rear-view mirror ghost-like… and saw Jaden staring and glaring right at her. No!… Yep!

Rico pulled to the side of the road; his lights were still flashing,… mulling over that blowup by a person he seemed not to know. Her voice wasn't like Sunshine's, nor… not even close to his precious Wendi. What didn't she understand? She sat next to him at the restaurant and heard General Hullinger order him not to change direction because spies surrounded him. He'd ordered Tammy to serve a DNA warrant on Kamryn if she ever turned up at her salon. Kam did, so Rico would have to play it like… business as usual. What else could he have done? The reason he had Kamryn transported all the way to Sacramento was that he hoped the traitors that worked for C.I.N. and Colonel Ruiz wouldn't have anyone at the jail.

A text came in on his phone 'sorry, babe. I didn't mean to go off on you, geez, I wasn't thinking; my bad…. you're only being true to yourself and doing what GBH 'General Bill Hullinger' had asked of you… forgive me, please. 🌀   Hey, I have a room for us at 'The Inn Above Tide' in Sausalito, right on the San Francisco Bay. I booked it for two nights seeya there later.' Rico read the text twice, then mused… talk about Schitzo? He smirked. It had been a few years since they spent time at that five-star Hotel, and he remembered it was a special time for them. How romantic it was... he texted back. "Babydoll, heck, if I'd known that, I'd delegate someone else to interview Wendi... I'm calling you....' Judea cleared her throat, realizing she was out of control when she'd just spoken to him... trying to imitate Wendi's sweet voice. "Hello babe, I'm sorry to have gone off on you. I must have a bug in my throat. I hope I'm not coming down with anything!" "Wendi, I'm calling Terrance. He's called three or four times. I will handle this Kamryn situation by delegating some dufus that I know that works at the Sac Jail." She laughed into the phone's speaker. Okay, I will cut short this gets-together at NIA and see you at the Hotel. Umh, in, let's say, an hour and a half. Oh hey, I still have that bottle of Toasted Head. We didn't even drink any...." "That's the plan, sweetheart; seeya there!..." Click.

<u>Conversation with NIA's CEO, Terrance Hallinan</u>

Jacob yelps from the front of the Limo, "Sir, you got a call from Rico on the mobile line." "Pass it through to the back." He wondered why he didn't call him back on his private line... "Hello, Mr. Captor..." "Why so formal, Counselor...?" "Rico, what are you doing arresting my niece? I thought all you wanted was her DNA?" "My Agent on the scene was there only to collect her DNA, but she was under surveillance and seen carrying a weapon, a pistol from the Salon. Kamryn was also carrying other bags out of the salon to her van...." "Since when is a Gun illegal in California? You only had a warrant for her DNA...." "Terrance, we found three bottles of formulas in her van and a few squirt guns, uh, most likely the poison used to kill...." "Rico, without testing the contents of the bottles, you can't just arrest her, uh, Kamryn, your... acting like vigilantes. I mean, the 357 Magnum is registered to Kamryn's sister Sara. She's had that gun for years. A beauty salon is always plumb filled with chemicals, dyes, and formulas. You can't just go in there and run roughshod over the employees and…" "Your correct it was improperly handled, but we both know that Sara murdered Carl and Bianca Sparks and the attorney, don't we?" Silence not heard.

"Terrance, I'll have her DNA collected at the Marin County Sheriff's Department; you can have someone pick her up from there… I'm sure it would be useless of me to try and interview her, for she'd ask for you to be present… She'd Lawyer up!" Oddly, Terrance and Jacob, who were listening, heard Rico cackle into a short reprieve of laughter. "Will that work for you, Counselor?" "Umh, yes, I'll be on my way to the Sheriff's Department to pick her up, and thanks for not being an asshole about this, Rico." It was his turn to laugh… Click.

Kamryn watched through the steel grate as the FBI SUV cruised West on Hwy 80.

Kam had tried in vain to speak to the two Agents in the front seat of the Black SUV. Thankful that she was no longer hogtied, only had handcuffs on her wrists and shackles on her ankles, chained to her waist. Like she was going to escape or harm someone, duh, this had to be more theatrics. Worried not for herself, shit she'd been through worse than this inside the Prison at NIA. Attacked, beaten, fought other inmates, drugged to oblivion, sexually abused by a Female Correctional Officer, the list goes on and on. This didn't bother her much. Been there, done that…! Kamryn was a veteran of abuse, no longer virgin material.

The Agent on the passenger side barked at the driver while listening to his phone. "Dammit, flip a bitch…. we're taking the prisoner to the Sherriff's Department in Marin. The driver was obviously an underling, subservient to his master, only nodded and said, 'yes sir….' I thought this had to be a good change of venue. I had heard they were taking me to Sacramento. I had shouted at the top of my lungs that the gun was legal. I knew that my uncle had bought it years ago for Sara. Heck, he'd taken us to firing ranges when my twin and I were like seven years old. That gun had to be thirty years old.

I sat uncomfortably on the bench seat, and my chains rattled when I moved. The only thing on my mind was my daughter Sonja. I knew when I saw the digital clock display on the dashboard of the Feds SUV that Renae was supposed to have taken Sonja over an hour ago out the gates of NIA. She had the code to get into my home in Tiburon and was probably waiting for me, not knowing why I hadn't finished up at Sara's Salon by now. I semi-sighed... at least Sonja was safe!

<u>Jacob parks the Limousine at the Marin County Sheriff's Department.</u>

Terrance had sent one of his attorneys who worked locally to Kam's Salon to engage the FBI Agent Tammy Fae, who was illegally searching the Salon. He contended that everything confiscated was done so without a proper Warrant. All the FBI had was a warrant for Kamryn's DNA. The FBI went hog wild, overreaching their authority after catching Kam with Sara's legal 357 Magnum, started searching the premises, and confiscated one of NIA's vans. Terrance intuited that something was wrong, highly suspicious, and peculiar Rico didn't make these amateurish blunders. To have his Agents search the salon without a proper search warrant meant that nothing that they seized was admissible in a Court of Law. Why didn't he simply advocate that his Agents park their Asses at the salon and lock it down till his patsy Judge would sign a Search Warrant?

Besides this blatant misstep, they had arrested Kamryn for a legal gun and were transporting her to Sac County, but in midstream, the decision was made that his Agents would drop his niece off at the Marin Sheriff's station. But as Terrance had learned, 'don't look a gift Horse in the mouth.' Jacob waited with him for Kamryn to be escorted into the Sheriff's Department.

Kamryn had noticed the vibes in the cab of the SUV had changed in her favor for the Agent in the passenger seat, who kept saying yes, sir, and will do, sir on his phone. The next thing that happened was the Fed mobile stopped at the curb, and Walla, the back door was opened... and off came her shackles and handcuffs
❋

"Jacob, can you try and get Wendi on the phone? I've texted her... she's not returning my calls or texts." "Sure, boss, oh here comes an SUV that looks like the typical FBI driver and could have Kamryn."

I sat forward, rubbing my wrists that were cut from the steel cuffs, we'd turned a corner, and I saw the Hummer Limousine that was my uncle's favorite Limo. Terrance was there, so this is why she wasn't taken to Sacramento... Terrance had pulled some strings and had her returned to Marin County. Suddenly a wariness struck her off-balance. Wait, I can't have him drop me off at my home in Tiburon. Renae and Sonja were supposed to be there; no way... how was I going to work this out. Uncle's email that Rocky had given her a couple of weeks ago to read was from a woman... Vadoma had told him to eliminate or Abort Sonja.

I'm let out of the SUV. The Agent tried to help me out, reaching his arm out, which I poked out of the way. My uncle spoke with the FBI driver and said, "Kamryn, don't say anything. They are going to be collecting your DNA. I will meet you inside the holding room." I mused, well, duh uncle, I've watched enough crime dramas, and with my family's derelictions, I was well aware not to mutter a syllable. The whole process took less than ten minutes, and I was swabbed and out the door. Embraced by Uncle, and even Jacob hugged me. Terrance said, "we'll drop you off at your home, don't worry about the van. I'm having someone pick it up. You have a few vehicles in your garage...." He smiled "it's been a while since you've driven your Corvette. Why don't you relax, spend the night and be back at NIA tomorrow morning at around noon."

What could I say to stop Jacob from driving to my residence? Renae had snuck Sanja out of NIA, and her automobile was probably parked inside the gates. Terrance knew what her Lexus looked like, and this could become a tragedy. "Hey uncle, can you drop me off at San Rafael Joe's Restaurant? I'm hungry, and I'll get an Uber home." He checked his Rolex watch and barked at Jacob... drop us off at Joe's. I could use something to eat." Then he leaned across the bucket seats and whispered, "why didn't you tell me you were pregnant?"

-57-

<u>Epilogue...</u>

<u>Kamryn tries to dodge Terrance's declaration.</u>

While Jacob parked at the curb in front of the restaurant, nothing else was said. Kamryn went straight to the restroom, having to pee badly. Thinking nervously, someone had betrayed her, and it could only be Rocky, Doctor Wei, or Liz. Hoping it wasn't Renae.

She scooted into the booth, knowing farewell they hadn't spoken since uncle had asked why she didn't tell him she was pregnant. Terrance bent his head towards her "well, Kam, why haven't you answered me? Why didn't you tell me you were pregnant?" I decided my best move was denial, "Please, do I look pregnant to you...." She stood up from the booth and twirled around. Some of the other customers at the restaurant who saw her Pirouette... smiled, and the waiter rushed over. "Is there something I can get you, ma'am?" Kam replied, 'yes can I have a Bikini Vodka Martini, please.' He bowed and hurried away. She sat back down with a smug look. "Wow, I didn't know I'd bring so much attention to myself spinning around out there?" "Yes, you did, niece. Now that your show is done answer my question, why didn't you inform me of your pregnancy? I am doubly disturbed and distraught, Kamryn, that you didn't trust me and kept this a secret, you poor child, then to bear the burden of losing your baby on top of it. Omg, I'm so sorry honey-bunny...." Terrance pushed his rear end over in the booth, reaching out with his left arm, and pulled her... close in an embrace.

Kamryn was freaked out, glad she'd doused herself with perfume and deodorant because she was perspiring like a sprinkler, afraid and anxious. She lowered her voice, trying to sound hurt and weak, and pretended that she needed his nurturing love. Kam was befuddled or, better yet, bewildered at why he thought she'd lost Sonja and had a miscarriage. Who was misleading him, who told him of her pregnancy.... it could only be Doctor Liz Honcho. Should she react spontaneously? No, she rethought that action. It was better to play it close to the vest and find out what her uncle knew about her baby. "I'm sorry, uncle, about not telling you about Brock's baby... if you can think back to when you didn't trust me. Unh, when you believed me to be Sara and wouldn't even return one of my dozen-plus calls, you never visited me. I hadn't anyone. Your NIA staff was punishing me, I was afraid... Frankly scared to death!"

She felt him squeeze tighter "excuse me, here's your martini, ma'am, would you like a heat-up of your coffee, sir?" Terrance shook no, and the table fell into silence. Kam didn't reach out for her Bikini Martini, only tried to shudder her body for effect. "I can't imagine what you went through. How horrible for you, sweetie. I mean, you were alone and with child." She had him backpedaling, so she struck. "Worse than that, uncle, I was forcibly drugged with mixtures of pharmaceuticals that were harmful to not only me but my baby. I was fed slop for food, physically attacked, beaten... chained and shackled to gurneys, and fed intravenously. Are you kidding me, uncle, huh? The stress alone could have killed my baby... I," He shrugged her away to get a look at her face, "I can't go backward, honey, I'm sorry..." Kam squinted, trying her best to have at least one tear... fall, "you know as well as I if the staff had got wind that I was pregnant I'd been forced into an abortion, I had zilch no one on my side. I was the venomous Vipress Killer Sara to everyone who looked at me. I was lucky to have a petite figure and could wear baggie overalls." He put his hand over her palm on the table, trying to see her eyes, but Kam's head was bent downward... so he tried to act sorrowfully. But was relieved that Kamryn had lost the baby. If not, he would have had to do something about the kid. Vadoma had made it clear that the baby Sonja was the Devil Incarnate.

"Again, I'm wretchedly apologetic that I didn't believe your assertion that you were not Sara. This will always haunt me, Kamryn. What was your plan if you didn't have that diabetic episode and were taken to the emergency room, where Liz discovered that you were pregnant? What were you going to do, niece... have the child by yourself in your cell? You poor baby, I don't know how you handled all of that. Then to lose the baby... Doctor Kathy Wei described how you fell over, your Water had broken, and you had a miscarriage. How fricken sad, sweetheart, for you." "For me, Uncle... for me, huh? what about my baby?" Then Kam bit her lower lip, geesh whoa, nelly, and spoke before Terrance did. "Uncle, I'm having a difficult time and wanted to open up to you and tell you what had happened, but the subject is so damn painful I've just Melted inside...." Kam was relieved; now she understood the players in the deception played out by Renae. Whew, that girl is my Hero.

Terrance scooted back away on the bench seat, knowing the onlookers had already had enough of a show. Terrance sipped his cool coffee, raised his hand, and waved a server over. Feeling a little beaten up and tired, it had been a hell of a rough day. He ordered an Expresso Martini. Then pointed at Kam's nearly gone martini, 'she'll take another also, please…'

He couldn't let it go, so while the kettle was hot, he ventured forward, "Kam, honey, there are a few things that bother me. I was under the belief that you and Sara had hysterectomies in your late teens or early twenties." Kam was prepared for this one… "yes, I hadn't had my period since I was like 17 years old and had a serious case of endometriosis and true uncle… Sara and I had decided never to have a child, for no one knows our bloodline like you. Our ancestors are the Who, Whose of evil entities, criminal psychopaths. Sara had driven me to this shady doctor, who had performed her hysterectomy, and I was rolled in and knocked out. Put under anesthetics and woke in bad pain, like someone had pounded a sledgehammer on my lower abdomen. Sara told me that I'd had the hysterectomy, and I thought that was it. Remember, I'd stopped having my period. I was super-duper surprised and didn't believe I was pregnant until the baby started growing inside me."

Terrance followed up on her impetus, "that's just another Sara thing. How sinister can a person be…" he cackled "yep, Sara is a one-of-a-kind perpetrator, a self-serving freakazoid for sure, Kam. But now that you know you can have a child, you must, before you continue a love life, have a hysterectomy, honey. It's the only way. I realize you think that I'm sort of silly believing in horoscopes and Fortune tellers and all that crap… Right?" Kam nodded, hoping he'd continue in this vein. "I was called out of the blue by our family prophetess, a soothsayer who prognosticated that you'd have a baby girl, and her name was going to be Sonja...." He stopped and gauged if he should continue. Still, she'd opened the can of worms admitting the family genetics were plumb filled with psychopaths, so... "Sonja, if she had lived according to my tea-leaf and tarot reader, would develop into the worse serial killer ever to exist, female or male." He said it, relaxed, and downed his martini.

Kamryn quickly brought her right hand together, holding her Bikini Martini to ensure she'd stop shaking. Bothering her to the max was the predated email she'd read that was given to her by Rocky from the Psychic Vadoma, who'd stated her baby's name before she knew it to be. Although how crazy could it be, little Sonja a Devil like her Aunts Valarie and Sara. Nah, no way! She remained silent, trying her best not to whimper, seeking.... for this subject to end. They hadn't even ordered appetizers yet. She was hunger-less and only wanted out of there. She wanted to meet up with Renae at her home and snuggle with her Angel... Sonja!

Terrance's phone vibrated, and he said excuse me, darling, for a moment... he read the text, 'boss, I got Kamryn's purse from the Fed's at the salon and just left Kamryn's home in Tiburon. I had cleaned up everything I could that I thought was left over by Sara when she lived there. It was like 49 degrees in the house, so I set the thermostat to 69 degrees. It's ready with the three bouquets of gorgeous flowers you requested 😊' 'great good job. When will you be here?' 'about fifteen minutes...' 'bring Kam's purse to her...' 'K.'

Kam fidgeted, impatiently not knowing the time, for she didn't have a watch. It was taken when she was arrested, along with her phone and purse. She leaned over and saw Terrance's Rolex. Dammit, it was already after 7 pm she was going to be late. Renae would just have to wait at her home with Sonja. She couldn't text her to let her know what was happening. "Uncle the Feds took my purse and...." "I know I have Jacob retrieving your stuff. Relax, let's order some appetizers. The waiter is starting to give us the evil eye. We're taking up his station, and….." "I think you are reading too much into his look. He's got to be happy with the bill so far. Heck, we've ordered three martini's already!" Kam hopped up "excuse me. I'm going to hit the head, ahh bathroom, Uncle."

Kamryn had memorized Renae's phone number and beckoned over a busboy, "can you tell me where the closest payphone is, young man?" He appeared dazzled, and his awestricken mouth opened. Nothing exited "ugh… well, I haven't seen one of those since I watched an old movie with my mother. I'm sorry." Kamryn disappeared into the restroom and sat in a stall on a commode, how was she going to navigate away from Uncle Terrance? After a long prayer, Kam skittered out of the lavatory. She shook her head unhappily while peripherally seeing her uncle coming into full view. Timing was everything, and in walked the big man himself, Jacob looking incongruent, waving a thick purse in his right hand, scanning the restaurant goers till he spotted them. "Here you go, Kamryn. I had a devil of a time getting this from that pesky Agent at the salon. She wasn't going to release it till she called Rico." "Thanks, Jacob. I'm going to the restroom, guys, so you can speak in private…." Terrance barked back, "what? Weren't you just in the bathroom…" "Uncle, I need to powder my nose, uhm, I've been crying." Kam, hurry up, we have nothing to say that you couldn't hear, darling… hurry up, let's order some food!"

They watched Kamryn disappear… Jacob stood like he felt like he was out of place, about to leave, then blurted out, "you know what, boss, I've had two disturbing calls to the limo, one from Wendi Feral and the other from Roma, Vadonna's daughter." Terrance rolled his head "yeah, I missed their calls, along with a half dozen others. I am with my niece, trying to enjoy dinner. What did they say?" "Ah, boss Wendi went off on a tirade about Liz and some medication she'd wanted to inject her with. She wants no more texting and to be left alone. She said I'm fricken fine. Stop this bullshit. The next call was from Roma, who went off on something like.... the baby lives. You must kill this baby... ughhhh, it's all insanity, boss." Terrance felt flushed.... and it wasn't the Expresso martini.

Kamryn sat on the commode, tapping away on her phone, texting after trying in vain to get Renae to answer her phone. She was dizzy and panicked, not knowing what had happened to Renae trying to get her baby out of NIA, hoping they were at her Victorian home. But weirdly, there wasn't one text from Renae on her phone. Terrance had made it clear what his feelings were about her having a child. Kam, in desperation.... went as far as to text Rocky, who hadn't gotten back to her. She had nowhere to turn other than back out of the bathroom. She had to get to her house at once, enough of this restaurant and Terrance's maunderings.

Kam saw Jacob's back as he left through the front door, then swiveled to see a scowl on her uncle's countenance, wondering now... what was up? Then her phone buzzed. A reply to her text... 'Kam, I just checked the security video Renae left a couple of hours ago, checked with the nurse's station, and Sonja isn't there. Renae has taken her to meet with you. I would assume....' 'K, Thanks, Rock.'

Renae escapes with Sonja out the gates of NIA.

Renae had to dot her i's and cross her t's. She knew precisely what NIA stood for. The memory of being strapped down on the gurney at the San Francisco Airport still lingered like a chronic cough. She had shivers bite her skin. She'd decided it was a combination of premenopausal hot flashes, but another realization shunned her. Nope, it was the vulnerability she felt... it was her reality in this make-believe world she'd existed in. A switch was flipped in her brain when Ronny, her husband, determined it was either her or him.... then he stabbed her with the hypodermic needle. Their relationship was in tatters. His career was what was important to him, and she wasn't going to be tagging along any longer.

Her best friend, Doctor Liz Houcho, her husband Ron, and NIA were guilty in her book of 'Gaslighting' her with psychological manipulations. Renae had at one time questioned the validity of her own thoughts and perceptions of what her reality was. She was no longer confused and had rebuilt her confidence brick by brick. The mortar had solidified, and her foundation was solid now... her self-esteem and mental stability were not in doubt. She'd not be a patsy anymore, and her dependency was finished. Instead of being perpetrated upon, she would be the perpetrator! First, she analyzed what had been done to her daughter and her before when she tried to leave NIA. Knowing Terrance and the NIA hierarchy were ruthless killers. They had put her daughter Candice under surveillance and threatened her life. Innocent Candice was in her final year at the University of Colorado in Boulder, CO. Over Christmas, Renae had finally convinced her daughter of the evil changes in her father. He'd become driven, uhm, addicted to the power of being a Public figure and dreamed of being the Governor of California. Ron was nothing but a Flea on NIA's ass and controlled like a weakened puppet by Terrance.

Renae had wrapped up Sonja, comfy-like, and had placed her on the floorboard of the passenger seat of her Jeep Comanche and was approaching the East gate exit out of NIA. She'd earlier met with her 'pro-life advocate' who was in charge of the gate this afternoon. All Renae had to say to her 'we got another baby, who would have been aborted if I didn't step in. I'm taking the precious baby girl to the adoption center...' Walls pulled through the triple gated enclosure and breathed in fresh freedom-laced oxygen for the first time in her 'Stepford Wives' like life. Candice awaited her in her Dodge minivan. She parked in the Safeway shopping center and unpacked after a long, lingering hug with Candice. Sonja was placed in the minivan's backseat in her flowered Graco infant Toddler car seat. Strangely in all the time she'd been around the baby girl, she'd never heard the child cry.

Renae tossed her life into a large black garbage bag, purse, phone, credit cards, license… anything that could lead to her. Candice did the same. They now had brand new identifications with legit licenses. The older minivan didn't have GPS nor an onboard computer system, no way of tracking her. It was purchased last week under Candice's phony name. Candice had worked with a Real Estate Agent in Santa Monica and had used a fake Power of Attorney agreement signed legitimately by Renae, who forged Ron's name on the legal document. They'd sold the Santa Monica beach house for bitcoins and had opened several overseas covert accounts; they'd live happily ever after like the Fairy Tales. Sara had given the beach house to her as part of the payment for helping her escape NIA. Renae and Candice had left Ron his part of the 7 million dollars divided by three. Inside, a suitcase in the back of the minivan held enough cash for the threesome to live life to the fullest. Then as a backup, they had the Crypto-currencies.

"Mother, this is way scary and exciting all at the same time. Dad is going to freak out when he discovers we're gone from his life!" "Yes, Candy, but what else could we have done? NIA had threatened your life. Your father is joined with Gangsters, immoral criminals, who would stop at nothing to get even with me… honey, uh Candice, don't forget that all I wanted to do was quit NIA." "I know, mother, we've been over this a hundred times. What bothers me is the baby. Why, since we are going to succeed in getting away, uuuh, why keep the baby mom?" "The child is our leverage, dammit, Candice… Sonja is Terrance's Grandniece or Great Niece. We will hold on to her until we are safe." "I kind of feel sorry for daddy…." "Don't. He's changed and is a clone now, pull over there. Let's change out the license plates, you know the shopping center had cameras, and we will be tracked there from my Lexis onboard computer system."

Liz finally comes through with Vadoma's cure for Wendi.

Terrance and Liz were texting... 'I'm at dinner with Kamryn in San Rafael. What's so darn important, Liz?' She texts back, 'Doctor Walters has finally got all the ingredients for the formula that your mystic gave you.' 'K, all we need now is to get Wendi back to NIA and inject her with two more doses at 24-hour intervals, and she'll be good as cured. Then that will end Wendi's side effects from your drugging of her.' 'Terrance, I only did what you wanted damnit 😣' 'Here comes Kam back from the bathroom. I will ttul.' 'ttul?' 'talk to you later....'

Rico and Wendi in Sausalito.

He flushes the toilet and wanders back to their bed, overlooking the San Francisco Bay. Checks the digital display. It was 3:49 am tried to slither into the warm bed without waking Wendi. Rico had fallen sound asleep after their loving session, and the conversation he'd had earlier with General Bill Hullinger was still reverberating in his mind. His skin crawled thinking of being in cahoots with Terrance, the man was a pompous contemptuous jerk, and they nearly never saw things the same. He felt her warm silky skin and cuddled up to her... switching gears 'what got into Wendi? She'd never been so wild in bed. She was on fire!' Remembering that one of the songs that Wendi had played on the Bluetooth stereo was "Sex on Fire' by the band 'Kings of Leon' during their loving session. Yep, it was fricken FIRE 🔥

Judea lay awake, looking away from Rico... her eyes staring out the Bay Window at the full moon, bickering with Wendi and Sunshine... *'he's going to figure out that I've changed, and you will be history...'* 'sshh now I've got to think.' Sunshine barked back, 'what girl, hum… Judea is that text from Liz bothering you, Darlin, huh?… You know they've been working on that concoction or remedy, uh injection.' Judea, in her short time in charge of Wendi, had learned one surefire way to shut up the peripheral chatter… she'd cross her eyes for about ten seconds… bam, done that. Judea concentrated and closed the adversarial compartments and lifted her butt into Rico's groin area. Time to sleep…

Valerie and Sara.

Sara rolled over again… "sister, what's up? Why can't you sleep? Everything worked out; Kam is at her house, right? They released her, Sara, so let's get some rest." "Val, I appreciate you letting me sleep with you in your apartment, but don't get me wrong…uhm, weirdly, I can't rest." "Valerie checks the time shit, girl. It's not 4 am what's bothering you?" "Kam's text seemed frantic. She asked me if Renae was still on site, wanted to know if I'd seen her… damn, it was like her third text." "So what? She's probably worried about her diabetes or something. Renae is her nurse, right?" "I guess so. Good night sister…."

Doctor Garza and Ann McClintock.

At that precise time, Ann McClintock, editor for the Documentary section of the NYTimes, was landing at the San Francisco Airport. Ann couldn't wait to visit with Doctor Garza, who had plenty to say about NIA…. his memory had returned. He was going to get even with the staff of NIA and Terrance and his sidekick Liz. Doctor Garza had been released on bond from jail. Ann had her camera crew filming. She wanted to bury the pricks that hacked into her Cloud, deleting all the evidence against NIA if it was the last thing she did… She wanted to put the Stake in NIA's Heart and would relish

the ultimate outcome of her upcoming documentary for
certain the corporation would be filing for Bankruptcy. Yes!

Colonel Ruiz.

After months, the FBI finally had the evidence in place, and
the arrest warrant was signed by one of C.I.N.'s benefactors,
Judge Delaney. Colonel Ruiz loudly cackled. The FBI's Swat
team would now raid NIA and had added search warrants for
Sara Amaya's cell. Her DNA proved positively associated with
the murders of Carl and Bianca Sparks and the attorney. It was
kind of a joke because Sara was locked up already, but her
original sentence was finishing up. This would throw a vice...
uuh monkey wrench into NIA's plans and keep them busy.
How he hated Terrance Hallinan and the NIA Organization!
Tomorrow morning he'd been assured there would be a
caravan of Law Enforcement Agents at the gates of NIA.

Wendi's parents.

*Ed and Barbara Feral were up in Vancouver, Washington,
their home, which wasn't comfortable any longer, Ed on one side
and Barb on the other pulling the blinds back and peeking out.
Barb said, "yep, they're still out there. You'd think they'd get bored
or realize we were not leading them to our bastard son. Mark
hasn't contacted us in years..." "I know, honey, but this is how the
FBI works. They print money, don't care how many manhours are
used, and you know how dangerous our son can be. Ugh, he's a
psychopath, darling."*

Jaybird and Sandi.

It had been a good night. Jaybird and Sandi abstained from
intimacy, but it was inevitable. They'd decided on a
rendezvous at one of Terrance's luxurious wineries for lunch.

They were comfortable, relaxing, and enjoying bites of their dessert when they both received the text. 'Get back to NIA 711' code for an emergency. Jay tossed a $50.00 bill on the table and asked the waiter, "Can you have the Valet pull our cars up? We have to leave and put this on Terrance's account thanks.' 😐

<u>Wendi... 'Jodee' awoke with Rico.</u>

Rico was driving her Audi 8, while Wendi sat back in the passenger seat, checking her phone. She'd used her tech skills and could link with Liz's cellphone and frowned while rereading the caustic text again between Terrance and Liz. 😐.

I'm telling you now, every text subject has lost it, I mean, okay, each case is different, but the dosage was the same that you gave Wendi. Please take a case-by-case analysis....' 'Terrance, I'm listening and am right here. Your preaching to the choir.' 'Okay fk, woman, what would you have me do....' 'uh, you need to get Wendi back in here. We have the remedy....We need her under observation hell; we've had three suicide attempts. Two succeeded in killing themselves, and they have already been cremated on-site! There's something toxic in that chemical formula I injected into her. Hell, don't forget the Horse tablet I jammed down her throat....' 'all right enough, Liz, I got this handled, she's with Rico, and she is dropping him off at the Fed building in Napa. I'll have her at NIA in less than two hours...' 😐

<u>Sofie and Nadia.</u>

Meanwhile, Nadia and Sofie were working on their presentation at the inaugural opening of the next class to attend NIA-U. They'd accepted their punishment and even looked forward to narrating their lessons to the recruits. Sure, they conceded it was going to be a nervous and scary time for them. Still, heck, they justified it by saying to each other that life was about sex. Without it, we wouldn't be here. In fact, civilization would have died with Adam and Eve, and Sex was essential for all living things. So what...? they were having unorthodox sexual intimacy. Hey, so be it. Get with life... or get lost! 'We're humans, and Sofie was convinced after reviewing the new class of students admitted to NIA-U that they wouldn't be prudes. The Holier than Thou fake clowns can shove it.'

It did help Sofie with her being in charge of the admittance department. She said to Nadia, "the majority of our new recruits are user-friendly, Nadia. All new recruits check marked positives about the LBGTQ community in the admittance questionnaires, which means they will not be casting stones at us!" "Okay ... right, Sofie... but your speaking first on stage!"

Brock Dane and Lacie Link.

Brock peered into Lacie's room... she was snuggled up to one of her body pillows.... he smiled. Damn, she had so many comfy stuffed animals that she'd used as pillows that there was barely room for her on the twin bed. Lacie's last conversation reverberated in his mind's eye. Yep, Lacie was coming out of her amnesia slowly but surely... "Brock, I understand that you'd seek out someone to love you; you're young and handsome as all get out. I get that you desire to love.... we were going to be married in under three months, and then our world just collapsed. Brock, I'm caught back in time. I'm in love with you, just as I was when I jumped from the third-floor balcony to get away from Sara! It's like I'm in a time warp.... I look at you and still see us. I love you!" Lacie sighed with a tweaked-out frown.

"I guess where I'm going with this is.... Brock, how could you want to marry, ughhhh, uhm, and fall in love with a woman that looks identical to the freak killer vixen Sara? I don't get it and never will, man. How could you day in and day out… look at the image of the person that put me into the hospital and nearly paralyzed me for life?" Brock seldom had his tuge stuck and glued… didn't try to embrace her, nor did he open his mouth to give her a rebuttal or concession. He didn't have an answer. Therefore, Brock left the outpatient hospital and went for a long walk alone.

Landing at the San Francisco Airport.

An entourage of Inspectors from Europe is hell-bent on arresting Valerie Amaya, DNA has been authenticated in the harrowing deaths of the couple that had adopted her, Valerie's DNA was found on one of the bloody daggers and on one of the restraints. MI5, Scotland Yard, BKA from Germany, AISI from Italy, and DGSI out of France… In total, there were eleven countries represented… Attorney Terrance Hallinan's Law Office had been contacted… Terrance hadn't replied as of yet. They wanted to have Valerie extradited back to England!

Kamryn is dropped off at her Tiburon Victorian Villa.

For a third time, Kamryn visited the woman's lavatory texting Renae and Rocky, her two only allies that knew the plan… the escape of her child Sonja from NIA. Kamryn wished she could call Sonja's father and future husband, Brock Dame… but his phone had been disconnected months ago. Kam even tried to call Renae, and her phone had just gone to voicemail like the last few times. Terrance had paid the bill and waited for her to rejoin him at the table. Jacob had pulled the limousine up to the front of the San Rafael Joe's restaurant. Valerie hadn't any way to avoid being driven to her home without causing suspicion. She'd texted Renae I'm on my way to my house… hide your car in one of my garages. The fob is hanging by my front door Renae. I can't wait to hold my baby… thank you for taking Sonja out of the prison… Kam…

They parked the minivan in long-term parking, took a rolling suitcase, and tucked Sonja inside a baby stroller at the San Ysidro port of entry. Walking nonchalantly along the border crossing following the signs 'Otay Mesa Pedestrian Crossing.' "Mother, what if U.S. Customs stops us?" "Relax, they won't, and besides, we're legal right… look in front of you. No one is being stopped… <u>Welcome To Tijuana, Mexico</u>… Yep!…

<u>Please check out the sneak peek of… 'C.I.N. Versus NIA.'</u>

'C.I.N. Versus NIA.'

Rocky stands at the podium in a subterranean conference room at NIA.

Rocky pounds the gavel down and then grimaces slightly. His eyes widen, itching his chin like he's pondering how to approach the next topic on the agenda, and then he decides just to spit it out, "some of you know Brock Dame, FBI Agent extraordinaire. Who has been in our outpatient Neurology Hospital recovering from Sara's attack? Let's just keep it there; he's made tremendous strides with our Stem-Cell Therapies and was paralyzed, unable to move nor speak... now in amazing shape? I'm told he's even approaching the plus side of his physical prowess before the Houseboat incident. I want to give everyone a heads-up about an upcoming article that an investigative reporter is working on at the San Jose Mercury News. It's an ongoing documentary. This should bring NIA's Neurological Hospital notoriety and applause from Scientists across our planet. Brock has had interviews with several renowned publications wanting his story." He pauses to let all that he said... sink in.

"Brock has recently enrolled in the next semester starting Feb 1st, only three days from now. He wants to be a participant and train here at NIA-U." Each person in the audience showed negative body contortions and facial features wavered, showing... strain. The expressions are not positively aligned, matching the body language. "We, being a private accredited 2-year University, can deny him entry. The point here is that we must decide which would be helpful for us. Should we allow admittance of an infiltrator spy, 'Brock Dame,' into our clutches instead of having Rico and the Feds continue to try and sneak them into our programs?" Jax stands from the front row and declares, "this is now up for discussion. We will step back into an informal format. Please remain seated. While we can chew over this issue, thank you."

Rocky Blake takes his turn advocating for Brock… "I will not waste your time describing my distinguished career choices" he waits and pauses. With a smirk on his face saw slightly faint smiles around him, then continued, "I've known Brock Dame for 17 years. We met at boot camp, became close buddies, and then went off to combat in the theater of war. We saved each other's Asses so many times I've lost count. He and I were special forces, Ops. I followed him with tenures in NSA, and the CIA finished up partnering with Brock in the FBI, actually signing on the same day. One thing I can maintain, and it surely proves itself out Brock is a survivor and Warrior. If we could land him here at NIA-U and convince him of the importance of our movement and belief system, he could only enhance our position and our teams. He is an unstoppable force, integrity-based like all of us," smiling at faces he's known for years.

"Sure, lately Brock and I haven't seen eye to eye, for he doesn't understand my loyalty to NIA, and honestly, I haven't tried to engage him with friendly banter or with a serious effort to recruit him. I have left him alone in his therapies, but in my opinion, he would make an awesome officer and leader for us. Those are some of the pros. There are cons, such as does Brock have ulterior motives for wanting to join NIA-U? Remember, Rico and Brock are very close. Actually, Rico was going to be his best man at the wedding of Kamryn and Brock, their bros. To sum it up, I'd assume that Brock would be an informant for the FBI and Rico. A caveat to be aware of … besides Rico, I'm his closest comrade, and I'd keep a watch over him. Umh, well, with all of your help, on the contrarian side, what would our excuse be not to allow him to join NIA-U?"

Wendi spoke up, "I've lived one door down from Brock and Lucie at the outpatient hospital for months, and every time I'd visited Brock, I saw how much they had advanced in their treatment schedules. Needless to say, he's made miraculous improvements. I'd speak to him daily, and I believe he has a mental impediment at this time. A mental block has compartmentalized what Sara had done to him on Lake Shasta, and he has no memory whatsoever. This is typical with head injuries. His brain's forcefield protection center has created a barrier to negative memories. Most often, this occurs and is diagnosed from military combat or enemy torture, a common syndrome of PTSD. Brock's mind has blocked out that segment in time. Aah, the question is will these memories stay locked inside his mind Vault, or will he remember what Sara did to him... we knew that Terrance has allowed his three niece's Valerie, Sara, and Kamryn, to start class on Feb. 1st, the same day Brock wants to join us!"

She looks around the room and see's Terrance, his chin bobbing affirmatively. "I will leave you with this. I recall back in the day that this was the same quandary we faced when Rocky wanted to join us. We all know how that worked out! We're in a Democratic system. But if it were up to me, I'd allow Brock entry papers and put him in Rocky's group of trainers he would report to him. Yes, Brock, no doubt, would be a tremendous asset... ugh, or he could become the worse thing to evolve within NIA-U since its inception. I will vote affirmative if he steps out of line, we expel him permanently, he will not have top secret clearance, not visit all our underground chambers be privy to what we're truly doing here. He would be a 2-year physical education major like 71% of our participants and be treated accordingly!" Terrance stands. "I don't know about any of you, but I need to relieve myself and grab another drink so let's take a 7-minute break to think about this latest proposal."

Jax waits... until after Terrance regains his seat and is about to rise when Wendi 'Judea' again stands. "I realize the intrinsic value I brought to NIA's squads, yet I'm not the physical specimen that some of our female cadets are. My skill set is Paranormal. As we all know, we are made of parts ok pieces, experts in their fields of land, sea, and air. Some of us are artful killers, characters of beneficial aspects take Sara who brings to our diverse group unmatched aptitude skills of Ventriloquism, makeup disguise Queen, an artist inside her skull with three uniquely skilled and intelligent personalities."

"Or Terrance's other Niece Valerie, who is the current Gold Medal winner in Archery and 3-time Olympian Champion, a silent killer who is highly proficient with Blow dart guns, throwing knives, spear guns, crossbows, and can take an adversary out silently with accuracy. Val is a remarkable talent and is a positive addition to our team. We are a collection of the world's best each additional asset builds our pyramid and human armory. We excel and are the sum of our parts. I believe adding Brock Dame is a definite positive until it proves otherwise." Terrance raises his hand "hey, we've already covered that subject. Still, thanks for..." she scoffed "please, Terrance, while I'm up here, let me Segue into this tremulous parallel subject matter. My boyfriend, man lover Yep Rico has asked a hundred times if he's asked once. He posed the question only this afternoon, 'Wendi, if NIA-U has nothing to hide, then allow me to tour the entire facility. I'm curious to see where you spend most of your rehabilitation time?'"

Rumbles, hems, and haws encompassed the large conference hall "um, yes, I can see some of you snarl with scowls and sneers, but I'm an advocate for just that. A benign walkthrough will not hurt us, and furthermore, our allowing Brock Dame to enroll here can only alleviate Rico's suspicious mind! Thank you." A few moments later, Jax finally calls for the vote to allow Brock entry into their program. _A 3 to 1 outcome to the positive side... abstaining from voting was Jaybird, Sandi, and Shon._

Newly conceived Judea allowed her 'minds to drift.' 'Sunshine and Wendi' had been silent, and still, she wondered how they would react on 3/17/18 when she was in a combat situation. Will she need the rough abrasive Sunshine's skillfulness and never say die attitude once again? Judea stares around her at the NIA Team leaders who were called in for this impromptu conference. She amuses herself thinking about how strange and diverse these people are, how her group couples up. She is in a relationship with arch-enemy Rico of course, doing double duty and enjoying keeping him distracted and busy. Looking around at the obvious budding relationships between Jaybird and her bestest friend Sandi wheeled her head back around, catching her platonic Buddie Jax, who was hot on Valerie. The odd couple, she couldn't help it to feel slightly jealous, not understanding why… Such a strange conundrum. She should be happy for him. Still, the aching came from within auhhh. Maybe it was Sunshine's emotional ties to Jax. Or something to do with my newly energized entity Judea? I felt an incomplete vibe of wariness.

The group nixes the visit by Rico, with only Wendi 'Judea' voting in the positive… Terrance stood and said, "If we allow Brock to enroll in NIA-U, then he can be Rico's eyes. That suffices in my book!" Then oddly, he displayed a wide solemn grimace, "okay, Jax, that brings up the next issue in order!"

Judea/Wendi wondered if or when General Bill Hullinger would consult with NIA alum, principally Terrance, and inform NIA's CEO that he'd had a conversation with Rico a few days ago. So far, Terrance wasn't acting as if anything had changed with his feelings toward Rico… The General told Rico to act as if it was business per usual, don't change up the hunt against NIA. Because C.I.N. was watching primarily… Colonel Ruiz.

<u>Mark Feral and C.I.N.</u>

At the very time that NIA was showing the Documentary of what C.I.N. had planned, Mark Feral was again perusing his conglomerate's profile 'Edgar Filings' and S.E.C. filings. The company he worked for... he kept tabs on after-all he'd had almost all his net worth invested in C.I.N. He Pushed his rolling chair back from his Walnut desk to think it's been less than two years since he left Jaybirds Montana faction well that's not entirely true he'd been working as a double spy for C.I.N. while still employed by Jaybird who was supplemented by NIA... He was slick and proud...Yup! He was encouraged by his quick ascension and advancement up the ladders of C.I.N. he was awarded for his merit, and he was confident that it wasn't his ego talking.

Mark, before joining C.I.N., was in charge of one of the dozens of satellite civilian militia outposts in America, a ground movement in Boise, Idaho. It was his baby, with over 1,300 soldiers at his beckoning call at one point. This was satisfying. He felt obligated ah, even indentured, yet glowed within with pride. Next, he wasn't so sure complacency reared its grizzly head! Mark contemplated back to the life-changing event. Was it fate or by chance, uh, accident, um, maybe plain ass luck, or was he Set-up? Sipping some Orange juice remembers how it all started; he was with Randy, Joe, Sammy, and Tank, and they were having cocktails at Caesars in Vegas. At the next table were some Arabs, older generation Americanized individuals. Mark was a well-known womanizer. Her name warmed his loins still when he thought of her, Cleopatra. He laughed now; she was so drop-dead gorgeous had to be a direct descendant. She was lusciously provocative, a cream-brown color with magnificent, enchanting eyes. He's fantasized about her since that afternoon... Yum!

Mark constantly analyzed his intentions questioning himself many times in the past before stepping into the unknown. Uh, again, was it luck or plumb fate or deviously orchestrated? Hindsight is 20/20. Mark had to concede that the woman, unh, played him. It's straight-up bullshit that women were considered the weaker sex. What a fricken folly that axiom was made up by a cunning girl. What makes a man weak is Testosterone… lust… kind of like an antonym… testosterone/ weakened his resolve, drops inhibitions, isolates, demolishes common sense um, blind to the chase & conquer… but who's the Conqueror? Did the hunter hunt the prey who acquiesces, or did reciprocal action occur? Did the prey hunt and circumcise the hunter?

Aah, it was nearly 5 am these lingering memories all collude 'figuratively thinking' collision pile up. Mark switched gears and pushed in the clutch, aware that he was a staple on the FBI's twenty most wanted list… killer and all that suitable garb, um, stuff. Glancing over at the Black sleeping beauty, her silky skin Ms. Cleopatra Nile exposed a salaciously sexy nipple, um yum, grinning time to do some rooting, bury some morning wood, then off to C.I.N. headquarters. He licks his lips before priming the pump knowing she trapped his ass… but what an Ass she has.

'The Trojan Horse of Troy was galloping ghost-like in the high desert of Nevada.'

On his drive to his military base, he smirted 'if the world only knew what the three letters umh acronym Really stood for, it wasn't what the world's stock markets thought. The symbol was one of the highest volume trading stocks on the New York Exchange C.I.N. equals '<u>Clairvoyant Interspace Nuances</u>' he chuckled into a warped cackle leaving a grimy squinted scowl upon his countenance ah clever name um moniker marketing genius provoking speculative thoughts. Touché!

Mark was now in the inner circle speaking of ovals. He doubled the guards that did a constant circuitous route around his facility for April fool's day, the first of April… loomed near. C.I.N. had lethal ulterior motives with the ways and means to bring them to fruition. Ugh, deadly serious, not the typical slow-moving smug communist Turtle. No, Cheetah like…

with a ton of momentum and more cash than was needed… an oxymoron in business. Yes, China, Iran, and North Korea, fitting and matching 'C' is for China, 'I' un Iran, and 'N' for North Korea, a triumphant 3-some. The Elko properties were 3 miles square of high desert with over a mile square under the Earth… ground. SpaceX's main and ample competitor, the guise, was fool's gold. C.I.N. was also competing against Virgin Galactic and Blue Origin and, at this time, was neck and neck with launches in the near future.

<u>Hours before the gathering at NIA's Amphitheater, where the Documentary was going to be shown/played on the humongous screens, the subject matter was 'C.I.N.'</u>

<u>'NIA… another mandatory conference.'</u>

One floor below the first floor of Hangar 1 A was the War room that spread the entire length and width of the Ginormous interior space of the three-storied building inside the 'Subpit' a name given to the basement was the leaders of NIA-U. Conference room # 1 was enormous, with all the luxuries of a fine hotel, with the exception of a grand view. This was an unscheduled gathering. They, per usual, met once a month. Wendi was the last to bring a mug of coffee to her seat.

The tables and seating were peculiar to most invited visitors and employees that were called to attend or testify. The Warriors of NIA were never comfortable when they didn't have their backs against the wall protected by a wall; better to be prudent, not paranoid, but always cautious not, leaving chances for the enemy to sneak up on them from behind. No, just not the trusting types, having seen too many others getting literally stabbed in the back in restaurants, café's, bars, and lounges, like the old mob movies, the gangster would face the doors or entranceways. Therefore you could find them up against a wall, their backs safe... eyes like a periscope scanning possible assailants and predators. They were always cogent and vigilant of their surroundings. At least in the War room, they could as a group relax knowing they were amongst friends, um, comrades for life, and their backs were Covered!

Thus the layout before them was separate round small wooden Mahogany tables side by side, backed up against the concrete block wall the tables wrapped around the room. In the middle was a moveable podium three steps up for the speaker or speakers to pose questions or make statements or, on rare occasions, for interrogations. Italian marble was laid on the floor, all colored a silver grey, with monitors adorning the open spaces upon the walls. At the entrance of the door on the left side, an alcove filled to the brim with computer banks and electronic gadgets.... etc.

There was no smoking, but that didn't prevent some from chewing cigars and gum. Terrance's busy stressed-out day continued, and he took a guzzle of his favorite drink, Cranberry juice, and said, "good afternoon. Thank you for attending this special session, as you are well aware that this entire get-together will be recorded and available on our closed-circuit network if you ever want to revisit any subject matter! I believe our General Jax will ceremoniously start us off. Please refrain, as... per normal, not interrupting our speakers until they have either paused or concluded their monologue, Thank you," he bowed, regaining his highbacked chair.

Jax walks over to the podium "make a note of the date. It's 1/27/2014, the time is 2:35 pm. Our regular bi-monthly meetings will be on 2/1/2014 and 2/15/14. As Terrance said, this is a special mandated meeting. We stand united for our Credo 'With our goals aligned, were Unstoppable' each member puts knuckles to the tabletops. Our format will be traditional. I will read off each matter at hand. I will outline the needs to be addressed in order of relevancy and importance.

We will all be afforded time to be heard, respecting our personal opinions and input. After full discussions, we will take a visual vote of fists. Each of us counts as one vote. The winning number supports the decision rendered, and a verdict or sentence will then be imposed. Rebuttals are time-sensitive, depending on the complexity of the situation. In some cases, a yes or no will suffice." Terrance raised his hand with a raised voice and emphasis and declared, *remember, I want all of us at the Amphitheater tonight. It will be an enlightening event for everyone and leads directly as to why our operation in the desert on March 17th is essential for mankind's existence."*

Jax taps the tablet on the podium, and three young faces appear on screens attached to the walls before them. "I realize each of you has already been sent these photos, and our intelligence report's proof is irrefutable. The three students are posers, ugh, informants working for the FBI and principally Rico Captor." Some of the members glance in the direction of Wendi, who nods acceptance nothing is a secret amongst them, like a blood vow each would die for the next, no reservations… united.

"I could spend five hours reviewing each of their transcripts, communications, clandestine rendezvous with their operatives, listen to the recordings, and list each of their crimes against us at NIA. Yes, they are pawns. Surely hindsight is 20/19. Perhaps our vetting process has to be revisited… we need to investigate the applicants more thoroughly. Maybe we need to make changes in how we analyze new applicants and participants. With that being said, I must commend our Admittance office and research teams, for only three spies from 1,713 enrolled is better than the U.S. Armed forces can pull off! Team leaders, you have had 75 hours to examine the files, have you not? Does anyone need more time?"

No one moved a hand for most of them… there'd already been too much talk… the overwhelming attitude was let's get on with it! Jax droned on, "In the past, we have issued the Death Penalty. Why should that not be a constant... unh? You might ask yourselves, are there any mitigating circumstances? I remind you this isn't so... If they were saving. It's a certainty the FBI employs them, done deal." A Frowl upon his face "there's no Diplomatic immunity here," most caught the humor with snorts and snarling cackles. He hesitates and sees Sandi's hands raised. She was holding an iPad. "Excuse me, Jax, as rhetorical as this will become. I failed to take roll call... silly but our protocol." He stares back at her and nods, "of course Terrance is here, Jax, Jaybird, Rocky, Shea, Wendi, Liz, Asia, and counting me, all nine of us are present, please continue." Jax rolled eyes others amused Terrance calmly stands "roll call might seem ridiculous with only nine of us folks here. But it will not be so ridiculous when there are 17 or 27 of us. We are growing fast. Roll call is procedural and ritualistic. Roll call gives credence to each one of us and will be part of every meeting we will attend. I'd like to think it adds more substantiation for each of us to hear our names aloud here in this room... we stand together. It adds emphasis within our Spirits, helping us to further bond 'We Are 1,' so yes, our names need to be addressed!" Swiftly fists pound the table. The vibes and ambiance are electrified blood pumping. Terrance sits back down, nodding to Jax, who says, "In that vein, we already have five more members to consider at our next meeting," Jax emphasizes, looking down at his Tablet. "Gladius, Javier, Moses, Angel, and Walter, head of security, will be up for votes then... yes, Sir Terrance, we're with you," he restarts. Jax waved his hand, holding the gavel and declares, "we can make this one quick... I recommend the Death Penalty for the three spies. If you're ready, we can take the vote at once!" He paused... "unless any of you feel compelled to voice opposition or another remedy, this is your time to speak up or forever hold your tongue!"

He started from left to right, and each negatively shook their heads, ready to call for the vote, until one member stood up. Everyone spun around, watching her walk forth. At the same time, Jax returned to his seat. Wendi 'Judea' took the three steps deliberately and rolled her shoulders in front of the podium. "Afternoon all, I don't stand opposed only as another voice of reason, um, mine that is... No Devil's advocate here within. In the past, we all know I voted for Death each and every time, as did all of you. And that includes the deaths of the soulless traitors that we've used in our classrooms, for teaching purposes... ugh, torture chamber victims." She makes a point of scanning her team members and best friends "perhaps I can share with you a unique perspective it's obviously called for in my opinion to foresee all variables in each terminal mandate now I'm sure your aware that Sunshine has been partitioned. So I'm Wendi Feral standing before you. Also, I'm well aware of the time constraints of speakers, so..." Terrance nods, raising his forefinger "no, I'm not overruling the clock. However, I want to remind all of you that we're still in deep water for the last assassinations of Federal Agents; please go ahead, Wendi."

"Okay, um, I'm sorry that I hadn't written down this presentation going to have to adlib it. Not making excuses, but it's been a whirlwind of events for me lately, speaking to the choir! I was hospitalized, umh, Sunshine and I, that is. I've also been spending my recovery time with one of our arch nemesis Agent Rico Captor. Many of you know him well, with the possible exception of Shen." Who raised his fist. "I met the man in question when your parents visited. He seems to be a driven individual." "Yes, most indubitably, Shen, ahh, I have a unique insight on how the man thinks even can intuitively read his mind's moves or objectives. We are closely bonded. No, I'm not a spy lol for us or NIA, but with that being extrapolated, if Rico meant us harm or was hellbent on destroying us, well, despite my love for him, my... my loyalty is with us!" Fists pound down sharply on the tabletops three times.

"Let me jump right in the deep end on the topic of the last two FBI moles, ahh, spies that infiltrated us. We all unanimously voted for the death penalty. We eliminated the male in Costa Rico Ziplining thanks to our compadre Shon," more fists. "The female on a dive in Hawaii, thanks to my B.F. Saudi for that deed," fists knuckle down. "The deceased infiltrators worked for Rico and reported to him. I'm sure most of you are unaware that Rico recently brought in the renowned 'Doctor Roble' for a second opinion about how the two had died. For those of you who are unaware of the Doctor's pedigree, she's the quintessential foremost Forensics expert and a renowned Medical Examiner. Both of the two moles' deaths were ruled accidental… but after her interference. The Death Certificates have been newly revised and issued with a Red Stamp, Homicides. The reports now are on the desk of three of Rico's top Agents and have the backing of Wash. D.C., the CIA is evaluating this change while we speak. Remember, friends, their only link before being murdered is they were attending NIA that was not nine months ago!" Terrance cleared his throat for emphasis, not muttering a word.

Judea, 'Wendi' continued, "C.O.S. um 'change of subject' NIA is still trying to mitigate the Sara escape and her diabolical swap out with her twin Kamryn. Her out-of-control killing spree included one of our employees Carl Sparks and his wife. In total, Sara snuffed out three humans in less than three weeks. Grand Jury DNA Warrants signed by a Federal Judge. They extracted DNA from Kamryn last week to be tested. We have no doubts that the DNA will prove it was Sara that committed those killings, uh… Who, by the way, was supposed to be under guard… locked up in NIA. I need not expound further but suffice it to say the last three months have been ugly… NIA's stock price is touching 52-week lows daily. With the latest Sofie and Nadia porn show, do we need any more negativity? Now the secondary offering is on the shelf...." Wendi eyeballs Terrance with that last tidbit.

Wendi gulps her Red Bull and adds, "the other evening Rico had left his main frame up and running again. This is only informational, do any of you..." glaring straight at Terrance. "Remember NIA's lead Internist Doctor Garza umh front pages social media sensationalized... we set him up with being a dealer of Heroin, Oxycodone then injected the poor fool with a special concoction to render him a resident in zombie land! This was only five months ago. I snooped on Rico's computer and read that Garza is beginning to be more Lucid and starting to articulate again. Let's not forget that before Doctor Garza's arrest, he'd been a foe with allegations leveled at NIA. He'd colluded with Ann McClintock, the NYTimes Documentary Editor, and Chief, who has made serious accusations against NIA. Luckily, we were able to delete her evidence from her Cloud account. She had all the information that Dr. Garza had relayed to her. If that's not enough... in the same vein, uhm, the same period, a Civil case has gone Viral filed against NIA alleged by a wife and three children. The litigation is starting next week... one of our Correctional officers, Bruce Glades, who was hooked to machines here at NIA... for months. Unfortunately, Bruce was injured on the job and recently expired. He was trying to restrain Kamryn... believing it was her evil sister Sara. He was accidentally stabbed with a contaminated syringe wielded by another employee Head Nurse Williams. Who buried the needle into a now... dead father and husband." Wendi swigged down the rest of her Red Bull.

"I've given you five open investigations, all not a year old. I believe if we vote to add three more accidental deaths or missing individuals, umh, or poison them or ensure their braindead, ahhhh throw in... maybe a spectacular plane crash, or what have you? Please, we're not made of Teflon... Think, truly, we all should self-commit ourselves to this insane asylum if we decide to muddy the water further. Just my opinion." Wendi abruptly walked back to her chair under the stares of the others, who were assessing her words and concerns, deciding if there were enough credence ahh valid reasons not to vote for the death penalty. Rocky, who doesn't speak much at these functions, raised a fist, rose to his feet, and paced over to the podium carrying his laptop. He looks back at Wendi and then down at his screen. "I have a few other points for us to ponder before we vote. I want us to rationalize this certainty that we have a Mission Impossible, which is a life-or-death struggle for most of Earth's inhabitants, well, at least starting with the first attack on North America. It is now a certainty that our informant's information has been vetted and examined. Our technical analysis with concurring pictures and videos of the underground installation is proof enough. No question, all this information demonstrates how caustic this situation has become, no doubt a mandatory emergency! Are all of you in agreement?" Everyone agreed by tapping the tabletops with their fists. There were no naysayers; Rocky had their undivided attention.

"Mankind will never be the same if we do not stop C.I.N., one of Jaybird's rivals who was employed at one of his Montana militias and the brother of Wendi. Uh, Mark Feral has now become as ridiculous as this will sound. 'Major Mark Feral' is in charge of the Elko Installation base and the underground Launch site. He is now Colonel Ruiz's right-hand man. I'm sure you are well aware that we have only 49 days and nights before we attack Elko. We need Rico and the FBI up our asses like 45-caliber pistols in our mouths. I'm done here. Think about it!" He walks back to his seat and takes a long draw on a water bottle. No one spoke till someone did. Terrance applauded. "I couldn't have disseminated it better. I could use you and Wendi as my assistants in the courtroom." He walked over to the scanner blows up several 8 X 11s.

"Every point Rock just elucidated upon is on these pages I was waiting to deliver essentially Rocky's soliloquy with the addition that Rico has had a hair up his Ass in regards to NIA for years. No need to go into these narratives, Rico and I have been butting heads ever since I met the man. Ahh, well, that's not entirely factual. We had a falling out when I defended my niece Sara on the Notorious Vipress case that was our undoing 'Bang' arch enemies, at least on his behalf. I hold no such ill feelings. As most of you are aware, I believe in the edict 'Live and let Die' let bygones be bygones. Please open the attachment on your Tablets named 'Elko' and spend a few minutes perusing it all. Anyways, Jax, you have the Floor!"

Jax said, "Okay, please take a look at that file when we adjourn for a break," checking the clock.

After a short break, he periscoped around, seeing all heads were at attention, and Jax went right back to work despite the change of directions that Wendi, Rocky, and Terrance traveled. He had to finish the voting process "all in favor of extermination raise their left fist above your head," waited, but no one did. He acknowledges this and adds, "all right, next, we will move to the penalty phase. We have propositions and sanctions that are in place for their offenses. Again let me reiterate that we have evidence that they have hacked into two of our computer networks, and now the Federal Government has the locations of 17 of our militia encampments and ranches. We caught them and inputed dummy fictional hierarchies of our leadership ladder. They were also able to locate other properties along with our Armory's/arsenals ammunition holdings of the 17 bunkers we saved 13 from the ATF raids." He paused. "If not Death, then what?"

Jax is about to slam his Gavel down in frustration when Shou puts his fist up "hey, might I have a few moments to tell you'll what I think?" Jax retracts, grinning "heck, what's gotten into this room? First, we have Wendi, then Rocky, and now you, Shou. I can't remember when any of you addressed this forum." Shon saunters up to the podium, "first, before we move on to the vote on other sanctions, I want to say I'm also worried and am concerned it is my opinion that our March 17th undertaking cannot be jeopardized. The last thing any of us need is a Swat team trying to feebly enter our domain attacking us here at NIA. Besides my belief that it would be a major mistake, something akin to suicide for them. I'd predict it would make 'Ruby Ridge' and 'Waco' look like dealing with Nursery school children. They'd Rue that decision. No, I propose we send the three undercover Agents packing like any other Ivy School or any reputable University, including military branches. If you don't cut the Mustard, you're discharged, umh, the wrong word, removed and kicked off the campus, exiled, or whatever. The other day I read that Google had an employee guilty of espionage, spying, and stealing high-tech secrets. Umh, caught Red Handed, their internal security force, escorted her off-site after she was fired! With zero severance pay, they packed her out, and she was finished. This happens in large companies such as Apple, Microsoft, and Facebook all the time. There inundated with spies." He takes a sip of water.

"So rather than bring more scrutiny on us, really, what pertinent information have they gleaned and passed on? Huh, we send them home, Blackball them ruin their credit, and names we hit them under the belt. They will never be able to buy a bag of Potato chips on credit. We could bring the three of them into the office and tell them we're sorry we're terminating their remaining classes. And that they don't meet our integrity and moral standards. We don't have to be specific. It's in our bylaws... this is a private University. It's a simple fix without repercussions." Shon pivoted back toward his seat.

Jax takes his position once again "does anyone else have anything to add?" Sandi rises and makes her way up "here's another viewpoint we could feed them fake information as we have been doing for some time, lead them purposely astray, use them as an advantage. The questions we must ask ourselves if it's worth the time and effort of playing the game in essence, continue doing what we have been since we discovered their infiltration…" she wobbles her head towards her B.F. "We do have the benefit of Wendi, who is tight with Rico. We've heard how he vents to her and questions her heck. He wants to have a tour of NIA-U. Hey, why not? I think if something were about to go down on NIA, Wendi would either get a heads up or catch the vibes."

"I also want to say I concur with Wendi's um assertion that we cannot "Take them out" drug them to oblivion or have the FBI issue missing person's reports because neither one of the three communicate with each other. They may not even know they're connected, but as far as what we've learned, the three work alone. So a planned accident with the three would be inappropriate and quite obvious to the FBI. We must be judicious and self-assured that the decisions we make today will brighten our futures. That's all I have to say. Thank you."

Jax starts to stand tentatively, slowly peering around for the next speaker doesn't bother to grab his gavel. Instead elaborates further, "taking the last points made by Shon and Sandi and fine-tuning them, we could always kick two of the three out, for if we boot all three, it will definitely bring suspicion on us, keep the least threatening here on site so let's bring in our top cadets and form a think tank then move forward… what do you think?" He walks back to the podium "all in favor of this plan of action that we excommunicate two of them or some variable of the same ending instead of the death penalty! Raise your left fist again." Simple math nine to zero… vote. "Have the record show the vote was unanimous. Now, who volunteers to take this action forward?" Shon, Rocky, and Sandi pump their right fists up. He nods his head "okay, done deal, we are adjourned for now. We'll meet back up at our regularly scheduled gathering on the 1st of February.

Take Care... power to NIA Forever." Pounding of the tables as the group starts to rise. Terrance takes a moment to add, "I'll see you all in the Amphitheater for the documentary film about C.I.N. later tonight! 'Take care... Long live NIA!"

***

C.I.N. Dilemma!

***

On Stage at NIA's Amphitheater, a Documentary to be shown to invitees.

Jax stands on the stage with Terrance in NIA's Amphitheater, along with a Viacom production manager in charge of Hollywood's Paramount division. She steps up to the audience, who are from all over the planet, many from the former Eastern Bloc countries. Most in the crowd were affiliates, employees, investors, or contributors to the NIA conglomerate. "I have the documentary loaded in our system Wilma. I want to thank you for being our Narrator for the evening. I agree with Jax that this biopic film you produced would be a headliner at the Sundance film festival...." "Thanks, Terrance. Without your help and being a steadfast proactive individual, this film would never have happened. Shall we do it...?" "yes, Wilma, let's do it."

Wilma was a wily vixen... smiling and working up the audience, expounding on further developments in the pipeline, such as the expansion into Europe of NIA's Neurological Hospitals. Then she stops in front of a bank of microphones. "For just the next 49 minutes, please remain in your seats. I need your complete attention. Please clear your minds of monetary gains and of to-do lists. Let's leave at the weigh-side relationship preoccupations, and please zero out your mind for what you are about to see. You're going to see a documentary this evening and will hopefully be enlightened and privy to what could end our existence on earth as we know it to be. Now since I leveled this shocking warning statement without giving any prior notice, you have 15 minutes to use the restroom, get some drinks, or whatever it is you need to do, all electronic devices are to be turned off. The show starts in 14 minutes, and change, don't be late."

Wilma struts backstage to speak to some of her production crew, spending time on lighting and special effects, see's Terrance wave her down, so she excuses herself and joins the small group that was gathered around a petite Asian woman. She had to be under 5 feet tall with her high-heeled pumps on. She was animated. Terrance held up his hand. "Wilma, I want you to meet Asia Wei. She is one of NIA's team leaders training our gymnastic division. The sister of OB/GYN Doctor Kathy Wei, here at NIA....." Asia lowers her head in greetings. Wilma says, "nice to meet you," Terrance motioned toward Asia... "please continue, Asia, explain what your concerns are...." Then out of nowhere, the production manager steps up. "Wilma... I'm glad I found you. We have some problems we must address before we start the film." *Wilma then hears the sound of music starting to play in her left ear. She hears three minutes to show time, turns, and says, "listen, our documentary starts in less than 3 minutes." Wilma left at a quick pace with the Production Manager.*

A few moments later, after Wilma had departed, she stepped up onto the stage where at least three thousand invitees waited patiently for the documentary to start. Terrance said let's go to our box seats! This should be enlightening for our invitees....."

Wilma steps from the drawn curtains and grabs her microphone. "Please watch this documentary that our film industry worked diligently on in the last three months. Pay attention to the Viable threats that C.I.N. 'China, Iran, and

North Korea 'has brought to our doorstep." The lights dimmed, and an invisible narrator began speaking with the allying video flashing across the innumerable screens.

"Since Nasa's meteoric obliteration and conversion from Governmental controls over space exploration to allowing private industries to take up the baton and run with it, companies have sprung up in the ever-challenging Space race competing not only against one another but the powers of the world who want to achieve the supremacy of the stars. SpaceX and Blue Origin with Virgin Galactic are to name several of these entrepreneurial enterprises.

Nasa, that is, the U.S. Government's political regime, had thought the competition was a positive approach to Space travel exploration Nasa was a Governmental monopoly. By opening up a bidding war for its employees, it helped proliferate an innovative new approach. The American way of Capitalism proliferated... 'Think Tanks' sprung up wherever wealthy investors with visions of grandeur invested. Some rationalized like a reality show who would man the first station on Mars. Remember, what brought the USA into power was and always will be our innovative minds, thinking out-of-the-box inventions and the 'what if's' funded with capitalism bringing forth our entrepreneurial Spirit. This way of thinking was initially pioneered in America and brought the USA into supreme power. Some private enterprises and companies went public trading on Wallstreet. They popped up and were cultivated with funds such ventures like SpaceX with Savant Elon Musk at the forefront. He was eager with relentless enthusiasm, not unlike other competitors in this 'Space,' pun intended!" Wilma peered around at the hundreds of faces, glued to the screens inside the Amphitheater, with optimistic leveraged thoughts. She felt partitioned knowing the content of the documentary... mulling over what the young Chinese woman Asia Wei had started to intimate earlier. Then fell back listening to the documentary...

"The competition was fierce. 'Cape Canaveral's' dormant Nasa oversaw much of the new breed of Space travel. In the beginning, the premise was to align these endeavors with an intense foundation of likewise competitive spirits. Think tanks motivated working relentlessly a predisposed rivalry existed among these Space exploration companies. Competition always seems to breed advancements in technology or any other facet of life for that matter. Examples are everywhere. Imagine having one automobile company manufacturing cars, with that being hypothesized… you can only purchase, say, a Ford vehicle. Without any competition allowed 'why would Ford strive to improve its products? It wouldn't be prudent. Why spend any more monies on R &D or elsewhere just keep churning out vehicles? Hey, it's the only show in town!" A monopoly…

Parts manufacturers, widgets… vendors ahh, airbags right down to the bolts that lock on the tires, products, and all standardized vehicle options are the same. The part manufacturers have no reasons to spend cash on R.&D. 'research and development' like a moratorium on new innovations… why waste time on that nonsense? Their customers haven't any choices, thusly they haven't any reason to better their products. It is what it is…. there will always be the human consumer, which only grows with population surges. Communism, Socialism, and Capitalism are ways of Governing people on this planet. Is it wrong to say that shrewd intrepid, energetically innovative minds be allowed to perpetuate to propagate to enlighten us all? Should we not be all that we can be and achieve exceptional results without restraints, for our lives are short-lived? Or should the powers to be limit progress and neutralize and squelch the gifted seekers and the inventors today of modern mankind?

Why we as a civilization should strive for improvements to our ways of life is a given but not a human right in many cases throughout history. From time's beginning, Prophets, intellectuals, and philosophers were governed not by their environment as much as by the societal regimes and systems that encumbered them. The governments they incubated within limited and weighed down such prodigies of inventions. This was, but a synopsis of the Forward in the C.I.N. prospectus's no one-line credos. Competition is what drives patents, inventions new technologies C.I.N. was not on the cutting edge. No, they already were… the Razors Edge!

<u>Computer-generated EMP attack by C.I.N. and Mark Feral on America.</u>

<u>A gathering of friends.</u>

Rocky and Shon were sitting abreast inside NIA's outpatient Neurological Hospital. Across from them were Brock Dame and Lucie Link. They were inside a private soundproof room on the third floor that was accessed through a moving wall, actually, a viewing chamber that was set up during construction to purview the adjoining four rooms. Brock was in shock.… "Really, I've been accepted by Terrance and the staff. This is exciting, Rocky. Wow, I'm so grateful to you and Shon…." "ah, bro, it wasn't just us. Wendi stepped up to the plate and…." Shon interrupted Rocky, "it was unanimous. Even the old codger Terrance concurred, your good to go, dude!"

Lucie still couldn't flex the left side of her face. It remained frozen, but her paralysis had improved by 1,000%. She looked on. "I can't wait till I can join Brock and train at the facility. Is there a chance that I can visit and work out there, Rocky?" He reached over and clutched her cold fingers. "Of course, now that Brock will have his own dorm room…." "No," said Shon, "will hook Brock up into a suite, and heck, you'll have a place to visit anytime, and after your therapy treatments, you can hang there all the time!" Her half smile warmed the three men, "Brock, we have some unsettling news, and this is so hushed you have to keep it under wraps. Total confidentiality that includes you, missy. If you disagree, then we will call an end to this private discussion."

Brock says, "well, hell yeah, you can trust me" Lucie dittos that. "all right, let's get to it, Shon" they unpack their briefcase's place them on a table, yanking out computers and a large monitor.

Rocky and Shon, along with the other Team leaders, had already viewed the presentation that was going to be shown later this evening at the Amphitheater where Viacom's Paramount producer Wilma Williams was going to engage a diverse audience of NIA supporters. They had decided to give Brock and Lucie a preview of the copied film and turned to the 49-minute documentary that was going to show on the 45-inch screen. It lit up, and Brock and Lucie sat back, watching the documentary.... they would never be the same. "Come on, Rock, let's get something to drink and let them watch it in peace, then we will put the ending touches on this presentation...!" "Wow, Shon, maybe you should be the narrator tonight...?" "Nah, no one is better than Wilma!"

They reenter with more drinks for Lucie and Brock, catching the end of the film seeing their expressions, Shon asserts. "Why such morose expressions come on, you guys, your acting like it's the end of the world" lol, he reaches out and clutches Lucie's thigh. Rocky taps the keyboard "all right, guys, I don't know if you're aware of what an EMP bomb is, but let's start by familiarizing you with what we're dealing with in the desert. Lucie looks up at Rocky.... "guys, really?" He allows a smile and declares "guy and girl.... okay, this is a bit dated, but it's a precursor to the video we'll play on YouTube. The name of it is 'How an EMP works' https://www.youtube.com/watch?v=X5X1oMw7KDY.
The video is about five minutes. This will further emphasize the documentary you both just watched."

They sat entranced and amazed that neither Lucie nor Brock had heard a word about EMP's and yet some of the most famous politicians and scientists were on the video. Then Rocky segued into one of the most proactive Presidents the USA has had. He pulled up an article for Brock and Lucie to scan over… Trump issued an executive order to prepare for an EMP attack. What is it, and should you worry? The Washington Post …the next 15 minutes, they sat and watched in disbelief that something so simple could end the lives of over 87% of Americans one way or another.

After the video, "Brock declares so this is bizarre. All that some splinter group or hostile country would have to do is fire a missile or rocket from like a freighter or cargo container ship up in the stratosphere above Central America, and all electricity is compromised. That's fricken crazy people with pacemakers drop dead, automobiles with electric currents stop, airplanes in the air drop to earth, and anyone hooked to machines at hospitals dies. Power is cut to all inhabitants. No more withdrawals of monies from banks, wires, or use of ATMs. It would cause a stampede of humans attacking the grocery stores for food and supplies. It would be mayhem, and chaos would reign, no more Wi-Fi, no Internet, no phone service, the list goes on…." "Yes, Brock, it's even worse than that… water would no longer pump, there would be zero electricity, no generators, no power to run anything. We'd be set back over 270 years ago when Alexander Lodygin and Harvey Hubbell lived. Heck, it was the year 1752 when Ben Franklin conducted his first experiment with a kite, a key in a storm!" 'Ok,' muttered Lucie, who still slurred and stuttered but was fully hypervigilant. "Is it temporary? How long would an EMP affect the USA?" Shon took this question, "that's up for discussion. Some say at least nine years, depending on the area you live in and the concentration of the Electromagnetic Pulse that the bomb discharges."

Shon shook his head "this is serious shit, boys uhh and girl. It's obvious that the US Government is aware of the possibilities heck, even Trump had brought it to the forefront, so the Government and Coast Guard are being proactive in checking out the Cargo Containers...." "Uh, what about shooting the missile down or...." "Bro, this is why we're here. There is a Terrorist group on American soil. People in the 'Know' seldom mention or acknowledge that the acronyms stand for our most unwavering enemies combined and, in collusion, China, Iran, and North Korea. Have you heard of C.I.N.?" Brock and Lacie vacillate, wobbling their bodies and heads nope. "Not until we watched the Documentary. Is this really possible...?" "Brock, I'll let you be the judge of that pal," sighs Shon.

"So what can we do? Why are you informing us of this? I'll tell you, in all my years in the military and law enforcement, I've never heard of such a thing as an EMP. This is wild. It isn't mainstream, or Lacie and I would have known about the possibility of some faction using the technology behind...." "Yes, Brock, get this... There have been over 15 fiction books written on the EMP subject. If you want to get caught up to speed, read this book...." Rocky hands two books to them "check this one out. It's titled '<u>One Second After</u>' and the author is '<u>William R Forstchen</u>' now, to answer your question, what can we do ahh, or better yet, how you and Lacie can help us?"

Shon pulls up satellite images of the massive installation in Elko, Nevada, with pictures and videos of only 35 minutes previously. He then tosses down a zoomed-in photo from that most recent reconnaissance. Lacie reacted first with a quick blush. They are shocked straight back in their seats. The photograph they saw was of a person that had been a mainstay in the FBI's five most wanted list for years. But after not surfacing had fallen off the radar as of late and was relegated to being ranked twentieth most wanted. 'Mark Feral's face stared at them... This brought heat collectively to their epidermis. When they actively worked for the FBI as partners.

They had hunted Mark Feral for years, and his last siting was up in Shasta County.

"Wtf," shouts Brock, "no way he's in with this terrorist faction. Well, hell, let's get our armed forces involved. Shit, blow a hole in the desert and annihilate them like yesterday. I don't get it C.I.N. has to be on our Radar. What are our military geniuses doing? Where are our special forces? How could a group the size that's in the surveillance pictures form without our Military's knowledge doesn't seem practical something is wrong..." ranted Brock.

Shon steps in front of them and opens his arms, asserting, "here's what we understand, the CIA suspects. Colonel Ruiz is in cahoots with C.I.N. along with other military leaders. It's essential to be cognizant that an EMP bomb only affects the area directly below where the missile explodes, dispersing electromagnetic waves. So all other countries remain unaffected... rumor is that Colonel Ruiz has been promised one of the small islands in the Caribbean for being a willing participant and leader of the C.I.N. forces on American soil. We think that Mark Feral works directly below Ruiz." Lacie sighs.

Rocky checks his phone. Time was wasting... "let's move on. What can we do? You ask us, Brock, well you're the closest man to Rico...." "Wait, Rocky... you are like his best friend too...." "No, we haven't been getting together ever since he found out that I'd joined NIA. He has been a bit standoffish. Brock, we need to bring Rico up to speed and get the FBI on notice, but that's not all. Before you or Lacie ask the obvious question, why not take this information to the highest authorities, such as Quantico, the Pentagon, the CIA, or the President of the USA? Simple and concise, we don't know whom to trust. Colonel Ruiz has compatriots throughout our Government and military forces. We can't afford to let it leak. We're on to C.I.N.s plans." A pause to let this all sink in "Our Tech team was able to decipher a coded message from the

Elko installation with a forwarding to three different locations in the USA 'April Fool's Day' will be for all the Fools' which we now assume is the launch date for the EMP. The problem we have is which installation of the three that we've discovered has the EMP. We did discover a humongous underground infrastructure below the encampment in Elko, but as of yet haven't located the substations of C.I.N. they could simply launch from another location." Shon grimaces "we can't just Butt rush them. Do you remember the song by 'The Who' 'I can see for miles and miles?' That's the problem, guys. Mark and his guerrillas, umh, insurgents or better yet, his screwed-up mutineers, can see anything coming at him for miles in the air or on the ground!" "Wow, Shon, I thought you only listened to Hip-Hop…." "Funny boy, I grew up 'old school' and enjoyed all music genres, so getting back on point, there's no way to disable the missile launch without alerting them that were attacking. Sure, we could blow all three of their installations to smithereens, but who's to say they don't have an EMP on a freighter or in another hidden bunker? We must be careful of whom we alert in our military, for Colonel Ruiz is connected to the roots. If he catches wind that we are in the know and are onto him, he might just fire off the EMP Missiles out of spite. The guy is known to be off-kilter and unpredictable. He's a crazy son of a bitch." Shon raises his eyebrows, matching his hands, and nods at Rocky.

Rocky adds with a grimace, "we have less than two months, 49 days, before we attack C.I.N. We have a Task Force formed, and Brock, if you're up to it, we'd like you to join us, but first, meet with Rico. Sorry, Lucie, you must stay on the sidelines for now, but you can be in the loop inside NIA's bunkers, watching and listening in real time. If you have any input, we will welcome it.…" "Thanks, Rock. I hope to recover soon. Can't wait to be back with the living!"

Shon flips the screen and points at a map… "the incursion into Elko with attack with removal and destruction of the installations is scheduled for 3/17/18. We just found another substation belonging to the C.I.N. network. We think it's not coincidental. It's the geographical center of the 48 contiguous States, situated about 2 ½ miles Northwest of Lebanon, Kansas. A missile silo is suspected on a rancher's property under one of the Wheat fields. The property owner is pro-military with hunting, and paramilitary training obstacle courses with shooting ranges on his acreage. All he's involved in is legally accomplished under the guise of the American Flag. He is a disciple of C.I.N."

Brock stood up and embraced the guys "you can count on me. I'll contact Rico and set up a meeting for the five of us," he kissed Lucie's forehead. Shon accentuated, "this is all hush and shush stuff, ah, information. Each of us is aware of the blatant Hatred Rico has for Mark Feral, who has tried several times to kill his paramour, um, G.F. Wendi. He will be ecstatic to hear we've pinpointed where the prick is. We need him on board!" Shon halfway smiled awkwardly "you know it's going to be strange indeed us working alongside the FBI and CIA..." Rocky verbalized "that's not a given, brother. You know it's mandatory to include Terrance in our get-together with Rico. He has no idea we're speaking and planning this out. Still, I'll inform him and see where it goes. Who knows, he may Nix the entire idea, and it will be just our NIA special ops um team that goes up against Mark Feral!"

Mark Feral consults with Colonel Ruiz.

Mark Feral sat in his secure bunker below the underground launch site in the state of Nevada, the City of Elko, on a 9-way Zoom call with C.I.N.'s leaders. Colonel Ruiz was speaking, detailing the Fool's Day EMP missile attack with Fervor and fanaticism. Some were on the edge of their seats, and many were standing... Mark daydreamed back to the earlier video call with Ruiz that he would be awarded as many courtesans, uhm, concubines as he could handle and live like a King on the other side of Colonel Ruiz's Island. He laughed at Ruiz's last words. 'Mark, what do you think of me naming the Island 'APRIL FOOLS'… Yep!

Approximately two years passed by… and Narrator Extraordinaire Wilma Williams was back at NIA.

January 23rd, 2020… Covid-19.

Terrance raised his hands above his head, wiggling his fingers towards him, miming everyone to… gather together. Wendi, Valerie, Asia, Jax, Sandi, Brock, and Lucie stood in a circle, with Jaybird and Rocky standing next to Walter and Shon. A somber, subdued dark cloud hung over them, which began only hours previously. Terrance said, "listen, I know what happened with Kamryn and Rico is weighing heavy on our minds and hearts; suffice to say, there is nothing we can do tonight to alleviate the pain and stress. I'm proud of you for having made it to this event. I need your support now more than ever. We will deal with Kamryn missing in action and Renae's despicable acts against NIA. We have the videos and pictures of Renae and Candice crossing into Mexico with the baby stroller. We know that over a year ago, the three of them had been sighted in Guatemala and had been rumored to have purchased a sprawling farm in Panama and have also been spotted in Costa Rico. We've got Amber Alerts out for Sonja and have our NIA tracking them."

Stone faces gazed back at Terrance, who declared, "let's table these controversial issues until later this evening. Believe me, if I could have circumvented what occurred yesterday afternoon, I would have, but we had no idea what Rico would do! It came out of right field. We will hold Sara responsible for these acts of negligence and stupidity now…."

Jax says, hey, Wilma is heading over here. Let's continue this conversation afterward." Terrance steps in closer to Asia... "Okay, you can trust Wilma... I've spoken with the NIA Board of Directors, and they agreed to fund an entire documentary about COVID-19. You have valuable, relevant information. Please feel free to divulge anything and everything you have already told us. I have prewarned Wilma.... is that okay with you, Asia?" "Yes, Terrance... no worries."

"Hello Wilma, I'm happy to see you once again...." Terrance re-introduced the group of NIA leaders. Wilma spies the bleachers and says, "come on, let's all have a seat. My dogs are crying out. I've been on my feet for hours.

Asia had been pacing in front of Wilma and her NIA friends for about seven minutes, rambling on and finishing up her rant. <u>"This killer virus was manufactured in Wuhan City, Hubei Province, China. I have relatives in that Province. The first medical case identified by "WHO..." "The World Health Organization' was held on December 31st, 2019, in Wuhan City. Then a week later, the Chinese authorities temporarily named the virus '2019-nCoV" or Coronavirus the date was the 7th of January 2020. That was less than three weeks ago, and I just received news that a complete section of the city has been cordoned off, and thousands are infected. I am asking NIA to help my family, which has left Wuhan City for Nanchang City, about 175 miles from the serious outbreak in Wuhan. One of my Uncles worked in a laboratory at the Wuhan University of Science and Technology. He told me rumors of something heinous being developed in the basement laboratories. Some suspected a form of germ warfare, a manmade disease created and propagated inside those walls." Asia pleadingly stares into their eyes "this virus if proliferated, has the potential and propensity to wipe out millions of humans. Please help me!"</u>

Wilma spins around to her camerawoman.... "did you get it all, Chir?" She nodded, "I'm so sorry, Asia. What you have detailed is catastrophic and could be life-threatening for all of mankind." Terrance stepped forward and said, "I agree with Wilma; we will do what we can to help your family Asia." Wilma repeats her earlier statement... "Asia, you can count on NIA's support... this is a certainty."

<u>Rantings from the Author.</u>

The next book in this series has been written and awaits editing. It's named for Kamryn's baby 'Sonja.' The story continues with all the unique characters you've visited while reading the books in the NIA series. 'Kam's baby, Sonja's adventures, will make her Aunts Sara and Valerie Blush.' $

Thank you so very much, and I hope to hear from you with suggestions on how the stories should unfold…! Contact me at my website 'Gembooksrock.com.' Thankyou.

Another novel soon to hit the publishers depicts the military action taken against C.I.N. If you're not into that type of Genre, please read… 'Sonja,'… Oh yeah… the subsequent phases of the story titled 'Covid-57' have also been written, but I need to edit the 700,000 plus words.' I find that editing is the most challenging obstacle I face when trying to bring my novels to the press. I plan to have at least five more books go to the publishing departments… before the end of 2023. Thank you so very much.

Sincerely yours… 'Glen "Rocky" Meyers.'
Not the Last Words… I hope! But yuh never know… do yuh?
$

If so desired, the natural sequence of books to read or listen to is as follows… 'Feral Eyes' then 'Feral Eyes 2.' Then Sara and the Kam books. Or if you want to jump right into the volcano… start with 'Sara' and then next on to the plate is 'Kam.' Most of the novels in the NIA series share original characters, but they are exclusively independent for the most part. I have added another few books to the NIA series. The titles are Covid-57 and 'C.I.N. Versus N.I.A…' Thanks to all of you!

I faced a quandary… wanting to publish each novel with approximately the same number of words… 200,000. This was my goal for multiple reasons: to keep the books priced reasonably enough for my readers and to keep the publishing costs down. I also wanted to keep each novel-sized at 6 x 9 inches. Therefore I decided to split KAM into two books.... To align my strategy... Three separate novels written in the Covid-57 series are ready for the publisher and will continue the Covid saga. Thank you. I hope this isn't as confusing as it sounds to me ☺... JL.

Just last night, 4/8/23, I awoke with an idea, then after mulling it over, I decided to follow through...I will publish 'Kam' and 'Covid-57' in stand-alone editions. I don't know what the size of the books will be, but I felt chided that my bookshelves wouldn't have the full-sized manuscripts in separate book bindings.

This is the 5th book in the NIA series of 13 that have all been written. Unfortunately, I am the sole Author without a team of Editors. I don't have a Literary Agent; I will be Self-Publishing,... it's just poor ole me. Therefore, the many errors in my novels are all mine; I'm sort of old school. I use a notebook and different colored pens for plot changes; I'm aware my punctuation sometimes stinks, although rarely, it's purposeful.

When I started putting pen to paper, I didn't know what an undertaking I was getting into. Whoa, this is Work!... with a Capital W! I wish I could hire someone to do the hard part of bringing my writings to fruition because... I honestly enjoy putting pen to paper.

I'd much rather write than do almost anything else, but this work formulating a Book is mind-blowing, and yet I step into Libraries and Walla; there are books forever; I am in Awe of them all.

I recently finished a Novel I've named 'Covid-57' for a simple reason. I envisioned the Pandemic we are trying to survive 'Covid-19', which could, in the end, be three times worse; thus, 3 X 19 = 57. I must declare... this one thousand-page-plus Novel reads like Non-Fiction, simultaneously exhilarating and ominous to write. It is the last book finished in the NIA series. However, 'Covid-57' isn't of the same genre mix as the other previous books. The protagonists remain true with several additions, and familiar characters bounce from the pages found in the NIA series. Speaking for the only person I can… me I enjoy and have fun and find creative writing super-duper rewarding and oddly an exciting endeavor, filled with exhilaration and pride. I will publish Covid-57 with five other completed books at nearly the same time.

I'm also hyped up… about a partially written book titled 'The Clinic.' I will soon add a preview of this novel based in San Diego and Mexico. Within the words and pages of 'The Clinic,' there is much truth about covert prison camps throughout Mexico; these establishments are supported mainly by relatives that pay the guards to keep their relatives alive and unharmed; I've spent time interviewing family members with inside information about this ongoing travesty.

Non-Fiction accomplishments 'Charity,' 'Take a Chance,' 'Take a Chance 2,' 'Take a Chance 3'… 'S.C.J Sacramento County Jail,' 'Savant Style Trading,' an informative book about trading the Stock Market, nuances, and how to profit, using basic algorithms…

Since this is a Lone endeavor or enterprise, I haven't many individuals to thank. Still, I have a single person I want to praise… Gerald Ward, employed by the Sacramento Public Library and the leading publisher at 'I-Street Press.' He just retired in December 2021. Gerry has been instrumental in this process of preparing my novels for print. Unfortunately, he's not an editor, but he is a fantastic photographer and knows his way around the Art of publishing… His extensive library of Photos has been used on the covers of the Feral Eyes books.

Last but Never Least, I would be remiss if I didn't Dedicate all my writing to my Dear Mother! 'Barbara Jean Hayes Meyers.'

As a small child, I watched her write page after page in notebooks; she wrote thousands of pages. Her Genre was Romance. She loved to write, always dreaming of one day publishing a book. Sadly never did. These books are for you, Mom... sorry, I am not talented in the Romance arena; perhaps one day, I will give it a College try.

Thank You for reading what I enjoyed writing. Oh, BTW, I include in many of my novels this phrase 'From the Corner of his eye' or my eye. The reason for this... is that it's my form of praise for one of my favorite books by 'Dean Koontz!'

I'm responsible for every error and mistake in my novels. I printed the first edition called an... 'ARC' book... or (Advanced Readers Copies) for some beta readers to let me know what they thought. Ugh, my first test books needed a lot of work... I had thousands of mistakes literally in my writing...The second edition will be cleansed, but it will not be perfect! Thanks for your time. Please visit my website, '<u>Gembooksrock.com</u>,' soon; I hope to have a business venture when offer for you, not costing you a penny, only time... enough! >Glen Rocky Meyers @ Facebook, Instagram. <u>Please visit my website Gembooks rock.com.</u>

<u>Thank you very much for your precious time...</u> <u>Respectfully... 'Glen "Rocky" Meyers.'</u>

Glen Rocky Meyers@ GlenAuthor' Twitter. Soon to have a Podcast on YouTube.

<u>Please visit Gembooksrock.com for the author's biography.</u>